A WYATT BOOK *for*

W

— ST. —
MARTIN'S
PRESS

Also by Linda Nevins

COMMONWEALTH AVENUE

LINDA NEVINS

Renaissance Moon

a novel

A WYATT BOOK
FOR ST. MARTIN'S PRESS ❧ NEW YORK

Design by Pei Loi Koay

Library of Congress Cataloging-in-Publication Data

Nevins, Linda.
    Renaissance moon : a novel / by Linda Nevins.
        p.   cm.
    "A Wyatt book for St. Martin's Press."
    ISBN 0-312-15200-0
    I. Title.
PS3564.E8544R46   1997   96-43467
813'.54—dc20   CIP

First Edition: April 1997

10 9 8 7 6 5 4 3 2 1

Est unus deus et una dea. Sed sunt multa uti numina ita et nomina: Jupiter, Sol, Apollo, Moses, Christus, Luna, Ceres, Proserpina, Tellus, Maria. Sed haec cave enunties. Sunt enim occulta silentio tamquam Eleusinarum dearum mysteria. Utendum est fabulis atque enigmatum integumentis in re sacra.

"There is but one god and one goddess, but many are their powers and names: Jupiter, Sol, Apollo, Moses, Christ, Selene, Demeter, Persephone, Tellus, Mary. But have a care in speaking these things. They should be hidden in silence as are the Eleusinian Mysteries. Sacred things must needs be wrapped in fable and enigma."

—FROM MUTIANUS RUFUS IN A LETTER TO A FRIEND

Renaissance Moon

Prologue

THE CULTS OF THE GREAT GODDESS

Cambridge, Massachusetts: April 1949

They were terrified of Sterling Catcher even before they began.

Naturally, no one admitted to that, but when the Chairman of the Classics department suggested the Dean's private conference room as a possible venue for the inquiry, that gentleman recoiled. He argued that his very own personal lounge was hardly suitable. It was not large enough to accommodate the various professors and deans and overseers who were expected to attend. It would not afford enough *distance* between the many participants from the faculty (who had every right to be there, after all) and the fearsome Sterling Alva Catcher himself. They couldn't be sitting in one another's laps; *that* wouldn't do. The library might be better, he said, more spacious and formal.

At that, and with a derisive snort, the grizzled old emeritus professor, who had been sitting silently by, listening with distaste, pointed out that the board of trustees had a perfectly fine sanctuary of its own—a vast, mahogany-paneled meeting room with heavy wine-red draperies and a crystal chandelier and portraits of John Harvard and the Marquis de Lafayette and numerous distinguished alumni lining the walls.

"If, gentlemen," he said with a sneer as he hobbled away, "you are convening a Star Chamber, you cannot do better. Why the devil don't you both just straighten up and agree to it?"

The location being thus decided, the trickier question of format was engaged and it was resolved, after due inspection of all options, that the Chairman, who was, after all, a respected classicist himself, should direct the proceedings. It was generally felt that he would be brisk, forthright, and unswervingly collegial.

"And don't forget," the Chairman himself pointed out, rubbing his palms together at the prospect of presiding over such an august occasion, "we've got that young Whatisname doing the work. Didn't you ask him to look into Sterling's activities?"

"Yes, but Sterling's a full professor," the Dean replied, suddenly doubtful. "And in living memory no full professor has ever been dismissed from the Arts and Sciences faculty. I think we're on shaky ground here, Horace. Very shaky."

"He's a damn devil worshiper!" the Chairman rejoined, his cheeks quivering with importance.

"Well, not exactly," the Dean pointed out, faltering. "That young fellow of yours said something about a Great Goddess . . . the Greek Moon Goddess, I think it was. *Greek*, after all."

"Pull yourself together, Stewart," the Chairman exhorted in return. "It's only an *inquiry*, for Christ's sake!" But that that cheerless Brahmin could be no match for Sterling Catcher apparently occurred to no one.

The "Whatisname" in question was an eager young Instructor, a recent Ph.D., who was a Californian and (this most notably) untenured. He had been given the initial task of preparing what some thought of as "the indictment." He did yeoman's work, gathering curriculum vitae, bibliographies, reprints of essays, and copies of Catcher's thirteen books on Greek poetry, drama, and theatrical tradition. He interviewed countless undergraduates, past and present, as well as colleagues by the dozen. Even the commandant of the small cadre of partisans who had held fast at a tiny but strategic stronghold in the Peloponnesus, where Catcher had spent a good part of the war, was run to earth and asked for his opinion.

The impressive documentation notwithstanding, Sterling's inquisitors knew little of his personal life beyond the fact that he had a wife (said to be considerably younger than he, though no one had ever met her) and two little daughters, born when their father was well along into middle life. All of them lived in an enormous house on an isolated tract of forest land out in the central part of the state. Sterling had purchased the property in the late thirties, and as soon as the war ended, almost four years ago now, he had taken a wife and hidden her away among the thousands of oaks and larches on that vast domain, miles from anywhere. What had become of their little daughters, whether they went to school or were quite well, no one seemed to know. Early on, the young Instructor got the bright idea of asking Mrs. Catcher for a private conversation, but was quickly dissuaded by the Dean himself. Instead, he decided to spy.

The difficulties had begun shortly after Sterling Catcher published a short monograph in verse form on an obscure middle-European cult of the old Goddess Hecate, Queen of the Underworld. In a preface to his poem Sterling had written:

> For thousands of years, time was reckoned in lunations; the solstices and equinoxes were calculated by their relation to the phases of the moon. Even now, it is on the darkest nights, when the moon is new and the worshipers are in the grip of their most powerful visions, that the greatest ceremonies of the cult take place. For if the glowing moon, the Great Goddess's symbol, inspires laughter and rejoicing, will not the dark of the moon compel a great and superstitious fear? Indeed, when the cycle comes round to darkness, we look, trembling, into the black bowl of the sky, the vast, depthless reaches of the heavens, and burn sacrifices to make the moon return.
>
> For *this* is the realm of the Enchantress—the third persona of the Trinity of the Moon Goddess—The Divine Hecate, Mother of Witches, Goddess of Incantatory Magic, beloved of demons and sorcerers, worshipped by Circe, Medea, and Morgan le Fay. She is the Crone—the nightmare vision known as the Lady of Spells, the Queen of the Underworld, as She Who Brings Destruction and Storms! She is every nocturnal, subterranean spirit come to life. Black is Her color and Her companions are the Eumenides, the very Furies of legend. She rises from the Underworld on nights when the moon is dark, running over the earth with Her pack of black wolf-dogs, Her approach signaled by their howling.

The poem was widely read and received with general alarm.

Shortly thereafter, it somehow came to light that Sterling was using his forest, and the field at the very center of the estate, and particularly the crossroads near the entrance to make offerings of some sort. On calm, moonless nights, he lit smoky fires that sent their plumes high into the sky. Whether these plumes had actually been seen by the ambitious young Instructor as he crouched in the tall grasses of the great, barren field was never clear. He may have made inquiries in the town; he may not have.

Then, during the summer of 1948, rumors began to surface that Sterling Catcher was doing something very . . . irregular. The people from Turn-of-River, the small village just a few miles west of his estate, told the authorities that they saw odd movements, fires burning and such, out there at night. Some of the townspeople complained of the stench of burning hair, or a sweetness as of burned fruit, and other smells, bitter and rancid, blowing toward them on nights when there was an east wind from the ocean, as if boiling salt, someone said, were mixed with rotted fruit and hair.

Not long afterward, in the fall, there were some desecrations in a church not far from the College, though the Dean and some of the elder gentlemen on the faculty doubted that Sterling had a thing in the world to do with that. They suspected he wouldn't go inside a Roman Catholic church for all the tea in China. But when, late the following winter, Professor Catcher gave a series of public lectures on ancient cults of the Great Goddess, they felt thoroughly vindicated in their decision to proceed with the inquiry.

The lectures were so well attended that they'd been obliged to throw open the doors of the auditorium, and the undergraduates stood listening in the snow—like Emperor Henry, barefoot at Canossa—risking their health to listen to his stories of the great neolithic deity.

"In the days when the world was stone," Sterling began, his deep, elegant voice rising with almost evangelical power, "the Great Goddess was Nature itself, the source of all the energies of life, the seed of all regeneration. And though She had one thousand names, She was only One. Never more than *One*.

"In Her youthful, blooming form, She is Selene—the manifestation of the Goddess in the sky—the Lady of the Upper Air. Selene is the maiden moon. She rides through the night sky in an ox-drawn chariot and Her crescent-shaped tiara is the glowing quarter moon. Her passage through the skies pulls on the tides and gives rhythm to the raging waters of the world. The Divine Selene observes; She protects and watches. But always from afar. She cannot be approached. She cannot be touched. Not by passion, not by the senses . . . not by anything. Selene, the chaste maiden, is the messenger; Her cold, distant light is the sign. But She is only the crescent, you see, only the beginning. *What is coming?*"

The young Instructor was there that night, disguised by a false mustache and a warm hat, anxious lest some of his own students see him lurking. Though it was cold as the bowels of hell, for discretion's sake he chose to stay outside so he could take copious notes and wear his hat without being too conspicuous.

But not long after, in February it must have been, the young fellow's investigation seemed to take on a life of its own when some of Professor Catcher's graduate students confided to him that Catcher was trying to convert them, though just to what they couldn't really say.

The following Sunday morning, after church, the Dean called the Chairman in a panic. "Horace! You can't imagine what they've told that young man of yours. They say Catcher actually *worships* her!"

"Who, Stewart?"

"Some pagan goddess—Artemis—I don't know. The naked one who—"

"I don't think we should—"

"Worships her, Horace. Makes sacrifices to her. It's indecent!"

"Hmm. Well, I suppose it's a good thing we're looking into it."

And from then on it was all just a terror of Sterling Alva Catcher and what he knew.

Professor Catcher had been requested to arrive at three o'clock. The Dean hoped that they might be done with the unpleasantness (as it would surely be) well before five when one of the emeritus trustees had promised sherry and snacks at his club, not too far away on Beacon Hill. No doubt a small, tasteful collation would be restorative after the exertion of performing what they saw, after all, as their duty. Initiating the possible dismissal of a tenured Harvard professor was hardly cause for celebration, but everyone agreed that a glass of decent sherry, perhaps a modest Scotch, would not put too fine a point on the proceedings.

At 2:58 P.M., punctually, the secretary to the faculty senate ushered Professor Catcher into the room. He was immediately offered a chair.

"I prefer to stand," Sterling Catcher said with a breezy smile. He folded his arms and leaned ever so slightly against the ornate molding of the doorway, looking down the polished table into the Chairman's small, moist eyes. "No offense, Horace."

Sterling's glance left the Chairman and slid up and down the table and across the filled leather armchairs that lined three sides of the large room.

As he looked at them, one by one, they were, collectively, as intimidated as many of them had been, individually, on those previous occasions that had led to this defining moment. Though Sterling Catcher did not socialize with his colleagues, over the years paths had crossed at numerous times and many members of the faculty still harbored unsettling memories of an icy glance, a curt nod, perhaps a phrase (possibly in Greek or Turkish, undoubtedly a curse) muttered in a deep, dismissive baritone. Not well liked, people said of Sterling Catcher. Not well liked at all.

Sterling was a large man, broad and tall, but with a lightness of movement, a perfection of proprioception, that was unnerving to watch. His hair, a heavy, deep silver now for several years, had once been a glorious blond, rich with glints of gold. His clothing, bespoke shirts and hand-finished jackets, was made for him, they said, in England and always impeccable in every way.

Sterling understood perfectly well that various of his colleagues had taken an interest in his activities. As a courtesy, he'd been informed of their concerns and a number of documents were made available, though not all (neither the most interesting nor the most damning), and this omission Sterling perceived and dismissed with vast amusement. It could have been terribly distressing had he cared a tinker's damn for their impertinence or their opinions. But one dark night last fall, he had himself seen that young fool from the junior faculty out beyond the obelisks at the entrance to the estate, alone and (so the idiot thought) unobserved.

Inquiries! More like the Spanish Inquisition dressed up with mahogany furniture and portraits on the walls! But Sterling knew they'd have his hide if they could get it, evidence or no, and, his amusement receding, he resolved to deny them that huge pleasure.

"Gentlemen, shall we get started?" the Chairman began, clearing his throat.

"Started on what, Horace?" Catcher barked, gripping the edge of the table with both hands and thrusting his large head forward, his shoulders bunched under the fine worsted of his suit. "On exactly *what?*"

The Chairman pressed himself against the back of his chair, though Sterling was a full twenty feet away.

"Professor Catcher..." He managed to croak out the words with some dignity, though he lost control of his breathing and his timing, and paused before continuing.

"...Sterling, you have certainly been informed of the purpose of this gathering. The Dean—"

At the mention of his title, more precious to him than his name, the Dean elevated himself slightly from his chair, prepared for whatever defense this not entirely unexpected show of defiance might require. As he did so, unfortunately calling attention to himself, the leather seat inflated with a small popping sound.

"Stewart!" Catcher cried, turning to the Dean, standing away from the end of the table and raising his arms in mock dismay. "*You're* responsible for this? *You?*"

"Sterling, please, we've barely begun," the Dean replied, returning his backside to the leather chair, which exhaled noisily. "It has simply come to our attention that your well-known interest in the cultural roots of Western..." The Dean looked at the Chairman, begging for help.

"...Western civilization, Sterling." When he spoke, the Chairman saw Catcher's eyes narrow, leave the Dean's mottled face.

"We're just interested in your new work, Sterling. This...this...goddess business. Evidently—"

"Evidently what? Is academic freedom, intellectual freedom, *religious* freedom an outmoded concept in these sacred halls?" Sterling's voice was soft, inquisitive, barely audible. "Shall we dispense with the reading of the charges, Horace?"

"Sterling, for heaven's sake. There are no charges. We merely—"

"No?" Catcher's large blue eyes turned to the eager, ambitious young Instructor, settled unobtrusively (as he thought) in a wooden chair near the window. "No? You sent that *boy* in the dark of night to look into my windows and *there are no charges?* I was a professor of classical literature when he was in diapers and he comes to watch my private activities from behind my own trees and *there are no charges?*"

Sterling's voice rose ever so slightly. "Do you tell me he came there on his own? Did you think I would be so *paralyzed* by my *visions* that I would not be aware that *boys* were skulking about on *my property?*"

"Sterling, please..."

"What I do on my estate is my business. It is not your business, Horace...nor yours, Cornelius...nor yours, Henry...Louis...Geoffrey... nor yours..."

The Dean rose to his feet, sick with the knowledge that important stones had been left unturned.

"...and certainly not yours, Stewart," Sterling said with a coarse, derisive smile, turning back and skewering the Dean with a glance. "'Goddess business,' you say? Goddess business? You speak, sir, of the Triple

Goddess of the ancient Greeks! The Goddess of the Moon, of the Earth, of Nature itself!"

"Sterling—"

"She is the oldest, the most sacred of all the symbols history has created. She has absolute power over birth and death and resurrection. For millennia, before and after the arrival of the barbarians from the north, the Greeks made sacrifice to Her. They blessed Her by dung fires and in the great hall of the Telesterion at Eleusis, whose secrets we may not know!

"I am initiate to those Mysteries," he roared, sweeping the room with his glance, his large eyes fixing each face for just a moment. "I have bathed and fasted and made sacrifice and *still* I do not know and will not know until some day the Goddess throws Her cloud over me. And over you, Stewart! She will throw Her cloud over you as well!"

"But Sterling, surely, you're an educated man..."

"And therefore, what? Therefore I cannot know anything on faith alone? It's true enough that I am neither scientist nor mariner. I am ignorant of perigee, syzygy, and declination. But I know that in the phenomenon of lunar force there is a cause and a metaphor for human spirit, human rage, the irresistible compulsions and agonies that govern us. As the moon waxes and wanes, so She blesses and curses, recedes and floods like the waters She pulls—not only the silt of ocean floors, but the delicate fluids in *our brains!* Tell me what is greater than the power to move the tides. Not even your Christian god can do that!"

The Dean looked around at the group. There was a faint shuffling of feet, a soft swell of coughs and murmurs.

"You have a Christian duty to your students, Sterling."

"And you are a bigger fool than I ever thought, Stewart, because you think the Christ is all there is. You know nothing of what may lie beyond this world."

Sterling paused and his eyes raked the room once more.

"Do you really think I care to be... one of you?" he said in a disgusted tone. "I tell you only this: it is the Great Goddess alone who wills the renascence of every living thing. Every living thing."

So saying, Sterling turned away from them. The little secretary, who had, despite clear instructions to the contrary, eavesdropped carefully from behind the door, opened it in the nick of time, and Sterling Catcher strode through without a backward glance.

His chauffeured car awaited at the curb and in minutes he was beyond the drive and past the river to the west. Sterling opened a small leather-bound book and lost himself in the odes of Apollonius Rhodius until, two hours later, the car turned off the county road and glided between the great stone obelisks at the entrance to his estate. As he stepped out into the freshness of the April evening, his elder daughter, Selene, three years old, came round the corner of the house.

She was a darling child, sweet and happy. Her bright, fair hair was wound in a pretty coil around her little head; her eyes sparkled when she saw her father. Laughing with joy, she ran toward him and leapt into his waiting arms.

Selene

Chapter One

Florence, Italy: April 1978

first met Selene Catcher during the time she was my cousin Piero's lover.

One bright spring afternoon, he phoned at my sister Carla's house in Florence to say he was taking the train from Venice the next day and would see us before sundown. He had an American friend with him, he said. A woman.

I'd been staying with Carla for the month or more since I'd left my post at the Vatican, having broken several bones in my foot playing soccer with some of our younger seminarians. As a man approaching his fortieth year, I suppose I should have known better.

But I'd also been feeling a distressing yet undeniable need for more secular companionship, which Carla certainly provided. Her beautiful house in the Oltrarno district of Florence was airy and bright, with a magnificent view of the Duomo across the river. Usually, the house resounded with the elaborate entertainments with which Carla filled her life, but she promised that we would be very quiet, just the two of us at little, perfect dinners. For several weeks I had been relishing that solitude, happy to be alone with my books and my thoughts. But I had just begun to confront the decision to return to Rome, or not to, when Piero called, peremptory and energetic as always, to announce his visit.

We hadn't seen him since the previous summer, but such a long break between encounters was not unusual for us. While Carla and I chose to stay close to home in Italy, cousin Piero roamed the landscape at will, devouring his part of the family fortune as quickly as the various accountants and advisors could replenish it. Piero traveled extensively, pausing from time to time to study something that caught his interest—mathematics, history, perhaps primitive music—and be off again, seeing the world and spending his inheritance.

Carla, Piero, and I are all that remains of a very old family that lived for hundreds of years in a villa north of Milan. The origins of the Corio fortune are obscure, not bearing scrutiny, perhaps, but we did know that long ago our ancestor had been the court historian of Ludovico Sforza, the notorious Duke of Milan who died, a prisoner of the King of France, in 1507. However dark his reputation, however, we in the family knew Ludovico as an important collector and patron of the arts, the man who had in fact virtually discovered Leonardo da Vinci, surely enough of a contribution to outweigh the many unsavory rumors of a cruel nature.

Late the next afternoon, the sun was just setting over the hills when Piero's taxi screeched to a stop in the gravel drive. He jumped out and kissed and hugged Carla, then embraced me as well, pounding my back with enthusiasm, while his American friend stood next to the driver, poised and relaxed behind a pair of movie star sunglasses, her mane of dark blond hair shining in the last rays of the early April sun.

"This is Selene Catcher," Piero said, drawing her toward us.

Knowing what little I do of Piero's history with women, I suppose I'd expected her to be what Carla's sophisticated friends would call *squisita*, as if an extraordinary physical beauty was essential to the task of catching and keeping Piero Corio's attention; and yet I can't really say she *wasn't*.

What she was, I think, was riveting; she was the sort of person who compels the attention of others, someone from whom you cannot take your eyes. She was extremely tall, almost six feet, and thin, a spike of a woman without discernible breasts or hips—although that was hard to tell because her gleaming black mink coat hung so gracefully from her shoulders, it could not do much more than suggest the woman underneath.

Her presence was absolutely arresting—a perfect posture combined with a perfect hauteur—but it was her eyes that drew me in, made it impossible to look away. They were of the oddest color—not yellow . . . gold, I'd say—a bronzy, tarnished gold flecked with an amber brown, the rims of the irises a deeper shade that reminded me of the heavy pieces of

Etruscan armor they have in the museum of the Palazzo Ducale in Venice. And clear as water.

They were set in a narrow, fine-boned face, the nose large but chiseled, defined, the mouth wide with pale, narrow lips. Her hair, which fell almost to her collarbones, was held back and away from her face by two handsome tortoiseshell combs. I sensed almost at once that that shining surface covered much that did not gleam, though it took me many years to learn that I was right.

Carla, making her welcome, kissed her on both cheeks, already chattering away. But then, when Piero turned and introduced me as "my cousin, Father Giovanni Corio," Selene held out her hand and gave me a warm, almost intimate smile. Though for several days we did not have occasion to speak except at table, from time to time I caught her looking at me and she would smile again with the same private expression, as if she found me intriguing in some way, as if she knew me.

For almost a week after her arrival, my brief encounters with Selene were characterized by intense though unexpressed interest on both sides. My sister feigned ignorance of that small, inconsequential drama, but one afternoon, observing such a moment, Carla threw her arms around my shoulders and tilted up my face with her plump fingers.

"Isn't he lovely!" she cried, caressing my flat cheeks, "this face—this marvelous silky hair. Too bad he's given it up, no? Ha!" I chuckled and pulled away, embarrassed (as Carla had intended that I be), but as I looked back, I thought I saw Selene wink at me, though I wasn't absolutely sure.

My gregarious sister was, and remains to this day, an extravagant and generous hostess who prides herself on her hospitality. Her spacious house, hidden behind an ornate fence, high in the hills near the Piazzale Michelangiolo, was beautifully decorated with eighteenth-century furniture and paintings (selected, I was sure, as much for the excitement of the acquisition as for the luster of the provenance), and it was constantly filled with an assortment of old friends and chance acquaintances.

The arrival of Selene Catcher fit perfectly into Carla's social enthusiasms. Carla adored her from the start and seemed quite willing to be dazzled by Piero's American friend, though she more than held her own in such glamorous company. In those days, Carla affected a glossy American style—expensive designer outfits and elaborate toilettes. But in spite of those efforts, Carla somehow could not help looking precisely like the Roman aristocrats Lotto and Raphael liked to paint, like our own ancestors perhaps—robust, self-assured, very direct. She loved to arrange her hair in ornate, fifteenth-century styles, coiled over her ears with strands of pearls all twisted through, as in Laurana's famous bust of Battista Sforza: the strong shoulders, the superb nose. Until I came up from Rome, Carla had people staying with her constantly; it was like a revolving door, new guests coming in the front while an army of used ones were going out the back. I'm sure many of them took advantage of her good nature, but Selene did not. They had formed an instantaneous affinity and the two of them were a delight to see.

Selene and Piero spent almost a month with us and their presence seemed to give Carla the pretext she'd been needing to break her vow to me of solitude and quiet meals à deux. Carla had always refused to indulge what she viewed as my intellectual excesses and insisted that I participate in all her extravagant pastimes, as if that might cure me of an extravagance of my own. As a consequence, I was thrown into Selene's society on a daily basis and was able to observe her relationship with Piero at close hand.

They were both exceptionally intelligent and witty and Piero's considerable learning and humor seemed as great a part of her interest in him as were his strong features and his powerful, athletic body. Nevertheless, it was clear that sex was the source and foundation of their rapport.

One day I was just coming out of the drawing room, planning to take a walk down toward the river, when I saw Piero and Selene sitting side by side on a brocade settee in the entryway of the house. Piero had his arm around her neck and the tips of his fingers were holding up her chin so she could listen as he whispered . . . whatever it had been. Startled at seeing such an intimate moment, I ducked back into the drawing room and went out another way, not wanting to be seen seeing them.

My fascination with Selene grew upon her air of mystery, inescapable in spite of her sophisticated talk and warm, vivacious personality. To my dismay, that fascination penetrated my most private thoughts and at length it occurred to me that I might exorcise it (as it surely deserved?) by talking to Piero.

One day I mentioned (oh, so casually) that despite her pleasant, friendly nature, I found her quite a mysterious figure.

"Well," he said with a small chuckle, "when you're that rich, you can do pretty much as you please and let people speculate at their leisure, can't you?"

We were on Carla's small terrace, a lovely little balcony off the study, which looked out over the dark ribbon of the Arno and across to the mass of the Duomo, glowing in the early evening light.

"How rich?" I asked, too intrigued by Selene herself to worry about the rudeness of my question. I poured a little more whiskey into Piero's glass and went into the study to turn on one of the tall lamps over the bookcases. I came back out and stood self-consciously by the balustrade, gazing across to the clock tower of the Palazzo Vecchio, unwilling to let him see my face.

"Oh, enormously," he said. "Enormously. Family money? Land? Who knows? But yes, very wealthy indeed. I've come to the conclusion that she's simply gotten bored with it all and taken it into her head to come over here for a while. It doesn't much matter why, does it? She has money and she speaks perfect Tuscan. Except for a sister, and possibly some old connections in Venice, I don't think she has any ties."

I was disappointed in that encapsulated description, but although Piero is famously uncommunicative, even in his most voluble moods, I'm not sure he knew much more. He did tell me, however, that Selene had been living in a small house in the Dorsoduro section of Venice since the death of her father, Professor Sterling Alva Catcher, late of Harvard University, an eminent author of many books on Greek poetry and drama. I was intrigued anew, having spent no little time in Cambridge myself, but apparently the father had left there many years before and we were not to know the details. At least not right away. Selene spoke of him very infrequently, but when she did—"Oh, yes, Father knew him...went there ...did that..."—it was in a factual tone that I found very hard to interpret.

That Selene Catcher and I—the charming, carefree heiress and the quiet, disaffected Jesuit—might have a point of intense convergence seemed impossible to me, until one afternoon several weeks after she and Piero arrived. It was early in May, only a few days till Carla's birthday, and I knew she would never forgive me if I did not mark the occasion in a suitably excessive way. Carla took special days very seriously, and I knew extraordinary gift-giving feats were called for. On a whim (or so I told myself) I asked Selene if she would be willing to help me find the perfect present. To my amazement and delight, she agreed at once and volunteered to be, as she called it, "the mastermind." My job was to pay.

"There's no point in looking anywhere but on the Tornabuoni," Selene said briskly as the taxi turned off the Ponte Santa Trinita and deposited us at the corner of the Via Porta Rossa. "This is Carla Corio we're talking about. No point at all."

The early afternoon was warm and sunny and we strolled up one side of the street and down the other, peering into the elegant window displays, getting ideas. There were beautiful silk scarves and gold watches and gleaming leather handbags. In one shop window, embroidered evening dresses dripped from the shoulders of a trio of impossibly thin, faceless mannequins—clearly not the best choice for my dear sister.

At that point we had been looking for more than an hour and both of us were beginning to feel a trifle disheartened, when, all at once, Selene pulled me by my elbow into a *gioiellerìa* about halfway up the street near the Palazzo Strozzi. There, instantly catching the attention of the proprietor, Selene demanded to see his rubies.

In a flash, necklaces, rings, bracelets, earrings, and brooches blazed up like a rosy fire from the velvet mat. I rather liked a small brooch that featured a ring of diamonds surrounding a perfect gem the size and color of a cherry. That it cost millions of *lire* seemed to make no difference to Selene. She picked it up and squinted into the ruby's heart.

"It really is lovely," she whispered to me in English, "nice and big. But nowhere near fancy enough for Carla, do you think?" She turned and peered around the shop. "Oh! Vanni! *Fantastico! Dai un'occhiata!*"

Selene's use of the old family nickname she'd heard from Carla and Piero had startled me for a second, but then I saw what had caused her outburst. On a round display table was an arrangement of small evening purses, jeweled and enameled, all shaped like animals and birds. They were, indeed, astonishing. With another cry of delight, Selene went over and picked up several at once. Drawing a disapproving glance from the proprietor, she hung their golden chains over her elbows and shoulders, opened their intricate hidden clasps, and examined the workmanship with care.

One, about eight inches wide, was shaped like a parrot, with a hooked gold beak and feathers made of glittering green and blue crystals and beads. Its red eyes were actual rubies, several carats each. Selene modeled the purse in the mirrored side of a cabinet; it swung in gaudy brilliance from her shoulder.

"*Perfètto!*" she cried, turning with a smile to the proprietor, whose displeasure melted instantly away. "*Perfètto!* Vanni, do you like it? Yes? It's Carla all over. An excellent choice." While I paid, Selene rummaged through a pile of heavy silk scarves and selected two as her own gift to Carla, one a gorgeous scene of a Renaissance wedding and the other a vivid design of flowers and tropical birds that matched the purse exactly.

Out on the sidewalk again, she turned to glance up and down the Tornabuoni and then smiled into my eyes. "Shocking price, no? How do they get away with it, I wonder."

I laughed. "Carla will love it. May I express my gratitude with an *aperitivo*? The Baglioni isn't far. Or Ballatóio's? It's just up near the Piazza."

"*Perfètto,*" she said again, and linked her arm through mine.

Chapter Two

It had been a sultry day, much too warm for early May in Florence, and we were glad to find ourselves quite alone in the cool dimness of the Ballatóio bar. It was a small place near the Lungarno Corsini and not particularly chic, but it was obvious that Selene didn't mind a bit. She sat back in the red swivel chair with a happy sigh and slipped off her shoes, fanning herself with a handkerchief she took from her purse.

After our drinks came, a Campari for me and a cognac for Selene, I tried to find a suitable opening for a proper conversation. We'd had plenty to talk about in the shops, but now that there was just the two of us, an entrée was hard to find. Still, as I felt it my gentlemanly duty to begin, I ventured a question about the only interest we seemed likely to share.

"Have you known Piero very long?" I asked, genuinely curious. Piero had told us that they'd met in Venice, but he never mentioned if that had been a month or a decade before. Laughing at the memory, Selene explained that it had been only the previous summer, at the studio of a mutual artist friend who lived near Selene's house in the Dorsoduro, just two streets from the Grand Canal. The two of them had been guests at a small lunch party and in the course of the afternoon they learned how much they had in common.

Both Piero and Selene had a wide circle of friends, most with considerable family money and ready to spend it on any excessive, self-indulgent thing their languid hearts desired. Although I knew how well my cousin Piero might be thought to fit into such company, I was surprised at Selene's frank description of their Lucullan existence.

Nevertheless, she did take some pains to point out that Piero appealed to her because he was so different from those spoiled brats (as she called them), who had begun to bore her nearly to death.

"To be sure," Selene said with a chuckle, "Piero can more than hold his own with the fools sometimes, but he's a genuinely educated person, someone who actually enjoys his education, his knowledge. It's part of him," she went on, more serious now, "part of his life, not tacked on as it is for so many people. I know his education was acquired in unconventional ways, but . . . well, so was mine."

After she said that, she frowned and sat in silence for a moment, looking intently at the thin curl of her cigarette smoke as it disappeared into the shade of the bronze lamp on the table. But then she laughed and looked at me.

"But Piero doesn't flaunt it, you understand, doesn't show it off, as my father so dearly loved to do. Piero knows better than to go around quoting Dante in restaurants." She raised her eyebrows in a humorous way, but the implied criticism of her father, about whom I knew so little, was impossible to miss.

"Piero told me that your father died not so very long ago," I offered, wondering if I had been remiss in not expressing even the most *pro forma* condolences before.

"Umm. Well, it's about three years now," Selene said with a slight wave of her hand and a mordant smile. Apparently, Sterling Catcher had been ill for many years and moved back to the family estate from wherever he had been living at the time—someplace in Greece, she thought, shrugging with apparent indifference—only when he became aware he was about to die.

"He summoned my sister, Elisabetta—Bet—to see him to his grave. He'd never shown the slightest interest in her before, but she came at once and moved into a small house on the estate. Bet and her husband have a beautiful, darling little girl. Her name is Carmen. What a wonderful child she is."

She lit up another cigarette and watched the match burn to her fingertips before she blew it out.

"Is that in Massachusetts, then?" I asked, thinking it likely since, as Piero had mentioned, her father had been at Harvard long ago.

She nodded briefly, not seeming to find my question an intrusion. "Our place is about two hours west of Boston, very isolated. Just a million old trees." She took a sip of her cognac. "Very remote. And quite enormous. My father bought it just before the war."

"My goodness," I exclaimed, completely forgetting my manners, "why did your father decide to settle out there?" I had imagined, at the very least, a town house on the top of Beacon Hill. "It must be very far from . . . well, culture, libraries, all that?"

At first she didn't answer me, didn't even appear to have heard the question, but at length she said, "My father was a citizen of the world, in the most literal sense. He traveled constantly, teaching, lecturing, having his own life, and he wanted his family completely removed from the world and all its . . . dangers."

"Your mother didn't mind the isolation?"

She tilted her head at my question, considering. "No . . . no, I've always believed it rather suited her. She and Father didn't get along all that well and I think she was probably quite content to be alone with us."

"You said your sister took care of him at the end. Was your mother not—"

"Oh, he and Mother hadn't lived together for years. She's a very devout Catholic, you see. As a matter of fact, a number of years ago Mother went into a convent, a cloistered order in upstate New York. She didn't take her solemn vows until she was fifty-six years of age. But in the deepest part of herself, I think, she's been a nun all of her life. And my father was the fire in which she was refined. Naturally, they never divorced, so when he died she was free to marry Christ."

I was astounded, but thought better of saying so. As Selene told about her family, there was an indifference in her manner that I knew could not possibly be real. But she seemed in a talkative, even confiding mood and I sensed it would be wise to keep my astonishment to myself and listen.

"Anyway, when Father died I was already living here in Italy, and I went back as soon as Bet called. The night I returned," she said, "I went out to take a good look at that piece of wilderness that was finally mine."

I heard in the words, and the tone, an incomprehensible satisfaction.

"He left it all to you?" I asked.

"All. Bet was chosen to watch him die, but he left the whole estate to me: every rock, every blade of grass, every tree and every leaf on every tree. Even the house Bet and Leon and precious little Carmen were living in. All mine."

She looked with some surprise at the empty glass in her hand. "Would you mind ordering me another cognac?"

When the waiter appeared, she lifted the fresh glass right out of his hand, took a genteel sip, and French-inhaled her cigarette. "Umm... lovely. But, Vanni, you must promise to visit sometime if you're ever in the States."

"Yes, well, I'll certainly look forward to it," I said with a dry smile, not thinking she was serious. Carla's friends issue invitations like falling autumn leaves, and they blow away just as easily.

"I'm perfectly serious," she said, her smile telling me she had read my thought. "We can sit in the *stùdiolo* and discuss... whatever."

"*Stùdiolo!*" I cried, overtaken by surprise, the word bursting from my lips. " 'Little study.' Like Francesco de' Medici's little hideaway in the Palazzo Vecchio?"

"Well, quite a bit larger, thank goodness, and with *windows*, but, yes," she said, laughing. "It was originally a nasty old barn filled with dreadful smells and rotten hay, but my father converted it into a study years ago. He spent hours in there, days sometimes. He loved being surrounded by the wonderful silence, the space, all his things. But when he took me away, he left it just like he left everything else—without a backward glance."

"What do you mean? Took you away? Where?"

"Away. Away from home. You didn't know that?"

How could I possibly have known such a thing? "On a trip? I don't understand. When was that?"

She shot me an odd, searching look and then seemed to recover her offhand, ironic manner. "We left the morning after Mother told me the Annunciation story from Saint Luke," she said smoothly, sipping her cognac. "At the time, of course, I had no idea there was a connection, but Father's decision seemed to have been made in an instant. Bet and I heard loud voices down in the parlor late that night, and the next afternoon a limousine came for us and off we went. I never even had a chance to say good-bye to Bet."

I could not understand why a story from Saint Luke would elicit such a response, but I prudently buried my expression in my Campari. If Selene was amused in any way she gave no sign. She merely glanced across the table at me, and away.

"I was almost twelve," she said with a shrug. "We went all over, following Father's lecture schedule around the world."

"And you traveled constantly?" I asked, trying to absorb what she was telling me. I knew, of course, that American parents are very competitive about what they like to call "custody" of their children, but such did not seem to be the case with the Catchers.

"Just about," she said in a flat tone, opening the small leather cigarette case she had dropped on the table. "Until the summer he sent me to a private *école* outside Lucerne. I spent the next two years reading novels and conjugating French verbs, and Father spent it on a dig in Yugoslavia, having the time of his life."

At that she broke out into humorless laughter that ended as abruptly as it began. She looked at me in a thoughtful way, as if deciding something. I had the sudden impression that our afternoon hunting birthday presents up and down the Tornabuoni had been a kind of initiation, some sort of test I'd passed.

"As our friend Piero may have told you," she went on, lighting her cigarette, "my father was the greatest classical scholar of his day. Actually, many of the standard translations of the classical plays are his; they're still used in universities today, or so I'm told." She looked up with an expression that may have been pride, or dismissal.

"For many years he enjoyed a brilliant career with it," she went on, "but in time—I'm not sure what the turning point was for him—in time his interest in the old religion, the old ways, the myths and rituals that many scholars think go back at least twenty thousand years, consumed him more and more. He got to the point where he was *obsessed* by the Eleusinian Mysteries and the ancient cults of resurrection.

"You see," she said, not missing a beat, "the old barn was not only his study. It was his temple."

I searched her face for irony, but found none. She gazed back at me without expression.

"Piero did mention that your father left Harvard quite some time ago," I remarked hesitantly. "Might there be . . . ?"

Selene smiled at my sudden discomfiture. "A connection? Oh, yes. The people at Harvard set up some sort of committee, examined all kinds of documents, held interviews with his graduate students. Father always thought it was nonsense, but I guess some of the mandarins on the faculty were starting to grasp the fact that Sterling Catcher really did worship the pre-Hellenic goddess, and that was a good deal more than their educated throats could swallow. Even long afterward, he loved to tell the story about the day he quit."

"*Mi scusi... moménto,*" I said. "Just a moment. You don't mean that was his... religion? He worshiped the Great Goddess?" I was embarrassed to show my surprise in such a blatant way, but Selene only smiled at my reaction.

"Artemis. Yes. Ereshkigal, Ashtoreth, Isis. Yes."

I set my glass on the table and leaned toward her, fascinated. "I thought... I mean, I assumed that he was a Catholic. Like your mother."

"Oh, my goodness!" she said, actually laughing aloud at the notion. "I can't imagine why you did. No, quite the contrary. I've often suspected there may have been a time, early on, when he thought he could convert her, but I think it's more likely that he married her to test himself, his own faith. He begged Artemis to give him a sign, some omen, not only that She favored him, but that She was more powerful, more to be feared, than Jesus Christ and all those Christian saints and gods and myths my mother worshiped. And She did."

"What do you mean?" I said. To this day I berate myself not only for the difficulty I had getting my mind around what she was saying, but at the awkwardness with which I let her see it. But Selene was unperturbed.

"My birth the next December, two weeks earlier than expected—on the night of the full Wolves Run Together moon—was that sign," she said in a matter-of-fact tone. "I'm sure Father must have believed that if he offered the Goddess my blank mind, my spotless soul, that She, in return, would not only reward him, but protect him from the gods worshiped by his wife. It was the simplest sort of appeasement."

"And you believe that too," I asked, though the interrogatory sound of it got lost somewhere and the sentence came out flat as fact.

"Yes," Selene said after a minute. "Yes, I do."

I knew, of course, about neolithic goddess worship and the cults that developed centuries ago around the idea of a powerful, life-giving female divinity. I knew, too, that Selene was the name of the maiden persona of the Triple Moon Goddess of the Greeks. Sterling Catcher's offering of his first child—symbolized of course by the name—may well have been a desperate act of propitiation, but in aid of what, I had no idea.

"But then, years later," Selene went on, "after he found out that Mother had told me that story from Saint Luke about the Archangel's announcement of the coming of Christ, he knew he had to get me away from her and from the threat of her religion. He'd underestimated the intensity of her faith, you see," she said with a wry pursing of her mouth. "Actually, I've never known how he learned she'd done it; maybe she told him herself—bluffed and lost."

So saying, Selene addressed herself to her cognac and took several small sips before raising her eyes and looking at me with the same vague challenge I'd noticed before. Her attitude was hard to interpret: Was she sneering at her father? Was she laughing at him? Was she acolyte or apostate? Scourge or follower?

"Over the years," she said, "we went to most of the important neolithic shrines in Europe and Asia Minor. Father especially wanted to return to Çatal Hüyük and to the limestone temples at Hağar Qim and to Tarxien on the south coast of Malta."

I had actually been to Tarxien as a student, but I said nothing.

"He was like a pilgrim," she said, glancing down at her hands and then at me. "I still remember the day he lay facedown on the stones at Ephesus. I can see him right now, like a priest at his ordination. He lay there for four hours, in that burning Turkish sun. And he never moved a muscle. I know. I watched him do it."

She smiled at me and blew some smoke into the air. Several exuberant people had just come into the bar and the waiter, perhaps anticipating the effects of our continued privacy on his tip, shepherded them off to a table in the farthest corner.

"Please do feel free to interrupt at any time," Selene said, a twinkle in her eye, "if I offend your holy office."

"Ah, prègo," I murmured with a small, dismissive gesture. "Please. It's fascinating." I tried (but of course failed) to imagine Sterling Catcher spread-eagled in front of the many-breasted statue at the famous Temple of Diana.

Then Selene laughed in the bitter way she had before.

"Please forgive me, Giovanni," she said in a strange, low voice, emptying her glass in a swallow and placing it carefully in the center of her little paper napkin. "I never meant to make you listen to . . . all this. I can't think why I rambled on and on the way I did. I do apologize. Shall we go?"

As she rose to precede me out into the piazza, I had the fleeting impression that what she had just told me was the shifting of some immeasurable burden, if not its loss.

Selene was silent in the taxi back to Carla's. As the car wound up the curves of the Viale Michelangiolo, I glanced at her from time to time, but her face was smooth, her golden eyes revealing nothing but her apparent interest in the lovely glow of the setting sun and the architecture of the fine villas set back from the road, protected by their ancient trees. For the twenty minutes it took to get to Carla's house, Selene said nothing at all.

I was silent, too, thinking about the conversation in Ballatóio's. Why would such a woman, independent, remarkably intelligent, accustomed to the most privileged style of life, reveal such private things to me? And, strangest of all, I sensed that her confidences had little or nothing to do with the fact that I was a priest. I was a comparative stranger, after all, and though I was beginning to feel that she did like me well enough, our level of intimacy was far below that required for such revelations.

When I handed her out of the taxi, she smiled as if at a chauffeur and went off into the house to dress for dinner, leaving me to pay the fare. When, a moment later, I ran up the steps to the entrance hall, Selene was nowhere to be seen.

The next morning, after Carla's long and noisy birthday party, Piero and Selene departed to a house party on the Adriatic shore near Rimini. According to Carla, they had accepted the invitation long ago.

We did not see them again until the early days of June.

Chapter Three

ne chilly afternoon, when Selene and Piero had been away only a few days, I was alone in the house, Carla having gone off for the day to some friends in Fiesole. I'd been invited (Carla made sure I was included in every one of the multitudinous social opportunities that routinely came her way), but declined as graciously as I could and spent most of the day reading in the small study off the balcony. But I was distracted and out of sorts. From time to time, I would get up to gaze across the Arno to the dome of the Cathedral, return to my chair, pick up my book, and moments later find myself staring across the room, not even taking in the small, priceless da Vinci drawing of a child, our number-one family treasure, which sits in uninsured splendor next to a grouping of cheap porcelain trinkets Carla found in a shop in Siena and could not resist.

By four o'clock, I was ready to admit defeat: I could neither read, nor think, nor work on the essays I had pretended to myself I would take the opportunity of my "convalescence" to write. The prospect of my daily therapeutic walk filled me with boredom.

I went to my room, paged quickly through my worn address book, and moments later the deep, cheerful voice of my old friend Avery French was booming at me all the way from Boston.

We had been casual acquaintances during my sojourn in the States some years before, but, surprisingly, our relationship had ripened into an enjoyable if not particularly intimate one, and we maintained it in a lazy way, mostly by letters and phone calls, when something needed to be said.

Avery was the editor of the moribund though still breathing *Renaissance Review,* a minor journal of essays on the art and culture of the period. He'd been at it for ages and was regarded as a person of considerable taste and discrimination, though it was generally agreed he was no businessman. I knew that the *Review* endured thanks to the contributions of a few old "angels," but Avery's personal luster had not seemed to dim despite the improvidence with which he ran his shop. Some thought it was little more than a wealthy man's toy, but I knew that Avery wasn't rich at all and that he cared deeply both for scholarship itself and for his reputation as a connoisseur. As a consequence of his indefatigable burnishing of that reputation, Avery also had a minor faculty appointment at Harvard. He taught no courses that I knew of, but he did have access to the services and libraries, and it was for that reason I had called.

It was midmorning in Boston and he answered the telephone on the second ring. I heard the sedate sounds of office activities in the background, but Avery seemed happy to hear from me and not in much of a hurry to ring off. We spoke briefly of family and friends, the weather in Boston and Florence, the state of his stomach (always a feature of his conversation), and, those formalities concluded, I asked my favor.

Avery chuckled richly and then paused, as if writing something.

"For you, my dear friend, anything. What's the name again?"

"Sterling Alva Catcher. As I said, he left Harvard about, oh, maybe thirty years ago, maybe a bit less."

"Heavens above. What'd he do to get himself sacked from Harvard?"

"I don't believe that was the case," I said, not sure of my facts but reluctant to get into it with one of the great drawing-room gossips of our time. I'm fond of Avery, but swearing him to secrecy is often ineffective. "Can you send it express?"

"Certainly. What I find. He taught what, classics?"

"Classics."

"Done."

I hadn't the least idea what Avery might find to send me, but less than a week later a large brown envelope arrived, accompanied by a scrawled note from Avery, who had heartily enjoyed his sleuth-like assignment. There was not as much material as I'd anticipated, just a dozen or so offprints of journal articles on Euripides's plays and Attic poetry. But tucked in behind them were two photocopied portions of what seemed to be an old manuscript. The copies were clear and sharp, even though the original had been handwritten. On top was a title page, written out with some flourish and signed by Sterling Catcher himself in a strong, spiky hand:

The Great Goddess in Myth, Fable, and Reality:
Sacred Rituals of the Neolithic Cults

All right, I thought, spreading the pages out on my desk, let's see what this is all about.

Sterling Catcher wrote that the "Great Goddess" was an all-powerful divinity who presided over the very essences of human life: birth, death, and resurrection. Secret cults, though forced underground, flourished through the centuries—far into the Christian era—in Europe, Asia Minor, and in parts of Africa. But for millennia before Judaism, Christianity, or Islam, before agriculture, or writing, or anything we know, the Goddess had been man's only hope of everlasting life.

Small artifacts, bulbous stone and terra-cotta effigies, had been discovered in crumbling megalithic structures unearthed in places with unpronounceable names—at Hacilar and Çatal Hüyük in Turkey, at Hağar Qim in Malta, and Musa Dag in north Syria—places Selene had mentioned when we had our drink. Images of a female power figure were found in monuments in Greece, Italy, Bulgaria, and France. The earliest went back perhaps twenty-five thousand years.

She was *Ashtoreth* to the Canaanites and *Ereshkigal* to the Babylonians. She was *Isis* to the Egyptians and *Ishtar* to the Sumerians. She was *Cybele* and *Tamar* and *Danu*. She was *Inanna* and *Amaterasu* and terrifying *Kali* . . . but She was only One. Never more than One.

How can it be that behind Her many masks, Her thousand names, the peoples of every corner of the world knew Her for so long? Millennia! She has been filled with Her power for more than twenty-five thousand years, though our bitter century conceals Her. But She was God. *She still is God.*

I turned the page and there, centered on the next sheet, printed in large, Greek characters:

ᗡᕁΤᕁΓΙᔕ

I stopped and ran my fingertips over the thick letters, quickly spelling out the Greek word to myself: *Artemis.*

> The neolithic Greeks knew Great Artemis as the goddess of the swelling moon and of the earth and sea. She was the first among the divinities gathered for the ceremonial pantheon: only the stars are older. As Selene is the Great Goddess in the sky, so Artemis reigns on the earth. She is queen of the forest and its wild beasts, but also of the great, foaming surges of the covering waters of the world. She has power over every animal on earth—those that wander the forests, those that fill the deeps, and those that sing and hunt and say they love.

Sterling wrote that cults dedicated to Artemis flourished wherever the ocean threatened—on the northern shores of the Black Sea, among the savage Celts and Norsemen, and in the sacred Aegean. "Even now," he wrote, "though Her cult is in shadow, wherever the water laps the land, there She will be found, a refuge for sailors lonely and frightened on the dark waters of the ocean seas."

According to Sterling, the silver fir is Artemis's sacred tree; all the vast woodlands of the world are Her domain. She is the patroness of all the fruits of the earth, and in the ancient days the offerings of the worshipful were found not only in the holy precincts of the great temple at Ephesus, but in simple groves as well, guarded, as Sterling put it, "by slavering dogs to warn the faithless out, but splendidly hung with vine tendrils and clusters of ripe, glowing fruits to make the pious welcome. For She favors those who obey Her with tranquility, fortune, and abundance."

Artemis has many names. She is called Maiden of the Silver Bow and Mistress of the Animals. Blind Homer knew Her as Mistress of the Game and Lady of Wild Things. Some called Her Artemis Brauronia; little girls came to Her sanctuary at Brauron dressed as bears to honor Her with dancing and sacrifice, for She is the patroness of girls and young women and mothers in childbed.

Sterling also wrote of the many legendary stories of Artemis's devoted servants: Daphne, the virgin nymph who, pursued by Apollo the Seducer, was turned into a laurel tree to escape him. And young Iphigenia, daughter of King Agamemnon, owed her life to the Goddess. She was to be sacrificed at Aulis for fair winds to Troy, the very knife was at her throat, but the Goddess descended in a cloud and carried her to Tauris to become Her greatest priestess.

"And many still sing of Hippolytus," Sterling wrote, "who loved the Goddess more than Queen Phaedra's flesh."

> Though he was ripped to pieces on the sharp rocks of the sea road, Divine Artemis saved him, too, caused him to be born again as son and consort. And what of Prince Actaeon, saved or savaged? He was hunted and overtaken—by Her dogs, say some, by his own, say others. But destroyed, having seen the chaste Goddess in Her bath.
>
> For the Great Artemis is always chaste. She resists every threat, every blandishment. There is no temptation which can alter that exquisite chastity. Those who worship Aphrodite, the Great Whore, are anathema to Her and She will repay. The Goddess is capable of terrible, retributive rage—fearsome revenge and earthshaking anger— as powerful as Her compassion for the wild things of the world.
>
> The rage of Queen Artemis accepts appeasement only in the coin of human blood; Her unforgiving nature is ever ready to wound and She must be placated. For here is yet another name, given Her by Ovid the great poet: *Merciless Diana*. Propitiate Her wrath, make offerings, remain chaste into your core—and live. Displease Her and be damned.

There followed a long section that was obviously a prayer. It was addressed to Hecate, the Moon Goddess's terrifying third persona. I knew of course that Hecate was the powerful sorceress for whom the witches in *Macbeth* create their spells. But Sterling described Her as an ancient Crone, the nightmare vision who rises from Her underworld domain only on the darkest nights, racing over the harsh fens with Her pack of rabid wolf-dogs: "She is the Enchantress," he wrote, "the Goddess of Incantatory Magic."

He explained that Hecate's power is over the unconscious, over instinct, over our most atavistic natures. She is known in ecstasies and dreams, in hallucinations and enchantments. Liquors and potions, such as She gave to the gods themselves, sweet poisons made from sacred roots and flowers—mandragora and wolfsbane, black poppy and dead men's bells and faery caps and the liqueur of the white-flowered hemlock—bring on those visions. She pricks Her fingertips on willow twigs and yew branches that She may use that blood to wreak Her bitter spells.

> The sacred number is Three. Three times three. Nine. The signature of the three-faced Goddess of Enchantments. Multiples of that sacred number bring Her forth. The old custom of sacrificing animals at a place where three roads meet honors this magic. The burned sacrifices are made only at crossroads, always under Her dark moon, gifts of fruit and hair, mysterious herbs, and black lambs and dogs still bloody from the knife. Hecate is unafraid of what cannot be explained.

When I finished reading the prayer, I got up and went to stand in the doorway to the terrace, grateful for the cool evening breeze on my face, waiting for my heart to become silent in its beating. I knew the symbols, of course, the themes; the chaste Moon Goddess was rooted in the culture I'd been part of all my life. She represented power, continuity, and regeneration. The myth of domineering Artemis goes beyond the seasonal flourishing of the forests and the phases of the moon virtually to nature itself. To Her ancient worshipers, She was the personification of the irresistible cycles of the natural world, the connection between the grand stirrings of the universe and the beating of human hearts.

But I had never thought very much about Hecate—the third part of the metaphor. Could Sterling have meant that She was the symbol of the dark of the moon, balancing Selene, symbol of the crescent, and Artemis, symbol of the full? Did She perhaps personify the earliest, most instinctual part of us—the swinging of human moods, the rising of human rage, the wildness in *us*?

I took a last look at the darkening sky and went back to my chair. I was astonished at how affected I was by what I'd been reading, material that was, after all, not unfamiliar to me. But these were all ancient stories—and, for that matter, *only* stories. Did Harvard force Sterling Catcher out because of *this*? Unsettling, yes, but a legitimate academic effort, or so it seemed to me. Still, odd that it should bother me, that I should find it so *spettrale*.

I took a deep breath and turned to the second sheaf of pages, which were filled with explanations of arcane rituals of worship. There were long passages that seemed to be either invocations or spells, meant to guide an earnest worshiper to proper propitiation of the all-powerful Goddess. I skimmed ten or twenty pages, but one portion in particular chilled me to the bone. At great and rather lascivious length, Sterling described the ancient practice of symbolic marriage, the consecrating of a "son-consort" for the Goddess. He wrote of the Stag King, a beautiful young man who would perform the duties of a consort to the temple priestess for one year and then be sacrificed and replaced. It was a custom that went back to the earliest times.

"It is one of the oldest ceremonies known to man," Sterling wrote. "The idea of the son-lover, the consort, is found in all the old societies. He is crowned only to be sacrificed. In the earliest days, men dressed in deerskins were chased and killed and devoured, and the ritual marriage with the Goddess is a development of that, for the Stag King, his function in the holy drama at an end, was sacrificed each Autumn and replaced, his successor doomed to the same."

The next page was elaborately decorated with skillful drawings of men disguised as stags, huge racks of antlers on their heads, skins hanging from their shoulders. With the tips of my fingers I traced the strong lines of the antlers and the expression of terror on the face of each sacrifice, perfectly clear even on the photocopy. The whole thing was surrounded by a series of jagged, toothlike designs interspersed with rather elegant, linear renderings of stalks of wheat and ears of corn. The design ran right off the page as if directing a reader to the final pages, at the beginning of which, written in fancy script, were the words: *The Sacred Mysteries of Eleusis.*

I was disappointed to find that the remainder of the manuscript was written almost entirely in Greek, and though I struggled through with determination, my Greek proved far too rusty for an adequate translation.

One short section, "The Resurrection Cult of Demeter," was in English, in Sterling's now-familiar hand. I read the four or five pages avidly, and when I was done I stared blindly across the room for several minutes, and then quickly put everything back into the large envelope in which it had arrived.

Enough, I thought, I have read enough. I don't need to know all this.

By the time Carla came home from a strenuous shopping expedition, I was, or so I thought, quite myself again. Carla was revved up, immensely stimulated by a long day of spending money and unwilling to settle for a quiet dinner at home. We went to a pleasant restaurant down the hill near the Pitti Palace, and by the time I crawled into bed four hours later I was exhausted enough to tell myself that Sterling's manuscript was of very little consequence. Impassioned and scholarly, yes, but truly not much more than the ramblings of the eccentric father of a mysterious and fascinating daughter.

But in those hazy, suspended moments before I fell asleep, I remembered what Selene had told me in Ballatóio's—that her father had taken her away from her home to *save* her (as he may indeed have seen it) from the malign influences of the Christian god. I thought of Sterling's chilling manuscript, his cold, factual accounts of the deeds of the Goddess, the horrendous ceremonies of the Stag King sacrifice, and of the powerful resurrection cults to which he, as a young man, had borne witness. That those had been Selene's childhood lessons was more than I could bear to think about, but even so—and despite myself and my exhaustion—I lay awake nearly until dawn, wondering how such a thing could be.

Chapter Four

ess than a fortnight later, Selene and Piero returned, unannounced and unexpected, from their trip to Rimini. It was close to midnight when they arrived. Carla, who had not been feeling well that day, had gone up to bed right after dinner, but I was down in the study in my dressing gown, doggedly reading Herodotus, trying to blunt the shock of realizing the disastrous state of my Greek. I'd been at it an hour or two every night since Avery sent me Sterling Catcher's manuscripts.

When I met them at the door, Selene gave me a light kiss on the cheek and went almost immediately to her room, looking calm enough but very tired and remote. Piero gazed rather soulfully up the stairs after her and then, putting his finger to his lips, motioned me out onto the balcony.

The lights of the city were dimmed by a damp mist that had settled in about eight o'clock. Piero stood by the edge of the balustrade, lit up one of his small, nasty cheroots, and stared into the thin fog off the river.

"What's wrong?" I asked. "Has something happened? We didn't expect you for at least another week."

He shrugged. "I don't know. I really don't. Not a clue."

"Well, were there problems in Venice? Carla mentioned you were stopping there afterward, something about Selene looking into renovations on her house? Carla said she..."

"Vanni. *Per favore*...I don't know. I wish I did. We didn't even go to

Venice. We stayed in Miramar a while and then, I don't know, we drove around, went to Ravenna... Ah, shit. She's been like this for a couple of days. I think she's just in a lousy mood. She gets like this." He puffed on his cheroot and turned slightly away from me.

"Is she ill?"

"Vanni—"

"Have you been beastly to her? You can be, you know. Is she angry?"

"Vanni, *stai zítto*. Shut up, please. She's in one of her moods. That's all. It's not the first time and it won't be the last. She said she wanted to come back here and I was just as glad to do it, believe me. Christ, I'm exhausted."

With that he stubbed out the cigar in a potted fern and turned to go inside. As he did so, he looked back at me from the doorway with a haggard, miserable expression in his black eyes, murmured an apologetic *"Buona notte, cugino,"* and went away. I realized I hadn't really understood, not until then, that he might actually love her.

I stayed out on the balcony until long after the lights of the cafés, those I could see, winked off and only the dome of the Cathedral quivered through the mist, dim and pale. I chided myself for my rudeness to Piero. Surely whatever might have passed between him and Selene was none of my business. Why couldn't a stunning and vivacious woman have bad moods, even fits of angry sadness, coming out of nothing? Of course, the little I knew—or imagined—of her background seemed to suggest a context; upon reflection, it was not so difficult to believe that Selene Catcher, so witty and engaging, might have a darker, less vibrant side.

The next morning, Selene seemed quite herself again. Piero was frankly relieved to see it, kissing her hands at breakfast, promising to treat us all to dinner at Sabatini's, and teasing Carla, who was feeling much better and positively elated to have her new friend back in the fold. I sat quietly sipping my cappuccino, watching in silence while the three of them laughed and chattered on about their plans.

Carla spent a long, busy morning, barely taking the phone from her ear, arranging all sorts of entertainments. She called dozens of her friends and by nightfall had orchestrated several lunches in the countryside, two "intimate" dinner parties (no more than thirty guests at each), and a large cocktail reception for her innumerable pals, who were, she claimed, all clamoring to see Selene again.

A week later, while the cocktail party was still rollicking along downstairs, I excused myself and crawled into my bed before ten o'clock. I lay there in a near-stupor, facing the fact that it was time for me to go back to Rome. My foot was healed, better than ever, and some days my "therapeutic" walk took me six miles or more, all the way to the back end of the Boboli Gardens and the Belvedere and home again through the winding streets below the Piazzale. And I had certainly had enough of Carla's friends to last a lifetime. My reading of Herodotus had, ironically, served only to freshen my guilt over the series of essays I had not even begun to write, and I was eager to redeem myself, if only by the attempt.

Nerved up by my thoughts, I turned on the light and reached for the small book of Greek poetry on the table. I had been reading for about an hour when I heard soft thuds and murmurs from the adjoining room—Piero's room. There followed a breathless silence, then an audible expulsion of breath from Piero and a light, soft rill of laughter from Selene. I did not press the pillow to my ears—nothing so Victorian. I lay with the book open in my hands and listened to them making love until, apparently, they fell asleep.

The next morning everything changed. We were taking a late breakfast when a telegram came from Selene's sister, Bet, in Massachusetts. Their mother had died in the convent two days before, leaving nothing behind but a small, gold crucifix for Bet and a message for her elder daughter: "Tell your sister Selene she is to continue to look for the Angel."

We were all instantly solicitous and eager to do anything we could to help her bear up under such dreadful news. But Selene would not let us comfort her, keeping to her room, rereading Bet's telegram, trying, as she later said, to understand why she could not absorb the shock of learning that her mother, whom she had not seen for so many years, was truly gone. She was completely overcome by the depth of her reaction.

I told Carla and Piero I thought it best that we let her recover her equilibrium as she would, silently hoping to myself that the peaceful quiet of the hills, the early summer air, the lovely views would do what friendship apparently could not.

That afternoon, Selene went for a long walk by herself. Piero, who had been trying valiantly to cheer her up, gently offered to walk with her, but she just shook her head and wandered off alone.

She did not come back for hours. I thought, fleetingly, of going to look for her, but quickly reminded myself that Selene was a grown woman, of an independent nature, recently bereaved (though in what way and to what extent I could not have known), and that, more to the point, Florence is a very easy city to get lost in if one sets out to do so. Though Carla fumed and fretted and Piero, tight-lipped, took himself up to his room with a bottle of American whiskey, I counseled patience even as I settled myself in my chair in the study, determined to wait up for her until dawn, if need be.

It was very late when I heard a car crunch onto the gravel of the driveway, and several minutes later Selene came slowly into the study. She sank into a chair and looked calmly across the room to me.

"Vanni. Still up?"

"Selene... Selene." I went close to her and got down on one knee by her chair, taking her hand. It was warm and firm in mine.

"Do you think I could have a little wine?" she asked in a clear, low voice.

"Yes. Of course, *con piacere.*" I got to my feet and filled a small glass from a decanter on the table. When I turned back, Selene had gone out the door to the garden and was standing in the middle of the mossy flagstones, her hands clasped in front of her. The slight breeze lifted her hair. When she felt my hand on her sleeve, she began to speak, though she did not turn to face me.

"You know," she said softly, "when my father bought the estate, years and years ago, he built a private road straight down from the pair of obelisks at the entrance and along the curve of the large field I told you about. But standing in the way was an enormous rock outcropping which was so big it was impossible to blast or move, so he left it there and built the road around it. It's granite... or, I'm sure it must be, and in some lights—at dawn, or when there's lightning with a storm—the mica in it shines like stars."

Her voice, low and almost musical, had a slight edge that frightened me. "Selene..." I began, touching her arm again, but she would not be interrupted. She moved to a small ornamental tree in the corner of the garden and fingered its leaves as she continued.

"When I was a girl I used to climb up to the top of that big rock and sit, sometimes for hours, and pretend that it was really a great sailing ship and I a sailor, curled up in the crow's nest, looking at the trees... the field... the moon.

"Many times, when Bet and I were little girls, and Father was away from home, Mother would take us up to the rock, even on days that were drizzly or cold, and we'd sit still as statues, listening to the birds or the wind while she told us marvelous, magical stories. She said that on the nights just before and after Christmas, there would be angels, announcements in the sky, and that for those few nights each year, if we paid very close attention, if we had faith enough to see, the angels might appear to us and bring announcements of glad tidings. 'Watch for them,' she'd say, 'all of your lives' ..."

Selene broke off with a small laugh, almost of embarrassment, as if she realized how impossible that must have sounded, how spooky and ridiculous.

"Of course, when I was a child," she said with a chuckle, "I thought she'd invented the angels, you know, just to entertain us. But she hadn't—it's an ancient story. In the old religion the period from Christmas to Epiphany is consecrated to the return of the dead."

I couldn't help it. I looked up into the black, star-filled sky almost as if I expected that the angels might have just popped out. I gritted my teeth and followed her gaze with my squinting eyes, but I saw only stars, and the glow of villa lights in the darkness. The earlier haze had lifted and the sky was clear as could be. A full yellow moon had risen over the hills.

"It was a night just like this when she told me the Annunciation story from Saint Luke," Selene said. "I remember how she took my head in her hands and brought her face close to mine and said, 'Look for these glad tidings, daughter, look for them all of your life, for with the Christ, nothing shall be impossible.' "

With those words, she turned to face me at last. "And now she's dead. Vanni, I haven't seen her since that night."

It was the simplest instinct to put my arms around her. She leaned gratefully against me for just a moment and then moved away.

"Selene, my friend, can I ask you? Where did you go today?"

She had taken only a sip of the wine, but she put the glass down on a small table and linked her arm through mine, as if holding on to me, on to anything, would make it easier to give an answer.

She told me that when she left the house that afternoon, she'd walked all the way down the hill, across the Ponte San Niccolò and through the busy streets to the center of the city. She walked quickly, distracted by nothing, engulfed in a complex wash of feelings in which guilt and longing seemed mixed in equal portions. Barely noticing how she got there, she found herself rounding the corner of the Palazzo Medici and took off at a run up the Via Cavour as if, she said, in some part of her mind she knew her destination. Minutes later she arrived, almost breathless, at the front gate of the Monastery of San Marco, the famous Fra Angelico museum.

It was lovely. Cool and silent. By then, it was late in the afternoon and the shadows of all the old trees were falling through the empty cloister. Selene had been there with some friends several years before, but though she'd gotten bored with the tour and spent most of the time impatiently waiting for the others to look their fill at the Fra Angelicos, somehow she still had a sense of where things were. She went directly to the long flight of steps that leads up to the monks' cells, climbed slowly up, and there— at the top of those stairs, in a fresco painting over five hundred years old—was the Angel her mother promised her.

Selene turned to face me and clasped her hands in front of her as she had before, looking at me with an expression that, even in the darkness, was bright with exhilaration.

"It was Fra Angelico's great *Annunciation*, of course, the announcement to Mary. Oh! I couldn't take my eyes away from the expression of utter rapture on her face. Fra Angelico painted her with her hands crossed over her stomach and the blue cloak held around her—like this—posed in an attitude of complete attention, sitting on a round wooden stool in the courtyard of San Marco itself. Every detail is perfection, down to the low wall between the arches and the designs on the capitals of the columns. And the Archangel Gabriel is *there!* Not in some cold Massachusetts sky, but *here*, Giovanni, in Fra Angelico's own city, five thousand miles from where I'd started looking!"

Selene pressed her body against the wall of the house, her palms flat against the rough old stones. Her eyes were fixed on the sky at a point somewhere above and behind my head.

"I stepped back and leaned all my weight against the opposite wall," she said slowly. "I imagined I could smell wet plaster; I felt the cool, smooth wall against my bare arms . . ."

After a moment, she cleared her throat and seemed about to reach for her wine, just a yard away on the table. But she didn't move, not a muscle, and I realized that the moment in San Marco had come again—she was reliving every detail, every sensation.

"I stood perfectly still, concentrating on the figure of Gabriel, and I saw that he looks *up* to the Madonna. The angel's line of sight in the painting is *upward*, and the eye contact is perfect. But though he was looking directly up at Her, at the Virgin, it was as if he was announcing something to *me* . . . just as my mother promised. The verses she recited to me that night long ago came alive for the first time: 'I am sent to speak unto thee, and to show thee these glad tidings.' It was like an announcement of the Renaissance itself."

I came out of my stupor, took a breath. In spite of my having known what she would see at the top of the stairs, I realized I could have had no sense at all of what she would have felt.

"Something seemed to have . . . come loose in me," she said, leaning toward me. "I'd been so cold before, but suddenly I felt a wave of almost unbearable warmth coming from the figure of the Archangel, as if his arrival in the cloister blew a hot wind toward the figure of the Virgin, and past Her to *me.* By the time I found a taxi and got back here, I was soaking wet from the heat. I actually sat on the front steps for a minute, just now, before I came inside. I was so hot."

She reached for the wine then, drank it all, slowly, deliberately, and replaced the glass on the small table. She went to the edge of the garden balustrade and stood looking out at the hills.

"Last night," she said, "after the party, when I went to Piero's room, he embraced me when I came in, but I pulled away . . . I didn't want to be touched. But Piero didn't seem to realize that. He grasped me to him, kissed me again and again and suddenly I . . . I . . . Oh, God! . . . I couldn't let go of him, I swear I couldn't."

I must have uttered some sort of sound, some thin, shrieking expulsion of my breath. I backed as far away from her as I could, as if to escape her words, to deny the truth of what I'd heard from my bed, my book of Greek poetry open on my chest.

But all at once Selene's voice became softer, her clenched hands fell to her sides, and she just stood, straight and slightly quivering, in the middle of the garden. Her eyes, which had been wide open just moments before, were now hooded and dark. I think it was several minutes before either of us moved.

"I absolutely could not . . . stop," she whispered, "because some-where . . . somewhere *inside myself,* I knew it was the last time."

With that she sank into one of the small iron garden chairs, her fingers pressed against her mouth. "Believe me, I know how this sounds. I know you don't understand. How could you?"

I roused myself somehow, opened my mouth to assure her that I did, but nothing came out. I stayed as I was, trying to regain what I thought of as my cool, cerebral self. A moment later, Selene came close to me and put her hand gently on my arm.

"I'm afraid I've shocked you rather badly. I'm sorry. I'm fairly shocked myself. But I did, Vanni ... somehow I think I did know it was the last time in my life I'd ever have sex with a man. And when I left the San Marco today I knew the Goddess expected me to give it up. I've been turning my back on Her for years, running away, living like a whore ... but that was the Archangel's announcement," she said in a groaning whisper. "The angel spoke for *Her*! And for the first time, there in front of that beautiful Fra Angelico, for the first time I knew that She's wanted me all along! But not as I've been! She wants me chaste—ready and *chaste*! I've never understood that before."

Her face had gone dead white with emotion and her golden eyes gleamed in the moonlight. She moved her hand from my sleeve and took a deep, shuddering breath. "I'm sorry," she said.

She turned and looked up into the sky again.

"Do you remember that day in Ballatóio's when I told you about my father and his ... devotion to the Goddess?"

"Of course," I whispered. Then I cleared my throat and said it again. "Of course I remember."

"Yes. And that he gave me to Her when I was born? Named me for Her virgin form? Selene, the cold, dispassionate, cerebral maiden goddess of the crescent moon?"

"Selene ..." I reached toward her, but her back was to me and she didn't see.

"And how he went to all the ancient sites, how he lay on the stones at Ephesus, praying, begging Her to notice him?"

"Selene, why don't we—"

"But all of it!" she went on, her voice rising with anger and emotion, "all of it—the pilgrimages, the sacrifices, the rituals, the great scholarship, *me*—it was all a hopeless, desperate, and ultimately pointless act of bargaining because the Goddess hated him and he knew it."

"But why?" I asked, knowing even as I expelled the words that I was actually *conversing* about the Great Goddess as a being with mind and motive. I supposed that my Jesuit brethren back in Rome would either be very proud of me—or very disappointed.

"He was an offense to Her because he was unchaste," she said, turning back to me. The gold had fled from her eyes, leaving them barely tinged with an ocherous, pale bronze. "She forgives many sins, many crimes. But not that. I've never understood before what an insult he was to Her."

Then, almost as if she were in pain, Selene reached out her hands to me and gripped my arms with a strength that surprised me. I could feel the tips of her fingers against the very bones of my arms.

"The Goddess had nothing but contempt for him," she said in a harsh, low voice. "He had no control over his ... needs. None. He had failed Her consistently and he must have known that whatever his talents were, how great his genius, the Goddess despised his powerful sexuality and that She was *right* to despise it. That's why he made that desperate act of propitiation when I was born. That's why he gave me to Her."

Curiously, as she spoke those words, she seemed, at last, to relax. I saw a loosening of the stiffness in her shoulders, and then, a second later, when she let go of my arms, she was, almost magically, as cool and remote as in the days and weeks before.

"As you know, Father Giovanni," she said in an odd, almost ironic tone, "when you are chaste you cannot be touched because you have dominated your own nature. Isn't that true?"

The next day she was gone, and I did not see her for more than a year.

went back to my post at the Vatican and
spent a satisfying summer and fall enjoying the scholarly life I'd once
thought I didn't want. In time, I understood that the months in Florence
truly had refreshed me as I'd hoped they would do, and I felt ready to
give my mind to what I had begun, once again, to think of as "my work."
My longtime fascination with the mystifying concepts of grace, penance,
and forgiveness had been damped down in my time away, but now I saw
them as embers, preserved in a paper cone, waiting to catch fire.

Though the simile was tortuous (and a little too self-regarding), it
seemed right to me. Whether my strange association with Selene Catcher
had played a role in bringing those embers back to glowing life, I had no
idea, but soon I found myself able to stop wondering what relevance such
ideas might have to me and my poor life, and to see them purely—
conceptual and uncluttered.

Late that summer, Carla returned to the family villa near the lakes
north of Milan. I knew that she missed Selene, had come to think of her
as a true friend and boon companion, but all she said by way of explanation for her abrupt move was that she was more comfortable in Milan,
soothed (as she put it to me in a letter shortly after she returned) by the
notion that generations of Corios had roamed those damp salons before
her. I let it alone, knowing she would take no advice at all from me.

Piero disappeared. Oh, we heard from him from time to time; he sent short letters to Carla, and the odd postcard from Tripoli or Bombay to me—but that was all. He had the money to do as he wanted, and the time. Though we three had, since childhood, always been the best of chums, our relations warm and loving, and though Selene Catcher had, naturally, been no part of that, her departure seemed to change the chemistry among us. The cohesion we had cherished seemed forever lost.

My return to Rome continued to stimulate me in a way I could not have anticipated. I was eager and sharp, and my first attempts at a series of essays on penance were right on the track I'd hoped for, though my guilt over such pride in what was, after all, a small accomplishment seemed to keep everything in balance. I'd lost my nerve for soccer, but I took long walks through the Borghese Gardens and the hills beyond, grateful and at peace.

So successful had been my resumption of my former life that some of my work soon caught the attention of others. More than a year after my return to Rome, I was invited to address a group of like-minded professorial types at a gathering in London.

In the last days of September, I checked into a small hotel on Curzon Street and went for a walk around Green Park. The air was breezy and fresh, and I loped along, enjoying the change.

A few days after the conference began I had a free afternoon. I lunched with an old friend from Cambridge days in a small restaurant at the end of Pall Mall that offered food only an Anglophile could love—heavy, tasteless, and very expensive. We came out into a sudden rain shower. My friend jumped into a cab, back to his office, and I ducked into the National Gallery, just across Trafalgar Square.

I walked slowly through the early Italian galleries—the backbone, as I was informed by the brochure, of the collection. I wandered past the great Duccio *Maestà*, the "Virgin in Majesty," enthroned with saints and angels, stood for several minutes before Bellini's famous portrait of Doge Leonardo Loredan, and then turned a corner into the Venetian High Renaissance Gallery to see their famous Titians.

And there, to my absolute astonishment, was Selene Catcher, looking very much as I remembered her: the heavy dark blond hair, a shimmering black mink coat draped over her shoulders, and the same riveting look when she whirled at the sound of her name bursting from my lips.

She was as startled as I, but came quickly toward me and without a word kissed me on both cheeks and stood back a pace, holding my arms as she had in Carla's garden on the night I'd seen her last—more than a year before.

"Vanni Corio," she whispered, not taking her eyes from my face. "Oh, Vanni!" I smiled and embraced her, the soft fur of her coat sleeves warm against my cheek.

"What have you been looking at?" I asked, just as though we had seen each other only an hour before and gone our separate ways through the gallery. Selene laughed and, slipping her hand inside my arm, drew me toward Titian's marvel, *The Death of Actaeon*.

"This."

The painting, glowing with the muted reds and browns of blood, tells the story of Actaeon, the unfortunate hunter who, entirely by accident, saw the Great Goddess Artemis naked in Her bath. Enraged at his intrusion, Artemis flung the water from Her wet hand toward him, and when the droplets hit, antlers grew from his forehead and his heart turned into a stag's heart, pounding with terror. But even then he retained his human consciousness; he knew how undeserved his punishment was, and yet his stag's heart was overcome with fear. He leapt away, trying to escape, but the dogs saw him and gave chase and overtook him.

Titian's painting was a perfect illustration of Sterling's story of the Stag King, the human sacrifice murdered and eaten as a symbol of power and continuance. Though I'd known of the picture for years, had in fact seen it before, I realized with surprise that it hadn't so much as crossed my mind when I read Sterling's manuscript on the Great Goddess.

"Look at Her," Selene whispered, her face close to mine, her free hand gesturing toward the painting. "Look at Her, Giovanni."

Conscious of the warmth of Selene's hand on my arm, I moved closer and stared at the Goddess, now clothed after Her bath, but with one, full breast exposed. Holding Her bow straight out in front of Her, She dominated the foreground of the picture; so much larger than life, I thought, even in the perspective of Titian's wooded scene. The powerful hunting dogs looked small and almost gentle beside the commanding figure of the Great Huntress.

I took a deep breath. "The original story is from Ovid's *Metamorphoses*," I said, turning to look at Selene's face. She was gazing, enraptured, at the painting, her amber eyes slightly narrowed, her lips parted. "He called Her 'Merciless Diana.'"

"Ah, yes," she said, with a small laugh, "and not without reason."

I peered back at the picture and saw that the figure of the Goddess seemed to be *running* toward the scene of the dogs leaping onto Actaeon, onto the stag he had become. Titian caught Her in midstride, full of force and movement. And poor Actaeon, savaged as he was, nearly dead, had partially regained his human form, but he still had a stag's head as he fell, surrounded by his own dogs.

"Their teeth tore him to pieces," Selene said softly. "They ripped him apart."

With that, she laughed, breaking the mood, and put her hand on my shoulder in a comradely way. "And what brings you here today of all days? It isn't raining, is it?"

I looked at her and chuckled. I'd been caught out for a dilettante. "As a matter of fact, it is. Or was. Have you been here long, I mean in the museum? Would you like a cup of tea? Something more?"

She smiled and looked at her watch. She reached into her pocket for a pair of black leather gloves and pulled them on. "Actually, I've been here since before eleven, just looking, walking. I'm cross-eyed from it. Tea sounds wonderful."

We went out into the wet, silvery air, through which the faintest glow of a misty sun could just barely be discerned. The people on the sidewalk outside the gallery were looking with surprise into the moist sky and folding their umbrellas.

We went into a small café not too far away near Leicester Square and I ordered tea, sandwiches, and brandy. Selene lit a cigarette and stared into my eyes with what I chose to take for delight.

"How wonderful you look, Vanni," she said, smiling across the table. "Handsome and fit as always. Carla would certainly say you're much too handsome for a priest," she added, enjoying my embarrassment at her remark. "But, Vanni, truly, *come va*? All well?"

I laughed and told her something of what I'd been doing since last we'd met in Carla's garden. "Now I'm here for a conference," I said, "loving London as always. But Selene, my goodness... I'm so happy to see you." Impulsively, I reached for her hand. She held mine firmly for a moment before letting go so she could pick up her brandy.

"Selene," I said in a whisper, "Selene, tell me how you are, what you've been doing all this time. Where did you go after that night in Carla's garden?"

"Well," she said crisply, stabbing out her cigarette, "the morning I left Carla's house, I checked into a hotel." She named a small, very discreet converted palazzo not far away from the Strozzi Palace. "I think you may know it, Vanni—it's a stone's throw from the Uffizi."

Calmly sipping the brandy, she told me she went to the gallery every single day for over a month. Perhaps no one knows exactly how many *Annunciations* hang on the Uffizi's walls, but Selene examined every one of them, day after day, from the gorgeous Botticelli with the red tile floor, to the da Vinci with the bench, to the sweet, courtly Baldovinetti, to the exquisite, Byzantine Martini, covered with gold.

"I spent nearly two thousand dollars on books and prints just in that first month," she said, "while I was still in Florence, before I left to pursue the Angel of the Annunciation across Europe."

Her odd phrase caught my attention and the déjà vu came out of nowhere. Suddenly, all I could think of was Hecate, seeing Her as Sterling described Her, racing across flat, barren wastelands surrounded by howling dogs, chasing . . . what? The Angel of the Annunciation?

Leaving Florence at last, Selene had traveled down to Rome to see Filippo Lippi's breathtaking *Annunciation* in the Galleria Doria Pamphili, and then to the Cathedral in Spoleto, where they have Lippi's pale, muted scene of the Angel making his announcement outside the wall of the Madonna's house.

"In the last year," she said, "I've been all over Europe—Paris, Naples, Bergamo, Venice, Munich, Ghent, now London—putting myself into the line of sight of every painting that I see. And finally, I think I'm beginning to understand about the act itself, the *announcement*, the moment when the truth of something is revealed . . . when everything is known."

She knew it was excessive, sick, perhaps. Concentration and discipline, she said with a small smile, which she had, in the early days, believed she'd seen in her father, had often thought about and yearned for, always seemed to be virtues. But the kind of *obsession* that had gripped her at the top of the stairs in the San Marco was altogether different.

She told me that for all the months since she had left Florence, until that afternoon in London with me, she had not spoken to a soul she knew by name. She explained that she had arranged with Carla to leave many of her things either at the house in Florence or in Milan, and for the last year had constantly been shipping packages of books, pictures, and notes back for safekeeping. I sensed that she had asked Carla not to mention anything to me, though she did not say why. I knew it was better not to press her.

"I haven't even looked at any painting that was not of the Annunciation," she said. "Believe it or not. Except for *The Death of Actaeon*. I think I'd been standing there for more than an hour when you found me."

She would not say where she was staying, but offered to "walk me home" to Curzon Street. The rain had started up again, soft and almost warm, but I had my umbrella and we went arm in arm through the crowds on Piccadilly and Regent Street and into the elegant fastnesses of Mayfair, talking nonstop as we walked. I asked her to join me for a celebratory dinner at the Mirabelle, but she declined and kissed my cheek in parting, saying she needed an early night.

"You see, tomorrow," she said, smiling, rubbing her lipstick off my cheek, "I'm planning to go up to the Fitzwilliam in Cambridge to have a look at the Veneziano *Annunciation*, and then back to Paris, just for a day or two, to check my notes on a Bellini I saw a few months ago. And then I'm going home."

"To Florence?" I asked, smiling hopefully.

"No, Vanni. Home to Massachusetts. It's time to write all this down and I think I want to do it there."

A few weeks later, we met again in Milan, and the next day Carla and I put her on the plane at Malpensa for her return to the immense, private wilderness she hadn't seen since she learned it was all hers. As agreed, we shipped off her many crates of books and prints and papers, tightly wrapped, care of the postmaster in Turn-of-River, Massachusetts. It was, Carla observed a few months later over a drink on the balcony in Florence, as if Selene thought she could send the Renaissance to America, air freight.

Three years later, Selene Catcher's book on Annunciation paintings was greeted with a fanfare that seldom accompanies an academic work, all the more remarkable because she had no academic affiliation whatsoever. Shortly after the book was published, she sent a copy to Carla's, and when I went up to Florence after Easter, it was waiting.

The book was oversize but thin, not quite two hundred pages. The morocco cover was smooth and soft, and embossed on it in gold, in exquisite lettering, were the words:

The excellent reproductions, on heavy enameled paper, were brilliant and glowing—Fra Angelico, da Vinci, Botticelli, Filippo Lippi, Carlo Crivelli. The book was absolutely gorgeous. I looked through at random, gently turning the pages one by one. Each plate was beautifully colored and mounted, each "moment of announcement"—that instant of supreme suspense, of grace, of faith, when the Archangel tells Mary that she will bear a special child—centered on the page within an elaborate gold border.

I read the book start to finish, lingering over the glorious reproductions, comparing each one with the analysis in the text. Selene was obviously in love with her subject and, more to the point, in command of it as well. She knew exactly what she was looking at, the meaning of every religious symbol, and the place in art history of every element of style, technique, and concept.

Many hours had passed when I looked up from the elegant Botticelli with the red tile floor. I sat with my finger in the page, staring out into Carla's garden. There, on that lovely spring night, almost four years before, Selene had told me what happened to her in the San Marco. The moon had been full that night, large and golden, but now the flagstone floor looked stark and cold and though it was not too much past five o'clock, the sky had gone silver in the growing dusk.

I have always disliked winter and its darkness, nervously marking the time until the days lengthen to show that spring is on its way. Spring had indeed come again, though with dismal skies and belated flowers. But I was oblivious to whatever omen that might be, for Selene's book seemed to warm my hand, and the brilliance of it to shine into my face.

Chapter Six

ver the next several years we had regular news of Selene's burgeoning celebrity: guest professorships, scholar-in-residence posts, even bona fide faculty appointments were offered in profusion, but she refused them all. She preferred, she wrote in a Christmas note to me, to stay in the *stùdiolo* that had once been her father's temple, deep in the forests of central Massachusetts.

Despite her success, Selene did not forget us. There were many letters, a few long, middle-of-the-night phone calls, and then, briefly and gloriously, a visit, more than six years after the publication of her book. One brilliant October morning she arrived at the tiny Florence airport on a shuttle flight from Rome, accompanied by her niece, Carmen, Elisabetta's daughter.

Carmen was a slim, lively teenager, willowy and a bit on the coltish side, with short bouncy hair and a cheerful expression, crowing with delight at every sight and sound, every new vista that opened up as Carla's driver zoomed down the Via della Scala and into the Renaissance center of the city.

Carla remarked somewhat later that Selene seemed to have an affection for the girl that bordered on adoration. At Selene's insistence, the three of them went everywhere together, shopping for all sorts of Florentine trinkets, and sampling the finest restaurants in the city and beyond. They went to Il Cestello and Enoteca Pinchiorri (Carla's treat—the cost, of course, supremely unimportant) and spent a long, happy day in Settignano, admiring the countryside.

When Carla and Selene would settle in for a long night of feminine gossip, Carmen was there beside them, not interrupting, exactly, but avidly watching her aunt's speaking mouth, stroking her hand, finally falling asleep on Selene's lap. When the two older women gave in to exhaustion and went up to bed, Selene would take Carmen to the room they shared, whispering to her as they climbed the stairs, kissing her face, and then tucking her into bed with murmured endearments.

On several of those occasions, as Carla told me later, she watched in fascination from the bedroom doorway, marveling at that effortless, nurturing devotion. It seemed to Carla that although it was tempting to dismiss Selene's love for the girl as the passion of a childless woman, such a simple explanation was not nearly adequate to the moments she had witnessed.

Carmen even accompanied them during an afternoon spent at the falling-down palazzo of the dreadful Princess Sgonfiotto, one of Carla's more frivolous chums. She sat at the princess's feet, seeming to understand most of her machine-gun Italian, and allowed herself to be pampered and fussed over. The princess gave her a pretty bracelet that she boasted had been in her family for ages and even Selene (who, as I subsequently learned, did not care at all for the tiresome princess) smiled indulgently and thanked her for making Carmen's visit such a memorable treat.

A few days before they were scheduled to leave, I was finally able to drive up from Rome to see them. It had been impossible for me to break away before. Of course, I was horribly disappointed, but there were students who demanded my attention and there was nothing I could do.

The night before the elaborate farewell dinner party Carla had arranged, Selene and I walked out in the neighborhood, making our way slowly through the hills, eventually coming to rest on a small bench on a widened part of the road high above the river, not far from the Ponte San Niccolò.

Earlier in the day, when I arrived at the house, I'd been taken aback by Selene's appearance. In some ways, she was more striking than she had been when Piero first brought her to Florence, but changed, somehow, profoundly changed, though I recall not thinking so at the time. It occurs to me only now, in a much broadened context, that the change was, in fact, extreme.

By then, of course, Selene was past forty, an age, or so Carla insists, when women make a decision about which way their looks will go. And indeed, Selene seemed to have decided. Gone with the mink coat were the perfectly cut clothes, the elegant sweaters and silk shirts, the splendid jewelry. That night, she wore plain woolen trousers and a heavy tweed jacket that looked as if it had been purchased by an elderly duchess in the Outer Hebrides. Her clothes were expensive as always, but undistinguished, almost unflattering. Yet she didn't seem to know, or to care. Her strong, spare hands were unmanicured. Her remarkable dark blond hair had turned a deep silver, the color burnished and uniform, looking as if it had the weight of the metal itself, as if, were she to put it up, it would make a massive coil, a crown, around her head. Years before there had been a few silvery streaks, yes, buried in the dark gold of her hair, taking one by surprise as they caught, perhaps, a sudden shaft of sunlight, of lamplight. But that night, in the late October moonlight, even pulled back in what Americans call a "ponytail," held in place by a black plastic barrette, it gleamed full silver, dense with the patina of what it had become.

But there was a stiffness in the way she held herself that seemed new to me, and I thought I saw a tightness in the fine lines around her eyes. Their expression was new as well, the former ironic serenity I remembered seeming now to verge on disengagement. She'd been happy to see me after so long (I did not doubt it in the least) but seemed unwilling, perhaps unable, to speak of her truest thoughts, to let me know her feelings. I was certain she was keeping something back, something important to her, but confused and saddened by my own feelings, I saw no way to compel a confidence she would not offer on her own. Selene had always had a superbly honed ability to keep another person at arm's length.

We soon climbed back up to the Piazzale Michelangiolo, emptied, at that late and rather frosty hour, of tour buses, schoolgirls, and souvenir sellers. We leaned on the wide stone balustrade and looked out to the minaretlike tower of Santa Croce and the glorious Duomo and the hills beyond, resting on our elbows, enjoying the silence. It was a fine night, clear and starry, not even the lights of the city stealing any of the shine from the sky.

A large, ocher moon had risen beyond the Duomo, and Selene gazed at it thoughtfully for several minutes before turning to me with a faint smile.

"Funny, isn't it," she said in a musing tone, "how for thousands of years people have felt some irresistible, almost superstitious need to give the moon a name? All cultures do it, even ours."

"Umm. And what moon is that?" I asked, smiling and pointing to the sky.

"That, my friend, is the Hunter's Moon," she said softly, "sometimes the Changing Season Moon. Do you remember I once told you I was born on the night of the full Wolves Run Together Moon?"

"Yes. I do, actually."

"Well, that's the Lakota Sioux name..."

"Ah, your *indianos?*"

"Yes. And it's also called the Long Night Moon because it's the full moon closest to the winter solstice, the longest night of the year."

When we got to the house, we stood still for a moment and Selene turned and looked up at the moon again, watching intently as it slid behind one of the tall, narrow cypress trees that lined the driveway. It then freed itself from their branches to sail across the sky in the direction of the hills.

"Even when She doesn't shine, She's there, you know," she said, turning and looking into my eyes. "She's always there."

After Selene took Carmen back to America, she wrote somewhat less frequently than she had before. More than ever, I relished the dry, sparkling wittiness of her letters, the trenchant observations, the news of Carmen and reports of the seasonal blooming of her sister's gardens. But at the same time, though her affection was clear and warmly expressed, she had a way of glossing over her own deepest feelings, seeming quite deliberately to avoid any mention of her inner life. I felt the same unhappy confusion I had during her visit and learned, in time, to content myself with those few confidences she cared to make.

Then, after a few years, there was only silence. I knew that Carla had invited Selene to come for another visit, but had received an answer only after the date suggested had long passed.

These had not been good years for Carla. Her plans to turn herself into "*la gran signora dell'alta società Milanese*" had fallen through, owing to her pride and intemperate character. She had neither husband nor career and seemed terribly out of synch with the times, destined to return to the era of the useless, beautiful woman who grows stout and goes to parties. In Carla's case, however, all this was done with her own money, and the irony grated. Lacking suitable companionship, she was upset at Selene's continuing refusal of her hospitality. She railed against the "hermit" Selene had become and threatened constantly to go to Massachusetts to drag her away from her unsociability.

I comforted my sister as best I could, but all the same I could not elude the suspicion that something was very wrong. I had the fleeting thought that Selene might miss the exciting period of celebrity that had followed the publication of *Annunciation Paintings.* But that did not ring true. Though she'd enjoyed her fame at the time, and had referred to it in her letters, I sensed that its loss meant very little. Something else was wrong, but we had no way of knowing what it was.

Carmen, with whom, perhaps surprisingly, I had struck up a delightful correspondence, had little to say about her Aunt Selene. In the early days, after their visit to Florence, I got a few girlish notes, but I answered each one, and as the years went by, her letters became more structured and mature, reflecting the growing charm and wit of the writer herself. One day I got a businesslike white envelope postmarked Boston, adorned with bright red arrows pointing to a new address I knew was not too far from Beacon Hill. Carmen had moved "into town" and had a job at a small, private library. "Oh, yes, yes, it's all SMALL!" she wrote. "The apartment, the job, the salary . . . all as tiny as they can be, but Father G., I'm absolutely thrilled with it all! Selene's not too pleased, though what in the world she thinks there is for me to do out on the estate, I can't imagine. After all, it's time I got my act together and I know it even if she doesn't."

My own academic life brought me fresh satisfactions. What I had once viewed as a penance had become a joy and I was very busy. I published two books of essays on themes of grace and forgiveness, and many articles as well. These ideas continued to fascinate me intellectually because I knew that faith alone would illuminate their meaning. I could continue to explore them my life long and never really come to grips with the possibility that contrition and God's love could combine to save so much as one miserable soul—if I did not believe in the mystery of grace.

However, not all of my work was so high-toned. I was unbecomingly proud of one small piece on the private chapels of the old ruling families of Florence. Some thought it rather shamelessly provincial, but others found it interesting and worthwhile. Encouraged, I offered it to my old friend Avery French when he came through Florence for a conference— one of those trumped-up junkets that give bedraggled art professors and editors a chance to take a trip to the Motherland (as Avery persistently called Italy) on the company's account. And he'd done himself proud on that occasion, checking in with a flourish at the Grand, right on the banks of the Arno (where, frankly, the rooms smell a bit of fish, but no one dares to breathe a word about it).

We met for dinner at Celestino's, a small place near the Ponte Vecchio, and spent a lively evening catching up on old times and old friends, Selene Catcher, of course, foremost among them. After *Annunciation Paintings* came out with such success, Avery had been among those editors who camped, in a manner of speaking, on Selene's doorstep, hoping for anything she might care to toss his way. He had written to me more than once to comment, not just on the coincidence of our having such an illustrious mutual friend, but on the brilliance of some articles she did on the paintings of Crivelli and Bellini, which he (brimming with gleeful satisfaction) had published in his *Renaissance Review*.

But when I asked him how she was, Avery fussed with the dressing of his *fagiòli bianci* and didn't answer for a moment. At length, in an uncharacteristically defensive tone, he admitted that he didn't really know what Selene was doing with herself. Just in the last year, he'd been forced to refuse an article or two of hers, though it cost him, as he said, "no end of grief." But the quality was simply not up to *Annunciation Paintings* or, for that matter, to the fascinating biography of Ludovico Sforza that had followed five years later. Her imagination had obviously been captured by the Corio family's old patron.

When I read it, I recalled something we'd always known in the family—that no portrait of Sforza was thought to have survived. Some people believed his man da Vinci might have attempted one, but if he had, it was gone with the dust of the Sforza family itself. For her book, Selene had commissioned some sketches from an unnamed artist, making the point that no portraits of "Il Moro"—the Moor, the Swarthy One, as Sforza had been known in his own time—were known to exist. At the time, I stared as if mesmerized at the drawings, feeling oddly like an interloper, as if I were looking at Selene Catcher's lover in some way . . . or at her fantasies, realizing only later that the sketches reminded me remarkably of Piero himself. The imaginary Sforza was heavy-muscled and dark, with gleaming black hair, though without my cousin's gentleness or polish.

Naturally, I had read just about every word Selene had ever written. She sent me copies of a few things, but I knew there were others and I made it my business to track them down—increasingly odd work, published in increasingly odd magazines and journals. After the Sforza book, her focus seemed to drift away and the only work of any length or substance she produced was an interesting monograph on Renaissance altarpieces that I thought splendid and ripe for development into a book.

Avery agreed. When he finished his generous plate of linguini carbonara, he sat back with his wine and assumed his "great editor" pose: stomach protruding, one thumb hooked into the Saks Fifth Avenue suspenders, regretful smile. "You know how she can be," he said, "imperious, unresponsive. I saw her in Boston about six months ago, but she didn't seem quite herself," he added in a confidential tone.

"Her work is getting rather *stranièro*," he said, misusing the word, not caring that he did. "I asked her to excerpt something for us from the section on the Portinari altarpiece—it's right here in town, as you know— but she was rather forcefully insistent that we take something else she'd just finished, a surpassingly weird piece on paintings of the naked, nailed body of Christ."

"Was it good?"

Avery took another gulp of his merlot and snorted with laughter. "I thought it was terrific, but it was a little too grisly for my distinguished editorial board, though I flatter myself I would have published it had the decision been mine alone to make. I still think so, but oh, my friend, it is to shudder."

"My goodness," I said with a small, uncertain laugh.

"I think what's so disturbing," he went on, more thoughtfully, "is my sense of what's going on in her head. You've read the Sforza, of course . . ."

"Selene sent us a copy when it came out. Remarkable."

"Yes. Ha! Book and subject—both of them short, bloody, sexy, and fascinating, what?" With that he choked off his laughter, perhaps feeling that my delicate priestly sensibilities could not withstand such an observation.

"What is she working on now?" I asked, feeling horribly disloyal. I had actually read the Christ piece, though I decided not to mention it. It was, as Avery himself said, a real "doozie," about representations of Christ's body after its removal from the cross, focusing rather erotically on muscle tone and limbs and eyes and wounds.

"I don't know," he said, obviously not liking to admit that. "It's getting odder and odder, though; I can tell you that. She's still interested in Crivelli, I believe, and Bellini. And she seems to be picking up some ideas from the preliminary work she did years ago for the *Annunciation* book.

That could be a good sign, don't you think? But I can't seem to shake the impression that the Renaissance has gotten twisted in her, contorted somehow in her imagination. That dead Christ thing is really unbelievable. I'll have my girl drop a copy in the mail when I get back."

The conversation then turned to his itinerary and we chatted for almost an hour on the terrific hotel deal he had gotten in Vienna.

I left him in the bar, just on the point of making a transition from merlot to grappa, and walked all the way back to Carla's, leaning gratefully into the hillside, eager for the strain, as if that amount of physical effort would translate to my mind somehow, make it easier for me to think.

I understood what Avery meant about the increasing strangeness of Selene's work. It was impossible to ignore the slight whiff of earthy vulgarity that seemed to infuse so much of what she wrote after *Annunciation Paintings*. The Sforza book had been nearly pornographic in sections, blatant and coarse, and it occurred to me that that in itself might be some sort of "clue"—though to *what* exactly, I had no idea. Sexual things, explicit or otherwise, have naturally never been my métier, but Selene's attention to the sensual seemed the opposite of that. She had a way of seeing (and exposing) the carnal in even the most cerebral situations. Certainly, I remembered the conversation after her experience in the San Marco, her confidences about the Great Goddess and Her loathing of Sterling Catcher's sensual excesses. But with the exception of the short conversation about the names of the moon, we had not mentioned the Goddess since, and I did not feel it my place to bring it up again.

Then, shortly after my dinner with Avery, to my immense surprise, I heard from him again. He had published my little piece on private chapels, but another short essay I'd done, one of my many efforts on the ideas of grace and forgiveness, had come to his attention. The word "obscure" does not do justice to the journal that took it, and I can't imagine why a man of Avery's pretensions and associations would ever notice it. Apparently, however, he loved it and had made a call or two to friends of his on the faculty of a small, fairly elite Catholic college there in Boston. A few weeks later, I was asked if I would consider a year in Boston as "philosopher-in-residence," I think they called it, though the phrase sends shivers through me even now.

I couldn't believe the luck, and speedily accepted. I took a leave of absence from my post in Rome, packed my bags, and called Selene Catcher at the estate to tell her I was coming to America.

Although Carla had made some fairly snide (though genuinely clever) remarks about my being asked to the States as a "thinker-in-residence" (I, who had been "in residence" at her villa time and again without having contributed very much philosophy at all), she was, underneath it all, bursting with pride. She came down to Rome to see me off, and invited a few rather nice old friends to dinner at El Toulà, a signature extravagance that she evidently felt would help me remember her—as if I could forget. When the liqueurs were served, she presented me with a Gucci shaving case on the account of which my vows of poverty were, it seemed, forever sliced to shreds.

When I said as much, offering a toast to Carla at the end of our sumptuous meal, everyone laughed at my neat metaphor and our hostess burst into satisfying tears.

Next morning at the airport, she put on her usual cheerful front when the little shuttle arrived to trundle the passengers out to the big Alitalia jet waiting on the runway.

"Love to Selene!" she screamed as I packed myself into the bus. "Love to you, *fratèllo mío!* Love to you!"

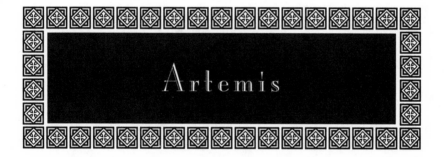

PART TWO

Artemis

Chapter Seven

y arrival in Boston was uneventful. There had been a few inches of snowfall the night before and it was still fresh and clean, sparkling in the afternoon sunlight as I got out of the taxi in front of the stylish Victorian mansion that my hosts maintained for visitors. Though they were a small college, very much in the wide swath of shadow cast by Harvard and the other megaliths of learning in the city and beyond, they were well endowed and able to provide exceptional accommodations for the visiting scholars, who, not unlike myself, claimed some ability to improve the young minds in their care. The spacious flat set aside for me was very handsome and I unpacked my bags with enthusiasm, delighted to find spotless linens, a full larder, and—that very evening—a dinner party to which I had been commanded by the president of the college. The party featured a glamorous mixture of local lights, and as I nodded and smiled my way through the evening, I thought how thoroughly my sister Carla would have relished my auspicious entrance into life in America.

My first days in Boston were filled with rounds of meetings and coffee parties, the faculty (singly and in small groups) seizing every opportunity to indulge in the most awe-inspiring political gymnastics. But I knew my way around such academic goings-on and settled in without making a fool of myself and sidestepping (with what I thought reasonable grace) any number of private invitations. My lecture schedule was light, the time to write (and, presumably, to "think") very generous, and by the time those first few days had passed, I was congratulating myself on my decision to come to Boston.

As my presence in a seminar room was not required for another week, I called Selene to announce that I was there, settled, and ready to visit.

"Vanni! *Meravigliòso!* You're here! You must come at once."

"And so I shall," I said, grinning into the phone.

The very next afternoon, armed with meticulous directions, my new Gucci toilet case tucked into a small bag, I set off in my rented car for the estate.

Everything was fine until I got to Gardner and turned south onto Route 68; it had grown dark so quickly that I'd barely made the turnoff when I had to put on my high beams. The charming Christmas-card dusting of snow we'd had in Boston did not prepare me for the heavy, trackless fall that hid every feature of the unmarked road. Proceeding at a snail's pace, I felt swallowed by the thousands of trees. Tall, dense, ancient, they were more than a forest—they were the land itself, the dominant life form. And all that time I passed nothing—not a car, not a streetlamp, not so much as the twinkle of a house light in the distance. At last I saw the left onto "Alt. 32," which *was* marked, and crept along exactly 3.8 miles to the county road, which finally brought me to the "place where three roads meet," Selene had described.

A full, golden moon had risen behind me as I drove, and when I turned off the county road and through the two stone obelisks of which I'd heard so much in years gone by, it suddenly loomed up over the trees as if to light my path.

It was just after six and I was not late at all, but I felt as if I'd been driving through forests of snow-laden trees for days. I stopped the car, rolled down the window, and stuck my head out, grimacing into the cold darkness. The narrow private road had obviously been plowed earlier in the day, but it was obscured by the additional few inches of snow that had fallen since.

Selene had told me to watch for the house about two hundred yards down from the crossroads, and far to my left, just beyond a slight rising of the land, I saw a light. I could tell, even in the darkness, that the house was very large. It was a collection of bold, rectangular shapes, the kind of structure not at all uncommon in New England. Yet in its very massiveness, it was impressive, tall and rather handsome against the endless trees.

As I steered carefully into a short driveway, my headlights caught an elongated black figure, erect and motionless, standing in the snow on a small, cresting swing of earth to the west of the house. Selene had obviously been waiting for me. When she saw the car, she waved and came quickly toward me, her tall, narrow figure seeming oddly spectral in the moonlight.

I hoisted myself out of the car and we embraced with laughter and much kissing of cheeks.

"Ah, Selene, Selene ... so long ... so many years."

"But you're here, my friend," she said, smiling into my eyes, "and it's like yesterday, no?"

"Yes. Oh, yes."

I reached into the backseat for my bag and followed her along the path and up several wide steps into an enclosed porch. She hung my heavy jacket on a peg beside her shawl and asked me to leave my boots, the snow in the treads already melting from the warmth of the vestibule, on a little square of carpet beside the outer door.

Inside, there was a large stair hall, brightly lit by a pair of brass sconces set high on the papered wall. There was a worn but obviously very fine Persian runner and several lovely antique pieces in the hall—a splendid fruitwood chest and a small damask settee. A large smoked-glass mirror, well polished, hung on the long wall between two paneled doors.

Selene watched with a smile as I peered around at the lush Victorian shabbiness. Then, with a small laugh, she set my bag down at the foot of the stairs and, linking arms, drew me along the hallway toward the kitchen.

Settling me at the heavy maple table, she moved vigorously about the kitchen, fixing coffee, taking from the refrigerator a large bowl of out-of-season fruits and a glass plate of crustless sandwiches.

I thought she looked very much as she had more than six years before in Florence. Her silver hair, now even lighter and more elegant, was still in a long ponytail, but there was a strange lucency to her skin I hadn't seen before, a kind of transparency that seemed different to me, as if she were not entirely real—not of this world. A remarkably silly thought, I know, and yet I thought it.

Selene didn't say much while I nibbled at my little sandwiches. She ate nothing herself, but drank several cups of hot black coffee while she listened calmly, with a faint smile, to my account of the drive out from

Boston and my impressions of the stark, beautiful landscape. We sat for over an hour in the warm, dry kitchen, discussing my move to Boston, Carla's most recent extravagances, and a funny story about her pal, the Princess Sgonfiotto, whom Selene remembered.

I did most of the talking, conscious of her perfect attention, her obvious pleasure in my stories. However, when I asked about Carmen, she sucked briefly on her teeth and glanced away with a sharp, glittery expression in her golden eyes.

"She's in Boston now."

"I know. She's written. I'll see her soon, I imagine, but I've been so occupied since I arrived, I haven't had a chance to do more than leave a message. Maybe next week?"

She ignored that, rose abruptly, put my plate in the sink, and offered to show me to my room.

"It was Bet's," she said, grasping the handle of my small bag and leading the way upstairs, "when we were kids. I think you'll find it very comfortable. Then we can go for a walk."

"Oh, in the dark, *cara*?" I began to protest, but she silenced me with a smile.

"No, Vanni. In the moonlight."

I laughed and hugged her to me with one arm. "Fine," I whispered. "Whatever you like. Give me ten minutes."

As she flicked on the small table lamp, I took my bag from her hand and lifted it onto a small rush-bottomed chair; when I turned back to the doorway, she had disappeared.

Bet's old room was small and pretty, cozy with a blue quilt and clean, white walls. I quickly placed my few things in the pine bureau and looked out the uncurtained window, gazing down over the sweep of forest that surrounded the house. The line of trees began not much more than thirty yards or so from the small side yard where the snow was glowing faintly in the light from the kitchen window.

When I came down the stairs, about fifteen minutes later, Selene was standing by the open door holding a large, square flashlight by its handle. She had her boots on, and the black shawl she had been wearing before was draped and tied around her shoulders. She turned when she heard my footsteps and smiled up at me. Small gusts of wind blew in the door and ruffled the strands of silver hair that had come loose from her ponytail.

"We'll go just down to the end of the road and back," she said, "give you a chance to see the property. The air will do us both good. Come."

We stepped out onto the stone walk and Selene pulled the door shut behind us, cutting off the light of the hallway.

The golden moon had risen high over the trees. I stood with my feet wide apart on the hard-packed snow as I peered across the road to where the immense open field Selene had described so many times stretched to a horizon fringed, far away, with another line of trees.

"Goodness, but it's *fine*, isn't it?" Selene said, handing me the flashlight. It was heavy and cumbersome and I almost dropped it into the snow. When I looked up she was already several yards away from me, gazing into the sky.

"It was fierce as could be this morning, even this afternoon," she called out, "but the wind blew itself out about four o'clock. Lovely, isn't it? Just grand."

With that, she whistled softly through her teeth, and all at once a pack of enormous dogs came running from around the corner of the house and bounded toward her at a gallop. In an instant, they had her surrounded, milling about her legs, and pushing against one another in a great, furry mass. And all that time, they were absolutely silent.

"Sit. *Sit down.*"

After some jostling for position, they arranged themselves in a row in front of her.

"Savo."

The largest dog—a huge beast I thought must weigh at least 150 pounds, and black as night, separated from the group. She was a good three feet tall at the shoulder, a mastiff, I thought, perhaps part Newfoundland. She came to Selene and lay down in the snow at her feet.

"Vanni, I want you to meet my girls." And Selene began, with a barely suppressed smile, to introduce these animals to me, knowing, without much more than the briefest glance in my direction, that I was thoroughly astonished and not a little frightened by the sight of so many large, black silent dogs.

"I . . . oh, *cara*, I had no idea . . . you never said . . ."

"Didn't I?" She turned to me, as if mystified to learn that she'd failed to mention these creatures in any of her letters. At the same time, she raised her hand ever so slightly, and Savo rose from the snow and came to me, circling me slowly, her tail twitching, her flat black nose sniffing almost every part of me, nudging my hips and my open, bare hands. Then she growled softly and went back to Selene's side as if she were, somehow, finished with her inspection of me.

"They don't care for men," Selene said in a matter-of-fact tone as she scratched Savo's ears with approval. "Generally, they don't allow men to come within twenty feet of me, but I want them to understand that you're different, that it's allowed."

I felt the oddest sense of relief when she said that. Any one of those dogs could have swallowed me alive, barely pausing to chew me up ... or so it seemed.

Then, one by one, they stood for their introductions. Selene came to me and put her hand on my arm. "And this is Leski."

A black-and-tan creature with heavy fur and a wide face, almost as big as Savo, stood and looked at me. "And Lorenza ... Mickey ... Tish. Tish is the baby, but even though she's small, we don't pamper her."

Tish was at least seventy pounds, I thought, black as Savo, and wiry with a shorter coat that, even in the moonlight, revealed sleek, powerful muscles.

"And Vinchy, Zaga, and Gallie, and ... Fitzi! Fitzi, come here."

Fitzi was probably half shepherd; taller than Savo, though not as heavy, she had a bright, intelligent look and glanced my way for the sake only of obedience. She did not care for me.

"As you can see," Selene said with a chuckle, "I named them all for the Renaissance."

"Oh!" Suddenly, I realized why the names had seemed so apt. "Savo is for Savonarola?"

"Yes, and—"

"And Galileo and Brunelleschi, Leonardo da Vinci and ... uh, the Uffizi Gallery? Selene, for heaven's sake ..."

She laughed and stroked Lorenza's pointed ears. "Yes. All nine of them. Ah, yes, my sweet bitches ... my sweet bitches."

I found the sight of nine uncollared, unrestrained black dogs extremely unsettling, but their absolute devotion to Selene was obvious and very reassuring.

"And are they coming with us?"

"Of course."

I turned to lead the way down the private road with the flashlight, but when I looked back, Selene and her dogs were just disappearing into the dense woods I had seen from the window of my room. Startled, I hurried after them through a slight opening in the trees and into the stillness of the forest.

Chapter Eight

he heavy boughs of the fir trees had kept much of the snow away from a faint old path I could just make out in the beam of the flashlight. Its glow reached a yard or two ahead of us and we walked along in an oval pool of yellow light.

"You know, this was a fabulous place at one time," Selene said in a reflective tone. "People thought it somewhat gloomy at this time of year, yet when these old trees are all burdened down with snow they're absolutely beautiful, don't you think so?"

"How much land is there altogether?" I asked, holding a heavy, snow-laden branch away from her face.

"Oh, probably about seven hundred and fifty acres," she said, "maybe more. Down at the end of the road, there's the original estate house. I'd say that's about a quarter mile from here with nothing but forest in between."

Selene had never mentioned the house before, or, if she had, I'd certainly forgotten.

"People used to call it the Wallace place," she was saying, "because the family lived there on and off for generations. But when Father bought the property, even though the house," she pointed into the darkness past the circle of light, "was vacant at the time, it was not included in the parcel."

I found that surprising. "Why not?" I asked. "Seems logical that it would be."

"I know," Selene agreed, nodding her head, "but it wasn't, and I've never learned why. But I do know that in spite of the hundreds of acres he already had—the field, the immense tract of forest, all this prime, wild land—Father never got the satisfaction he assumed he would because no matter how he maneuvered, he never got the original house."

Her words, and the unechoing way they hung in the still, cold air, made me even more aware of our isolation. It was as if we were surrounded by a kind of curtain that hung from the very branches of the trees, shutting us off from everything beyond.

I looked around at the dark trees and the shadowed spaces between them, past which no perspective could be grasped, and wondered how anyone could choose such utter solitude. It was like living on the moon. But then I recalled what Selene had said about her father wanting his family removed from the world, and somehow, at that moment, I could see the lure of it—the splendor of the isolation.

As we continued slowly along the faint old track, Selene appeared to glide over the snow rather than through it, as I was so laboriously doing. I hurried after her, but my own momentum sent me skidding off the path, my legs plowing shin-deep through the fresh snow. Suddenly flat on my back, I found myself staring up in terror into Fitzi's disapproving yellow eyes.

"Oh, Vanni, do be careful!" Selene said, coming back and taking my elbow in a firm grip, helping me move ahead of her into the center of the path. The dogs backed away, but even though I was then standing, Fitzi looked at me with a low growl of warning.

In a few minutes we came to a slightly wider part of the forest path. It seemed to dip as it took a gentle curve between two enormous trees, and then, just at that point, it curled into the road itself and ended. Leaving the embrace of the forest, we had come out directly across from the great, saucerlike field. It seemed to glow like a giant amphitheater, the icy skin of the snow glistening in the ambient light from the sky. The stark whiteness of it was almost blinding compared with the darkness of the forest; the perspective suddenly opened up and I saw that, as the crow flies, at least, we hadn't come that far at all. For some reason, Selene had deliberately led me the long way about through a thicket of snow and darkness.

My eyes soon grew accustomed to the change of light. The moon was then behind us and I looked straight up into the black sky, feeling strangely comforted to see the stars. At first there seemed to be just two or three, but then, as my eyes accommodated even more, millions of them.

I stood absolutely still, mesmerized, imagining that more stars were revealed by every instant of the earth's turning, as if the frictional movement of the planet against the fabric of the sky skinned a layer of the darkness back, revealing the infinite numbers of the stars shining underneath. I was enthralled.

Selene came close to me and put her hand lightly on my arm, gently rubbing the sleeve of my jacket. As I turned toward her, dragging my tearing eyes away from the stars, the flashlight swung with my movement and caught a looming shape a short distance down the road that blotted out the sky and the stars. Sterling Catcher's rock.

"Selene!"

"Yes," she said in a laughing voice, delighted with my startled reaction. "Isn't it terrific?"

As Selene had told me on that evening long ago in Carla's garden, the rock was about the size of a three-story house, but narrow and almost pointed toward the top. From where I stood it appeared smooth as slate.

"It's shining," I said, looking up the sheer face of the glittering rock.

"Yes, it's just riddled with mica, all through, or maybe that's ice, too. Could be."

We approached almost with reverence, as if to a cathedral. Even the dogs, following in single file behind Savo, moved more slowly.

Selene sank down on one of the smaller boulders that lay jumbled at the base of the rock and motioned me to sit beside her. She leaned slightly against me and I could feel the warmth of her right through my heavy jacket.

It was on this very spot, perhaps, that her mother had told her the Annunciation story from Saint Luke, had implored her to watch the sky for the heavenly messenger. Overcome by the thought, I looked up, half-expecting to see angels hovering in the clear, moonlit air above, but I saw only the millions of stars.

"When Carmen was a child," Selene said, as if reading my thoughts, "she always wanted to hear my mother's angel stories. She never tired of hearing them. She'd beg me to tell about Archangel Gabriel and his announcement.

"After I came back from Italy for good," she said, slipping her arm through mine, "Carmen and I used to go for long walks almost every night. We'd start out right after dinner, no matter what the weather, and walk all through the woods and down to the river with the dogs."

The creatures in question had arranged themselves in a wide semicircle around us. I realized with a small shudder that had I tried to go away they might not have let me.

"And sometimes we'd sit right here not talking at all. It was just the two of us together, watching the sky. Ah, Vanni, I miss those days."

Intrigued as I was by the silence and the icy, remote darkness, as heartened by the fact that the dogs obviously obeyed Selene without question and had not as yet offered to eat me alive, I was nevertheless somewhat weary and a glance at Selene's face told me that she was as well.

"Shall we save the old Wallace place for another time, my dear?" I said gently, reaching for her hands to help her to her feet. She seemed startled, but then breathed out with a deep sigh and stood up.

"Yes . . . yes. Tomorrow is time enough. Right now I could use a drink." She stepped back onto the packed snow of the road and set off toward her house, the flashlight swinging from her hand.

We walked along in silence, Selene slightly in the lead, I staring in fascination at the great white bowl of the field. We soon rounded a gentle curve and, far to the left, about two hundred yards away, I saw a lighted window, glowing as if suspended in the darkness. But just then, before I could call out or say a word, the dogs stiffened and surrounded Selene, then sank low to the ground, their hackles bristling, low growls rumbling in their throats. A moment later, the branches of the trees at the side of the road parted and a tall man emerged from the forest.

"Dwight!" Selene cried, not without pleasure. "Dwight. What a surprise. How are you?"

"Okay," he mumbled, jamming his hands in his pockets. "Okay."

"This is my friend, Father Corio. He's visiting here for a couple of days. Giovanni, our neighbor, Dwight Desjardin."

Dwight Desjardin was a tall, lean young man, wearing jeans and a khaki T-shirt under his open wool jacket. He was as powerfully spare as a stripped branch, no waste on him at all. Even in the dim light of the averted flashlight and the glowing of the moon, I could see that he had a fine, prominent nose, arching from a thin bridge, set in a face that might have been handsome if there had been something behind the eyes.

Though he kept his hands deep in his pockets, Dwight acknowledged

Selene's drawing-room introduction with a bob of his head and a tightening of his shoulders. For no reason I could think of, I somehow knew that he'd been following us from the shelter of the trees, perhaps since we'd left Selene's house, more than an hour before.

"How do you do?" I said, convinced of the absurdity of the situation.

His eyes, perhaps gray, perhaps a pale, lifeless blue, flicked up into mine for only a second. The dogs rose from the snow and circled him on tiptoe, gliding slowly around and around him. Though they growled and slunk slowly closer to his legs, and although Selene did nothing to stop them, it was as if Dwight were unaware that they were there, showing neither fear nor even interest.

"Lido needs me," he mumbled then, and without another word turned off toward the lighted house, cutting through the deep snow of the field. The dogs followed after him, but when Selene softly clicked her teeth, they wheeled back and streamed past us toward her house.

Selene saw me looking after Dwight's retreating figure. "Poor, sweet Dwight," she whispered.

"Who is he?" I asked, mildly curious.

"Just a neighbor. He lives with his sister in that sty of a place over there," she said, gesturing vaguely toward the light I'd seen. "It belonged to their father."

"Desjardin." I tried the word out on my tongue. "Dess-jardin," I muttered again, anglicizing the pronunciation. "Is it French, then?"

"I suppose. Peavy died a couple of years back. He was ninety at least. When Bet and I were kids, my father hired him as a caretaker. He was really an interesting old guy. Never went anywhere without a shotgun or a rifle. Actually, I think he was famous in the area as a hunter, a woodsman, as they used to say. Bet and I always got a big kick out of following him around in the forest. One time we snuck in that house over there and saw all his guns hanging on the wall. Scared us to death!" Selene laughed aloud at the memory. "Just before Father died he sold the house to Peavy for a dollar. About what it's worth."

"What does Dwight do?" I asked.

"Do? Nothing. Most of the time he lies on the ground in the forest, staring at the trees."

"Selene. Surely not."

"Well, he also does various chores for Lido, his sister, and for me," Selene said. "In fact, earlier this winter he built a wonderful set of bookshelves in the *studiolo*. I never asked him," she said, turning calmly to me, a faint and enigmatic smile at the corners of her mouth. "He offered to do it."

"Really?"

"Yes," she said in a matter-of-fact tone. "But he would do anything I asked of him. Anything at all. He adores me."

I stared at her in what I'm sure must have been frank disbelief, but she didn't seem to notice.

"Dwight was strange and remote even as a boy," she said as we turned into her short driveway, "but the last few years he's gotten worse." She turned and looked up into my eyes with a strange, ironic expression. "About a year ago he took a boning knife out of Lido's kitchen drawer, brought it into the woods, and used it on himself in horrible ways. They sent him away for a while and he's been back only a short time now, just since last fall."

"What? No. Oh, Selene, good God! Cut himself?"

She cleared her throat and stood perfectly still in the drive, finishing her thought. "I understand his treatment was fairly medieval," she said. "Shock therapy . . . I don't really know. I think Dwight believes there can never again be anything as atrocious in his life as what he's already gone through, but his preparedness for the possibility that there *could* be seems so limitless, so . . . *poised*."

"But he has a sister," I offered, "some family—"

"Oh! His witch of a sister? That goddamned Lido Desjardin?"

Selene said the name with such revulsion that I was momentarily startled.

"She looks exactly like a Botticelli painting come to life, but don't let that fool you. She's a disgusting little bitch."

Selene's words had been *expelled* somehow, not merely spoken intentionally. But she recovered herself almost at once and I thought it best to pretend I hadn't noticed. Then, with an angry look at the full, hanging moon, she turned away from me and went into the house.

Chapter Nine

efore I followed Selene inside, I went
to the car to get the case of pinot noir I'd brought along as a house gift.
I had forgotten about it when I arrived, and I lugged it into the kitchen
then and there, apologizing for having overlooked it before. But although
she kissed my cheek and graciously thanked me for the gesture, Selene
went directly to the cupboard over the sink and reached for a black bottle
of cognac, pouring a generous splash into a big goblet, sipping quickly. I
saw several more bottles on the shelf before she closed the cupboard door.

She looked at me and pointed to the cognac. I shook my head.

"No? Sure? Well, don't wait for me to open the wine, Vanni. Here,
take the corkscrew and the bottle, dear; we'll have our drinks down in the
stùdiolo."

The large, shingled barn was about fifty feet away at the end of a path
made of terra-cotta tiles, many of which were missing, many chipped, but
all swept clean of snow. Seen in the softness of the winter moonlight, the
barn seemed simple, even cozy, a perfect New England postcard. It was
easy to forget that it had once been a pagan temple.

Selene moved ahead of me, her long hair flying out in the fresh, cold
wind that suddenly gusted around the corner of the house. I followed her
down the path and through the heavy *stùdiolo* door. As we entered, my
gaze was drawn instantly upward to the bow of a cathedral ceiling with

a many-paned skylight near the peak. Tall, narrow windows were set every few feet all across the southern and western sides of the huge room. I judged it to be about thirty feet wide and twice as long. A small lamp with a perforated metal shade glowed on the antique mahogany desk, shooting long slivers of light around the room.

Scores of framed pictures filled every inch of space between the windows on the south and west walls. Placed from above eye level down to a ridge of molding set about two feet from the floor, they were all extravagantly framed, crusty with gilt and silver paint. All were perfectly square to the window moldings and each other, some less than an inch apart, and all, or so it seemed to my quick glance, were from the Renaissance.

Selene took a box of wooden kitchen matches from the desk and knelt before the logs already laid in the screened alcove of the hearth. The enormous fireplace, set slightly back in such a way that I hadn't been able to see it from the door, was sheltered by a heavy stone mantle that must have been over eight feet wide and almost as high from the floor.

"So how do you like my *stùdiolo*?" she asked, looking up at me.

"Homage to Isabella d'Este-Gonzaga?" I said with a grin, waving my hand at the walls of pictures. When I said that she smiled, pleased that I had remembered how much she liked to talk about the late, great Isabella. Years before, at one of Carla's famous dinner parties, Selene had held the guests spellbound with her stories of the great Renaissance *patronéssa* of the arts. Isabella was the eldest daughter of the house of d'Este in Ferrara and the wife of Francesco Gonzaga, Marquis of Mantua. A woman with limitless money and blazing intelligence, she had become, at a very tender age, one of the greatest connoisseurs in Italy. Second, some said, only to Lorenzo de' Medici himself. That night at dinner, Carla's jaded friends had sat entranced, their aristocratic lips inches from their forks, mesmerized by Selene's explanation of the accomplishments of the elegant Marquesa de Gonzaga. I knew, of course, that she was related by marriage to our own ancestor, Ludovico Sforza, and Carla did, too, but we kept our mouths shut for once. Selene Catcher was not the sort to be one-upped.

As if remembering the same dinner party, she laughed and handed me a full glass of pinot noir. "Of course," she said with a chuckle, "Isabella held court in hers, but even though it's fairly solitary here, at least I can look at my pictures in peace. I doubt poor Isabella ever could." She went over to tap one small pastel of a Madonna and child another millimeter into line, and switched on a tall brass floor lamp I hadn't noticed in the corner. Suddenly, all the pictures came to life, glowing as if they were real.

"They're obviously just reproductions," Selene said with a smile. "There's nothing valuable here, though some of the frames are probably worth something."

"Are they all from the Renaissance?" I asked. "The Italian Renaissance?"

"Oh, yes . . . well, a few Van Eycks, an early Holbein . . . see, over there? But yes, Italian. Everybody's here, from that old Brunelleschi rendering near the window to that tiny little Tintoretto of the crucifixion," she said, pointing to the far southwest corner. "Isn't it sweet? That one's really late, though they're not in any particular order. I just put them where they fit."

"You bought these when . . . when you . . . ?"

"When I was 'chasing the Angel'?" She laughed when she said it, knowing I would remember the phrase.

"And . . . yes?"

"Ah, yes. Many of them."

"Wonderful," I whispered, my eyes moving over the deep colors of the scenes and the richness of the frames.

There was a grouping of old furniture arranged by the west wall—an overstuffed blue sofa, a tall cane-back rocker, and an easy chair covered in a lively chintz. In front of the sofa was a low table piled high with books and manila folders.

I put my glass down and went over to pick up a portfolio that had fallen to the carpet. It was a set of pictures I recognized at once as a collection from several of the important galleries in Florence. Unable to resist, I leafed through eight or ten beautiful prints of some of the most exquisite paintings ever made. I pulled out a reproduction of Fra Angelico's *Annunciation* and held it up to the lamp on the desk.

Selene came up beside me and for several moments gazed lovingly at the Archangel. Then she crossed the room and reached toward a picture that hung between two of the windows behind the sofa, running her fingers in a caressing motion over the glass. It was the famous Byzantine *Annunciation* by Simone Martini, the one from the Uffizi.

"Now, this picture is quite early, you know," she said, turning to me for just a second. "A hundred years before the Fra Angelico. And very different."

I went over to stand next to her so I could see what she was looking at, what she meant. And realized, astonished, that the whole central section of the west wall was filled with *Annunciations*. Dozens more than had been included in her book. I supposed I had not adequately appreciated the obsessiveness with which she'd chased the Angel across Europe all those years ago. I couldn't believe what I was seeing.

"This Martini is the central panel of that magnificent Siena altarpiece they have," Selene was saying. "As you can see, even in this old print, the halos really *are* gold. The Angel's robe is gold, the cloak flying around his shoulders is gold, his wings are gold. The Virgin doesn't sit on a little wooden stool as She does in the Fra Angelico . . . look here."

I looked. Martini's Mary was sitting on an inlaid Byzantine chair, opulent and richly decorated. The difference in the two paintings stunned me for a second before I remembered something from the text of Selene's book: that the same great event could be seen in very different ways. Even the glory of a heavenly messenger was subdued in the Fra Angelico, the colors muted, the attitude less vibrant.

"And of course there's that charming Baldovinetti," Selene said, pointing above her head. "That's also in the Uffizi, and there's the Andrea del Sarto from the Pitti Palace that I just love, the one with the Angel on the right, which is so unusual . . . over here, dear, look, holding a lily. Now, that's about two hundred years later than the Martini."

"They're wonderful," I said, "wonderful. It's as if your book has come to life." There was an empty space, about eleven inches square, next to the Baldovinetti. "Selene, *cara*, what was here? Oh, the Fra Angelico, perhaps?"

"I gave it to Carmen when she went to Boston. One of these days I might frame the one in the folder and put it there. Or not."

She watched as I walked slowly along the walls, my eyes jumping from one picture to the next. In addition to the remarkable *Annunciations*, there were dozens of the usual Madonnas and saints; martyrs and crucifixion scenes; bleeding, perforated Christs and naked, chubby little *putti*. The very stuff of the Renaissance, of course, and in all styles, all periods.

But in one section, filling the wider space between the two center windows on the long south wall, was a collection of portraits: the living, breathing people who lived through it, who were there while the Renaissance was going on. There were gents in red hats, and ladies with plucked hairlines wearing stiff, forty-pound dresses with gold-embroidered sleeves. Rich old merchants with heavy neck chains and vulpine expressions were side by side with arrogant, overdressed teenage aristocrats riding beautifully harnessed horses, their manes and tails plaited with ribbons and flowers.

A collection like this had taken much more than money, much more than time—or even love.

I turned back to her, shaking my head. "*Cara*, it's wonderful. What a beautiful room. How happy you must be here."

She smiled faintly and sank into the swivel chair behind the desk. She took a cigarette from her pocket and lit it, striking one of the kitchen matches against the edge of the desk. I hadn't seen her smoke since I arrived, though I remembered how inveterate a smoker she'd been in the old days in Florence. But then I saw the wide scar in the mahogany veneer where many matches had obviously been struck before. She sat, quietly sipping her cognac, while I continued slowly around the room.

The entire east wall behind the door was covered to within inches of the ceiling with overflowing teak bookshelves, obviously the ones Dwight Desjardin made for her. And there, hanging at the far corner where the shelves ended, almost hidden in the small space between the doorjamb and the wall, was one other picture. It was a print of *The Death of Actaeon*, the Titian she'd been staring at that day I'd come upon her in London, the one that had so vividly reminded me of Sterling's story of the Stag King. Somehow, in the subdued light of the *studiolo*, it looked terribly sinister, particularly in its obscure spot behind the door. I went close and looked at it carefully, marking the tall, angry goddess and the doomed prince, his stag's head thrown back in terror, so close to death. When I turned back to Selene, she got up and went to one of the windows and looked out over the gleaming snow; I could see its brightness around the silhouette of her figure. She covered her face with her hands for a second and when, a few moments later, she came back to the desk and reached for the glass of cognac, her face was a mask.

"You might like to see what Carmen looks like now," she said a bit abruptly, but with a small smile in which I saw the fathomless affection I remembered and on which Carla still, occasionally, remarked. "It's been years since you've seen her."

She reached for a small, framed photo that was propped on an easel in the middle of the clutter on the desk.

"Ah!" I exclaimed, taking it from her hand. "And the famous Bet, no doubt."

"None other."

The photo was of a slender, pretty woman about Selene's age, perhaps a few years younger. Her pale blond hair was simply coiffed, her skirt and blouse a lovely shade of blue. But there was nothing of her elder sister's vibrance in Elisabetta's face, none of the stunning glamour that not even the years and the silver hair had managed to subdue. Bet had her arm around a serious-looking young woman with chin-length light brown hair who leaned against her shoulder with an inward, even misty expression through which a sharp intelligence was clearly seen, apparent even in the photograph. This grown-up Carmen was not especially pretty, but there was a look of thoughtful contemplation that gave her small face a distinction, a fineness that the cheerful, bouncy teenager I remembered had not had. The nose was a trifle blunt, the complexion pale, but with the gentlest flush, and the hazel eyes, now more brown than green, and alert as could be, seemed to be hiding something intensely private. A huge, black dog—Savo, of course—had its muzzle on her knee, and in her lap, balanced against her chest, was the Fra Angelico in a plain, dark wooden frame.

"When was this taken?" I asked.

"The day Carmen left for Boston," Selene replied in a tight, low voice, her eyes on the thin curl of smoke from her cigarette.

"You sound like you're not too pleased," I said, carefully sipping my wine, even as I watched her out of the corner of my eye.

"Well, no, I was completely against it, and frankly I made no bones about it," she said. "But Carmen was so determined, what could I do? Bet and Leon thought it was a great idea. Imagine? But I've gotten used to it. I visit occasionally ... not too often."

She looked up and her glance fell on the photograph in my hand. "That was the day I gave her the picture, just to 'announce,' you see, the beginning of a new life for her—independent, full of new experiences. She keeps it in the little hallway of her apartment in Boston."

"Hmm. Will I be seeing Bet and Leon, do you think, while I'm here?" I asked, setting the picture back on its easel.

"Sadly, no," Selene said, staring at the picture with a frown. "No. They went to see some friends in Dalton and Bet called earlier this afternoon to say they've been snowed in."

"Oh, too bad." I was genuinely disappointed.

"Next time. Oh! Wait, I think I have some other snapshots from that day." She rummaged in a drawer of her desk and drew out an envelope from which slid ten or fifteen other photos. She handed me one of Bet, smiling happily into the camera, and another of Carmen, on the floor of the *stùdiolo* with three of Selene's dogs, wrestling and giggling, her legs in the air. When I laughed myself, Selene chuckled, too, and riffled through the other pictures, tossing several on the desk.

One caught my eye. I picked it up and found myself looking into the green eyes of the most extraordinarily beautiful young woman. Selene saw what I was looking at.

"Oh, goddamn it!" she cried, snatching the photo out of my hand. "Christ, I forgot I had that."

"Selene, what is it? Whose picture is that?"

"Lido Desjardin. She was here that day. I couldn't very well refuse; she and Carmen have been best friends since they were kids, but . . . oh!"

Lido did, indeed, look like a "Botticelli come to life." Selene's bitter comment had been no exaggeration. The perfection of feature and coloring was remarkable. Even in the photograph her apricot-colored hair glowed like a cloud around her head. Her image filled the frame with no context to detract from her exquisite face.

With an expression of absolute revulsion, Selene scraped the hard blue head of a match against the worn rim of the desk. She held the photo in the tips of her fingers and thrust it into the flame, then got up to toss it into the fireplace, adding a small log from the basket on the hearth. As the dry wood caught, the fire blazed up with a brief shower of sparks.

"My God, how could I have forgotten that?" Selene muttered, standing in front of the fireplace with her hands on her hips, watching the picture curl up and turn to ash.

I had, of course, no context for such an outburst and Selene neither explained nor apologized. Satisfied that Lido's picture was no more, she returned to the desk, filled up both our glasses, and carried them to the low table by the sofa. We sat and sipped and talked of other things for more than an hour. We spoke of Carla, and one of my more recent articles, in which Selene expressed great interest, and even of Piero, who had recently taken a position with a firm in Paris and who seemed, at long last, well into middle age, to have found something to do.

I carefully scrutinized her expression for evidence of anger, or disinterest, or even pain, but Selene commented only that Carla and I must be glad to see him settled, his boundless, restless energy channeled, at least for now.

"Yes," I said, frowning. "Time will tell, eh?"

The topic seemed to bring the evening to a natural close. Selene said she wanted to stay in the *stùdiolo* a while, but that I should get my rest and treat her home as my own. When I rose, she tilted her face up for a kiss and I softly pressed my lips to her forehead before I went out into the icy dark.

The dogs were clustered on the swept tiles of the breezeway, overflowing onto the snow-covered lawn at the edge of the path. As I closed the *studiolo* door behind me, they chuffed and growled, but only Savo got up. She walked close beside me and waited while I opened the kitchen door and went inside. When it was firmly closed, I looked out the window, unnerved to find her looking up at me. Then she turned and trotted back to her pack.

About three o'clock in the morning I was wrenched awake by a terrifying dream. I was clinging for dear life to the side of a gigantic chariot, studded with strange silver symbols, which raced through a black sky while crystals of snow smashed into my face. Blinded by the swirling storm, I could only look downward to the white waste far below me, and there, as if keeping pace with the speeding chariot, I saw the wolves, dozens of them—a shadow, a dark, swift current—gliding, streaming over the snow.

I sat straight up in bed, waiting for my mind to tell me it had only been a dream, and at last the panic receded, leaving me damp and breathing hard, but exhilarated with relief. A moment later, the last racing wolf loosed its hold on me and fell away.

When I woke up again, many hours later, the sun was pouring through the clean, uncurtained window, seeming already quite high in the sky. I remembered that I'd dreamt . . . something, and tried to call the dream to waking memory, but though no more than the vaguest fragment seemed to stick, I remained riveted by the effort, and gave it up only with reluctance.

Chapter Ten

I did not see Selene again for quite a while. We spoke on the telephone a few times, but she seemed distracted and impatient (though not necessarily with me), and I thought it best not to press her. I was somewhat lonely, I suppose, and I must confess it. I missed Carla more than I would have believed, her flood of cards and phone calls and tins of *biscotti* notwithstanding. I'm sure Carla would have screeched with laughter to hear that I was, at such a late date, learning that I was not entirely the solitary, cerebral creature I'd always claimed to be. She would have accused me of pride, self-deceit, and worse, and she might well have been right.

In early March, the students were away on a retreat and as my services as chaperon were not required (they were thought to be perfectly safe with the Sisters of Poor Clare), I rang Selene to invite her to spend a weekend in Boston, even volunteering to drive out to collect her, but she was abrupt and taciturn on the phone. Not even my promise of the fanciest Italian dinner the city had to offer could change her mind. I kept my disappointment to myself (and took some pride in that), though the truth was I had anticipated that we would see a good deal more of each other than we seemed likely to.

About three weeks later, Carmen called and asked me to have lunch at her apartment. We'd seen each other several times since my visit to the estate, usually at restaurants. I hadn't been to her little place before and accepted the invitation with pleasure.

Our burgeoning relationship had become one of the chief joys of my new life in Boston. Selene was in the most uncommunicative of moods, Avery French (whom I had tried, unsuccessfully, to visit) was on a trip abroad, and I had been loath to establish personal relationships with my new colleagues, fearing to be ensnared in their endless rivalries. I was invited, of course, to teas and dinners and parties by the bunch, even to an evening at Symphony Hall, which was a splendid treat, but the political cauldron rumbled and boiled and I thought it best to stay away from the splashing.

But Carmen Poynsetter made the difference, and it had been with her that I'd spent my most satisfying free afternoons and evenings. Her post as a cataloger at a minor private library-cum-museum in the Back Bay was utterly undemanding, and she was free to meet me at odd times and on short notice for a cup of coffee or a sandwich at one of the small, popular bistros on Charles Street near her place of work. Our initial encounter, about a week after I visited Selene, had been far from the dull, obligatory courtesy I had anticipated. Carmen revealed herself on that occasion to have grown into such a lovely young woman I soon found myself seeking out her calm, witty companionship more and more.

The day of our lunch, I strolled the several blocks to her apartment. Spring was just rousing itself in Boston. I'd been told it was late that year, the winter having been unusually brutal after a decade of light snows and disappointed skiers, but it was definitely on its way. The cozy neighborhood where Carmen rented three rooms in an old, nineteenth-century brownstone was filled with ancient flowering trees just budding. Though the pink and white magnolias would not be out for a fortnight or more, a few spindly forsythia had made their appearance and I saw, in one tiny, iron-fenced yard, a bed of pink and blue hyacinth just poking through the dirt.

Carmen was waiting for me on the wide stone steps of her house and ran down the walk to give me a hug of welcome. She seemed to grow prettier each time I saw her, though "pretty" was never the right word for Carmen. She had decided to let her hair grow, and had taken to wearing a bit of *maquillage* around the eyes, but it was her warm, unassuming nature, nicely spiced with a directness of manner and a crisp way with a phrase, that I found so appealing. She would never be a beauty, but she was, even at her tender age, a *person*—fully formed.

That day, she was wearing a soft caramel-colored sweater and brown trousers, an outfit that was most becoming with her shining light brown hair and smooth complexion. I presented my bouquet of daisies and in exchange received a kiss and a whispered confidence:

"I have a surprise for you."

"Oh? Might it—"

"Oh, no. Don't try to guess," she said in a mysterious, dramatic tone. "All in good time."

Arm in arm, we went inside and up the ornate, curving staircase to the second floor.

Her flat was lovely. She'd repainted it in a sublime shade of pale green and the furniture, mostly gifts and castoffs from her parents and Selene, was just what she needed—all of it pretty, simple, and comfortable. The bright, decorative touches were Carmen's own—some silk flowers, perfectly arranged and placed; several skillful line drawings on the walls of the small bedroom, which she told me with a wink she'd done herself; and bright pillows everywhere. It was as charming and welcoming as Carmen herself.

While she saw to our lunch, I wandered through the rooms inspecting her quite respectable collection of books, mostly fiction, I noted with a frown, but very well chosen. I saw a number of small porcelain figurines, many of which Carmen said (with an affectionate laugh and a shake of her head) had been her mother's. I instantly realized that the shepherdess and her microscopic lamb and the apple-cheeked balloon seller were not to Carmen's taste, but the fact that she'd made her mother's old treasures welcome in her home showed a grace and a kindheartedness that was lovely to see. Not for the first time, I reflected that the chatty, giggling teenager I'd met years ago in Florence had bloomed into a subtle and loving woman. That (as Carla would have quickly pointed out) is not always the case, but I was happy to know that Carmen was a most gracious exception to what was possibly a rule of human nature.

The Fra Angelico *Annunciation* was nowhere to be seen. Selene had mentioned that Carmen gave it pride of place in the entryway, and I'd remembered to look for it, but it was neither in the foyer, nor the short back hall, nor the living room. When we sat down to a nice lunch of fresh garden salad and chicken crepes, I asked Carmen what she'd done with it.

"Gave it back," she said in a brisk tone, putting down her fork. "Last week."

"Really? Carmen, I'm surprised."

She was not as sanguine about it as she had at first pretended. She sighed deeply and looked out the window for a moment before she told me how that had come about.

She said that about a week before, on the first day of spring, she had returned to the estate for a visit. "I haven't gone back as often as I planned," she said with a rueful smile, "certainly not as often as Mother and Selene expect me to, but the time had definitely come, so I rented a car and off I went."

Though it had been a chilly, bleak Saturday morning, Carmen said she was determined not to let the disappointing weather make a difference. She spent a couple of hours with Bet, chatting in the kitchen while Bet did some baking, and then went over to the *stùdiolo*. It was almost noon. When she opened the *stùdiolo* door, Carmen found Selene at her desk, books and papers piled high all around her.

It was no secret that Selene had not written a word for months and was eager to make a solid start on a new book. A short article, as she'd told me herself, would not content her; she wanted to do something splendid and ambitious, on a par (at the very least) with *Annunciation Paintings* or the Sforza book. Throughout the winter she had done quite a bit of reading, had taken out old folders and notes, stacked her gorgeous art books on the desk, and hoped thereby to find her inspiration. But though she spent hours in the attempt, thus far she had been unable to focus her ideas.

On that morning of the vernal equinox, oblivious to the gloomy weather, Carmen was in a marvelous mood, chatty and bright. She gave Selene a smacking kiss and a hug and poured herself a cup of black coffee from the pot on the desk before handing over, with a great flourish, the Fra Angelico *Annunciation,* reframed in ornate gilt, wrapped in fancy paper, and tied with a blue ribbon the same color as the Madonna's gown.

"I think this might become our new family symbol," Carmen said with a warm smile and a chuckle. "We can trade it back and forth, use it for all announcements—such as writing new *books.* Just an example, of course." She laughed gaily and sipped her coffee while Selene slowly untied the ribbon.

Though Selene looked at the picture in absolute silence, Carmen could see at once that she was not at all pleased to have it given back, no matter how loving the thought, or how beautifully Carmen had reframed it.

Despite her great love for her glamorous aunt, Carmen had struggled for years with Selene's incredibly powerful personality. That Selene, in her turn, loved Carmen so much only made it worse. Bet was content to love Carmen and to guide her, offering whatever help Carmen might ask of her. But Selene's devotion was different. She had come to think of Carmen as an extension of herself and never doubted her prerogative to order Carmen's life, to make all her choices for her. Carmen, loving girl that she was, had twisted in the wind of Selene's passionate nature for years, desperate not to appear ungrateful, but equally desperate to set off on her life's path all on her own.

Carmen knew that the situation was not at all unusual, but that didn't make the problem any easier to solve. She loved Selene too much to risk hurting her volatile feelings. But the Fra Angelico seemed a way to change things; with the return of the picture, Carmen felt that she had found a subtle, even witty way to announce that she was on her own at last. In all innocence, she was trying to make her own announcement—that true independence could come only with her own action. But to Carmen's dismay, she realized (only after the gift had been unwrapped) that it was a most unwelcome announcement.

Nevertheless, as if determined to disguise her reaction, Selene cheerfully suggested they go for one of their long walks, and Carmen readily agreed. Together, they started out along the forest path, moving easily through the tangled undergrowth. Carmen was eager for all signs of the new season, her searching fingers seeming to find even the tiniest pale green bud, though spring was only hours old. The dogs ran ahead of them, strangely agitated that day, perhaps by Carmen's visit, or maybe by the tug of the full Sap Moon, rising unseen above the low, gray clouds that churned in slow circles across the sky.

"We followed the dogs all the way to the river," Carmen said, her mood suddenly quiet, even pensive.

"We stayed there a long time, just sitting on the smooth boulders by the bank, watching the water. I told Selene a little bit about my life here— my job, a few new friends. It's fine, Father, not very dramatic, but it suits me, it really does. Lido Desjardin's my best friend, and has been for a hundred years, and my living here hasn't changed that. I mean, we still get together almost every week. But I was trying to show Selene that I *like* my life, that I'm content. At least for now."

I smiled at her calm, though perhaps somewhat wistful, expression. She saw me looking at her and smiled back, saying she thought that Selene might have been, in spite of herself, reassured by that description of a life that could, surely, pose no threat at all.

Eager to make amends for the Fra Angelico (though Selene had not said an unkind word about it), Carmen got up and wandered along the riverbank, plucking the miniature purple flowers that had already sprung up there in the dampness, presenting Selene with a sweet bouquet.

"First of the season," Carmen whispered as she handed it to Selene with a hug and a quick kiss on the cheek.

Though it was still the middle of the afternoon, the sky had darkened and a few crisp flakes of spring snow danced through the air as they started back, the dogs running ahead of them as before. They came out of the forest behind the estate house and the remains of the enormous formal garden, impressive even in ruins, that had once been Eugenia Wallace's pride and joy.

The garden had been an imitation, in miniature (as Selene had heard it from her father), of the great public garden at Chichester in England. But now Eugenia's exotic plants were gone and the marble paving stones that had once formed the curving walks were broken and scattered, littered with last season's leaves.

The dogs had chased a small deer into the center of the garden, a young doe that had lost its way, but though Savo lunged forward, teeth gleaming in the dim afternoon light, she could not, apparently, be bothered to kill it, and at her signal the others let the doe escape. Selene and Carmen watched from below the wide veranda of the house as the terrified animal bounded away into the forest.

Earlier, I had mentioned to Carmen that I never did have a chance to see the estate house during my brief winter visit to Selene.

"We planned to," I said, accepting a cup of excellent coffee, sitting back in my chair, "but it didn't seem to work out."

"Well, I think in its day it was a gorgeous place," she said. "Mother mentioned just the other day that some Wallaces lived there when I was a little kid. But they moved out."

"Vacant all this time?"

"I believe so." Carmen went back to the kitchen, soon returning with a plate of sliced fresh fruit and a big bowl of real whipped cream.

When I protested (even as I spread my napkin on my lap again), she laughed and gave me a large portion.

"You're trim as can be, Father G.," she said, laughing. "Downright skinny. C'mon. We can be good tomorrow."

But just as Carmen seated herself at the table, ready to continue her story, the doorbell rang several times, and she jumped up again and ran to answer. Apparently, my "surprise" had arrived in the form of another guest.

It was none other than Lido Desjardin. Carmen brought her friend into the room and presented her to me with an amusing mixture of ceremony and delight.

Lido gave me a long, appraising look before she let go of my hand, then turned away to hang her jacket in the closet, allowing me a moment to collect myself before the three of us sat down to the sliced strawberries. Selene's photograph (of which, in any case, I'd caught only a glimpse) did not prepare me for Lido's vivid perfection.

The gods cast the die of beauty with artless, indifferent hands. Sometimes a single millimeter can make the difference between the ordinary and the dazzling when, as if by magic, every relationship, every proportion is as sublime as it is unforeseen.

Lido Desjardin was like that. I think she was the single most beautiful woman I have ever met face-to-face. I can't speak to her inner beauty (convinced as I am that the very concept was the invention of someone both virtuous and ill-favored), but physically, at least, Lido was, as Selene Catcher herself had said, like a fifteenth-century painting—a Botticelli—come to life. But Lido was not a mere Flora, or one of the Graces from the *Primavera*. She could have been Aphrodite herself.

Carmen explained that she'd been telling me about her visit with Selene, and Lido raised her hands in a gesture of mock horror, as if Carmen had pulled a gun on her.

"Oh, hey, don't let me interrupt *that!*"

"Well, you were there, too, Lido," Carmen said, winking at me, the only hint that she might know I was aware of Selene's opinion of Lido.

"Oh, you mean at your mom's house. Yeah."

She turned her brilliant green eyes to me for a moment and then nodded vigorously. "Yeah, Carmen and Madame Selene were just going up the steps to Bet's kitchen door when I saw them. Lookin' for those frosted brownies, weren't ya?" she said, ruffling Carmen's hair. She gave a somewhat ironic laugh and reached for the largest strawberry on the plate.

"Bet had spent most of the day baking, you see," Lido said, turning to me to be sure I understood. "She wasn't there when we went in, but all the stuff she'd made was on a tray in the middle of the table, cooling off. A minute later we heard the car door slam and Bet came in through the living room. She didn't even have her coat off when she said..." Lido broke off with a cackle of laughter. "Remember, Carm? 'Big news, everybody,' she said, 'I've got big news'!"

Lido grinned, stuck her finger in the whipped cream and licked it off.

"We all wanted to know what the 'big news' was," Carmen said, laughing, too, "but Mom was enjoying herself too much to spit it out. 'Just wait,' she said, 'just give me a second.'"

After Bet hung up her things, she filled a pan with cookies and brownies, added a few of the dog biscuits she always kept in the pantry, and placed it on the back stoop where the dogs were milling about, whining and growling at the smells from the kitchen. Savo, who adored chocolate, nearly knocked Bet down trying to get at the brownies, but backed away with a whimper when Selene came to the door. Bet scratched the fur around Leski's ears, stuck a gingersnap between Fitzi's bared teeth, and closed the door against the cold. She washed her hands at the sink, put up a pot of coffee, set out four cups, and finally sat down at the kitchen table.

Carmen jumped up on the edge of the sink and leaned against the cupboard. "Okay, Mom," she said, taking a small bite of a lemon bar, "let's have it."

"Well, now," Bet began, enjoying the moment of suspense, "I was down to Turn-of-River this afternoon and dropped in on Wanda Stoner in the store. Well, we got talking, and after a bit her Earl came in from out back, and the three of us——"

"Bet, for God's sake," Selene said in a bored, impatient tone.

"Sissy, give me a chance, now," Bet said with just a touch of good-humored annoyance, smiling over at Lido, who was leaning against the refrigerator, sucking on a gingersnap. "So there we were chatting and Wanda told me... wait'll you girls hear this. Wanda told me that the Wallace house has... been... sold!"

When Bet said that, she laughed aloud at the expressions on their faces. Carmen, somewhat indifferent, tried to show some excitement at her mother's news, but Selene got up from the table and stood stiffly in the doorway. Lido nibbled at her cookie and watched the three of them with interest.

"Well, that's terrific, Mom," Carmen said, with a quick glance at Selene. "Who bought it?"

"His name is ... oh! wait, wait, I want to say it right," Bet said, still chuckling with pleasure. "I want to get it right. It's *Italian*, Selene; isn't that interesting? Let me see ... his name is Victor Bellacéra, and Earl says that as far as he knows, Mr. Bellacéra is a single man! Isn't that something? A single man! Earl says that agent down in Springfield wouldn't tell him any more, so we don't know the details, but isn't that *some* news! Isn't that just *some* announcement!"

"Oooh, an Eye-talian," Lido said in a low, ironic tone, looking pointedly at Selene. "How about that, ladies?" She turned her attention back to her cookie, but not before she was rewarded with a poisonous look from Selene.

Bet's hands were clasped over her chest; she looked happily from Carmen to Lido to Selene and back again.

Just then Selene turned from the doorway. "Are you sure?" she said sharply. "Does that idiot Earl Stoner know what he's talking about?"

"Oh, absolutely, Sissy," said Bet, her face glowing. "Earl also told me a few things have already been delivered. He says a real telescope, and some fancy antique bed, and a tree, imagine? An actual tree. They're keeping them for him in that big shed out behind Wanda's store. A single gentleman, honey," she said to Carmen. "Won't that be fun?"

"Think he's cute, Carm?" Lido said with a playful wink at Selene. "And if so, exactly how cute?"

"Oh, Lido, honey," Bet chided. "Earl and Wanda didn't say anything about *that*." She laughed. "But they believe he's moving in within the month."

Lido, finishing Carmen's story for her, snatched the last two strawberries from the plate, dunked them in the whipped cream, and gobbled them down. She was the most extraordinary combination of exquisite feminine perfection and the sensibilities of a twelfth-century peasant, and I watched with fascination as she licked off her fingers and, completely at ease in Carmen's apartment, got up to look in the refrigerator for more fruit.

"An odd story," I offered, pulling my eyes away from Lido and turning back to Carmen. "I didn't have the impression Selene cared so much about that house."

"She doesn't," Lido said, coming back and lounging in the doorway behind Carmen's chair. "She doesn't care at all. Not about the Wallace place, anyhow. She just doesn't want anyone else to get what she can't have."

"Aw, Lido," Carmen said, "come on. She's not like that."

Lido shrugged, bored with the topic, and with a Dionysian lack of self-consciousness, bit off a few green grapes from the bunch clasped in her hand.

Chapter Eleven

f I may be permitted a meager pun, my lunch with Carmen and her friend Lido gave me considerable food for thought. Meeting the fascinating if inelegant Lido Desjardin was in many ways the highlight of the visit, but more than anything I was troubled by the news that Carmen's relationship with Selene, after decades of devotion, might have moved onto shaky ground.

Naturally, I knew how possessive Selene could be. "Domineering" (a word Carmen had carefully avoided) did not do her justice. She was accustomed to having her way in everything and I suspected (though the subject had never come up) that her outright ownership of the estate lands might have been imperfectly distinguished in her mind from control of the souls who lived upon it. Particularly Carmen.

But the notion was dreadfully harsh and did not give Selene her due. I knew she had cherished Carmen from childhood, always speaking of her with pride and devotion. There was no doubting the depth of Selene's affection, but, yes, that was only a part of her nature—only a part. That very devotion, completely sincere, was also, as I knew from Carla's analysis and from my own observations, ferocious as could be—passionate and unrestrained.

My conversation with Carmen did not leave my thoughts for days; I hated to see the dear girl so obviously upset at her aunt's displeasure. And of course my thoughts drifted continually to the ineffable Lido Desjardin and her clear reciprocation of Selene's intense dislike. That there was some history there I did not doubt—a past hurt, real or imagined; some female imbroglio I could not possibly have understood. But it seemed unlikely that Lido, despite the closeness of her friendship with Carmen, could have posed a genuine threat to Selene's assured dominance over Carmen. All the same, a friend, offering ideas, influences outside those Selene herself controlled, would not be welcome. It was all of a piece with Selene's irritation over Carmen's move to Boston.

A few days after my lunch with Carmen, Bet Poynsetter called and invited me to dinner. We chatted like old friends with an immediate, completely spontaneous ease that delighted me. Before I could express the thought myself, she said how "ridiculous" (her very word) she found it that we hadn't met in all the years I'd known Selene.

"Selene can be so impossible, you know? She doesn't think of things sometimes. But not to worry; the opportunity for us to meet at last just came along, Father. We have a new neighbor, as Carmen told you, and I've invited him for a little family dinner party and I would *love* for you to join us."

Then, with an almost girlish giggle, Bet confided that she hadn't wasted a second inviting Victor Bellacéra to dinner.

"He said yes just like *that*, Father. I think it'll be fun. Please say you'll come."

It was clear that Bet was not to be deflected. She told me she'd already decided on the Saturday one week hence, hoping the weather would be nice and warm so they could have the dining room windows open during dinner.

I couldn't help but laugh at that outpouring of an invitation and said at once that I'd be most happy to join the party.

"I'll look forward to it," I said, smiling into the phone. "Shall I call Selene, then? Let her know I'm—"

"No, no. Your coming is the only thing she likes about this dinner. Believe me. She's expecting you."

On the Friday afternoon before Bet's dinner, I saw Avery French for the first time since my arrival in Boston. Although I'd been told that he was out of the country for an extended period, when I called again I learned that that had been a fabrication, meant to conceal the sad fact that he was quite unwell and had been home and at rest these many weeks.

When, very distressed, I called his home, his wife explained that he'd had a slight stroke after Christmas. Though it had been touch and go for a while, he was doing better. Seconds later, Avery himself got on the phone, imploring me to stop by for a visit. I knew that despite my weekend plans, and a number of errands to do before I drove out to the estate, I couldn't possibly refuse.

I arrived at the small town house on Beacon Hill at the appointed hour. Avery met me at the door himself, looking frail but chipper. When I came into the small foyer he embraced me, his grip terribly weak but his eyes shining with pleasure.

Though the weather had turned cooler during the week, we sat by the open French doors to the garden, sipping tea and nibbling small almond cookies. A decanter of whiskey was within arm's reach on the low table between us—in case of emergency, Avery said with a droll chortle.

We caught up on my new post and his "temporary indisposition." His bright, peremptory tone did not deceive me at all; he was plainly very ill and grasping at any chance for a diversion. My heart went out to him. We spoke of Florence and some recent scandal in Boston politics and other inconsequential matters, and then we got to Selene. When I mentioned my first trip out to the estate, and the edgy, elusive behavior that had followed, Avery nodded, not surprised at all.

"She's having a rough go, and damned if she'll tell anybody why," he said, looking furtively over his shoulder as he took a big bite of a cream horn that I guessed (correctly) he was not supposed to eat. It had been set out as hospitality for me.

"Typical, though," he said, wiping his lips. "Just like her." He reached for a small chocolate bonbon and popped it in his mouth.

"I'm not supposed to eat these poisonous delights, but screw it," he said, licking cream off his fingers. "I can't live forever."

I helped him up and we took a short turn around his tiny, walled garden. The day was bright, though with a cool breeze that rustled through the dry branches of the dwarf dogwoods that lined one side of the garden. Avery leaned heavily on my arm, though he refused to go in when I suggested it.

"Clarice'll have my hide, but *tant pis*," he said with a cackle of laughter that turned immediately into a harsh coughing fit. I quickly led him back inside and settled him into his deep chair, worried at the flush that the exertion had caused to spread over his thin face.

"Think Selene would come see me?" he asked as I poured out a small portion of the whiskey. He took it with a trembling hand.

"Of course, yes," I answered, though I did not think so at all. "As a matter of fact, I'll be seeing her tomorrow. Her sister's having a dinner party and I'm driving out in the morning. I'll mention it to her, of course. I know she'd love to see you."

"Hmm. Maybe yes and maybe no," he said. "Well, I know how she can be. She's in one of her moods now. No saying how long it'll last."

We talked for a few more minutes but he was obviously very weary. Time to go. But as I slipped on my coat and prepared to say good-bye, Avery, in an odd gesture, stretched out his hand toward me. A random ray of sunlight forced its way through the dusk to sparkle on the star sapphire of his cuff link, but his blue eyes were completely serious.

"I do have one piece of free advice, Giovanni, if you'd care to listen to a sick man's intuition."

I smiled and took a plaid wool blanket from a chair, covering his knees. "What's that?"

"Just this. Try not to leave her alone out there too much. Sure, she's got her sister, but that precious Carmen of hers is living in town now, right?"

I nodded.

"Yes, well, that was hard on her. Everybody knows she dotes on the girl. All that solitude's not good for someone like Selene. Don't let her keep you away."

I did not arrive at the estate until midafternoon. Selene had been at Bet's all morning, trying to help with preparations.

"The table's been set since breakfast, she's so nervous," Selene informed me without preamble when she greeted me at the porch door. "You'd think the queen of bloody England was coming at the very least."

Mean-spirited, yes, but when I laughed at her intensity, Selene suddenly chuckled herself and gave me a rueful, reluctant smile. But she was clearly in a foul mood. She seemed angry and tense and yet unable, certainly unwilling, to confide in anyone at all. Perhaps it was my own pride (always my cross), which made me think she'd tell me, old friend and fellow scholar, what was on her mind. But she showed no sign of doing so. I remembered Avery's parting words, but thought it best to keep my own counsel—for the moment.

I understood that Selene had not admitted to herself that Bet, mother of a daughter, after all, might have had a private point of view where the new neighbor was concerned. When she dropped in on him with her dinner invitation (almost certainly, I thought with a private smile, bringing him a pan of her famous brownies), she must have given herself the little maternal treat of imagining a match. Mr. Bellacéra might have been completely unsuitable for any number of reasons, but Bet's girlish enthusiasm on the phone had told me he was *not*. No mother lets an attractive man slide away unevaluated where a marriageable daughter is concerned. As Carla has explained to me during numerous conversations on the subject of her friends and their daughters, feminism flees such a prospect.

"And will Lido be at the dinner party?" I asked, when I joined Selene in the *stùdiolo* for a drink.

"She would not enjoy herself," Selene said with an unamused curling of her lip.

The fact that Lido had not been invited, I thought, was probably Bet's doing. Perhaps she had believed (as most women surely would) that Lido, the "Botticelli come to life," could distract that new neighbor's attention from Carmen, who, bright and charming though she was, might not have appeared to glisten quite so much with the lovely Lido Desjardin for comparison. Yet it occurred to me as well, almost as an afterthought, that Selene, reflecting, thought it might have been the wiser course to have the "Botticelli" there after all—a Judas goat of sorts, to keep the man away from Carmen. Somehow, the fact that I had not yet met either Bet or Victor Bellacéra himself did not seem to contradict my reasoning.

While I sat in the chintz chair by the west windows, Selene rattled on, tense as a cat, and though I continually eyed the stacks of books and papers on the desk, longing to ask her what she was working on, she said nothing about it, preferring to complain, almost compulsively, about Bet's party.

She paced the room, touching the pictures, the furniture, smoking one cigarette after another. At last, she came to rest by *The Death of Actaeon* and stood rubbing the tips of her fingers back and forth over the edge of the frame, staring at the figure of the Goddess in the picture. All at once, she turned and glared at me, and for just the briefest moment I saw Artemis in the strong squaring of her shoulders and the swish of her long, silver hair. The expression in her eyes was a perfect replication of the Goddess's anger.

She walked slowly away from the Titian and leaned, finally, against the windows, looking toward the line of trees beyond the yard.

"That night of the equinox," she said, "after Bet told us about the house being sold, very late—it must have been two or three in the morning—I went out walking with the dogs. We cut across the field past the rock and came out opposite the estate house. The downstairs lights were out, but I saw a shadow cross behind the blinds in the front room."

"And?" I had come up beside her, looking out toward the shimmering late afternoon sky.

"And nothing. I saw it, though. I did."

The shadow might have been Victor Bellacéra, I supposed, but it was more likely only her imagination.

A moment later, she went abruptly to her room to change for dinner, leaving me to wonder yet again why the advent of a new neighbor had upset her so. I believed Lido's assertion that Selene didn't really care all that much about the Wallace place. Was it a metaphor, then, for loss of absolute dominance over the affairs of the estate? Yes, possibly. But there was more. I knew Selene too well to doubt it. I looked around the *stùdiolo*—the retreat, the sanctuary, the temple—and was suddenly brought to mind of Sterling Catcher and his passionate belief in the transfiguration of the Goddess: maiden . . . huntress . . . crone.

And though it defied everything I believe, the certainty and faith I've tried to nurture all my life, I knew that some time during that night, of which she'd spoken with such angry bitterness, the aloof, intellectual Selene had somehow turned into Artemis. It was as if she had become the Huntress . . . Merciless Diana.

Chapter Twelve

bout seven o'clock, the day's bright sun beginning to sink behind the trees, Selene and I went across the wide lawn that separated her house from the Poynsetters' small, square saltbox home. It was neat and trim as could be, painted a clear, serene gray with white shutters on every single window.

"Pretty, isn't it?" Selene said with a slight pursing of her lips. "Look at those funny little flower boxes... so charming. Even in winter Bet keeps them filled with greens and berries, poinsettias. Let's go round the back."

I followed her to the back porch, an old-fashioned enclosure with wide, screened windows along which ran a redwood shelf that was filled with identical terra-cotta pots of African violets and impatiens.

By way of announcing our arrival, Selene slapped at the wind chime ornament that hung by the kitchen door, and we entered to the gentle clanging of dozens of tiny metal birds. Our hostess, a flowered apron snug over her pearls, hurried over to me and took my hand in both of hers.

"Father Corio... Oh! at last. We are so honored, so honored," Bet said, looking up at me, her wide blue eyes shining with pleasure. Having seen her photograph, I already knew that the sisters did not resemble each other in the least. Bet had none of Selene's imperial glamour, the powerful sense of self that had survived the silvering of the hair and the abandonment of makeup, jewelry, and gorgeous clothes. But in early middle age,

Elisabetta Poynsetter was femininity itself. She was pliant and soft, polished and natural at once, and I could see in the subtle perfection of her toilette the sort of gentle beauty that is both unnoticed and unforgettable. I think she was the kind of woman I would have chosen had I not chosen God.

Leon came forward to be introduced and shook my hand with a strong grip. Leaning forward in a conspiratorial, man-to-man fashion, he wasted no time in offering me a drink.

"Can I interest you in a nice double bourbon, Father?"

"Indeed you may," I answered with a smile. "Thank you."

Leon Poynsetter was a soft-spoken man, about fifty years of age, I thought, large and fleshy, with a ruddy face and a thatch of salt-and-pepper hair cropped close above his ears. Carmen had frequently spoken, lovingly and with an engaging forthrightness, about her parents. I knew from her that Leon performed his role as paterfamilias with an affecting strength of purpose, wishing only to keep his adored wife and daughter happy, regardless of any personal expense to himself. His job as foreman at a small factory nearby brought him home every night by six on the dot, back to his family.

Where his sister-in-law was concerned, Leon was entirely out of his depth, and knew it. He accepted, without illusion and without demur, that Carmen and Bet were precious to Selene in ways he, despite his own devotion, could have no hope of understanding. But if Leon worried about that, he did not say so, neither to his daughter, nor to me, at any time.

The bourbon bottle was produced forthwith and generous portions splashed into three gold-rimmed tumblers. Bet already had a little glass of sherry, half full, on the windowsill above the sink. She picked it up and the four of us stood, perhaps a bit stiffly, toasting one another, and Carmen (who was nowhere to be seen), and the fine, clear evening.

"Mr. Bellacéra should be here any moment, Father, but I thought you might like to see the house before he comes," Bet said, her blue eyes moist with hope.

With a knowing smile at me, Leon resumed his fastidious construction of the salad, cutting mushrooms and bell peppers into slices of unnecessary thinness. Selene sat down at the kitchen table, peevishly refusing to accompany us, but Bet ignored her (with what I thought was admirable panache) and gently pushed me ahead of her into the meticulously arranged dining room. She paused to fuss for a moment over the centerpiece, but then remembered herself and led me through to the living room.

Bet Poynsetter was obviously a woman who had given years of loving attention to the management of her home. Everything was spotless and neat as could be. Fresh spring flowers, no doubt from Bet's own garden, were placed in pretty vases all over the room.

As I followed her up the narrow staircase to the second floor, Bet paused suddenly and looked down at me with worried eyes.

"I hope you can get Selene to tell you what's on her mind, Father," she said without preamble. "She won't tell me, but I know she loves and respects you so much she might say something if you ask her outright. I'm worried sick."

Fortunately, her heartfelt plea did not seem to require a response. Without another word, she turned away and continued up to the landing at the top of the stairs.

Two bedrooms faced each other across the tiny hall. Carmen's door was closed, but I heard the sound of a hair dryer and some soft music from inside her room. The master bedroom was as charming and tidy as the downstairs rooms, but I quickly covered the smile that came to my lips as I imagined Leon Poynsetter lumbering in his undershorts past the violet-sprigged wallpaper with the matching bedspread, nearly invisible under a great collection of hand-embroidered pillows.

With a shy, gentle smile, Bet blushed slightly, closed the door, and led the way downstairs.

"So what do you think?" Selene said a minute later, looking pensively out the window of the dining room. She reached into her pocket for a cigarette and dropped the match, still burning, into a vase of tulips on the sill. "Sweet, isn't it?"

"Yes. Yes, it is." I smiled. "In a way it's almost like a doll's house."

"Yes. Oh, darling old Bet ... sweet, darling Elisabetta ..." Selene frowned and stared thoughtfully out into the yard before she motioned me beside her.

"That's Bet's rock garden." She gestured with the cigarette beyond the window to an oval structure about the size of the dining room table, rising about four feet off the ground. The rock wall was perfectly smooth, the masonry quite perfect.

"It's unusual," I said. "And very pretty. Did Leon do it for her?"

"Um, he built it about three or four years ago. Bet putters around out there until the sun goes down, March to October, digging, pruning, poking at the roots. It's a wonder anything grows at all, she fusses so."

"What does she plant there?" I said softly, leaning against the window frame next to her.

"Oh, let's see, there're tulips now, of course, but sometimes delphinium—one year she had California poppies—gloxinia and asters in season, even lily of the valley. Every year Carmen says there's too much sun for them, but they grow in whatever leaf shadow they can find. The proportions are lovely, aren't they?"

Bet came in to shoo us out of the dining room so she could flutter over the table one last time. She plucked one barely wilted flower out of the centerpiece and moved two or three of the wineglasses a millimeter to the left.

"Wanda Stoner told me he's getting his groceries from her," Bet said, joining us back in the kitchen. "Isn't that nice? And Earl's helping him get his garden in." She took the knife away from Leon and started slicing some black pitted olives for the salad, nervously eating half of what she cut.

"I can't imagine why you people are knocking yourselves out this way," Selene said in a sour tone. She took the bourbon bottle from the counter and splashed more whiskey into her glass.

Leon smiled indulgently at his wife while he wiped his hands and buttoned the cuffs of his white shirt.

"Well, now," he said, checking the knot in his tie in a small mirror above the sink. "Lido tells me this new neighbor of ours is a very friendly sort, sister-in-law. You might just find yourself taking a shine to him. Might not be impossible."

"I think we're all set." Bet was carefully removing her apron, smoothing her blouse as she did so. "I think it's going to be just delicious. Selene, come look at the . . . oh, honey, not ready yet?"

Carmen had just come into the kitchen. She was wearing her bathrobe, and her hair was still in curlers. But her eyes were quite dramatically made up with a pale green shadow that enhanced their color and black mascara, which looked remarkably sophisticated.

She greeted me with a big kiss and a wink, but after a minute or two of standing around, fussing with Bet's pearls and poking into the salad, Carmen popped a couple of the black olives into her mouth and went upstairs to dress. Leon put his salad in the fridge and led us into the living room to wait.

Bet insisted that Selene sit on the sofa. She tucked one of her crocheted pillows in behind her, making her comfortable, and leaned down to give her a soft kiss and a pat on the shoulder. "Be nice, Sissy," she whispered in Selene's ear. "Please."

Sipping my drink, I went over to the front window. Far across the broad lawn, the setting sun was slanting off the south windows of the *stùdiolo*. The long panels of glass glowed orange and gold in the late light. A lamp had been left on and it shone outward into the dusk, illuminating the large room where Sterling Catcher had once performed archaic rites in celebration of his Goddess.

Chapter Thirteen

ictor Bellacéra came into the Poynsetters' small living room with long, powerful strides. He was a tall man, an inch or more over six feet, strongly built, but lithe and graceful in his movements. He had the quintessential Roman face one finds so often repeated in paintings, sculptures, and medallions. His eyes, observant, intelligent, dark as olives, looked calmly about the room.

It was apparent at once that he was completely at his ease in any company, greeting his hosts with a confident charm, his gestures smooth and economical, his smile genial but brief.

When Bet introduced him to me, he shook my hand and nodded, not so very impressed, I thought at first, at least not with my Roman collar.

"Victor Bellacéra. My pleasure, Father."

"Giovanni, please."

"Of course."

I had the immediate sense that I'd seen him before, knew him from somewhere, but I think it was only that he was the sort of person who appeared as if one should have known him. There was a sense of such utter self-possession about him that at first I was certain he must be either a well-known actor or the celebrated heir to some incomprehensibly old fortune. And then, a moment later, I realized I was reminded of my cousin Piero.

Victor Bellacéra was not as heavily muscled as Piero; he was leaner and more sinuous. But his hair was black as coal, just like Piero's, and his skin, darker in the way of southern Italians, as fine and luminous. But most of all, the resemblance lay in his complete assurance of his own presence, that startling sense of self that brought Piero Corio so vividly to mind. In short, Victor was, or at first inspection seemed to be, an American version of my accomplished cousin, polished to a hard, true shine.

Leon bustled around everyone, serving drinks. Whiskey sours were Leon's specialty and he had the makings all arranged on the sideboard: maraschino cherries, slices of orange, and a big bottle of the best Canadian whiskey.

The new neighbor insisted that they call him Victor and he smiled, rising from his chair in a courteous way when Leon offered him the cocktail. Bet, a second later, produced a tiny napkin to slip under it. She had been utterly charmed by Victor's gift to her, a small jade tree, almost a bonsai; he said he'd grown it from a cutting of a plant he'd had for years. "A love of horticulture," he said with a smile, "seems to run in the family."

"Oh," said Bet in that breathy way I'd noticed before, "and how interesting that your family is of Italian extraction. Father Giovanni and his sister have been friends with *my* sister for many years...."

That seemed to capture his attention, though I couldn't imagine why it would, and in response to his question, in as offhand a way as I could manage, I told him a little of my family. Victor was familiar with the name of Ludovico Sforza and though I sensed he had spent considerable time in Milan, appearing to know the streets, the atmosphere of the city, he did not say when he was there, or why, or for how long.

Bet evidently thought then that the history of the estate was sure to entertain him and she chatted on for several minutes, speaking of her father and the road, the old estate house and the rock, while Leon grumbled at his watch with a paternal smile and wondered where his princess, his girl was.

"She's getting all spruced up, uh, Victor. You know how girls are."

When Leon said that, Victor laughed softly, showing strong, perfect teeth. There was no doubt he knew exactly how girls are.

Selene was unable to take her eyes away from him. She seemed fascinated by the dark line of his jaw, the curve of his thigh muscles through the fine fabric of his trousers as he sat on the edge of Leon's wing chair, the calm, knowing intelligence in his black eyes. Victor seemed surrounded by an aura of smooth, elusive darkness, of mystery and force, something liquid and silent cloaking an irresistible sensual power. Yet there was great gentleness in him as well, an obvious sunniness of disposition that seemed ill-matched with mystery or (more accurately) unable to hide the deep-running sexuality that underlay it all.

To my intrigued eye, Victor Bellacéra looked as if he'd done everything there is to do—had loved, fought, and grieved, had persuaded, rewarded, and avenged—and remained untouched by all of it. A skewed kind of chastity, I thought at once, but of course I kept the observation to myself.

Thinking back now to Selene's reaction to him, I find I cannot say what struck me most—her languid greeting, the piercing focus in her eyes, or her rigid posture. But I know it was because of the rhythm of her breathing that I absorbed, as she surely had not intended anyone to do, the impact of the moment of meeting. It was like the first afternoon in the San Marco for her, I think. The same astonishment, though (as I soon learned) instantly denied.

And all the while she sat posed on the sofa as if she were Isabella Gonzaga herself. She sipped at a glass of straight bourbon and, with apparent disinterest, let the conversation flow around her, but I saw her staring, with neither shame nor awareness, at the strong, steady hand with which Victor held the delicate stem of his glass. I watched her watching him and realized, not a moment too soon, that I was doing it. When, a second later, Victor reached out to set his glass on the coffee table, his movement broke the tiny spell and I realized he had known Selene was staring at him.

He turned to her and mentioned that he knew her beautiful book on Annunciation paintings.

"My uncle," he said with a slow, affectionate smile, "my father's elder brother, was an amateur scholar, and a great lover of the Renaissance. He treasured your book."

When he said that, Selene seemed to recover herself and leaned forward to take a cigarette from the pack on the table.

"Would I know your uncle's name?" she said, in a tone that suggested she didn't in the least care about the answer.

Victor looked at her, turning his long Roman profile ever so slightly. The muscles in his throat contracted over the perfect collar of his shirt as he took a swallow of his whiskey and began to tell us about his uncle, an old man who had loved the Madonna, revered Her as his *patròna*. For him, Victor said, the book on the visitation of the Archangel had brought the holy moment of the Annunciation to life.

"'Santa Maria, patròna mia,'" Victor quoted, smiling gently. He looked up, about to continue with his thought, but just at that moment, Carmen came into the room.

I had not known she could look so beautiful. Her light brown hair was smooth and heavy on her shoulders, and the dark green of her silk dress was the perfect complement to the makeup I had been startled by before. Her eyes shone with pleasure as she paused in the doorway. Then she looked across the room to Victor with an expression of complete and instant recognition.

Victor rose to his feet at the very moment Carmen looked at him. He moved toward her as if he were in some sort of dream, his concentration as perfect, his gaze as unwavering as hers. He offered his hand just as Carmen offered hers, and the two slid together from fingertips to wrists, as if carved by a master sculptor. As they stood there, no word of greeting having been spoken by either one of them, Bet's introductions unheard, Victor looked down into Carmen's eyes with an expression of such welcome, such ... *rapture* ... that I could not help but catch my own breath.

A few minutes later, we were settled in the dining room. Bet brought out the big tossed salad, then a platter of veal scallopini (which proved absolutely delectable), and the bottle of *Chianti Classico* Victor had brought, confessing to Bet with a grin that he had asked Wanda Stoner if she knew what Bet was serving.

"We've seen you working on that house of yours," said Leon, pouring wine. "Fine old place."

"Nice to have someone living there again," said Bet. "Isn't it, Sissy?"

"Marvelous," Selene said dryly, putting a tiny mushroom in her mouth, looking into the flames of the candles and then across the table into Victor's eyes.

Victor looked back at her, frowning slightly, his fork halfway to his lips. The glowing candlelight of the dining room defined the laugh lines at the outer corners of his eyes, the grooves just beginning in the hard planes of his cheeks, and around the wide Mediterranean mouth. I could see the flashes of silver at his temples.

Ah, so he's not that young, I thought with a quick glance at Selene, who ignored me. This cool and polished Victor Bellacéra, this bringer of wine and jade trees, is no boy.

"Bob Wallace took good care of his property," Leon offered, breaking into my thoughts, "even though it's run down quite a bit over the years. Looks like you're making a lot of changes, though," he continued. "High time."

"I've traveled so much in the last few years," Victor said, looking away from Selene and down the table to Leon. "I'm just as glad to settle down, for a while, anyway. I grew up in Massachusetts, but I've been away a long time and it's good to be back. The house is just what I was looking for. I must say I'm enjoying the work, all the renovations."

"Well, I think you could get Dwight Desjardin to help," Leon said. " 'Course, you can't always tell with Dwight, he—"

"Yes, I've met him," Victor said, wiping his mouth with a gesture Selene watched with complete attention.

"Oh, poor Dwight," Bet said, leaning into the circle of candlelight. "He hasn't been too well, you know."

"I know," Victor replied, putting his napkin in his lap.

For a few minutes, we all attended silently to our food, passing serving dishes, sipping from the wineglasses that Leon kept filled to the brim. I felt very alert to currents and nuances, though I didn't quite know what to do about them. Carla, I thought, would have broken the silence by asking Victor some dreadfully personal question, but I knew I could never do the same.

Carmen was eating very little, though she sipped frequently from her glass of Chianti. She hadn't said a word, but I'd already noticed that her eyes met Victor's constantly across the table. Victor was too courteous, too sophisticated to stare, but he glanced continually back at her. Every time he made a remark to Leon, or smiled and said something to Bet or me, his eyes paused on Carmen's face, as if in reassurance. If he looked away even for a moment, he seemed to be telling her, it was only because custom and courtesy demanded it.

At last, Bet, who had seemed oddly oblivious to the atmosphere, asked Carmen to pass the salad to Mr. Bellacéra.

"Thank you," Victor murmured, rising ever so slightly to grasp the bowl she pushed an inch toward him. Their fingers were on the bowl at the same time and I had the most fanciful notion that I could hear the lead crystal ringing under their hands.

"There's a great deal of work to be done," Victor said with a glance at Leon, picking up the thread of the conversation. "I'm planning to add on a large room against the back of the original house, but first I want to repair the fireplace in the old living room. I've already begun to—"

"Oh," said Bet, her fork poised and empty, "that huge stone fireplace! Bob Wallace had a dreadful stag's head in the—"

"Twelve points, Betty," Leon said, chewing. "Don't forget that. Our old friend Bob," he explained to Victor, "loved to hunt. He and old Peavy Desjardin, Dwight's dad, bagged, well, more than their fair share," he said with a bark of laughter. "Got that buck back in the sixties, I think it was."

"Well, I gave it to Earl Stoner to dispose of," Victor said with a chuckle and a warm glance at Bet. "I'm afraid it was a pretty moth-eaten specimen, twelve points and all."

"Do you hunt?" Selene asked suddenly, forcing Victor to look at her. Her mouth was partly open and I saw her tongue flicking at the corner of her lips as if she were tasting something irresistible. I'd never seen that devouring expression on her face before, as if she could eat raw meat and relish every bloody bite. Even her voice, when she asked the question, was low and harsh, devoid of its usual warm elegance.

"I have," he said, putting a small portion of salad on his plate, "in the past. Not anymore."

"Bob Wallace used to love to read Hemingway aloud, remember, Sissy?" Bet said with a shy giggle. " 'The Snows of Kilimanjaro,' all the Africa stories."

"Umm. Fancied himself one of those white hunters, one supposes," Selene said, looking straight at Victor, testing for *his* fantasies.

I had spent some months in Africa in my younger days, the obligatory missionary experience all young priests attempt, and offered an anecdote or two from that time, hoping to redirect the conversation and the mood.

"In those days," I finished, "central Africa was not the hell on earth it has become. I wasn't there very long, only a few months, but the experience has stayed with me all these years."

"And now?" Victor asked, looking intently at me. I was somewhat surprised to see he was sincerely interested in my reply.

I laughed. "Now," I said, "I spend most of my time in libraries, or in my rooms. Reading, studying, writing." I shrugged, suddenly not too happy with being the center of attention. When I said something about my book on grace and forgiveness, Victor leaned toward me across the table.

"And can that be?" he said, as if eager for a factual answer. "God's forgiveness is real . . . *real*?"

I nodded. "I believe it can be—is. Yes."

"But would He forgive anything at all? Can God love whatever we do?"

"Perhaps He only loves what we *are*," I said, intrigued anew at Victor's interest in my work. "The miracle is that He loves us without propitiation, without sacrifice."

"Without slaughter, then?"

"Or so we believe," I said carefully. "May I ask, were you raised as a Catholic?"

He shrugged away the idea. "They tried, but I preferred something I could see—like stars," he said, turning to Bet with a calm smile.

"Oh, yes!" Bet said in a reedy, tense voice. "Victor showed me his telescope the other day, Leon. So interesting. Are you an astronomer, by any chance?"

I learned later from Bet that Victor hadn't told them what he "did for a living." Not even the Stoners, who were, according to Bet, indefatigable rooters-out of personal information, claimed to know. The new neighbor had not been observed going off to work, though he had (as it was told on the rialto of Turn-of-River) paid cold cash for everything from groceries to trucking, possibly even for the house itself. No one, or so Bet confided to me, her eyes twinkling at the idea of having such a mysterious, compelling new neighbor, knew a thing about him.

Victor laughed and inclined his head in Bet's direction. "Oh, it's just a hobby of mine. That old telescope is decent enough, but really nothing special. I've been interested in astronomy since I was a boy. I suppose you could say that *my* fantasy was that I imagined myself as . . . well, as Galileo."

I was bemused at that, at the notion that a man of such seamless self-possession might have a fantasy at all, that anything he might think or do or wish for was not real.

"I now hunt only stars and planets," Victor remarked with a small laugh, "not beasts." He looked again at Carmen. "Perhaps some time you might enjoy looking at the constellations," he said. "Do you think you would?"

"Wonderful," said Carmen, looking back at him as if she had simply been waiting for the invitation to be spoken aloud. "Of course I would."

"Well, maybe tomorrow night, then?" he asked, looking intently into her eyes. "How would that be? I've barely unpacked anything else, but the telescope is all set up. And the dark moon is tomorrow so there won't be any interference."

"We may see the Pleiades," Carmen said softly, surprising everyone but Victor, who smiled and leaned eagerly toward her.

"Yes, and Venus, I think..."

"Until She sets," Carmen added, her eyes glowing.

Selene's glance darted from Carmen's radiant face to Victor, watching as he began arranging the salt and pepper shakers and fallen flower petals into constellations right there on Bet's tablecloth.

As Victor explained all the wonders they might have a chance to see, Selene's face was a mask of lust—and anger. Suddenly, as I watched, she caught her breath with a sharp sound, almost a cry. Her cheeks were flushed, and her eyes, in the moment before she had the presence of mind to look down at her plate, lost all their focus. They went inward and dark in a second.

I took a sip of my Chianti, almost trembling with relief that—as everyone else was watching Victor's "constellations" forming in the center of the table—I was the only one who witnessed what had happened to Selene.

Chapter Fourteen

et served dessert and coffee in the living room and Selene, refusing to resume her pose on the sofa, sat in the wing chair with another whiskey and a cigarette. She watched while Victor put a raspberry in his mouth and crushed it against his teeth with his tongue. Then he slowly licked a bead of juice from the corner of his lip. He caught Selene looking at him when he did that, but I noted with some surprise that he was the first to look away.

The conversation turned to Eugenia Wallace's garden, then to the sundial Victor was having shipped from France to dominate its renovation. He said that he had a fondness for such instruments, that one of his prized possessions was an astrolabe that was said to have belonged to Vasco da Gama.

"My goodness, not many of those around," said Carmen, who was sitting between Victor and her mother on the davenport, eating her berries with a spoon. "Do you have to be out on the ocean to use it?"

"Well, it helps," he said, leaning forward, his elbows on his knees. The lamplight glowed on his black hair. "An astrolabe is for determining the altitude of the sun, or other celestial bodies, so it's nice to have a level playing field," he said, looking into her eyes. "I believe the word is Greek for 'star finder.'"

"Yes," Carmen said with a lovely, spontaneous smile. "It's called 'taking the stars,' isn't it? Do you think Columbus had one?"

"I don't doubt it," Victor answered with a grin. "Maybe two."

"In case one fell overboard," Carmen said, laughing.

"I've heard Columbus spoken of as the ultimate Renaissance man," Victor said, still smiling, turning to Selene. "Would you agree with that, Ms. Catcher?"

But she did not answer him. Nor did she get to her feet when, some time later, the Poynsetters accompanied their guest to the door. Leon was smiling in his gentle, self-effacing way, and Bet, her arm around Carmen's waist, was blooming (as if there could possibly be a single bud left in her *to* bloom) under Victor's thanks, his praise for her fine dinner, his offer of reciprocation.

Selene did not rise to join them, but I did, just catching the angry look she threw my way. The five of us stood in the open doorway, half in, half out, while Bet and Leon made their good-byes. Carmen and I said nothing, but as he turned to go, Victor took her hand in his and reiterated his invitation to watch the stars.

"Tomorrow, yes?" I saw him gently, slowly rubbing his thumb over her knuckles as he spoke.

"Yes," Carmen said, her eyes shining.

"Wonderful. Good night then." Still holding Carmen's hand, Victor turned toward the living room. "Good night, Ms. Catcher," he called, raising his voice a little.

But Selene did not respond, and a second later, with what seemed great reluctance, Victor let Carmen's fingers slide out of his and went down the two shallow steps to the path.

I was already standing on the lawn, having thought it more polite to get out of the crowded foyer, and when the screen door slapped gently shut, I moved to the edge of the driveway, entranced by the cool, clear night, those millions of stars.

"Beautiful, aren't they?" Victor said, pausing beside me, inhaling deeply through his nose.

"Beautiful," I agreed.

The two of us stood there, arms folded, looking calmly up at the sky. For the first time that day, I felt completely peaceful and at rest.

"I never get enough of it," Victor said in a soft, wondering voice. "Since I was a kid. I don't know why."

"The stars, you mean?" I asked, smiling and turning to face him.

"Yes. And the sky...the sky..."

"Have you done any flying?" I asked. I had no intention of prying, but the question asked itself.

"Not for a long time," he said, and I saw him frown in the darkness. "Well, except as a passenger. I prefer looking at it from down here."

There didn't seem to be anything more to say, so we didn't force it. We shook hands and looked carefully at each other.

"I hope to see you again, Giovanni," he said. "Do you visit often?"

"Oh, I imagine I'll spend some time here now that the weather's improving."

"You must come and see my house when I get it all fixed up. Will you?"

"I'll look forward to it," I said, releasing his hand. He chuckled, squeezed my elbow, and moved away into the darkness.

Half an hour later, Selene and I went back to her place. The dogs were lined up outside the *studiolo* door, eagerly waiting for her, their plume-like black tails swishing low to the ground, little grunts and growls rumbling deep in their throats. They showed no interest in me (for which I was duly grateful), not even when I put my hand on Selene's elbow for a second, though I saw Savo stiffen, alert as a living thing could be, when I did that.

I'd brought Selene a bottle of Benedictine as a gift and she poured some into a little glass for me. I took a sip and settled myself on the sofa. As we spoke about the dinner party, Selene paced the room, touching everything she passed—a chair, a table rim, the edge of the parchment lamp shade. She'd done that before, as if trying to drain her tension into the objects around her. The cigarette in her other hand burned down as she talked, and at last she ground it out in the marble dish on the desk that served her for an ashtray.

"You didn't care for Victor?" I asked. "You didn't like him, trust him? What?"

"Oh, he's nothing much, Vanni," she said in what I had begun to think of as her "Isabella" voice—the aristocratic assumption of superiority, even of sovereignty over other, lesser beings. "An uncivilized American nobody acting as if he were Lorenzo de' Medici himself, a perfect Renaissance man at ease with literature and travel, good food and wine, hunting, astronomy, exotic gardening. Oh, it was so obvious. Leon and Bet were charmed, of course, but I certainly was not," she finished with a short burst of laughter.

I watched her carefully as she spit all that out at me, intrigued to see where this was leading. Her protestations, and her scorn, seemed excessive.

"I lost interest in the evening very quickly," Selene went on, finally coming to rest in the chair by the desk. "Naturally, I understood that he was only trying to impress me, showing off almost like a schoolboy, but Galileo and *Columbus*. Really! He had the cheek to speak to *me* of Renaissance men, as if he imagined himself in their company, I suppose. Ha!"

She laughed and splashed some of the Benedictine into a glass, drinking most of it all at once. When she raised her head, she looked over at me with her golden eyes shining and her wide mouth, still moist with the wine, slightly open, and once again I caught a whiff of something so coarse, so erotic that I drew in my breath a little at the realization that this was the same woman who had chased the Angel of the Annunciation halfway across the world.

"It really wasn't very subtle of him, was it," she said, "to show his interest in that manufactured, oblique way? An old Italian uncle. *Really!*"

"Interest?"

"In me, in my work, my reputation. It's obvious that in his own small way he's a man of the world, not easily impressed. Oh, he did seem to have made a genuine effort to be nice to Carmen, but I'm sure simple girls are not to his taste. He did his best to conceal it, though, to disguise his attraction with courtesy toward everybody else."

"But you saw through that."

"Oh, please," she said with a laugh, tucking her long legs under her, smoothing back her hair with a languid hand. She looked especially fine that night—her color high, her heavy silver hair twisted somehow and tied with a black silk ribbon. Her pale gray silk blouse reminded me of the exquisite clothes she used to wear long ago, in Italy.

"Of course I did. How could I not? After all, Giovanni, I'm not all that much older than he—maybe ten years, maybe somewhat less. Inconsequential."

Where the devil was this going? I wondered. What in the world was the matter with her?

"Very frankly," she said, uncoiling her legs and leaning toward me, "I think it's just a matter of time before he . . . approaches me."

I thought I hid my shock rather well. I'm chagrined to say that in spite of what I thought I'd observed at the dinner table, I hadn't guessed for a moment that such thoughts would cross her mind. But why wouldn't they, after all? Why wouldn't any woman, even one with Selene Catcher's mind and history, her fierce and unconventional devotions, look with interest at a man like Victor Bellacéra?

Selene sat back and lit another cigarette, scraping the match across the scar on the desk. "He was obviously dazzled. But of course it's unimportant and I'm much too tired to think about it." She waved her cigarette back and forth in dismissal, her eyes fixed on the thin cirrus cloud of smoke that seemed to flow from her hand.

Not long after that, we said good night. Selene locked up the dogs and went back to the *stùdiolo* for another drink, and I made my way up the dark staircase to my bed, alone. Though I was very tired, perhaps a trifle overfed, both with veal and spirits, I couldn't sleep. I lay on the smooth, cool sheets with my arms behind my head, waiting, but my brain churned on.

It disturbed me terribly that in just the last few hours something had seemed so different in Selene, so unexpected. Her behavior in the *stùdiolo* had been absolutely fascinating. I hadn't seen that posturing before, that crooning pretense. Not even her description of the last night with Piero had evoked the self-absorbed sensuality I saw in her eyes when she spoke of Victor Bellacéra.

Who in the world ever has a clue where passion comes from? Etymologically, of course, it comes from the Latin word for *suffering*. That may well be instructive, for there is an irrationality to both passion and suffering that dominates the mind and heart as reason, by its very nature, cannot. But no one is ever ready for it—as anyone who's felt it, *suffered* it, emerged from it may be happy to tell you. My own life, I thought, with a strange sinking of my heart, had given me small chance to learn about it for myself. Even as a randy boy, I had been loath to educate myself except by surrogate.

But was all this simply about passion? Only that? All-consuming, mind-altering sexual passion? Would that be possible for a woman like Selene, I wondered, remembering again the remarkable conversation we had had years ago on the night she came back to Carla's house from the San Marco. Despite the vow of chastity she had hinted at that night, she was also, and had remained, a vibrant woman in the prime of life. Yet she'd spoken of Victor as if all she felt for him, for his impressive appearance and his polished style, was mere contempt.

Distressed by my thoughts, I got out of bed and went to the window, looking out at the dark shadows of the trees, the black sweep of lawn. And there, in the side yard, I saw Selene, surrounded by her dogs, just setting off down Sterling's road, the thin beam from her flashlight probing the ground ahead.

All at once, I remembered something I'd read about years before—the romantic idea of a spontaneous mutual passion, an instant's meeting of the eyes that explodes into an irresistible *knowing*—a sharp exposure of the future. I was sure that something very like that had happened between Victor and Carmen. They had been unable to take their eyes from each other all evening long, had seemed to lean toward each other as they said good night in the doorway, their clasped hands almost a metaphor for what they felt.

But even though Selene could not have missed the stunning affinity that blazed up so quickly between them—*did not,* as I remembered, miss it at all—her stalking movement down the road revealed, as nothing else that night had fully done, that the nail of such a passion had pierced her as well.

And what, I wondered, as I watched her move through the darkness and out of sight beyond the trees, might the Goddess—the chaste, implacable, Merciless Diana—think of *that?*

Chapter Fifteen

he next morning the sky was like slate and the air was noticeably warmer. A dripping kind of day—windless, dank, English. The clammy gloom was almost an insult after Saturday's brilliance. My throat felt parched and tight even in the humid air.

Before I went downstairs, I paused in the open doorway of Selene's room. The narrow bed was covered with a white wool blanket; there was no decorative spread or comforter, just the blanket and a single pillow in a white flannel case. The oak chiffonier held only a plain silver tray, well polished, on which was placed a shallow silver bowl, also unadorned and very shiny. There were no pictures on the walls, no books on the low table by the bed. A spare blanket was neatly folded on a ladder-back chair; the pegged wooden floor was bare. The room made the small cell where I lived during my first days in the seminary look like Versailles.

I called Selene's name several times as I went down the stairs, and paused on the bottom riser, listening for movement, but the whole house was empty, warm and silent. But in the kitchen, scrawled on an index card and leaning against a half-full jar of instant coffee, was a note: *"Working all morning. See you for lunch or later. Make yourself some coffee."*

While the water boiled in the kettle, I stood in the kitchen doorway, deciding what to do with myself. I had originally planned an early return to Boston, and had mentioned that to Selene the night before. She had either forgotten or was hoping I would stay. As I had no obligations in Boston until evening, I decided to go for a nice ramble over Sterling's vast property, looking forward to the spectacle of a New England woodland in early spring—even under the day's unreflecting skies.

The instant I stepped outside and turned onto the estate road, I was surrounded by the dogs. They seemed to have come from nowhere. My heart leapt into my throat and I instinctively thought of either useless flight or ignoble retreat, but they kept their distance, though their eyes never left me for a second. Heartened by that, I foolishly stretched out a hand to the closest one, a great black creature with a long, lolling tongue, but my friendliness was rewarded with a low, intense growl from all of them and I snatched back my hand, still whole, and shoved it into my pocket.

Cautiously, I took their slightly increased distance for a sign of permission and set off with a bold step along the road. A furtive glance told me they were following in single file, Savo in the lead, but they were at least fifty yards back and I determined to ignore them, reasoning that if they were set on mayhem, they would have let me know already.

At first I thought I could use this morning of unexpected leisure to pay a visit to Victor Bellacéra, to see what kind of conversation we might have when no fascinated women were around. Naturally, I knew nothing of his habits, but I imagined he might well be up and about his renovations on that gloomy Sabbath morning. Yet, on an idle impulse, I changed my mind, and when I got to Sterling's rock, I veered off west into the forest.

It was rough going for a while. The warmer air had already softened the chilled spring earth; pools of moisture stood around the roots of the trees, and a muddy slough filled every depression in the ground. I had to grasp the boles of smaller trees for balance as I splashed along.

Though the first hundred yards or so were faintly marked, perhaps a continuation of the old path Selene and I had taken all those weeks before, in no time at all it disappeared and I realized with some consternation that I had no idea where I was in relation to the road, or Selene's house, or Victor's. When I looked back, I noted that my escort had disappeared. Perhaps they'd lost interest, having merely seen a way to amuse themselves for a short while at my expense.

A few yards farther on, the ground began to rise a bit and I soon realized that I had climbed a kind of crest in the forest to a natural plateau. Though it must have been approaching eleven o'clock or even later, the sky had not brightened. The branches of Sterling Catcher's great trees, though still bare of leaves, were thick and woody overhead, creating a bowl of air in which the sound of the dripping boughs seemed unnaturally contained and dense, as if shrouded invisibly in velvet.

I leaned gratefully against a tree, catching my breath, and looked up into the dome of the space. There was a seductive oddness to it and I stood perfectly still, trying to get a sense of what was so intriguing. After a few minutes, I became aware that the cathedral-like area in which I stood was a nearly perfect oval, some sixty feet across. Though at first I saw no tree stumps, no evidence of a human hand in forming it, I felt a sense of symmetry and enclosure, as of an architecture not entirely natural. I gradually noticed that the perimeter of the space was ringed with large, regularly placed black stones. They were perfectly round, wet and faintly gleaming, worked almost to smoothness.

I made my way slowly around the oval, brushing some soggy fallen leaves away from the tops of the stones with a small bare branch I'd found. The stones were of uniform size though uneven in height and inclination, as if they had settled into the earth. How long must it have taken for them to sink like that?

The oval space enclosed by the stones was not quite invisibly trisected by three faint tracks, which seemed to divide the area into equal sections. Frowning with curiosity, I began to cross the diameter of the oval, and suddenly slipped, flailing my arms to keep from tumbling into the depression hidden in the very center, where the three barely marked lines converged.

My heart thudding with the adrenalin of having avoided a fall, I went as fast as I dared over to the other side and nearly fell onto the stone across from where I'd started. Clutching my knees, I breathed slowly through my mouth, my eyes flickering from stone to stone and to the sunken area in the middle, now a messy slush of the old, dead vegetation that my frantic feet had churned up from underneath.

I stood up and with my bare fingers brushed the dead, damp leaves and one sodden pine cone off the stone I'd sat on. The top felt as if it had been sheared off flat. I squatted down and brought my face to within a few inches of it, feeling it carefully, smelling it: the surface had recently been burned. I stood up and moved slowly clockwise around the outside of the circle, looking at every stone I passed. Each one had a small flattened area on top. Each one seemed rough from burning.

I went back inside the oval, careful to slide my foot along the ground before I put it down, lest I plunge into whatever unmarked pit was there.

A step at a time, I made my way to the center and found that at its deepest point the depression was not only very gradual but shallow as well, no more than shin-high relative to the surrounding level ground.

Carefully, I prodded the hollow area with the wet toe of my boot. It was filled with old leaves and forest debris, which frothed up to reveal layers of ancient vegetable matter. Had the day not been so gloomy, I might never have seen the dull gleam almost under my foot. I bent down and dug through a clump of rotted leaves and mud with my bare hand, searching for the source of that dull shine.

It was a plain silver basin, about eight inches across, crazed with a million tiny scratches but not tarnished, as if the dense rot in which it lay had kept it clean. The bowl was exactly like the one I'd seen on Selene's bureau. Holding my breath, not particularly proud of my furtive, if intrepid, behavior, I plunged my fingers into the hollow where the bowl had been. At first, I found only more dead leaves and clumps of moss, but then, from deeper down, I drew out a small bundle wrapped in a bit of sacking, held together with a black silk ribbon, which I carefully untied. It was a collection of half a dozen tiny, brownish bones, cleaned and perfectly preserved.

Somewhere, I found the presence of mind to rewrap the bones and replace them in the slushy hole. Then I put the silver bowl back and scooped dead leaves over it, gathering palmsful of the rotted mush and packing it down, as if I could disguise what I had done—and seen.

I stood up and cleaned my hands on my handkerchief and looked around the oval. Focusing on a small fir tree directly across from where I was, I got my bearings and counted carefully: there were twenty-seven stones.

Turning in my own footprints, my heart beginning to pound just a little, I counted the stones again to be sure I'd done it right the first time.

Twenty-seven.

A multiple of the sacred number three. Of nine.

Three times nine.

The trinity of the Moon Goddess: Maiden, Huntress, Crone.

The upper air, the earth and sea, the underworld.

Selene . . . Artemis . . . Hecate. Sterling had written that nine was Hecate's number, the signature of the three-faced Goddess of Enchantments.

I had known for years of Selene's fascination with the Great Goddess, and thought I had come to understand that she worshiped the neolithic Mother as I revere the Virgin.

But it had taken considerable reflection (much of it conducted on some semiconscious level, often at times when I was unaware of thought) for me to get my Christian mind around the *possibility* of what Selene believed. If I accept Jews and Hindus, I asked myself, why can I not, why *will* I not, accept the Goddess? Is Merciless Diana too terrifying for me, a poor Jesuit father relying on my overeducated brain and Christ's love to make my way to my grave with some aplomb?

But my speculations over the years had never included any expectation that I would some day find myself in an actual *place of worship*. Perhaps because of their almost melodramatic tone, Sterling's manuscripts had seemed little more than stories, only fables and dark fairy tales. He himself had always seemed ancient and remote to me, his rhetoric from another time. Not even the savage rituals he had described—sacrificing animals to Hecate at a place where three roads meet, the brutal Stag King ceremonies—had seemed quite real. My long relationship with Selene notwithstanding, it seemed impossible to me that anyone might actually worship the neolithic Goddess in this day and age. But for the first time, in that dank, dripping oval of black stones, I knew at last that Sterling and his ideas were an integral part of Selene and the way she chose to live her life. She'd learned it all from him. But her mother—the woman who had taught her about the Angel of the Annunciation, who died a nun's death—what of her? What did Selene take from her? Something, *surely?*

In the calm elegance of Carla's drawing room in Florence, in my austere sanctuary in Rome, even in the flat in Boston—places where events had moved me to take out those limp, photocopied pages again and again over the years—Sterling's ideas had been chilling enough. But here, on the edge of what was (all too obviously) a ceremonial oval, deep in an ancient forest, in the cold, seeping gloom, the very word "neolithic" conjured up images of a firelit band of hot-eyed people, draped in uncured animal skins, gripping their stone knives and circling a terrified man, bound with animal gut and sinew, the rack of antlers jammed onto his skull. Ten thousand years ago, somewhere in central Europe on the night of a new moon, they had danced around him, offering the living sacrifice to a great stone effigy, all breasts and buttocks, the eyes bulbous with knowledge. Desperate times, the neolithic age—desperate people.

And I knew that I—priest, intellectual, skeptic—came from those ancient Europeans; the blood that runs in my veins once spilled from someone who had given himself to that ugly, erotic stone Goddess, someone who prayed to Her and expected Her to grant the prayer, someone who was prepared to offer Her just about anything at all, propitiate Her by any means, if She would only answer.

I sat heavily on one of the burned stones, my face in my hands, trying to understand.

Could there be, even now, a secret, cabalistic cult performing such ancient rites in the dark of the moon, at crossroads and in the depths of primeval, Artemisian forests? Do they slaughter lambs and let fruit rot so it will be pleasing to the Goddess? Where are the temple maidens and the stone knives? What are the symbols and the signs?

Who is the son-consort this year? Who is to be sacrificed?

When they've done with the Stag King, how long do they wait before they eat him?

Which sacrifice will satisfy Her most?

What will She give Her priestess in return?

I took a deep, shuddering breath and pulled my hands away from my face . . . and saw the dogs.

They were spread out in a broad semicircle across the oval from where I sat, spaced perfectly at every other stone. Only Savo was inside the circle. She stood between two of the converging lines, about twenty feet away, her teeth bared, her black fur bristling.

When I stood up, Savo came a pace or two closer, her tail twitching slightly. One by one, the dogs moved into the circle beside her, shoulder to shoulder, facing me.

With careful nonchalance, I looked once again around the dark, wet glade trying to guess if Selene was likely to see the mess I'd made before I went back to Boston. And what if she did? What would she do if—when—she found out? Slit my throat and leave my blood-soaked body at this crossroads with rotten fruit piled on my chest? Ridiculous; on the face of it, impossible. But in that one bursting, surrealistic moment I felt the ceremonial knife at my own throat. Without thinking of the stupidity of what I was about to do—without thinking at all—I succumbed to the absolute terror that I felt, and ran.

I crashed out of the space, leaping over tiny bushes and fallen branches. I had no idea if the dogs were behind me. Swept along by fear and imagination alone, I raced down the sloping forest floor, gaining momentum as the land fell away, but just as I was about to lose my footing altogether, I crashed, full weight, against a tall, tilted sapling, my arms tight around it, my hands clasping each other on the opposite side, my cheek scraped and wet from the bark. My breath wheezed through my throat and teeth, sounding to my ears like keening, a thin, disgraceful wail.

I have no idea how long I stood there, embracing that small, comforting tree, but when some time had passed, I moved away and stood up on my own, my legs still quivering a bit but holding. I found my soiled handkerchief and wiped my cheeks and chin, relieved to see no blood, though the skin of my face felt tender and sore to the touch. I took a deep breath and ventured to move a little way apart from the tree, turning to get my bearings.

And the dogs were there. Silently, they had followed me all the way down the slope. Again, Savo moved out a short distance from her pack. As she watched, I brushed off my jacket and went slowly down the incline, holding on all the way, until I felt the level ground and could no longer hear my heart. Concentrating on each step, I made it through an area of low sedge and thornbush, where the land flattened and sank, and came at last to the edge of a small clearing surrounded by trees that grew more sparsely, their topmost branches no longer touching.

And they were still behind me. They had come no closer than before, but they had not dispersed either. Suddenly, I knew that I was being not so much pursued as led. They were herding me, perhaps back to Selene. All at once, but soundlessly, they came to a kind of attention, ears pricked up, their growls held in their throats. Led by Savo, they turned and trotted away into the trees. What had they seen or heard?

In the clearing the ground was level and flat, as if cared for by a loving, purposeful hand. The small area was almost entirely occupied by an oblong bed filled with spring flowers, some already in bloom—jonquils and snowdrops rimmed with miniature hyacinth. And at the end of the tiny garden was a polished wooden board, almost four feet tall and half as wide. It was a tombstone. The flowers grew right up to the base, might have sprung from it.

I stopped short and instinctively ducked behind one of the larger trees just as a person carrying a basket entered the clearing from the other side. Although I was many yards away, and well hidden, I shrank back and peered around the curve of the trunk, hoping I could watch from there unseen.

It was Lido Desjardin. She was dressed in boots and a gray anorak, her red-gold hair frothing out about her head in a great ruff. She paused in front of the grave-garden and knelt for several minutes; then she rose, reached into the basket, and took out some small gardening tools—a hand rake, shears, a little hoe—and went to work tending the grave. Though I squinted and strained, the wooden tablet was too far away for me to read. When she was done with her weeding and pruning, Lido gathered up the small cuttings, put them in her basket with the tools, and stood up slowly. She put her basket down a little distance from the grave and vigorously ran her fingers through her hair.

As her hands untangled it, the hair streamed down, so vivid as to be resistant to the strange gray light, and fell in a cloud of gleaming ringlets to her shoulders. Even at that distance, even in the gloomy light, even with the shapeless jacket, Lido looked like a Botticelli portrait come to life.

Though I clung to the rough bark, making a conscious effort to remain unseen, at the same time I was seized with the impulse to run to her, but knew I must resist. She knelt again, her face in her hands, and remained motionless as if giving me a chance to make my decision.

But it was out of the question to speak to her. There was my pride to consider—and her privacy. But when she didn't move, I found myself sinking to my own knees, my hands gently grasping the trunk of the tree before which I knelt, and at last, feeling under my clothing for my crucifix, I took it in my hand and bowed my head.

I told Selene nothing of the incident at the circle of stones, nor of the dogs. Certainly not a word about coming upon Lido in her clearing. When I got back to the house, we ate a modest lunch at the kitchen table and, in the middle of the afternoon, I drove back to Boston, leaving many things unsaid.

A few days later, I sent Selene a note, rather formally inviting her to come into Boston for a special concert one week hence. A string quartet was playing Monteverdi and Mozart at Symphony Hall and I already had the tickets. She called to say she'd be delighted, and we made fairly elaborate plans for dinner, the concert, and for a drive along the ocean the next day. But on the morning of the concert, she phoned again to cancel, her reasons vague and almost careless. I was embarrassed to go in search of another companion on such short notice. Instead, I went alone and put my damp raincoat on the seat beside me.

Chapter Sixteen

ne morning, toward the end of May, I sat down at my desk as usual and opened a folder of notes I'd been working on for days—a new essay on the ambiguity of sin. I'd scribbled page after yellow page of half-formed ideas on intention and inadvertence, on accident and irresistible compulsion. It has always seemed to me that there can be an element of happenstance in sin—that the power of events may carry us beyond the confines of our normal principles and restraints, which are not, in any case, the same as virtues.

The ideas fascinated me and I tortured myself and them for almost an hour, trying to say exactly what I meant, but it seemed impossible. Overcome, I threw down my pen in disgust. I was irritated and bored and, the truth be told, feeling a little sorry for myself. All sins of a sort.

When the phone rang, just as the pen bounced off the corner of the desk and into the wastebasket, I leapt to answer, thinking blackly that I'd have a conversation with *il diàvolo* himself if he was as amusing as I'd always heard. But then I actually laughed aloud when I heard Carmen's voice.

"What's so funny?"

"Nothing, my dear, nothing. Forgive me."

"You sound like you were expecting someone else."

"Ah, no . . . no. A man in my position has few expectations."

"Oh, good grief! You're in a lousy mood, aren't you?"

"No worse than usual." Of course I was grinning like a madman into the phone, glad she couldn't see my face.

"Well, how about a nice walk in the Public Garden, then? It's gorgeous out and they said on the news it's going to rain tomorrow."

We agreed to meet at two o'clock by the statue of George Washington. I put away my notes on inadvertent sin, retrieved my fountain pen from the wastebasket, and read "The Snows of Kilimanjaro" in Italian while I ate my lunch.

After half an hour or so of aimless strolling, which we spent admiring the plants and searching for the perfect place to sit, Carmen and I settled down on a quiet bench shaded by an immense linden tree on the Beacon Street border of the Garden. She'd brought along a thermos and two plastic cups and we sipped the sweet iced tea in a companionable silence. Elegant dark red azaleas, fully in bloom and set in a lovely sun-washed bed across the path from our bench, reminded me of the flowers Carla sometimes kept in her small terrace garden in Florence. Early in the season, she would place entire bushes in some beautiful ceramic pots she'd purchased long ago from an artist in Montefiesole, and they bloomed, red and fragrant, as though unaware of their confinement.

Carmen told me she had recently been back to the estate on a short visit. "Father G., it was so wonderful, I wish you could have come. The trees were almost—not quite, but *almost*—in full flower and Mom's lilacs are glorious this year. She didn't want to cut them back, but I talked her into it and they're *fabulous.* Oh! Like lavender clouds against the house."

"Ah, my poetess," I said, squeezing her hand.

She blushed, but gave me a charming giggle before she continued. "Well, spring's so beautiful this year, they're all getting into it."

Lido, she went on with a grin, had been spending hours on her knees in the dirt of her herb garden, tending the circular beds of marjoram, rosemary and dill, salvia, smilax and oregano she had planted on the eastward side of the yard.

She also told me that Victor had been working diligently on his house. Carpenters, glaziers, and landscapers came in a steady stream down the road. After many days of watching from the shadows of the forest, Dwight ventured forth to ask if he could help. Victor, who had seen him hiding there, accepted at once, and the two of them worked side by side with the hired laborers, constructing a huge steel skeleton against the back of the original house. When that was done, they brought in cranes to move the twenty-foot panels of tinted glass into place, creating the spacious, sunny salon pane by pane. Though the Wallace living room might have been thought to be more than adequate for any entertainment, Victor, for reasons he did not discuss, wanted something unusual and grand. If it was an indulgence, he did not apologize. He had the money and the inclination. At the far end of the large room, he built a platform for his telescope, set several feet above the floor and placed in such a way that the lens would focus in a long angle past the trees. Near it, against the original wall of the house, was a long table with specially built shelves for his maps and celestial charts. A rich man's fantasy, Carmen thought, offering her comment with a wink, but now come fully, expensively to life.

She had been there on the day the work was finished. Victor, exhausted as he was, took Carmen out for a special dinner at a restaurant a few miles past Turn-of-River.

When they came back to the estate it was nearing midnight. Indifferent to the late hour, they went for a walk through the forest, their slow steps lit by a waxing crescent moon. They went up the slope I'd climbed myself, up to the plateau of the worship oval. Carmen, seeing no way to deflect him from that route, stood by one of the great trees on the perimeter as Victor slowly paced the circle, his lips moving slightly, his face calm and remote.

"What did he say?" I asked.

Carmen shrugged. "Nothing. He just walked around the whole circle, looking, thinking. I had the impression he understood exactly what it was, but he didn't say anything at all. He just kept walking, shaking his head a little. After a while he came over and put his arms around me for a minute and then we . . . went away. Mom said don't worry about it, don't get into it with him. And I haven't. I won't either."

I saw no reason to interject the fact that I'd been there some weeks before, nor that I had reacted in a rather different manner. It was impossible to tell if Carmen suspected, or wondered, or hoped I had seen the circle.

"And Selene?" I asked. "How is she doing? Do you see her?"

"She's okay. Working—at least she seems to be. The *stùdiolo* is a royal mess, if that means anything." Carmen seemed about to add something more, but did not. She wanted to, I could see that, but whatever she might have said, both loyalty and love forbade.

"Anyway," she went on, getting up from the bench to tuck the cups and thermos neatly into her canvas bag, "Mother and Daddy are settling in for summer. You should see them, Father G., they're a riot. Mom and her flowers...Lord. Daddy has Red Sox tickets, but they're going on vacation next month, so he'll probably miss some of the games."

"Going where?"

"Maine, I think. Canada? I might go with them, I'm not sure. But Victor wants to go to the Cape. I don't know...maybe."

She sat on the bench again, the canvas sack clasped in her arms, and turned her shining, happy eyes to me. "I never thought this would happen to me," she whispered, suddenly on the verge of tears. "I hoped, you know...wished...who doesn't wish, huh? But..."

"But what, *cara*?" I said softly, looking, not without some concern, into her face. "*Che cosa?*"

The tears spilled, one by one. "Oh, Father, he's wonderful—*wonderful!* And I think he actually loves me back. Imagine?"

As the semester drew to a close, I spent hours trying to come to terms with all I had to do. There was the enduring question of going back to Italy for a while, or for good, versus the more appealing option of staying in Boston for another year. An offer had been made, along with improved opportunities to write and study, which were a powerful temptation.

But I was also rather worried about Carla. Piero had visited, briefly, and was off traveling again, in the Orient. His departure had left Carla depressed and richly dissatisfied. She had called more than once with disingenuous questions about my "plans for the summer."

There were, in fact, some family business matters that might benefit from my attention. Carla's profligate use of money had given her the better head for figures, but my annual signature was required on whole sheaves of documents. They could have easily been expressed back and forth across the ocean, and no excuse to go was needed, but the papers provided a neat one all the same. One dark morning, I was puttering about my flat, trying to work through to a decision, when the phone rang. I picked it up without enthusiasm.

"Giovanni. It's Victor Bellacéra. How are you?"

"Ah, Victor. Good morning...good morning."

"I'm at Carmen's. We're going up to Gloucester for the weekend, but she's just called to say she's delayed at work, so I thought I'd impose—if it's no imposition," he said, laughing.

"Please, come and have coffee. By all means." I was delighted at the prospect and said so. Twenty minutes later, I was letting him in the door.

He looked more handsome than he had the night of Bet's dinner party. An odd observation, perhaps, coming from me, but the fact was that in spite of his quite prepossessing appearance on that earlier occasion, and notwithstanding his effect on Selene, Carmen, and our hostess herself, he had seemed more than merely handsome.

That Friday morning, however, wearing well-cut beige slacks and a dark blue shirt open at the collar, an expensive sport coat thrown over his arm, he was masculine beauty itself. The black hair was (or so I thought) a bit more slashed with silver and his skin was deeply tanned and taut with confidence and good feeling. He looked powerfully, fully *alive*.

He came in with a quick, energetic step, looking around my study with genuine interest. At a glance, he took in the books and the one or two pictures I'd brought from home, the excellent carpet on the floor, and the furniture, which, reviewing it through his eyes, was really rather fine. I hadn't particularly thought about it before. It was comfortable and exactly what I needed, so I hadn't paid attention to the good lines of the pair of armchairs or the attractive inlay on the marble fireplace.

"Maybe I should have stayed a Catholic," he said with a dry smile, tempered with a friendly wink and a laugh in which I heard not only a generous admiration for my surroundings but also (perhaps?) a whisper of regret.

"We'll be glad to take you back," I said cheerfully, leading the way to the kitchen. I turned on the pot of coffee I had prepared after his phone call, and we stood in easy camaraderie watching it burble while he told me that he'd asked Carmen to join him there.

"Do you mind, Giovanni?" he said, all seriousness. "It more or less popped out when I called her back to tell her where I'd be. I hope it wasn't too much of a liberty."

"But of course, no," I said, struck as I had been at Bet's by Victor's remarkable combination of an arresting physical presence and old-fashioned good manners. "*Con piacére*, I am always happy to see her. Always."

"Good."

We took our cups into the study and sat in the matching armchairs, now revealed as handsome and solid.

"I was sorry you could not come to my party," he said, crossing his long legs and leaning back in the chair.

"Ah. No sorrier than I, Victor, believe me. But it was impossible." I said a word or two about my penance of a schedule, and the end-of-term hysteria that grips all academic institutions in the spring. He nodded as if he really did know what I meant. When I mentioned my still-tentative plan of going back to Italy for a visit, perhaps short, perhaps long, possibly permanent, he looked at me with a frown and, yes, alarm.

"You might not come back? I'm sorry to hear it."

I shrugged. "Who can say? In any case, I may be walking along the Lungarno and drinking Florence city water fairly soon. My sister is eager to see me, and I her. But, I am unsure. At any rate, I do apologize that I could not be there to celebrate. Carmen's told me how hard you worked on your house. It must be a great satisfaction to you to see it finished."

"Umm." He took a sip of his coffee. "The party was all right. Nothing too big, just an afternoon buffet for the neighbors, a few people from Turn-of-River, the Stoners . . . oh, my goodness, what a pair!"

"Selene was there?"

"Oh, yes. Indeed she was."

He needed nearly no prodding to tell me about it, and in a matter of minutes I realized he had invited himself to my house that morning for that very purpose. As he talked, he sat unmoving in his chair, his strong, fine hands folded on his knee.

"I just felt, you know, that I wanted to do something nice for all the people who've been so kind to me," he said with a brief smile. "And Carmen was a delight. She volunteered to be a sort of unofficial hostess. Ah, Giovanni, what a lovely woman she is."

To my embarrassment, Victor confided that he'd been nearly unable to take his eyes away from her. He said that in the weeks since she had come into his life, Carmen seemed to have bloomed like the flowers in the great field. It was as though (and he smiled in an indulgent way when he said it, not embarrassed at all) even her lovely party dress had been made of all their colors—blue, fuchsia, and the pale gold of the wild irises that grew near the rock and filled the vases in the soaring glass salon where the guests had assembled.

Selene Catcher had sat regally in a white damask chair, as far from the glare of the glass wall as she could, picking at a plate of sliced fruit that Victor had brought to her himself. He explained that he only intended to show her the respect due a woman of her age and accomplishment, but her silent stare unnerved him. She wore a flowing white dress that day; her silver hair was tied back with a white silk ribbon. Her only jewelry was a heavy silver pendant of a strange, ceremonial figure, and though Victor could not keep himself from staring, he was chilled (as he put it) by the distinctive oddness of it, the crudity of the design defeated by the richness of the silver from which it had been fashioned. He did not speak to her for most of the afternoon, busily attending to his other guests, but he glanced her way from time to time and found her eyes upon him.

Everyone left before sundown, bubbling with thanks and promises and good wishes. Victor looked around for Carmen—they had planned a private *coda* to the party—but she had disappeared without a word. In a matter of ten minutes (displeased, he was not quite sure how it had happened), he and Selene had been left unexpectedly alone. He did not see how he could ask her to leave, and, hoping she would refuse, he invited her to share a bottle of wine he said he had been saving. When she said she would, he fetched the wine and fresh glasses, and there they were, at dusk, alone in the circle of light cast by the small crystal hurricane lamps set every few feet around the platform for the telescope, talking about the Renaissance.

Victor had mentioned casually that it was the politics that interested him most: the finances, the cloth trade, the power that patronage conferred. He said he was fascinated by the wars with the French, the treachery of popes and princes alike.

Selene seemed terribly irritated at that. In her clear, elegant voice, tinged now with a superior annoyance, she spoke of the rich, hot, smoky atmosphere, of Mantegna and Raphael, of sculpture and cathedrals. Victor answered that he was more intrigued by the shady beginnings of the great fortunes of the Medici and the Visconti. She praised Isabella d'Este-Gonzaga for her love of art and he replied that he revered Columbus and Galileo.

As they chatted on in that awkward fashion, Victor sat tense and unhappy in his chair, occasionally running his hand through his hair, wondering where Carmen was, how long this unwelcome tête-à-tête might last. Beams of light slanted through the louvered shades. He got up to open them, finding the dimness and the lamplight far too intimate, too unintended, but just then, the door from the old part of the house burst open and Carmen and Lido, laughing and calling to Victor, spilled into the shuttered room in a flood of sunset. The sky behind them, orange and gold, seemed to catapult a beam of evening light across the floor.

"Victor!" Lido cried, laughing over her shoulder at Carmen. "Victor, look what we brought you!"

Smiling, eager, Victor left his glass on a table and went to greet them, pulling them into the salon.

"Ah! Wood nymphs; look, Selene," he called to her, laughing. "Arms full of flowers, how beautiful..." He reached toward Carmen and drew her and the overflowing bouquet of flowers toward himself, bending to smell the sprays of wild columbine and purple loosestrife balanced in her arms.

"They're not weeds, are they?" he said, starting to laugh at his own small joke.

"Oh, Victor," Carmen said in a low, teasing voice that sparkled, rippled with little rivers of pleasure, "my goodness, you can be so silly. Oh, hi, Selene, still here?"

He and Carmen took the flowers into the kitchen and as she placed them carefully in the sink, Victor came up behind her, inhaling the beautiful fragrance of her hair, his arms embracing her from behind. Carmen leaned back against him, humming, murmuring, and in the second that he looked up and out the kitchen window, Victor saw Selene, her arms flung wide to the rising moon, run headlong down the old road toward her house.

When he finished his story, Victor sat perfectly still for a moment, and then, seeming to come to himself, reached for his coffee. He took a deep breath and looked up at me with a faint smile, which he could not possibly have meant to seem so strained.

"Selene Catcher is a very unusual woman," he said in a dry tone, not without some admiration.

"Without a doubt." I watched his face carefully.

"You've known her many years, I believe. Bet said something at supper the other night."

"Seventeen years," I answered, still unsure of his mood, his attitude. "We met at my sister's home in Florence. You can't imagine how dazzling Selene was in those days."

"Yes," he answered with a light laugh. "Yes, I can."

Chapter Seventeen

armen joined us about an hour later. I had gone into the other room, for a reason I've forgotten, but when I came back I saw that Victor had heard her gentle knock and let her in. They were standing in the foyer, her face tilted up to his, his large hands gently smoothing back her long, windblown, honey-colored hair. Though their embrace was brief, there was an intense intimacy to it, and I stood rooted to the carpet, feeling as if I had somehow surprised them in the act of love itself.

Carmen seemed to have brought the sunshine with her. Earlier, the skies had been cool and moist, but the light suddenly streamed over the housetops on Commonwealth Avenue and down my street, burning away the morning's fog with its luminous, still hazy warmth. All at once sunshine flooded the room, lighting up the small pieces of colored glass that made a pattern of fruit in the leaded ornamental windows high above my desk.

"Sorry you missed Victor's terrific housewarming, Father G.," Carmen said, leaning out of Victor's arms to kiss my cheek.

"He's just been telling me about it," I said. "I'll look forward to seeing all those renovations."

We talked on, quietly, the conversation so relaxed as to be nearly desultory, unmotivated, or so I thought. Carmen was in a pensive mood, but I soon sensed that she was trying to find a way to tell me something she believed I would not want to hear. Something Victor knew already.

At last, she shifted in her chair, gave Victor an odd, inquisitive look, and went to the window. She idly parted the lace curtains with her fingertips before turning back to me.

"So did Victor tell you what Selene did that night?"

"Carmen..." Victor's voice was low and almost sad, but he could not bring himself to chide her. Indeed, she ignored his warning, sat on the edge of my desk, and turned unhappy hazel eyes to me.

"Did he?"

I shook my head. "What are you talking about, *cara?*" I asked in a whisper.

"She spied on me..." Carmen began, but her voice thickened as she tried to speak. She sniffed and took a tissue from the box on my desk.

"Oh, Carmen, I can't believe it," I said, feeling the faint thud of my heart.

Carmen took a deep breath and blew her nose again. "But she did, Father, she definitely...did. It was really, really late, but Lido and I were too revved up to go home, so we were sitting in the moonlight on those stones at the base of my grandfather's rock. You know, on the side by the old road?"

"Of course," I murmured.

Carmen sighed deeply and, looking over her shoulder at Victor as she went on, told me that she and Lido had been there for almost an hour, talking in hushed, intimate tones about the first sparkling intimations of what was happening with Victor. I was sure that a young woman does not normally reveal to the gentleman in question the romantic secrets shared with an old chum, but Victor's face revealed no displeasure at all. On the contrary, he seemed relieved that Carmen's story was being told at last.

That night, Carmen was exhilarated both by the fun of the party and by the wine she'd drunk with a bit too much abandon. Lido, exhausted but utterly relaxed, laughed at her. "Time for you to get some sleep, my friend. Ready to go home?"

But Carmen was still too full of energy to sit. She jumped up from the boulder and walked back and forth along the road, wondering aloud if she had ever guessed that being in love would make her feel so itchy.

"Was I ever like this before?" Carmen said in a laughing voice. "Do you remember?"

"God, I'm sure I would have," Lido said, laughing too. "Look at you. You better lay off the sherry, miss."

They laughed together at that. Carmen was a little the worse for Victor's expensive Spanish sherry and knew it. When he'd kissed her in the kitchen after they brought in the flowers and grasses from the field, he said he could taste it on her lips.

"You didn't tell me what you thought, though," Carmen said, throwing the flower in her hand into Lido's lap. "Earlier tonight. What was she doing there?"

"It makes no difference, dear heart," Lido said. "None at all. Zilch. Zero. Don't worry about it." If Lido had an opinion about finding Selene in the salon with Victor, she was keeping it to herself.

"You and I never talked about this kind of thing," Carmen said in a more serious tone, "years ago. I think we must have been too shy, too young."

Lido snorted with laughter. "Shit, what'd we have to *say*, for God's sake? Big nothing."

"I can't believe all this is happening," Carmen said. "Oh, Lido, I think maybe I'm going to have a life, a *real* life. You know, that night we were up in her circle of stones—remember I told you?"

"Uh huh," Lido said, nodding.

"He told me he thought I was beautiful. Me! Can you imagine?"

She held her skirts up with her fingertips and danced, little prancing steps along the road, laughing over her shoulder.

But just then, twirling toward Lido again, Carmen thought she saw something move behind the rock. She blinked and looked again. Yes.

Saying nothing to Lido, she hiked up her skirts and danced farther down the curve of the road, ten yards, twenty—enough to get a clearer look at the field side of the rock. Selene was spread-eagled against it, leaning toward the very boulder where Lido still sat listening to her slightly tipsy friend go on and on about Victor.

Astonished, Carmen forced herself back along the path, retracing her steps those twenty yards to Lido. Even from there she could see that Selene, obviously unaware of being seen, had ventured a few feet past the rock and stood nearly on the rim of the road itself, one hand out for balance, not ten feet behind them.

"I just hope the old bitch doesn't find a way to screw this up for you," Lido said, idly picking the leaves off a long stem of Queen Anne's lace.

"Lido . . ."

"Well, don't worry, babe. Victor won't let her. Trust me. I don't know what's up with her, but she's gotten weirder than ever the last few—"

"Oh, Lido, please don't." Suddenly, Carmen put her face in her hands, holding her palms tight against her cheeks as if to keep the very bones together.

"What, hon?" Lido said softly. "What? Oh, Carm. Jesus, don't cry, honey." Lido got up and took Carmen in her arms, rubbing her back in gentle circles. "He won't let anything go wrong," she said with more urgency than before. "How could he let anything happen? How can he care about the past, about anything when you're so—"

"Beautiful, he said," Carmen whispered. "He says I'm beautiful."

When she finished her story, Carmen turned to Victor and I saw him blow her a little kiss and mouth the words "you are."

"And Selene heard all that?" I said, as Carmen slid slowly off the desk and went to prop herself on the arm of Victor's chair, resting against his wide shoulder. "You're sure?"

"Yes . . . yes. I saw her. The dogs were there, in the grass, but it was me so they didn't move, didn't warn her. But she was *lurking* behind the rock like—"

"Perhaps it was a mistake to tell you," Victor said softly, getting to his feet, drawing Carmen up with him. She leaned gratefully against his side.

"I'm sorry," he said, "but you're her oldest friend, Giovanni. Probably her only friend."

I looked at him. He took a deep breath, swallowed his saliva. "There's something wrong with her. You know that. Maybe you can help her."

They left soon after that. Though they invited me to join them for lunch, I begged off, claiming term papers and manuscripts. True enough, but an easy way to be alone with this information I had not asked for and certainly did not wish to know.

Selene following people in the dark of night? Selene hiding and lurking? It seemed ridiculous, impossible, almost a drawing room farce, though in a bitter mode. How could the vibrant, glossy, brilliant woman I had known—and for so long—turn into a witchlike creature with a pack of dogs, invading the nighttime silence of the forest with her private pain?

Chapter Eighteen

y conversation
with Victor and Carmen was terribly unsettling. I had expected to go to
Italy within the week, but it was all too clear that I could not possibly
leave Selene as she was—or as she seemed (were their stories to be believed) to be. My problems were added to by a call from Princess Sgonfiotto.

The woman evidently considered it her proper place to berate me, long
and loud, for my selfish indifference to Carla. When I (foolishly) protested, explaining that I planned to be there very soon, she raged on,
informing me, with self-congratulatory glee, that she, the better Christian,
had taken Carla into her house in Fiesole so she would not be alone. My
own sins, whatever they may have been, were suddenly beside the point:
I would not allow my sister to remain impaled on the princess's tender
mercies too much longer.

Somewhat dreading the possibility of further feminine recrimination,
fearing the worst, I phoned Selene to invite myself for the approaching
weekend. To my surprise, however, she was delighted to hear from me
and apologetic at her failure to propose it on her own. The timing, she
said, was actually quite perfect. "It's been much too long, and besides, I
have something to tell you."

When I mentioned my need to get to Italy as quickly as practicable, she was genuinely upset to learn that Carla was not doing well.

"She's not staying with that bitch—that repulsive Serafina Sgonfiotto!"

"Well, not for long," I said, unhappy with the conversation. "That's why I'm fairly eager to get over there." Selene knew that Carla had a tendency toward melancholia; she would understand that my visit to Italy was not only overdue but critical.

"Well, fine. Short and sweet, then," she said as we rang off. "I can't wait to see you."

The June morning was sunny and dry and I reached the estate feeling more optimistic than I had for days. As I pulled in her short driveway, Selene ran out to embrace me, taking me somewhat aback with the urgency of the hug she gave me. I held her shoulders firmly, and looked into her face.

A stranger would have taken her mood for one of cheerful, almost combative energy, but as I let her pull me into the house, and watched as she filled two glasses with lemonade, spilling almost as much as went in the glasses, I saw her vibrance as a manic, nearly desperate effort either to ward off anger or to express it. She was as *distraite* as I'd ever seen her and her face glowed with an excess of feeling I could not identify.

We spoke of Carla, of my travel plans, and many other things. But as we talked, she kept looking away from me, her eyes darting to the window, the corners of the kitchen, back to my face, and then away again. At last, unable to tolerate her barely reined-in tension another minute, I suggested we take a walk down to the river I had yet to see.

She agreed at once and we set off in the bright sunshine, saying little as we went along under the fluttering canopy created by Sterling's great trees, now fully leafed. It was cool and hushed in the forest and I had almost lost myself in a reverie—of what I cannot now remember—merely following Selene along the path, when all at once we came out into the clearing where I had seen Lido Desjardin weeks before. I realized we were on the side opposite to where I had hidden myself behind a tree that day, watching Lido tend her father's grave.

Selene paused and then went into the center of the clearing and walked slowly around the small garden plot.

"Peavy Desjardin's buried here," she said in an odd tone. Earlier, I had been too far away to read the inscription, but now I saw the deep, beveled initials—P. L. D.—and the dates, carved by hand into the polished slab of wood.

"Dwight carved the marker before his . . . incident with Lido's knives," said Selene. She bent to pick up a small, broken flower that had been plucked or blown from the border of Peavy's garden. She twirled the stem between two fingers and dropped it carefully on the center of the grave.

"Creepy place, don't you think?" she said with a small frown, coming round to link her arm through mine and bearing me along beside her toward the northern edge of the clearing. We reached the rim of trees, and then moved away through the oaks and larches. Selene led the way with confident strides.

Ten minutes later, we came out of the forest into a wide, banked area beside a rushing river. Thirty or forty yards upstream I saw the water come swirling past a hump of shiny stones, actual white water tumbling around a gentle bend and then bounding toward us in the straightaway, portions of the stream curling off into shallow little pools.

"How beautiful!" I cried, turning to Selene with a grin.

"It's just showing off for you today," Selene said, chuckling at my expression and settling herself easily onto a broad stone at the leaf-clotted edge of the river. The stone had sunk well into the soft bank and was tilted by the centuries into a perfect spot for sitting, for allowing oneself to be fascinated by the speeding water.

"It's lovely," I said, choosing a flat stone nearby, from which I brushed some dry leaves and tiny branches before I sat.

Selene seemed, almost magically, relaxed and calm, a confusing contrast to her earlier agitation. She sat in an easeful posture on her stone, watching the water. She pulled her knees up to her chin and stared across the river to the trees on the far bank.

Then, remembering the simple solemnity of Lido's ritual, though judging it wise to say nothing of what I'd seen before, I asked Selene when Peavy Desjardin had died.

"Two years ago April," she said, sitting up straight and lighting a cigarette. "In spite of the fact that he was so old, it was really a very sad occasion. Everybody liked Peavy. He died on the night of the full Sprouting Grass Moon."

She swung her legs over the side of the stone and looked thoughtfully down into the water. "I remember that because the grasses were coming up in the field, the forsythia behind the *studiolo* were just getting started.

Lido and Dwight had a little ceremony for him in the clearing and I came here afterward, right to this very spot, in fact. I remember I spent most of the day listening to the water, watching the leaves bud out, take hold of their branches. I stayed until the moon came up, just after dusk."

We sat in silence for a few minutes, looking at the beautiful, mesmerizing water, absorbed in our own reflections.

"I was disappointed, by the way, to have missed Victor's housewarming party," I said after a while, hoping, however clumsily, to lead her to the topic.

She didn't answer me at first. She drew slowly, meditatively on her cigarette, not willing, I thought at first, to give in to my possibly too blatant invitation.

But then she threw the cigarette, half-smoked, into the speeding water, watched it disappear downstream, and turned to me.

"It's just as well you didn't come," she said in a low, bitter tone. "You would not have seen me at my best."

I'd understood as much from what Victor and Carmen said, but I was surprised to hear Selene admit even to the least of it. She told me frankly that she hadn't wanted to go, but agreed to after Bet gave her a piece of her mind about the importance of neighborly feeling.

But almost from the moment she walked in, she said, it was obvious that the buffet, disguised as a casual party for the neighbors, a way to thank them for their help and friendship, was really meant to be an offering to *her*, a way to impress her, to show her what Victor had, what he was, what he could do. The marvelous food, the splendid room, the attention to detail were both metaphor and promise. Though Victor had closed the enormous wooden louvers, designed to darken the salon into an observatory, the blaze of afternoon sunshine was too powerful to banish and beams of yellow light filtered through tiny imperfections in the panels and cast golden patterns through the room. It was almost, Selene thought, an imitation of the shower of gold in which Zeus had accomplished his ravishment of Danaë, and she smiled as she said it, remarking on how suitable a metaphor that was for a seduction so artfully begun.

As Victor himself had told me, he and Selene were left alone after the guests departed. In Selene's view, Victor had arranged their solitude, eager to talk, to begin his approach to her. She was irritated, though, that he seemed to insist on discussing the Renaissance, as if there were nothing else to talk about. As the conversation moved along, she watched as he ran his fingers through the heavy black hair that fell over his forehead.

She saw the flashes of white between his fingers, and watched his speaking mouth without hearing a word, and stared at the hard muscles of his face, thinking of Andrea del Sarto's portraits of aristocrats with dark, strong chins, and of the sensitive young man who once sat for Titian with a careless glove thrown across a powerful thigh.

Seeing the faint gleam of Victor's tongue as he glanced up at her and unconsciously licked the last drop of wine from the rim of his glass, Selene knew that he was falling fully, willingly under her spell, looking at her with a greedy appreciation she had not seen in a man's eyes since Piero Corio had screamed at the pain of her teeth on his shoulder and pleaded for more. But that had been many years ago, and here was Victor Bellacéra, radiant with the same intelligence, but more exciting than Piero had ever been.

Just as Selene suspected he was about to confess his feelings, Lido and Carmen came rushing in with all their messy flowers. They had seemed so foolish to Selene, irritating and childish, giggling over their great bouquets as if they'd brought some sort of splendid gift instead of armfuls of weeds and dried-up wildflowers. But after Victor and Carmen went into the kitchen with the flowers, Selene was, to her immense distaste, left alone with Lido.

Lido, holding her own bouquet of lilies and yellow celandine, reclined like a cat on the cushions of a large sofa, and smiled faintly at Selene. Without the smallest indication of self-consciousness, Lido raised one knee and let her long skirt fall in a drape to her lap, exposing the smooth, taut skin of her thigh. Her mass of gleaming hair was held up off her neck and out of her face with fancy barrettes, crusty with sequins and fake crystal. She brought a swaying stalk of day lilies to her face, inhaling, and then moved her arm, seeming to be unaware of what she did, and used the lily to push loose tendrils of hair out of her eyes.

As Selene watched, her attention sharpened by her terrible anger, Lido became, inch by inch, Titian's *Venus of Urbino*, the left hand curled so slightly into the well of the lap, the right hand filled, not with Titian's roses, but with the heavy lilies. Lido's chin was perhaps a millimeter to the side, but her eyes were as calm, as satisfied as those of the false goddess in the painting. The bright mottled light from the closed louvers threw beams across her breasts and thighs, obliterating the thin fabric of her dress. Selene could see her pale nipples through the gauze of her bodice.

"Did we interrupt something?" Lido said softly, looking across into Selene's eyes. "Were you two discussing . . . *art?*"

Selene put her glass down and rose into the room, feeling as if she filled the space, as if her head were pressed into the pitch of the ceiling.

"Or was it something else?" Lido whispered with the tiniest smile as her upper lip rose away from her small, white teeth.

"That little slut makes me sick," Selene said, striking a wooden match against the dry surface of the rock. She lit a cigarette and blew a stream of smoke into the air.

"I knew myself to be a compelling object of any man's desire," she said, curling herself into a sitting position on her sunken boulder. "And that was what Victor felt, of course. But he didn't dare let it show, certainly not to them. Actually, I was amused at how deferentially he treated me that afternoon, knowing he had to hide his passion behind his educated conversation, his courtly words, those black Sforza eyes. I left at precisely the right moment."

She uncoiled herself with a slow, lazy movement until she lay full length on the stone. "It was just a matter of time before he would reveal his feelings. When I had a moment to think about it, of course, I realized that the girls' childish interruption meant nothing. Nothing at all."

She smiled at me in the same lazy, confidential way. "Sex no longer motivates me, Vanni, as you know," she said in a voice trimmed in the tiniest soutache of boredom. "After all, I have been chaste for many years. Absolutely celibate."

She said it with such hauteur, such insouciant pride that I found myself surprised, not so much at the fact that she was telling all this to *me*, but at the suggestion that chastity and celibacy are the same. Chastity cannot be willed; there's a great deal more to it than abstinence. And of course Selene knew that.

"There have always been plenty of women for whom the seat of consciousness is in the ovaries, the womb, the nipples," she said in her Isabella voice. "Think of Lido lying there on that sofa, imitating the Great Whore she worshiped. So obvious. So repulsive."

I was curious as could be about anything to do with Lido Desjardin, and watching the furious expression that crossed Selene's face when she spoke Lido's name intrigued me as always.

"Does Lido have a man, a boyfriend of her own?" I asked. It seemed impossible that she did not.

"You may believe me when I tell you I take little interest in Lido

Desjardin's vaginal affairs," Selene said with an angry look, instantly pulling her eyes down to her burning cigarette. "Never did."

I was sure Selene knew I'd met Lido in Boston, though neither of us had ever brought the subject up. Carmen had surely mentioned it at some point; it was not a secret. "She's very lovely," I observed. "It's hard to imagine she's never gotten involved with a man."

But Selene only laughed, that marvelous, full-bodied laugh of hers, and wound up choking on her cigarette smoke.

"What? What's so funny?" I said, smiling.

"A man would have to be out of his mind to become 'involved' with a tramp like that. She'd eat him alive. She would devour him. That vulgar display she put on was certainly proof enough, wouldn't you say? But it had nothing whatever to do with what was happening between Victor and me. Mind you, I'm not saying I put much stock in that particular encounter—some heady talk about the Renaissance and a glass or two of merely decent wine. There's much more to come."

I was frankly appalled at that, at the self-serving self-deceit of it, and at her attempt to shock or offend me with such coarse talk. My feelings must have shown plainly on my face, but Selene was uninterested in my reaction. She slid off the rock and went down to the very edge of the water, her shoes sucking slightly against the soft bank. She reached down to scoop up a handful of small pebbles and threw them, one by one, into the purling water. Then, without another word, she started back into the trees, toward home.

The sunshine had dimmed while we were talking; the sky was almost white. A convoy of clouds gathered high above us, piling themselves into thunderheads. In the sudden absence of even the weakest beam of sun, there were no shadows and the woods loomed bleakly around us. Even as I watched, following Selene back to the main forest path, the air thickened with humidity. I suddenly felt claustrophobic and oppressed, weighted down by the air, enclosed by leaves too thick to shoot an arrow through. I looked back at the wet riverbank, and across the expanse of water to the other side, before following Selene through the trees.

At length, we came out of the forest and onto the road, somewhat east of Victor's house. The glass salon seemed to rise above the landscape, tall and bold in its setting, but flattened into the monochrome of an old sepia photograph by the odd light and the absence of clear shadows.

Chapter Nineteen

hen we came in from the river, Selene pro-
duced a bottle of ancient Tennessee bourbon from the depths of her
kitchen pantry. She put it on a tray with some glasses and a small bowl
of ice and I carried it down the tile path to the *studiolo*. In minutes, we
were settled in beside a fine, roaring fire.

I immediately noticed Carmen's reframed Fra Angelico, set on a small
easel in the center of the desk, realizing with some surprise that it hadn't
been there on the occasion I'd been back for Bet's dinner party, though
Carmen had returned it some weeks before that. The new frame was
gloriously gold-leafed, embellished with vines and tiny flowers. At first,
its opulence seemed unsuited to the reverent simplicity of the scene, but
as I turned it, easel and all, toward the weak light, I saw that it was
perfect. The dull gilt of the frame warmed the cloister where the Madonna
sat waiting for the Angel; the thin wash of rosy color on the carved surface
seemed almost not to be paint at all, but a reflection of the Angel's robe.

Selene moved the tray to the low table by the sofa and mixed highballs
for both of us. I sat down across from her in the flowered armchair. After
taking a few gulps of her drink, she continued the story she'd broken off
so abruptly by the river.

Almost without transition, she told me that after she'd come home
from Victor's party, staying here in the *studiolo* for more than an hour, she

had wrapped herself in a light shawl against the chill of the May evening, whistled to Savo, and set out across the field. The full Flower Moon, small and white, was high above them.

The knee-high grasses and the lengthening stems of Queen Anne's lace and wild foxglove swayed silently as the dogs slipped through on their padded feet. But as they approached the rock, still on the field side of it, Selene was surprised to hear voices, borne toward her on the silky wind.

The dogs, sensing her sharpened attention, and hearing the familiar voices even more clearly than she could, came closer, fanning out behind her like a circling army, fully alert, their bared teeth gleaming. Savo stayed beside her, leaning slightly against her hip as if to counsel caution, but Selene, ignoring her, crept silently to the east face of the rock, holding her breath to listen as Carmen and Lido spoke of Victor Bellacéra.

Selene moved slowly, inch by inch, carefully making no sound at all, around the bow of the rock to a point where she could see them from an angle, and listened with impatient, reluctant sympathy as Carmen fought, not so much for the specific words, but for a way to convey the *idea* of the thing she sought to tell. That she loved Victor. That he found her beautiful and loved her in return.

Hearing Carmen's urgent words, fearing to hear more, Selene covered her mouth with both hands and pressed her skull against the rough surface of the rock. For years, from the time she returned from Italy to find Carmen grown into a lovely preadolescent child, Selene had wondered if it would ever come to this. How much she had denied she wasn't sure, but she knew that somewhere in her mind she'd always known that someday a man would fall in love with Carmen.

But having faced, for that one breathless instant, the beauty of what Carmen had become, Selene drove the thought away lest she be forced to face a further truth. She stood paralyzed behind the rock, embracing the great boulder as if it were living muscle and bone. She pressed her face against it and rubbed her cheek back and forth across the grain of the granite surface.

She was aware only of a deep, shuddering *frisson* of intense feeling so powerful that all she could do was grind her forehead against the rock, her fingers nearly bleeding from their grip on the clumps of glittering mica. Slowly she began to realize that the girls had started up the path.

"I moved backward to the east face of the rock," she said in a low voice, "so they wouldn't see me as they walked away."

"What did you think was going on?" I asked, as matter-of-factly as I could. "What did you think it meant?"

"Well!" said Selene, sucking in her cheeks and giving me a first-class Isabella look as if the answer were obvious, "naturally, I blamed that goddamn Lido for putting such ideas into poor Carmen's head! I was livid—*livid!* How do you think I felt? They'd obviously been talking for months! For all the time since Carmen moved to Boston, away from me, Lido'd been filling her head with trash about sex and men and ... *love.*" She nearly spat when she spoke the last word; she took a gulp of her whiskey as if to clear her palate of the thought itself.

"Oh, of course I can understand a girlish crush, a little curiosity, perhaps. Victor is quite attractive, after all, in many ways the epitome of what women think men are—or ought to be."

She shrugged as if she found the subject tedious. "But a man for all of that. Only a man."

Remembering the recent conversation with Carmen and Victor in my study, unhappy at the realization that Selene felt no regret at all for what she'd done that night, I offered as bland a response as I could manage. "And you think Lido was—"

"Well, Carmen doesn't have the experience to deal with such things on her own. It was all Lido's doing, don't you see? And now, I'm definitely going to be forced to intervene, to protect her from Lido, from Victor, and from herself. She knows nothing *whatever* about what men are like. But my goodness," she said, laughing, "I suppose boyfriends are one thing and men like Victor Bellacéra are quite another."

That crass remark left a strange, metallic taste in my mouth. Selene's patronizing dismissal of the idea of a boyfriend for Carmen seemed a bitter mixture of scorn and anguish. Perhaps blaming Lido for "putting ideas in Carmen's head" made it possible for Selene to deny that something was indeed developing between the intoxicating Victor Bellacéra and the precious girl she'd protected all her life.

Oblivious to my musing, Selene got up and threw some small pieces of wood on the fire. They sparked up, snapping, and then settled down as she rearranged them with the ornate poker that she kept beside the hearth.

"Of course, I wasn't particularly surprised to learn that they'd been in my oval," she said, a strange lilt in her voice. "Every time I leave it, I arrange twigs and moss in a pattern that an intruder would disturb. I must say, you made a dreadful mess of it the time you went there, didn't you?"

When my eyes flicked up, she gave me a long look and then broke into a spasm of choking laughter. "Oh, Vanni, for heaven's sake, did you think I didn't know? There were wet leaves and bits of moss all over the dogs' feet that day! On *your* feet!"

She picked up her glass of bourbon, sipped, and then folded herself gracefully into the rocking chair beside the sofa. We sat in silence for a minute or two and then our eyes met. Hers were golden and serene, even benevolent. She had let me know, and with a sangfroid I was hard-pressed to match, that she'd been aware all along that I'd been in her sacred place. Under the circumstances, however, I thought my answer showed impressive self-possession.

"Were you going to take me there?" I said, breaking the silence. "If I hadn't come upon it by myself?"

But she didn't answer, only smiled her Isabella smile, drained her glass, and set it with exaggerated care onto the table.

"Now then," she said, uncrossing her legs and leaning toward me. "Do you think you could bear up under a very fine dinner?"

"Dinner?" It was the last thing on my mind, but all of a sudden I realized how hungry I was.

"We shall have a *bon voyage* celebration and I will tell you some fascinating things, just as I promised on the phone. What do you say?"

With that, she got to her feet in a quick, lithe movement. "They've got a new restaurant just a few miles past Turn-of-River. I can't vouch for the food, of course, but it's supposedly *French*, if you can believe it. And after all," she finished with a small, ironic smile, leaning down to whisper in my ear, "even someone as intellectually stimulated as you, my dear, must eat, *n'est-ce pas?*"

Chapter Twenty

uring the forty-minute drive to The Inn at Stone Mill, Selene, energized by the prospect of an evening out, held forth with enthusiasm about restaurants she had known in days gone by. I did my best to concentrate on the darkening road while she regaled me with elaborate accounts of exotic meals she had eaten from California to the Caucasus. The detail she offered was as exquisite as the foods must have been, her memory of her own intense pleasure so clear, so complete as not to be memory at all.

I could almost taste the creams and sauces, feel the alien meats ripping in my own teeth, so vivid were her stories. I felt as if I had actually seen the breezy veranda, set high above the Dardanelles, where sliced melons were eaten with antique silver forks; fancied I could hear the obscure Grieg sonata that had accompanied her dinner of salmon fillets, taken in the mirrored dining room of a small seventeenth-century castle on the shore of a tiny lake deep in the Norwegian hinterland.

"I always ate that way," she said, "before you knew me."

But even as I listened, enchanted though I was, I smiled because I had indeed been present on some of the occasions she described, yet she had remembered them as something that had happened only to herself.

But, as so often, I was struck by the powerful ambiguity of her personality, the thunderous sensuality that, so far as I could see, still motivated her, and the introspection—often verging on disengagement—with which, it seemed, she was able to turn her back on anything she did not care to face. But above all, it was clear that in every sense she had been, and was, and would forever be an epicurean to her core.

It was after eight o'clock when we rounded the last blind curve, about ten miles past Turn-of-River, and the carriage lamps on the immense gate of The Inn leapt up in the headlights. Moments later the valet was reaching for my car keys and we were sailing up the steps and into the Federalist splendor of the foyer.

The entire restaurant was decorated for summer. In the lobby, hanging over the elaborate archway to the dining room, was a spectacular wreath—five feet across and fashioned of fresh green linden boughs (they must have replaced them almost every day), dripping with fantastical arrangements of yellow and white flowers, among which were threaded strings of tiny white lights that twinkled as if for a summer Christmas.

This masterpiece was echoed in the large dining room itself by a series of curved swags, constructed of the same greens and flowers, placed at intervals along the damask-covered walls, and in a massive bouquet set in a silver basket upon the mantelpiece.

Despite the fact that we had no reservation, we were given a choice table by the wide French doors and settled into our chairs by the maître d' himself. Our table looked out over the dark shapes of the old mill house and the great wooden wheel, just faintly visible in the twilight behind the reflection of the dining room. The draperies had been pulled back from the glass, and tiny gusts of warm air from outside blew the long lace curtains into the room. I thought to myself that if the food was even half as wonderful as the decor I would be well satisfied.

Selene was quite stunning that evening, eccentrically costumed to be sure, but elegant nonetheless in a long black tunic-like garment made of a silky fabric that flowed from her shoulders nearly to the knees of the matching trousers. Around the high neck of the tunic she wore a necklace of beaten silver, thick and flat, from which hung an oval amulet, large as a baby's fist, ornamented with an embossed figure I thought I might have seen before: a praying Navaho? A martyred Druid warrior? And over the entire ensemble she had draped a black-on-black silk-embroidered shawl, which gleamed in the lights of the room. Her silver hair was twisted into a coil at the back of her head, skewered with a vaguely Asian-looking spike made of ebony, chased with silver. A few brilliant strands of hair fell loose about her face, lifting slightly in the currents of the air-conditioned room.

From the moment they were handed to us, it was clear that Selene considered the hand-penned menus with their calligraphic swirls and glued-on pearls the merest fiction. Whatever might be written there could not be expected to pertain to her or to her appetites. She set hers aside with a dismissive gesture and after an (I thought unnecessarily intense) inquisition of the mercifully dull young waiter, our food was ordered and, in due course, beautifully served from gleaming chafing dishes.

Selene looked at my Lobster Sarah Bernhardt with narrow-eyed distaste and quickly turned away, sipping at her tiny glass of ice-cold Absolut with pursed lips: the Sarah Bernhardt of the Renaissance.

She swiveled sideways in her chair and ignored her own dish, which she had not yet touched. It was a made-to-order vegetable plate, appetizingly arranged with carrots, longitudinally sliced and perfectly arrayed across the asparagus spears, surrounded by mushrooms, pea pods, and broccoli flowerets. It was not exactly *tournedos* of wild boar with black cherry marinade, but it did look delicious.

At last Selene picked up her fork and pierced a small piece of broccoli, dunking it into a *saucière* filled with *crème moutard*.

"How is it?" I asked, cracking a claw and digging away at the meat inside.

"Wonderful," she mumbled, slowly chewing the crisp broccoli. "Wonderful. Delectable. This is what you should be eating at your age," she said, spearing a crisp pea pod and holding it aloft like a Saracen's impaled victim. With her other hand she poured a splash of the excellent Pouilly-Fumé into my glass.

"Molto grazie, signora," I said with a chuckle, picking up the slender, pretty glass and settling back for a short rest after my assault on the lobster's claw. "And are you indeed going to tell me why you brought me out here to this wilderness?" I said, smiling. "Or do you plan to ply me with expensive food and assume I'll forget your promise?"

She flung me an amused, almost mischievous glance. "Have another popover, *Padre,*" she said, thrusting the warm basket toward my side of the table.

We ate in silent pleasure for several minutes, but after only a few bites of her elegant vegetables, Selene signaled the waiter for another Absolut and then smiled radiantly across the table with a look that only having one's wishes instantly attended to can summon up. Dared I believe a sumptuous evening was all it took to bring that glow to her face? But she did seem, at least for the moment, at her ease and in fine spirits. While I ate everything in sight, enjoying myself immensely, she began at last to tell me what was on her mind.

But, as so often, she crept up upon it from behind, as if her story were prey that had to be cornered and trapped before she could attack it. "For a start," she said with a sigh and an ironic lifting of her eyebrows, "the weather has been absolutely filthy since the beginning of June—sultry, humid, simply ghastly. You know how I hate that."

She said that the heat spell had left her speechless and lethargic. She would sit for hours at a time in the *studiolo* surrounded by sheaves of old notes and thick, dusty books, beginning each day with the conviction that she had a plan, an idea for her new book. But though the mornings were dim and almost cool, by the middle of the afternoon the sun poured like liquid through the tall windows and she wound up staring at the pages in wordless desperation. We had had a cooler time of it in Boston and I looked up from my tomato salad in wordless sympathy.

Only a few days before my arrival, though, the weather had broken at last with torrents of slashing rain that sluiced down the long windows of the *studiolo* and soaked the gardens. Bet ran frantically across the lawn to fetch Selene and, together, wet to the skin, they spread sheets of plastic over the huge peony bushes and the Aquitaine roses that lined the driveway, hoping to save them. And, mercifully, the storm blew east and away and cooler weather followed for a day or two, refreshing everybody's spirits.

The morning that the Poynsetters were due to leave for their vacation, Bet stood on her green lawn biting her lips and frowning at the cosseted roses and the pampered peonies, worried lest they sicken and die in her absence without the daily doses of encouragement only she could give them. She and Leon were on their way to Maine and the Maritimes for two weeks, maybe longer, Leon said, if all went well.

"As if that were in doubt," Selene said, laughing and snapping her fingers for another Absolut. "As if their itinerary might take them to the edge of the known world, thence, by accident or fate, into a *terra incognita* desolate of clean bathrooms, gas stations, and real coffee."

I chuckled at her dramatic rendition of the conversation. "I reminded Bet that they were only going to Maine," Selene said, "not Mozambique."

But after she said that she frowned and pushed her plate away. She lit a cigarette and stared pensively at the glowing tip before continuing her story.

That night a hot wind blew in from the south, and Selene climbed into the forest with the dogs, making her way up through the dense trees to her clearing. But even at that altitude the humid air had settled in, transported by the shards of intense sunlight that pierced the covering of leaves for long hours every day, shooting to the forest floor through all the intervening weave of leaves and branches.

At dusk, she lay on the ground inside the oval of twenty-seven stones. The depression in the center was carpeted with layers of sphagnum moss and ground pine, old leaves and fir needles that had nearly disintegrated over the years into a resinous, springy powder that clung, sweet and pungent, to her clothes and hair. Surrounded by her dogs, Selene placed herself in the very center of the oval, and Savo, thick-furred even in summer, reclined behind her. Selene lay her head on the silky withers, feeling the huge dog's wild, slow heartbeat in her neck and shoulders.

The search for a worthy subject for her book, for a way to begin again, had oppressed her for weeks. She begged the Goddess for an inspiration, a sign, her eyes searching the dark sky for the waning Strawberry Moon. And then, all at once, when she had begun to fear she'd missed it, had miscalculated the phase and the angle, the hard, white moon slipped from behind a cloud and shone directly on her face.

When full darkness came, the dogs, led by Savo, disappeared among the trees; they silently killed small animals and sleeping birds, ripping out their throats, and returned to the clearing to lay these poor, eviscerated tributes at Selene's feet. Facedown in the very center of the oval, Selene offered them to Artemis, whispering promises.

Selene's eyes were a glassy citrine color in the light of the dining room. A large slice of Sacher torte had been set before me while she was talking, but I hadn't so much as picked up my fork, stupefied as I was by her story, and by the assertion that the Goddess had answered her prayer for inspiration, had responded to blood sacrifice.

"Everything changed after that," she said softly, taking a sip of her coffee. "Everything. She *gave* it to me, you see, that night in the forest. I know She did."

Selene saw my expression, the sad disbelief that must have shown clearly on my face at the thought of the pagan Goddess sailing through the night sky, seeking Her servant's gift.

"Oh, Vanni dear, eat your dessert," Selene stage-whispered, reaching across the table with her own fork, cutting off the tip of my piece of cake and popping it into her mouth.

"Selene . . ."

"Everything's wonderful, darling, never better. Coffee?"

She filled my cup from the silver carafe on the table. She looked spectacular just then, flushed with satisfaction, the tiniest morsel of chocolate frosting in the corner of her lip, her golden eyes smiling into mine.

She saw me looking at her, winked, and snapped her fingers for the check. Of course it came at once, in a small filigree basket. The maître d' stood somberly at a safe distance as Selene stood up and reached into some hidden pocket deep inside her clothing and produced two one-hundred-dollar bills, which she dropped into the basket from shoulder height. I had no idea how much of that, if any, was the tip. She rearranged her shawl around her shoulders in a wide *véronica* and swept from the room, her silver hair gleaming under the chandeliers.

Moments later we were standing beside the wide stone *porte cochère* under a clear sky from which all but the last streaks of an amethyst sunset had departed. Looking about her with a bright, happy gaze, Selene seized my wrist and pulled me with her toward the flight of stone steps that led down to the riverbed.

From the top of the stairway I could just make out the fancy sign that hung from a crossbar by two chains in front of the small clapboard structure on the opposite bank:

ORIGINAL 1825 MILL HOUSE AT STONE MILL
STATE HISTORIC SITE—ADMISSION $2.00
MAY TO OCTOBER

The huge mill wheel itself turned ever so slightly, creaking as it rocked. The shallow water burbled through the lower spokes, making a bright, chuckling sound.

"Let's go across and sit for a while," Selene said, eagerly surveying the rocky shore and the charming little *faux* Japanese bridge that crossed the narrow waist of water to a similarly inspired bench beside the sign.

It was a trifle cooler than it had been earlier in the evening and the wind, though somewhat stronger, was still gentle and refreshing. I held Selene's elbow as we went slowly down the steps, across the little bridge, and into the lee of the cottage.

"Marvelous!" she cried, throwing out her arms as if to embrace the lovely, rustic scene. "Ah! Glorious!"

I settled myself on the fancy bench and stretched out my legs. The chandeliers in the dining room glowed far above us. From my perspective at the riverbank, I could see that there was only the narrowest ledge outside the French doors where we'd been sitting; it was just a foot wide, maybe less, and then it dropped off into nothing, onto the deadly jumble of the rocks that formed the riverbed. A person could throw open those French doors, eyes focused on the giant mill wheel, the claret sky, and step off into nothing, into death. As I watched, the maître d', shielding his eyes from the reflection of the room in the glass, peered, grimacing, out into the darkness for a moment before he closed the velvet drapes.

"So, cara," I said, leaning toward Selene's shoulder. "Shall you continue with your story, or keep me in suspense?"

She laughed at that, well aware of her earlier promise. "Oh, Vanni, I've broken through, I really have."

"Selene!"

"After that night in the oval, yes, I'm sure I have. The next few days were dismal and wet, but oh, so much cooler. It was wonderful."

She told me she'd spent those days poring over her enormous collection of art books and the scores of prints she'd never found the time to frame. She spread many of the pictures out on the desk, each one held down with a stone or a cup or a shell, and studied them for hours.

One afternoon, she was, as usual, alone in the stùdiolo, but feeling very quiet, very calm. She got up from her chair and stood back from the desk, trying for an overarching view of what was there, placed in seemingly random order on the desk. And, astonished, she saw what she had chosen:

Every single picture was of the Maestà configuration: The Madonna in Majesty. Here was the Virgin enthroned, surrounded by Her worshipers, with the Child—the Son, the Consort, the Sacrificial Lamb—standing in Her lap, already waiting for His destiny to catch up with Him. Indifferent to the bone-deep ache in her shoulders and to her stinging eyes, Selene held each picture under the glare of the desk lamp, the fabulous altarpieces from great churches and galleries all over Europe.

Anchoring the ideas of all the others was Mantegna's gorgeous Madonna *of the Victory,* finished in 1496 for the Gonzagas of Mantua. The artist had placed the Virgin on a marble throne under a *baldacchino*-like structure of espaliered orange trees hung with gourds and fruits and a coral branch suspended from a rosary. In the painting, the Lady is surrounded by the military saints, George and Michael, and the kneeling Marquis, Isabella's husband, arrayed in fine armor.

Selene stared at the *Madonna della Vittòria* for almost an hour, and then turned her attention back to the Frari, Barbadori, and San Zeno altarpieces, all showing the utterly calm and powerful central figure, worshiped by saints and heroes, by noblemen, martyrs, and angels.

"I was so transfixed, Vanni, I had no idea that night had come," she said, reaching for my hand. It had grown completely dark but for the stars and the muted lights of the dining room high above. Selene's hand was warm and motionless in mine.

"I barely heard the rustle of the trees, a sudden rain shower that pattered on the skylight. I was absolutely absorbed in what I was doing."

Late that same night, toward dawn, perhaps, she ran to find her copy of the life of Isabella Gonzaga, knowing exactly what she was looking for, knowing that Isabella herself—the great *patronéssa*, the lover of myth and legend—had seen these parallels five hundred years before. And now she, Selene, saw them too—the links, and then the chains they made.

At first she could not believe it had taken her so long. Of course, she'd been too close, had cared too much, and so had lost her way. All the world believed that the regal, blue-robed Queen of Heaven was the same girl who had received, with such trembling reticence, the great news brought by the windswept, gold-winged Gabriel. She was, of course, the same, but in disguise.

The world called Her Madonna, Saint, Lady, Mother, Virgin—and so She was. They called Her Stella Maris, "Star of the Sea," to keep Her secret safe from all but those who still believed. Even the artists who created the wonderful panels and altarpieces had preserved the fiction, painting Her that way to keep Her secret. The Christian emperors had destroyed Her temples, yes, but not the cult and not the truth. For the character of Saint Mary had been created only as a surrogate, and within that lovely metaphor they hid the Goddess Herself: patroness of sailors, ruler of the moon and tides and all the rhythms of nature. Thus had Her followers, and the great artists among them, thrown the cloak of Christian myth over Her, to protect Her through the centuries.

And now Selene saw clearly what Isabella Gonzaga herself must have known: that the Great Goddess, disguised as Mary—immortalized in hundreds of fabulous *Maestà* paintings—had been immanent in the life of the Renaissance. She was the patron saint of the Renaissance itself. The time had clearly come to give Her the obeisance She had been denied.

When she'd told me all that, Selene suddenly hunched forward with great nervous intensity. As she did so, her silver amulet dangled free, swinging with a mesmerizing slowness from the thick silver chain, catching random beams from the security lights on the mill house bridge and the chandeliers glowing behind the closed drapes of the dining room.

"Oh, Vanni!" she cried in a hushed, ecstatic voice, "I saw it...I saw *Her*! I saw a way to begin again. She had been denied for *centuries*—but not really, not completely. She lived on in your Madonna!"

Selene leapt up from the bench and stared down at me, her golden eyes wide and ecstatic. I knew instinctively that however astonished I might feel, I had to focus on what she was telling me—that through blind faith and effort and need (oh, yes, such compelling *need*) she had, or so she believed, discovered that the Goddess and the Virgin were the same. She seemed to be reliving the exhilaration of the very night of her discovery.

"I hadn't seen it before," she murmured, sitting down again, holding my arm with both her hands. "I never did, not in all these years. But She deserves to have Her power known, the continuity, the force of it!"

She stood up again, pulling me with her. Her elegant silk shawl, loosened, sailed out around her in the wind, and her face was luminous as I hadn't seen it in years, filled with joy, radiant in the starlight.

"And that will be my new book—the Goddess in the Madonna. She's there, Vanni, in the center of every altarpiece, every *Maestà*, every Mother and Child! Oh, Vanni," she said, putting her hands on my face and beaming up at me, "She has let me see it. She gave this to me."

Chapter Twenty-One

wo days later, feeling smugly secure about leaving an inspired Selene alone with her developing manuscript, I went off to Italy to see about the other woman in my life.

My fears for Carla soon proved exaggerated; I was frankly surprised at myself for not having seen feminine manipulation at its most adroit, and for having forgotten how resilient my sister can be when, almost as an exercise, she puts her mind to it.

It was true enough that Carla had a dire penchant for melancholy, usually kicked off by an unhealthy speculation on her own tragic circumstances. She liked to feel sorry for herself, and to let me know she did. There was more than one Sarah Bernhardt in the poor priest's life! But though her unhappiness could be real enough, it was transient at best, and Carla, in her less self-dramatizing moments, was (or so I have always believed) aware of that. She viewed herself in turns as a childless spinster, forsaken and forlorn, or as a rich, utterly unfettered *grande dame*, well positioned to have her own way in everything. Of course, I loved her completely in spite of all that *behavior*, and well she knew it.

My visit to Italy was well timed, if only as a salve to my own ragged feelings. The months in Boston, productive but demanding, and my growing involvement with Selene and her family and neighbors had taken an emotional toll I hadn't truly thought about until Carla's driver swung my luggage into the back of the Mercedes and whisked me up the winding Via San Domenico to Fiesole. I was eager to see how big a mess Carla had made of things by moving in with the insufferable Princess Sgonfiotto. But I was quite taken aback to find, as the car swiftly negotiated the dizzying twists and turns of the road above the small piazza, that my resourceful sister, true to form, had solved the problem on her own. She had moved out.

"The woman is a beast!" Carla screamed as I came through the garden of a charming little house at the crest of the old Etruscan road. "A beast! How could you let me do it?"

"Let you! Carla, for God's sake . . ." And we were off. We laughed and argued all through a splendid dinner and two bottles of a lively local wine that Carla had brought in by the case. The rooms of her new house were airy and bright and in back there was a terrace, smaller than at the much grander Florence house, but open to the surrounding hills. It was a jewel, enhanced with pots of bright red flowers and with a view, far below, of Florence nestled in the lovely Tuscan landscape.

Most mornings, the city was hidden in a haze that seemed to grow from seed in the dark hours of the night. Then slowly, almost magically, through the morning hours the mist rose away from the city, and by lunchtime the elegant bulk of the Duomo was revealed, dominating everything around it. I never tired of looking at it.

I spent quite a few of those fine, misty mornings seated at the glass table on the terrace writing to Selene. I produced long, exhortative letters about life and art and writing and the importance of confronting whatever pains us most. My excellent surroundings notwithstanding, I was troubled by what I thought of as my old friend's escape from life as it is lived. She had locked herself away in her forest far too soon. But I mailed only the mildest and most loving of the letters and fretted on my own about the rest.

And then, about four weeks after I arrived, a new idea began to come, so obvious that I wondered how I could have failed to think of it before.

Carla had been invited to a very chichi private party in the wonderful *Salone dei Cinquecento* —the Hall of the Five Hundred in the Palazzo Vecchio, down in Florence. Of course, she dragged me along as her escort, insisting that I leave my Roman collar home and keep my big mouth shut about my profession. The *crème* of Florence society was there—artists and musicians, patrons, critics, restorers and collectors of great and near-great art, politicians, and a few strays from the Italian diplomatic service. It was all as *ultra* as could be. The wine sparkled, as did the ladies' jewels, and Carla was quite in her element. I less so.

Embattled by the rich conversation and the even richer guests, I wandered as far as I dared from the hot, molten core of the party and found myself at the door to Francesco de' Medici's *stùdiolo*, the small, windowless room Selene had mentioned to me years ago, laughing as she compared her old barn with the duke's extravagant, neurotic hideaway.

I had been there before, but not for many years, and I tiptoed in with happy anticipation. Francesco's tiny room is covered with splendid late-Mannerist paintings set in panels, at least two of which disguise secret doors that open onto dark, twisting stone stairways leading up to the even more claustrophobic chamber where, it is said, the Medici hid their treasures. I thought it impolite to stay too long in that beautifully oppressive room, particularly as I had removed a red silk rope to do so, but when I came out to the brilliance of the *Salone* again, the idea struck me with almost theatrical force and I occupied myself for the remainder of the evening thinking it through.

When we got back to Fiesole, I wasted no time mentioning my great idea to Carla. "Why don't we invite Selene to come here to Florence, as our guest, to work on her new book?" I said, grinning with excitement. "It will get her out of that forest, bring her back to the marvelous atmosphere she loved so much. *Brillante*, no?"

And Carla was enthusiastic, too. At first.

"Yes! I will let her use the Oltrarno house. Why not? I'm happy here. The air is cleaner and nobody bothers me. (*As if Carla wishes to be left alone.*) Perfect!" she crowed.

But later, as we were having a last brandy on the terrace, looking at the Duomo, the lights of the city forming an almost perfect oval at our feet, Carla, having had a chance to give the idea some consideration, kissed my cheek and pointed out the principal shortcoming of my plan.

"The idea is wonderful, Vanni. Even obvious, as you say. But I'm not so sure she'll come."

"Oh, I think she will. I'm going to ask her as soon as I get back."

"*Ah!* Stubborn as hell, that one. You'll have a hard time convincing her, my love. Maybe, though, if she brings her lovely Carmen with her, *forse . . .* perhaps . . ."

I had told Carla, and readily, of my growing affection for Carmen, but had said nothing at all of Victor Bellacéra. It occurred to me that in omitting any mention of him I had denied him the unquestionable influence he was exerting over events at the estate. I was positive that because of him Carmen would never be persuaded to come. But Selene? Would she come without Carmen? *Forse... forse...* perhaps.

Chapter Twenty-Two

he day I returned, it was hot and sticky in Boston, a rude shock after the breezy air at Fiesole. I'd written to Carmen from Italy, a few oversize postcards with scenes of the Pitti Palace, the Ponte Vecchio, and the Boboli Gardens, all of which she had specifically requested. I'd also sent a letter; it started out as a humorous note, but quickly evolved into four closely written pages filled with little more than idle news and random speculations, though deeply—oh, yes, deeply—felt.

Of course, I'd mentioned the date of my return, and when, on a steamy afternoon at the end of July, I pushed open the door to my stuffy flat, a huge bouquet of bright orange day lilies—Carmen's welcoming gift—was waiting for me on the desk, along with an invitation to lunch a few days hence.

Naturally, I called her that very night, not a little bemused at my own delight in the increasing closeness I felt for this sweet young woman who seemed to have assumed the role of treasured niece virtually when I wasn't looking. I have frequently had what people of my age like to call "young friends," but my affectionate feelings for Carmen were warmer than I would have thought.

However, we never did have lunch. Carmen called on the morning in question to say that she had decided to go out to the estate for the weekend. First thing I knew, impromptu arrangements were made and soon I was pulling up to the front door of her brownstone, ready to drive her and to spend a day or two myself visiting Selene, with whom I'd spoken and who seemed glad enough to have me back.

Carmen was waiting for me on the steps. She looked wonderful, tanned and rather slimmer, I thought, than she had at the end of May. Her hair was now quite long and sun-streaked and drawn up rather elegantly with wide tortoiseshell combs. It was almost a déjà vu of that long-ago spring evening in Carla's driveway in Florence, the day Piero first brought Selene into our lives. In those days, Selene had worn her hair like that, but Carmen was bouncy and cheerful, as Selene, with her mordant sense of humor and her impenetrable hauteur, had never been.

Carmen was wearing a red blouse and a soft cotton skirt that swished in colorful folds to her ankles. Multiple silver bracelets shone against the tanned skin of her arms. I was pleasantly surprised to find Victor standing on the steps beside her. Evidently, his pickup truck, in which he had driven to Boston only the day before, had unaccountably broken down and he was obliged to leave it at a garage for repairs. My return had coincided most happily not only with his need for a ride home, but with this unforeseen opportunity for a good, solid chat à trois.

The day was steamy and hot, the air-conditioning in my leased car most welcome. At my suggestion, Victor drove, and I was quite content to relax in the backseat and let Carmen catch me up on the summer events I had missed. As we cruised along, Carmen, her fingers gently twining through Victor's black hair, told me that the family had returned from their vacation on the eve of the Fourth of July; the station wagon had lurched up the driveway an hour before sundown. Selene apparently saw them from the stùdiolo window, because she came out into the sunshine and hurried across the wide, unmowed lawn to greet them just as Leon pulled up to the dead peonies.

Carmen knew Selene was surprised to see her. They had not so much as spoken since the day of Victor's party, back in May. Carmen had thought of calling, but each time she picked up the phone, she remembered Selene behind the rock, eavesdropping on the conversation with Lido, and, awash in feelings she could not name, let it go and did not make the call. Her reaction had tormented her for weeks.

She climbed out of the backseat and went over to give her aunt a hug, just as if the last five or six silent weeks had never happened. "You look tired, Selene," she said with a warm, indulgent smile, stroking Selene's shoulder. "Feeling all right? Maybe you just need a little sun on your face."

"I'm perfectly fine," Selene replied sharply. "Completely fine."

"Well, good. By tomorrow ... Oh, Daddy, wait. Wait!"

Leon was struggling with a large wooden crate, half in, half out of the tailgate of the station wagon.

"I can do it, sweetheart," he said, puffing, reaching for his handkerchief. "I got it ... I got it."

Bet had been standing in the driveway, smiling at their efforts. She was carrying her tote and a big L. L. Bean shopping bag filled with enormous, filthy pine cones.

"Hi, Sissy. Ummm!" She placed two smacking kisses on Selene's pale cheeks. "Surprised, aren't you? I know you hate surprises, dear, but I couldn't resist. We called Carmen from Campobello and she took the bus up to Tenants Harbor in time to meet us for lunch on Thursday! Oh! we had a ball, we ... Leon! Why don't you get Dwight, dear, he'll—"

"I got it, I said!" Leon was bent double over the crate that he and Carmen together had wrestled to the driveway.

"What's in there?" Selene said, watching Carmen and Leon as they finally managed to set the crate onto the asphalt. It fell the last few inches and water splashed out and ran in streams down the sloping driveway.

Bet had dropped her parcels on the grass and reached for the soft, limp peonies, now almost completely brown. She plucked a few of the remaining petals with her gentle fingers, frowning.

"What's in the crate?" Selene asked again.

"Live lobsters—eight of 'em—for tomorrow."

"*Live?*"

"For the picnic, Sissy. You didn't forget? Tomorrow's the Fourth of July! Isn't it marvelous? Leon made such good time."

"We had it on the back lawn behind the porch," Carmen said, hooking her elbow over the seat and swiveling around to smile at me. "Daddy was all freaked out because there wasn't any corn. Every year he says he can't wait for summer, just because of the corn!"

Victor laughed, glancing up at me in the rearview mirror. "Bet had food for an army, Giovanni, all of it just delicious. But yes, no corn!" Chuckling at the memory, he said that Bet barely listened to Leon's complaints. She was busily dishing out Wanda Stoner's ready-made cole slaw, brushing a bee away from the Waldorf salad.

"It's only knee-high by the Fourth of July," Bet pointed out, "just like it says in the song. We've got heaps of food, Leon, not to mention all that lovely lobster. We'll have plenty of corn on the cob next month," she said, reaching across the table to pat his flushed cheek. "I'll get all I can carry at the farmers' market next month. I promise."

Leon, still pretending to grumble, put his beer down and went back in the kitchen door to check the lobster pot, thundering ominously on the stove.

Selene sat in a lawn chair under the shade of the porch awning; Dwight squatted on the grass beside her, his gray eyes feral and cloudy. He would stare up at her from time to time, get no response, and look away again with an unreadable expression.

Victor reclined on the grass between Lido and Carmen, relaxed and smiling, full in the glow of the late sun that beamed from beyond the trees. Carmen touched the long hair at the back of his neck; she twirled a lock of it in her fingers and whispered something in his ear that made him laugh.

Lido loved summertime with a passion, the steamier the better. She reveled in the annual blooming of the long-stemmed flowers that grew wild all over the estate. She would gather armfuls of the most brilliant and decorate her house and porch with vases and jars filled with their lush colors, their hot scents. She had been making flower leis all that afternoon, weaving together the stems of white clover and goldenrod, fleabane daisies and black-eyed Susans. She had used a great white star of Queen Anne's lace as a centerpiece for Carmen's wreath, and she dropped it over her head and sat back on her hips to admire the effect.

Nodding with satisfaction, she reached into her basket and withdrew another garland, this one made entirely of the heavy, dark red lilies that covered the field and grew in every crevice of the estate. Years before, when Carmen was a little girl, Selene had told her that these flowers gave their name to the Red Blooming Lilies Moon of July, and Carmen had been struck by the image. She thought about it this time every year.

When Lido placed the lei on Victor's shoulders, he smiled up at Carmen, who bent down to kiss his cheek, and then, slowly, his mouth, before she straightened up as if to move away. Victor, with a small cry, reached for her and with the tips of his fingers managed to grasp a fold of gauzy skirt. Lido laughed, a deep, throaty sound, as Victor pulled Carmen down beside him on the grass. And all that time, Carmen said, she knew Selene was watching them, like a bird of prey, from the shade.

By eight o'clock the shadows began to lose their definition. Carmen, still wearing her flower wreath, helped her mother clear the table while Victor and Lido folded up the tablecloth and followed them into the house. Dwight thrust his hands into the pockets of his jeans, and slipped away into the forest.

"We only have time for one piece each," Bet called out moments later as she stepped sideways out the kitchen door, carrying her pedestal cake plate while Victor held the door, and then her elbow, and Lido followed with the napkins and dessert forks.

"Your favorite, Sissy," Bet said, coming to the table with a tall white angel food cake; choice blueberries and cherries formed a discernible if rather impressionistic Old Glory on the top.

"You barely touched your supper, Selene," Bet said, bringing a plate into the shadows. "Here's an extra big slice, dear—eat it all, now."

While everyone else had a piece of cake, Lido sat on the grass with her guitar and plucked at the opening strains of "Black Is the Color of My True Love's Hair," letting the tune wander to a sprightly "Turkey in the Straw" before coming back to the phrase *"his face is something wondrous fair..."*

She sang it softly, slowly, in a deep contralto, looking from Carmen to Victor, and then across the grass to Selene, who didn't move, her cake fork motionless in her fingers.

Then Bet, urged on by Carmen and Leon, offered a wavering soprano rendition of "Paper of Pins" with Victor joining her for the second verse in a light, silky baritone that was almost a lyrical extension of his speaking voice, warm and natural.

Apparently no one had known that Victor could sing, or that he ever would, and Lido, delighted, poked him gently in the chest with the frets of her guitar and begged him for a solo.

"A solo!" he repeated, playfully grabbing his throat and then pretending to hide behind Carmen, holding her shoulders with both hands as if to use her for a shield against Lido, who, laughing, pleaded again for a song.

"C'mon, now. You must know lots of songs! Vic-*terr!*"

"Ah, Lido, no." But Carmen slid her arm around his waist and leaned against him. She whispered softly to him while Bet and Leon laughed and applauded in advance.

At last, out voted but smiling, Victor consulted with the minstrel and began:

> *Might I be the wooded fernbrake*
> *At the end of a lovely day,*
> *Where my shepherd girl reposes,*
> *There doth Love her homage pay.*
>
> *Could I be the gentle zephyr*
> *Sighing 'round her charms so sweet,*
> *Or the air her lips are breathing,*
> *Or the flowers beneath her feet.*

"Sing it in French," Lido whispered at the chord change. During the second verse Carmen had drifted over to the peony bushes near the driveway. When Victor came to her, she lay her arms languidly on his shoulders and her hands rested limp and open against his back the whole time he was singing:

> *Que ne suis je la fougère,*
> *Où sur la fin d'un beau jour,*
> *Se repose ma bergère,*
> *Sous la garde de l'amour.*

Leon stamped his feet and whistled through his fingers, applauding wildly, poking his laughing wife with his elbow.

"That's great! Isn't that great, Betty? That's a fine voice you got there, son," Leon said, opening another beer under cover of all the applause and general hilarity.

"All right, everybody, it's nearly time," Bet said, wiping her eyes and leaning down to kiss the top of Leon's head before she took the remains of the cake into the house.

"Oh my, yes, time to go," Leon said, looking up at the magenta sky and then down at his watch. He and Lido carried the table around to the side yard and Carmen, sliding out of Victor's arms, ran up the kitchen stairs after her mother.

"It was a wonderful party, darling," Victor said as we drove through the obelisks and onto the private road. I'd been so absorbed by their story, I barely realized we'd arrived.

"It really was," Carmen said. "I just ... Oh, there's Daddy!" she cried out, leaning across Victor's lap and waving wildly to Leon, who was out in the yard, the garden hose hanging from his hand.

"Daddy!" Carmen jumped out of the car, gave her father a hug and a big kiss, and ran into the house.

Leon reached into the car to shake my hand and patted Victor's shoulder in an affectionate way.

"Victor, where's your truck, son?"

Victor explained about his fan belt, as Leon grunted in sympathy.

"Giovanni's going to drop me at the house," Victor said, smiling up at Leon, who was wiping his damp face with a paper towel. "I'll be over later, hour or so."

"Father Giovanni," Leon said, leaning in to address me. "You'll come by for dinner, o' course."

"I don't know what Selene has planned, Leon," I said carefully. "But I promise I won't miss seeing you and Bet before I go."

"Okay. Whatever the Queen Bee wants," Leon replied with a resigned expression. "Interesting woman, that sister-in-law of mine. Defy anyone to say different."

"No disagreement here," said Victor with a dry chuckle. He backed out of the driveway and two minutes later we were pulling up in front of the estate house. The freshly painted white veranda gleamed in the late morning sunshine and swept in clear, beautiful lines to the upper story, where three Palladian windows faced out over the field. It looked for all the world like a plantation house from nineteenth-century Georgia.

"Will you come in, Giovanni?" Victor said.

We were standing on a widened part of Sterling's road, which swooped out in a fan shape in front of the huge house. I shaded my eyes with my hand and looked across to the line of ancient trees that rimmed the far end of the field. The tall grasses swayed and glittered in the light. Behind us, to the left of the veranda, was the formal garden I had heard so much about. Unable to resist, I walked a few yards toward it for a better look.

The dimensions of the restored garden were impressive, the proportions perfect. Even though Victor had replanted it completely, there was still a European, piazza-like feeling to the space and I was sure that old Eugenia

Wallace, who had, no doubt with an army of assistants, created her garden out of the living forest, would still be able to recognize it as her own. There were tulips and dahlias and large, heavy dark purple flowers I had never seen before. At the far end, I could see the restored ruins of an ornamental iron fence, five or six posts topped by curved rims with spike-like finials, all that was left of an old line of demarcation between the cultivated and the wild. It was covered with the late roses.

"Really, Giovanni, please come in," Victor said with a chuckle. "It would be my pleasure."

"Ah," I said, "sorry, not at the moment. Selene expects me." I had been hoping for a tour of Victor's renovations; Carmen's descriptions of the rock-faced wall in the salon, the elegant, overstuffed furniture, and the colorful abstract paintings, many done by Victor himself, were tantalizing and I'd been frankly curious. "Another time, perhaps."

I turned to get in the car, but Victor put his hand on my arm. "I didn't want to mention this in front of Carmen," he said, "but there's something I think you should be aware of, a problem. Well, I don't know, I..."

His decision to say what little he did had obviously been impulsive, and was as quickly reconsidered.

"Victor, what is it?" Then: "Something about Selene?"

He shrugged, obviously sorry he'd spoken. "Ah, you know how Selene is," he said, not ungallantly. "But, something happened that night of the Fourth of July party and, well..."

"Victor," I said, "you know I'll keep it to myself."

"Well," he said, still hesitant, "it happened after everyone helped Bet carry all the picnic things inside. Selene and I were alone in the yard. I couldn't think of a thing to say, so I asked her where we were all going, even though I knew."

He said that Selene had looked pointedly away from him before she answered. "Fireworks," she said, obviously irritated. "They do it every year over at the lake. I never go."

Victor, who was standing several feet away from her with his hands in his pockets, did not reply. Selene got up slowly and came close to him, running the little finger of her hand back and forth over the smooth edge of his shirt pocket.

"Why don't you and I go to my library instead?" she said in a low voice. "We could have a little cognac while I show you what I've been working on."

When he didn't answer, she drew her cheeks together with sudden displeasure and turned slightly away.

"I've begun a new book," she said, "and I've discovered something very interesting. I thought you might like to—"

"Well," he said, carefully clearing his throat and moving just out of her peripheral vision, "ordinarily I would, of course, but it seems that tonight...I know Bet and Carmen would be delighted if you came along."

Without another word, Selene turned down the driveway toward her own house. The dogs were all sitting at the edge of Leon's asphalt, lined up side by side in a furry row, waiting for her. Just then, Carmen came out the front door. She had changed her skirt for a pair of pink linen slacks and her flower lei for a lovely crystal necklace Victor had given her.

When Carmen saw the dogs, she grinned and ran down the driveway past the station wagon toward them. Lorenza and Savo stood up, planted their legs wide apart and whined for kisses, though they did not come closer. Carmen embraced all nine dogs in turn, murmuring little greetings, gently pulling Mickey's wagging tail, and then turned to Selene, who was already standing in the road.

"We're going to the fireworks, Selene. Aren't you coming?"

"Carmen, you know better than that."

"Yes, but don't you think you could make one exception?" Carmen said.

"I'm sure I don't see why I would, Carmen. I have no time at all for nonsense."

Carmen moved slightly, as if she were about to protest, but the movement turned into a shrug. "Well, it's up to you," she said in a soft voice in which Victor heard no expression. Selene snapped her fingers at the dogs, who galloped down the road toward home, and without so much as a nod to Victor or Carmen, she set off after them, not looking back.

After he told me all that, Victor sighed and leaned his hips against the trunk of my car, squinting into the sunlit field. Except for the faint hum of busy insects in the white ash trees that surrounded the veranda, it was silent all around us. The breeze had died down to a whisper and the tall grasses and flowers that filled the field swayed so slightly they might have been a painting.

"Later that night," Victor said in a low, hoarse voice, "while the rest of us were off at the fireworks, Selene went in my house."

"How do you know that?" I said softly. It seemed impossible that she would do such a thing. Yet, after what Carmen had told me about seeing Selene eavesdropping by the rock, I was (I am so ashamed to say) unwilling to denounce him.

"Giovanni, it was obvious...obvious." He turned briefly to me and then away, touching my sleeve with a tentative, apologetic gesture. "She'd done it before, too."

"Oh, Victor, surely..." But what could I say to that? What could I possibly say? Still, I might have stopped him then, and we both knew it. I could have refused to listen to such tales about my dear old friend, but all I did was look sadly into Victor's eyes and, with a gesture, allow him to continue.

He had been away for a while, he said, since the middle of June, but had returned very late the night before the picnic. Just after midnight, passing Selene's house, he thought he saw a shadow move away from the trees, but he wasn't sure. When he slowed down for another look, he saw her clearly in his rearview mirror, a tall figure dressed in white.

When he got home, he went directly to the salon. The house was stifling hot, something he had not anticipated, and he often slept in the large, airy salon on a chaise purchased for that purpose. He undressed and spread a clean sheet over the chaise, glad to be home at last. He lay down and put his hands over his exhausted, stinging eyes.

He must have slept, for some time later—it could have been an hour or a minute—he awoke and lay perfectly still, sensing a nearby presence.

One small lamp glowed dimly on his map table, just enough for him to see there was no one in the room. But outside the great glass panes, near the wall where the salon joined the original house, he saw someone moving. Whoever it was, a figure in white, was pressed against the glass.

Victor didn't move. Didn't dare betray his wakefulness. At length, the figure moved away and he, sick at heart, without a notion what to do about it, was still awake and wondering when dawn came rising in the east.

"And then," Victor said, "the next night, the night of the Fourth, she came again."

He opened the trunk and took out his small satchel and some boxes and other parcels he'd taken from his broken pickup truck. He set his things on the gravel and turned to me where I stood, shaken and silent.

"Again. I realized later she must have come in the kitchen door because I'd left it unlocked. I mean, out here..."

He broke off and closed the trunk, very gently, took another deep breath, and jammed his hands in his pockets before he spoke again.

"I don't think she touched anything in the kitchen or in any of the downstairs rooms, but she was in the bedroom, sure enough."

"How do you know that?" I demanded, aghast at what he was saying. "How could you possibly know?"

"Oh, Giovanni, because all my shirts were disturbed, badly disturbed. I keep them lined up very neatly, and in fact I'd only recently been to the laundry and there were at least a dozen there, I knew there were. But when I looked in the closet that night, after the fireworks, they were completely in disarray, some off the hangers, all of them crumpled, and one was... wet. Damp. I don't even want to think with what."

"Victor, please, think what you're—"

"And there was that smell, that faint scent of cigarettes and cognac and a light perfume that... ah, Jesus."

He sank down on the hood of the car and put his face in his hands. "I can't believe I'm telling this to anyone, but I'm so afraid that whatever is going on with her could hurt Carmen in some way. I don't know how. Some way."

He took his hands from his face and looked at me. "I swear to you, I'll kill her if she hurts Carmen." He was deadly serious.

He pushed himself away from the car and carried two of the larger parcels up onto the veranda, as if needing something physical to do. When he came back, he seemed about to say something else, but just took another load up the steep steps to the veranda.

He was a man clearly at his wits' end, ashamed of what he was telling, but compelled to tell it all the same. His apparent trust in me was a tribute I did not relish.

He came back again and stood beside me, his hand on the roof of the car. "I think she's crazy, Giovanni. Plain and simple. I think she's out of her mind."

"Victor, my friend, I don't know what I can do," I said, looking into his sad eyes. "What can I do?"

"You can get her the hell away from Carmen," he said, his voice suddenly thick with anger. "That's what you can do."

Chapter Twenty-Three

hen I left Victor, I drove back down Sterling's road, through the obelisks, and out onto the county road toward Turn-of-River. I was taking a chance that Selene hadn't seen me pass her house, but I had to be alone with Victor's dreadful story. If necessary, an excuse could be fabricated without too much effort.

Absorbed in my jumbled thoughts, I drove most of the way to Turn-of-River before I slowed down and let the car slide to a full stop on the shoulder of the road. I knew I needed a moment to rest, to collect myself before facing her.

That I might think of my dear friend in such terms upset me. I had looked forward to this visit since my conversation with Carla in Fiesole. In my valise I had a wonderful bottle of Tuscan wine, Carla's gift, and a package from me as well, meant to be not so much a gift as a clever way to pose our invitation for Selene to come and spend as much time as she liked in Carla's house in Florence.

Victor's story had left me badly shaken. I judged him to be a man not at all given to idle speculations, a man entirely without susceptibility to the more spectral side of life. But his belief that Selene Catcher, whom I had known for almost twenty years, could be a danger to the young woman we all loved was horrifying.

It troubled me most of all that Selene's devotion to the Great Goddess might somehow have played a role in the chilling behavior Victor had described. All the time I'd been in Italy, I had been plagued by thoughts about Selene's plan for a book that would reveal the Great Goddess as the true Madonna, vibrant and real in the life of the Renaissance. There, half a millennium ago, brilliant men had made the Renaissance, and Selene believed they had done it for the Goddess.

I knew from Sterling's manuscript that Goddess cults were still flourishing in Anatolia, in Italy, and in the Aegean area as late as the fourth or fifth century, and probably even later. I had absorbed that information with ease, so why was it so hard to accept Selene's idea that Goddess worship continued through the Renaissance? From Ashtoreth and Ereshkigal to Mary by way of Artemis: was that so big a leap? Why should it be impossible to believe that the original identity of my precious Saint Mary was to be found in the ruins of the Temple of Diana? And why should I resist believing that such faith exists, when I do not doubt my own?

I knew that Selene worshiped the Great Goddess precisely as another person would believe in Jesus Christ or in the Buddha. She prayed to Artemis as one prays to Yahweh, to Allah, to any god. Why was a circle of burned stones any less a sanctuary than a mosque, a synagogue, or the basilica at Santa Croce? Piety takes more than architecture. Perhaps it was the intensity of Selene's belief that so disturbed me, her cabalistic, conspiratorial view of the persistence of Goddess worship through the centuries, the artful, secret devotion of Her followers.

I took a deep breath, put the car in gear, and crept off down the county road toward the estate, feeling a little bit more settled, I suppose, but really no less pensive than before.

If Selene had, indeed, witnessed the two passes of my car, she gave no sign, greeting me with enthusiastic kisses on both cheeks and a warm, strong hug of welcome. The dogs, clustered close behind Savo, stayed several yards away, snarling softly as if eager to rip my throat out, but just marginally lacking the immediate motivation to do it.

Even when I helped Selene carry our lunch into the *studiolo*, they kept their distance. When Fitzi (who had taken an unaccountable and particular dislike to me) darted past the pack to snap at my legs, Savo herded her back, viciously biting her shoulder in the process. Were they saving me for later?

In the *studiolo* we divided the food onto two white porcelain plates, poured out Carla's wine, and settled ourselves by the low table. Selene seemed fine to me. Her golden eyes were calm and bright and I could scarcely credit Victor's story. We spoke animatedly of Carla and my weeks in Fiesole, Selene responding with the appropriate laugh or frown or clicking of her tongue to every little tale I had to tell.

When the bread and cheese were crumbs on the tray, and most of the grapes had disappeared, I put a large, brown paper-wrapped package in Selene's lap and sat back with a fresh glass of wine, watching her.

She put a grape in her mouth before she pulled open the length of string with which I'd tied the package. I heard the grape burst and snap between her teeth.

"Open it," I said.

"What is it?"

"It won't bite you, *cara*. Open it up."

My gift to her, my invitation, was a huge book, bound in heavy watered silk of a rich burgundy color, the corners mitered to perfection, the front cover embossed right through the padding with the elaborate escutcheon of the ancient Farnese family of Rome. It was the book of Odoardo Cardinal Farnese's collection.

The pages were all hand-cut, feathery at their edges, the gatherings perfectly aligned in a quarto format one doesn't see anywhere but in rare book rooms and museums. Large linen leaves were hand-sewn between every gathering, and affixed to each one was a glossy photograph of a painting or a piece of sculpture, a jeweled reliquary, or an ornate chalice or crucifix—items of astonishing beauty and unconscionable splendor.

"Oh, Vanni," Selene said in a breathless voice. "Vanni, the Farnese treasures. My God."

She turned the page to a life-size photograph of a pair of velvet gloves embroidered with gold thread and enormous black pearls arranged in the shape of a cross.

"My God," she whispered again. She closed the cover and gently fingered the shield and crest embossed on the silk cover. "As far as I know, there are only twenty copies in the world, no?"

I nodded happily, indulging myself with a small inhalation of intense pride, thrilled with her reaction; not too many people would appreciate this book, and Selene Catcher was one of the few. The hushed reverence with which she'd touched the pages was everything I'd hoped.

"Isn't the Palazzo Farnese closed up? Abandoned?"

"It's closed now, yes."

"Umm. I thought so. I was there once," she said, opening the book again, "long ago. The rooms and galleries were all absolutely crammed to the rafters with the cream of the Roman Renaissance."

She turned a few more pages with her fingertips; opposite each plate was a discussion, in Italian, of the treasure in the photo. Each initial capital letter of the text was illuminated as in a medieval manuscript, but more gloriously so, the elaborate geometric swirls and bestiary designs bearing a more sophisticated, late-Renaissance look.

"What a gift," she murmured, "unbelievable. Oh, look . . ." On the linen pages in the center of the book, which folded out to quadruple width, were wide-angled photographs of what appeared to be ceiling panels or frescos. I stood behind her as she unfolded each leaf, looking over her shoulder as she explained that they were meant to represent a panorama of the most erotic love stories of the gods of classical antiquity.

"The frescos were commissioned," she said, "from the Carracci brothers. They were supposed to help the Cardinal compete with the popes." She chuckled, pointing to scenes of muscular divinities engaged in voluptuous sexual athletics, and chubby, sexy children playing with opulently harnessed tigers and rams.

As she spoke, Selene ran her fingers over the striving musculature of the gods' bodies, seeming to caress them, to feel the warmth under the paint. In one panel, the sleeping shepherd, Endymion, a stylized drape covering his genitals, was embraced by an intent and avid Selene, his head gathered to the goddess's rounded shoulder. Their figures were surrounded by writhing, tortured nudes, eyes closed either in imitation of Endymion's endless sleep, or in a paroxysm of unsatisfied desire.

Selene put the book gently on the sofa, got up and took my face in both her hands, and kissed me softly, briefly, on the mouth and returned to her chair.

"Now. Vanni, my friend. Tell me why you have given me such a gift."

I shrugged as if the book were a trifle, little more than a box of chocolates or a nice scarf. "It's an invitation, Selene. Carla and I want you to come to Florence, to her house. For as long as you wish. To work on your new book."

She had been leaning forward to take a cigarette from the pack on the table, but stopped, astonished by my words. Smiling, I got up and lit her cigarette with one of the long, blue-tipped wooden matches. I pushed the tray back and sat at the end of the coffee table, holding her free hand in both of mine.

"Selene, your new book will be your gift to all of us who love you.

Why not take six months, a year, even longer? Do it in Florence. Think of it, my friend—museums, libraries, marvelous conversation! Carla will give you the whole house."

When she didn't answer me, I let go of her hand and moved away to the windows, carefully watching the back of her head, thinking hard.

"Of course," I said, "we hope you will bring Carmen with you. If she wishes to come, *cara*, she would be most welcome. It goes without saying, no? Imagine our dear Carmen loose on the Tornabuoni with Carla!" I said, laughing. "Ah, the frocks! The *gioiëlli!* While you and I go off to Rome to sneak into the Farnese!"

I suddenly stopped laughing and knelt in front of her. "Selene, please say you will consider it."

Selene said nothing. She smoked the cigarette down to the filter, ground it out, and got up to look for something. As I watched, on edge but curious, she dug in a chest of drawers in the far corner of the room and came back to her chair holding a small leather box. It was filled with pictures she had saved of the grand old times in Florence.

They were completely out of sequence—odd photos of landscapes, a small, pretty ruin that was unfamiliar to me, a few blurred party scenes. Selene shuffled them as if they were playing cards and fanned them out across the table. There was one little bunch of about ten snapshots, held together with a limp rubber band, of Carla and Piero and herself seated behind a table littered with bottles and plates of cut fruit, surrounded by five or six laughing people I could not remember, though I may well have been the one who took the picture. There was another of Carla alone, smiling over her shoulder at the photographer and pointing at something with one long, vermilion-lacquered fingernail.

Frowning, Selene dug toward the bottom of the box. And there, in a small cardboard folder, she found what I supposed she had been looking for all along: a candid shot of my own younger self, leaning over the balcony railing at Carla's house in Florence, looking pensively away into the middle distance. My fair hair (of which there is now somewhat less) was smooth across my narrow Corio skull; my cheeks were just beginning to show the faint creases and lines that Carla now tells me are distinguished.

I took the box from her, placed it on the desk, and took her hands in mine. "Dear friend, I know I presume, but it distresses me to think of you locked away in your forest when you could be in Florence with us. Why not do your book in Italy? The idea's fairly obvious, after all."

She pulled her hands away and lit another cigarette, saying nothing.

"I think it's time for the *principessa* to leave the castle," I said in a more serious tone. "You need to look the Renaissance in the face, my friend. The Pitti Palace, the Bargello, all the churches. You're probably getting ready to tell me that Giotto's *Enthroned Madonna* is in your nice book on Renaissance painting, but you know it's hanging right this minute on a wall in the Uffizi. This book of old Farnese's loot is only a clue, Selene, a taste. Only . . . *antipasto.*"

She got up, moved away from me, and went to stand by the south windows, watching as rain clouds gathered and darkened in the late afternoon sky. The dogs were rolling around on the damp grass, fighting in a bored way, taking occasional disinterested swipes at one another and then galloping over to the trees and back again. Selene watched them for a few minutes, then went to the desk and sat motionless in the chair, thinking of things I could not possibly know.

Chapter Twenty-Four

excused myself and went upstairs to change. When I came back, maybe half an hour later, Selene was leaning over a large, tattered map of Italy spread out across the desk. When I put my hand on her shoulder, she looked up at me with a wide, luminous smile. We had finished most of Carla's Tuscan wine and I had with me a fresh bottle of cognac and two glasses. We drank a toast to Florence and the Medicis as we studied the map under the cone of light from the desk lamp, tracing routes from Venice to Rome and back to Fiesole. Selene was radiant. Perhaps it had been a good idea to leave her alone for a while; she had obviously been pondering my invitation.

"Now, will you help me with something?" she said, getting up from her chair to kiss my cheek.

"Of course. If it doesn't require physical labor," I said with a grin.

She laughed at that. "Actually, it does," she said, going to the fireplace and pushing a small chest away from an alcovelike space beside the hearth, paved with the same rough stones that formed the enormous fireplace surround.

Behind the chest was a large, old-fashioned canvas trunk, cinched with rotting leather straps.

"I just remembered this yesterday," she said, tugging on a strap. "It's all that's left of what Father sent back from Greece before he died.

It's just now occurred to me there might be some useful stuff in here. Years ago . . . Oh, Vanni, pull that end, dear . . . when I myself came back and redid the room," she said, sitting down on the floor, "I just shoved it into the alcove. I didn't even give it much of a look. But you never know, huh?"

Together, we opened the trunk and Selene brushed away the grit and cobwebs with the back of her hand.

The old trunk did, indeed, contain Sterling's last effects. There were letters from Graves and Seznec, written in Greek, French, and English; remnants of the manuscripts of an old Hebrew cabalist whose work he had admired, now faded and illegible; and a pouch containing a tiny relic, a shard of a statue of the Goddess, stolen, as he'd told Selene on the one occasion that he'd let her see it, from the ruin at Tell Azmak in Bulgaria.

There, too, at the bottom of the trunk, were all the preliminary notes for *The Cults of the Great Goddess*, and notebooks filled with spells Sterling had created himself, hoping to summon the Goddess, to enjoin Her favor and forgiveness.

There was a small journal, bound in marbled paper, recounting his first trip, years before Selene's own birth, to the famous Telesterion, the great hall at Eleusis, where the most secret of the rites of the Mysteries were traditionally observed. As we looked through, Selene told me that the ceremonies were not only still performed, and still kept secret on pain of death, but illegal as well, absolutely forbidden by the Greek government. Aloud, sipping at her glass of cognac, she read out the passage describing the day Sterling bathed in the sea by Eleusis and became initiate to the Eleusinian Mysteries themselves. Her own father!

It was full dark by the time we found another thick portfolio, unmarked, bound with a cord. It had been partially hidden under the cotton lining of the trunk. When Selene opened the portfolio, sheaves of shiny paper spilled out across the desk. They were all images of Aphrodite, portrayed in every medium and form. There were scores of them, the slick paper slipping through our hands like falling leaves.

Right on top, wrapped in a large sheet of onionskin, was Clouet's famous portrait of Diane de Poitiers, the notorious mistress of Henri II, her naked body framed by the red satin draperies of her bathing chamber. Her breasts, milk-white, firm and pointing, were exposed to the light of the foreground, her eyes disinterested and calm. In the background, a coarse serving woman suckled a fat child with her great red melon of a breast. Selene gasped when she saw it.

"Is this a joke?" she cried, flinging the picture from her. It sailed across the room. "A riddle? From Diane, to Artemis, to breast, to sucking child, to *naked in her bath*? Did that old bastard mean for me to find it?" she screamed, tearing through the rest of the portfolio, horrified to find it filled with the Aphrodites of the Renaissance itself, reclining nude courtesans radiating full, vulgar consciousness of what they were. There was Giorgione's *Sleeping Venus*, the one from Dresden, almost an imitation of the Titian fastened to it with a rusty paper clip, the master's great *Venus of Urbino*, which I had stared at as a boy, long ago, my shoes silent on the floor of the Uffizi.

In the Titian, Aphrodite was awake as she could be, her fingers curled in toward her vagina in the exact same pose Selene had described when Lido Desjardin taunted her in Victor's salon weeks before. Was she protecting? Masturbating? Offering? Aphrodite's gaze was fixed on the helpless viewer, forced to stay outside the frame, unable to respond to the bold invitation in those eyes.

"What the hell am I supposed to think about this *shit!*" Selene flung the Titian to the floor.

Looking at what her father had truly worshiped—the portfolio of pictures mirroring the mind of the man the Goddess had despised—Selene sprang up from the desk chair, roaring, screaming, exciting the dogs, who began to rake their claws against the closed door of the *stùdiolo*.

"Slut! Harlot! *Whore!*" she howled. She shrieked the words over and over as she grabbed handfuls of the pictures of Aphrodite, snatching them up from the desk, the floor, the chair seat and twisting them in her strong fists, cracking the enameled paper, ripping all of it to shreds, the rosy flesh, the globes of breasts and mounds of pudenda, the wild apricot hair raining to the floor in a whirlwind of gigantic confetti.

But even in that tearing rage, in which all thought was nearly gone, Selene's glance fell upon a large piece of *The Birth of Venus* that had fluttered to the carpet, barely creased. So fine was the print that Botticelli's scallop shell seemed to be real, three-dimensional and wet, rising from the ocean floor with its alabaster goddess and her flowing hair, surrounded by the frolicking nymphs and prostitutes and demon satyrs who welcomed her birth with laps full of flowers. Selene grabbed that, too, and tore it into tiny pieces, shrieking.

But just then, underneath the stacks of Sterling's folders that covered the big desk, I saw part of a large picture, a bower of dark green leaves, shown in great detail—glossy, thick, botanically perfect. From the leaves hung dozens of exquisite oranges, full and solid as if made of gold. It was Botticelli's magnificent *Primavera*, possibly the most famous Renaissance painting in the world—Aphrodite and her court.

Even I could almost believe that Botticelli had seen the opportunity for a bitter joke. He had portrayed Aphrodite as a Renaissance virgin with a sweet, pretty face, her abundant hair carefully arranged. She stood with seeming modesty in the center of the painting. Her right hand was raised in a travesty of Christian benediction, but her round breasts, clearly defined by the artist, betrayed her true nature: here was the procuress, the mistress of the dancing harlots to her right and the smiling blond slut to her left, who reached so artlessly into her lap, from which flowers were already tumbling. Botticelli had known exactly what he was doing.

Groaning under her breath, Selene looked at it over my shoulder, her hands over her mouth in actual horror.

"No!" she cried in a deep, harsh voice. "*Noooo . . . !* Oh, God, how could this happen? What did he want with this? It's a mockery!"

And it might well have been just that—a sick, vulgar mockery of all the *Maestàs*, all the altarpieces of the Goddess.

Selene grabbed a single-edge razor from the desk drawer, snatched the *Primavera* out of my hands, and slashed at it again and again and again, weeping in shrill, breathless gasps. She threw the pieces into the cold fireplace and set them afire, watching with glittering, wet eyes as the paper scorched and burned.

As I stood by, helpless and sick at heart, she ran back and grabbed from the floor two handfuls of the cracked, torn pieces of Sterling's Aphrodites and threw them into the fire where the Botticelli, already black and curling, smoldered in its own ashes. I recognized torn scraps of the Titian, the Giorgione, of the portrait of Diane de Poitiers with her obscene, pointing coral nipples.

Selene went back for more, slashing with the razor, screaming in guttural wails of anger. I remembered that night at the Inn when, thrilled, she told me she'd finally recognized the Goddess in Her guise as the Madonna, had understood that She was the *patròna* of the Renaissance itself, Her power intact after twenty thousand years. But now she knew that the Great Whore, and the terrifying threat she posed, was also never silent.

All at once, I saw that there was blood all over Selene's clothes, her hands, the pictures, but she didn't seem to realize she was bleeding. When I went to her, trying to take the razor, she shoved me away and continued to rip and shred the fragments on the floor into smaller and smaller pieces. As she tore into them, the muscles in her face quivered with revulsion and rage.

"Selene!" I reached for her again, succeeding this time in seizing her shoulders, pressing one hand to her forehead; she was absolutely burning up. "Selene, my God." I poured out a couple of fingers of cognac and she gulped it down, still trembling.

"Oh! The bastard! The filthy bastard! No wonder She hated him! He bathed in the sea at Eleusis, for God's sake! He was an Initiate as I will never be! He was the one who betrayed Her, but She's making *me* pay for what he was!"

Suddenly, with a loud cry, she wrenched herself away from me and the force of her movement slammed the heavy desk chair all the way back against the bookshelves.

"Those fucking pictures! All those filthy, hideous pictures of the one he *really* worshiped!" she screamed, running hooked fingers through her wild silver hair.

Selene's eyes, bronze-dark with hysteria, were burning in her face. She brandished her heavy crystal glass about with violent, purposeless swipes, just wanting, I thought, something hard to hang on to. The remaining portion of the cognac splattered over the Persian carpet. Finally, with a loud groan, she threw the glass itself across the room, and it smashed into the wall high above the framed *Annunciation*s, shattering into sparkling fragments.

"Selene," I shouted. "Selene! Please, no!" I tried to catch her again but she spun away from me, sending the shards of crystal skittering across the floor.

Her screams had turned into harsh, ragged breaths, the terrible, rasping inspirations of air exhaled in wheezing gasps. When I tried to approach her from what I thought was her blind side, she struck out at me and the unexpected power of the blow sent me reeling back against the desk. Dazed, I clung to the edge of it, my breath knocked out of me.

And then she lit the first match.

She took it from the pocket of her sweater and scraped it hard against the wood of the window frame.

As the blue head ignited and blazed up, she shrieked again and threw the burning match at the Farnese book, which was still on the sofa, open to the panorama of the *Loves of the Gods*.

"Selene! *Stop it!*" Somehow I got up from the floor, lunged toward her.

But a small, dense *poom* of sound came from the book, and bright yellow flames shot up like a bouquet from the dry pages. I grabbed a carafe of water from the table and threw it toward the burning book. Mercifully, the fire sizzled out, but Selene had already struck another match and tossed it toward the book again. It fell short and dropped, still burning, to the floor.

"I should have burned them years ago!" she bellowed. *"I should have known!"*

I ran around the sofa toward her, trying to step on the second fire on the way, but she had lit yet another match and was holding it straight up in front of her.

"Selene! No!" I grabbed her with both arms and pulled her against me with a strength I never knew I had. I could feel the heat of the lit match against my chest, but I didn't let go of her until I was sure the flame was out.

All at once she shuddered violently and sank in my arms.

"Oh, Selene," I whispered, "Selene." I stood holding her, smoothing her hair, feeling every inch of her body against me. I whispered to her in Italian, softly, the same words over and over: *"Andrà bene, cara, andrà bene* ... it will be all right."

I led her to the large flowered easy chair and settled her into it, still smoothing her hair. I poured some cognac into my glass and gave it to her. She drank it all and lay back against the soft cushion of the chair, weeping softly through closed lids, her face contorted. "Oh, Vanni, the book ... the beautiful Farnese book ..."

"It's all right, *cara*, it's all right."

As I leaned over her, our faces were nearly touching and I smelled cognac and cigarette smoke and the scent of the extinguished match, with which I was absolutely certain she had been prepared to set us both afire.

I knelt beside her chair and held her as best I could in such an awkward position, until, with one final shiver, she seemed to come to herself. She sat up straight in the chair, yanked her fingers through her long silver hair, and twisted it back into a rope.

"I'm just like him, you know," she said, lifting her wet face to me. "Just like him."

"Selene. No. You mean your father? Oh, no. What a terrible thing to say."

"Terrible? Of course it is. But it's true enough, Vanni, true enough."

Chapter Twenty-Five

After I got Selene into bed, and satisfied myself that she was actually asleep, I went in the bathroom and checked the front of my shirt. Of course it was smeared with dried blood from Selene's slashed fingers, but there was also a charred, ragged hole about the size of a quarter right at the level of my diaphragm. I looked carefully, but though my undershirt was slightly singed, my skin was not burned at all.

I splashed cold water on my face and then went downstairs to deal with the *stùdiolo*. The dogs, clustered on the tiles at the end of the breezeway, whined and backed away as I approached. Suspicious, I looked anxiously at Savo, but she only growled softly and trotted away across the grass, her pack close behind her.

In the *stùdiolo*, jagged pieces of crystal and large flakes of ash lay sodden in the tracked-up puddles of cognac and wine and water, but there was no fire, no smoldering—the real disaster had been (at least temporarily) averted. I poured the remains of Carla's wine into a fresh glass, swallowed without tasting it, then swept and wiped the floor and took the cups and glasses back to the kitchen. But there was nothing I could do about the book.

It was completely ruined, blackened and wet. I wrapped it in a towel, just as it was, and, not knowing what else to do, left it on a shelf in the pantry. I had the unhappy thought that now there were only nineteen of those books left, only nineteen of that exquisite private edition of the Cardinal's hoarded treasure. If that. Who could say what had happened to the others? Was there a horrifying story for the destruction of each one? Were the other copies of this record of the fabulous booty of the House of Farnese burned, stolen, buried, hidden, shredded—lost forever? Perhaps cursed by the Cardinal himself?

Back upstairs, I looked in on Selene and then went to my own room. I undressed and got into bed and lay there wide awake, trying to gather my wits and my sense of proportion by thinking over the events of that day and all the others since Selene had first told me about the Goddess and the Madonna. And in time, only a few minutes, perhaps, I felt my breathing slow and the sheer puzzle of it all start to engage my mind.

I was wary of convoluted psychological explanations; it would be so easy to jump to the tempting conclusion that Selene's idea of the transfiguration of the Great Goddess into the persona of the Virgin Mary was a way to reconcile the faiths of both her parents. But I had been schooled all my life to mistrust that kind of facile reasoning.

I thought it more likely that her new book was an act of genuine devotion, of worship, and, yes, above all, of *propitiation*. It was a plea for forgiveness, more extravagant in its way than anything Sterling himself had ever done.

My own idea was quite arresting (possibly because it was my own), and I knew I might be making too much of it. But the idea seemed so right to me. Selene's creation of a lasting testament to the power and importance of the Goddess might be a deliberate, even desperate beseeching of Her mercy. But what was the sin?

If Victor's belief that Selene had been stalking him, entering his house in the small hours of the night, yearning in some voiceless way for his attentions, was as well founded as I feared, then my notion would indeed make sense. Selene herself had told me that imperfect chastity was the sin the Goddess hated most. And I knew (maybe better than most) that avowal meant little: the *will* to chastity, an *interior* sustaining of such a vow, must remain unbreached.

I thought it likely that Selene, her father's heir in so many ways, might also have inherited that powerfully sensual nature that could not be restrained. It was undoubtedly why she had become hysterical at the sight of all the images of Aphrodite. The hypocrisy of Sterling's probable devotion to the goddess of physical love, of sexuality, had been too much for Selene. She had clung for years to her own impulsive vow of chastity. That Sterling had insulted the Goddess with the indulgence of his own erotic nature (although I had only the evidence of Selene's word for that) both offended and frightened her.

But there are sins and sins, as my decades of scribbling bear witness. I was far more concerned with the possibility that Selene's greater sin—her *Christian*, her human sin—was a knowing betrayal of the young woman she loved as her own child.

Knowing?

Could it possibly be that Selene did not realize that Carmen and Victor were passionately in love with each other? She *must* know, I thought. How could she not?

Lord above, *I* saw it. I knew without a doubt what was going on between Carmen and Victor, adding layer after layer of depth and feeling all that spring. From Bet's dinner party, when they first met, to Victor's housewarming and, most compellingly, to the Fourth of July picnic with its songs and kisses and leis of field flowers, their intimacy had grown. I remembered the easy tenderness with which Carmen had, only that morning, sat in the front seat of my car, twining her gentle fingers in his hair.

Could Selene *knowingly* betray that lovely girl? Unthinkable on the face of it, yet even I—cool, passionless creature that I knew myself to be— had recognized Victor Bellacéra's erotic fascination well enough to understand how even fear of the Great Goddess's wrath might be eclipsed by such a passion. I knew that regardless of the motivations and undercurrents which the discovery of the Aphrodite pictures had stirred up, getting Selene away to Italy had become essential.

The next day we had an early lunch with Leon and Bet. Carmen and Victor were not there, having gone off somewhere together for the day, but Carmen had left both Selene and me big bouquets of the wild red lilies. Mine was accompanied by a little scribbled note in which she promised to call within the week.

Bet served a delicious vegetable omelet, accompanied by fresh fruit salad, sweet muffins, and her excellent coffee. The conversation was lively enough and I found myself enjoying the company, the warmhearted kindliness of our hosts, and Leon's slightly salty sense of humor. For that, his wife chided him with frequent blushing, but I sensed it was a game they'd played for years, growing increasingly skilled at the fine art of relishing each other's companionship.

I was surprised, and very pleased, that Selene joined in with a good temper and a few stories of her own. I was reminded of our early days in Florence and of the charming and vivacious role she'd played in those jolly dinner conversations long ago. She looked marvelous that day, rested and even happy, and though she ate little but the fruit, and seemed to play constantly with her bouquet, stroking the lily petals and stamens over and over with her long fingers, she was in a splendid mood.

Bet held forth at length on the farmers' market, coming up in just two weeks, a local festival that had been celebrated annually in the area for many years.

"Father Giovanni, you'll be here for that, I hope," she said with a smile, passing the plate of muffins my way. "It's the middle of August every year, just about the time of the Feast of the Assumption of the Blessed Virgin. Everyone goes," she said; "it's just a wonderful day. They've been doing it since . . . well, since when, honey? Since the war?"

"Before, I think," Leon said, considering. "Must be more than fifty years. Didn't do it *during* the war, of course, rationing and all, not that I can remember that far back. Ha!"

When I expressed some doubt that I would be able to join them, the feast being a Holy Day of Obligation, they all expressed sincere regret.

"It's the biggest thing hereabouts," Leon said, "except Christmas. Too bad you'll miss it."

Despite that disappointing note, our lunch proceeded with much laughter and anecdotes of markets past, and though I glanced frequently at Selene, expecting her to drift away into boredom or indifference, she did neither. After I thanked Bet and Leon for their hospitality and got my little satchel from my room, Selene walked me out to the car.

"You know, Vanni," she said, "I can definitely live without another farmers' market in Turn-of-River. I might surprise you and show up in Boston."

"Do you think you would?" I said, kissing her cheek, looking doubtfully into her bright eyes. I was reluctant to show too much enthusiasm. I'd invited her times without number in the months I'd been in Boston and she'd never once accepted.

"You never can tell. The Feast of the Assumption falls on Diana's Day this year," she said with a wink, giving me a brief hug and opening the car door for me. "It might be fun to celebrate with a little pagan revelry, hmm? I'll call you."

The next two weeks flew by in a haze of work and preparations for a visit from a prominent cardinal, for which I was expected to remain on display, chattering and praying in turns. In an interval between a convocation and a cocktail party, I called Avery French to see how he was getting on. To my surprise, he announced he was back at work, and one afternoon I took a walk over to the decrepit French revival mansion on Marlborough Street that houses the *Renaissance Review*.

I found Avery in his private office, settled into a massive green leather chair behind a fine old Hepplewhite desk of solid vintage. Across the room hung a well-framed print of Crivelli's *St. George and the Dragon*.

"The original hangs in Mrs. Gardner's house," he told me with a proud chuckle, "right here in town. I don't mind telling you, Giovanni, some days the dragon wins, but you get to a point where you more or less expect it."

I laughed with him, of course, happy to see him in good spirits, but his voice was less booming than of old, and his backside no longer fit the capacious chair quite as snugly as it must once have done. I suspected (rightly, as it turned out) that before too long, in deference to his health, Avery would be obliged to retire from his post and the Crivelli would be hanging in the house on Beacon Hill.

But he was in fine form that day and we gossiped for well over an hour. I'd said nothing whatever to Avery about Selene's new book, but when, on an impulse, I mentioned the likelihood of her coming to Florence for an extended stay, he feebly slapped his hand on the desk with approval.

"In that case, we just might find ourselves making dinner plans at Sabatini's," he said, brightening at the prospect.

"Oh?"

"Well, my wife and I have said more than once that the air in Tuscany could be just the thing for my condition. We've got our eyes on a villa that's for rent not far from San Casciano. We're giving it a lot of thought. That's strictly *entre nous*, of course, but it could be there's a reunion of sorts in our future."

As I got up to leave, he came with me to the door and concluded our visit on a more serious note.

"I think you're wise to get Selene the hell out of here, Giovanni. She's made herself some sort of prisoner out there on the estate, and nobody knows why. But a year or so in Florence should straighten her out."

That night, brimming with hope and good feeling, I called Carla to report on my visits with Avery and Selene.

As it happened, the day of the farmers' market came and went without Selene. Fool that I am, I had rung up to remind her of our conversation, but she disappointed me once again. She was filled with fresh inspiration, she said, working day and night. She feared to break the tenuous thread then forming. I was unhappy, of course, but chose to take her refusal as a sign that she was getting herself geared up for Florence. Though she hadn't actually accepted our invitation, I felt sure she would.

But I had no chance to indulge my anticipation. My presence was required at various festivities surrounding the Mass of the Assumption of the Blessed Virgin. I sat with the grandees of the Boston church as the cardinal celebrated the bodily ascension of Our Lady into heaven. The fact that it was also (as Selene had pointed out) Diana's Day—the pagan festival celebrating the birth of Artemis herself—did not find its way into the cardinal's remarks.

Late in the afternoon, many of us gathered for the traditional feast at the Back Bay home of one of the wealthier supporters of the Church, a local politician who gave (or so I was told) handsomely each year. Contemplation of the connection between that hearty gentleman and the princely merchants of Renaissance Florence, competitively contributing to the building of chapels and cathedrals, gave me considerable entertainment as I prowled the buffet, making something of a pig of myself in the process. Fortunately, I was almost incognito—merely one of dozens in a black suit and Roman collar.

Afterward, I went for a long walk around the neighborhood. It was a warm, clear night and I sat on a bench on the Commonwealth Avenue mall, watching the full moon climb ever higher in the sky. I remembered Selene having said something about it being the Grain Moon, harbinger of the harvest. I thought about the sacred observances of the morning and wondered if the birthday of the Goddess had been transmuted, centuries ago, into the Assumption of the Blessed Virgin—if all the rites and rituals, all the piety and wit, did indeed converge.

It was very late when I took myself home to bed. At once, I fell into a deep oblivion in which my dream of the Goddess was both startling and elegiac. I saw Her perched on the shining horn of a crescent moon, Her little son in the crook of Her arm, a stag's head mask hanging from his tiny hand.

I have no idea what time it was when the ringing phone roused me from my dream. I fumbled for it, vaguely aware of the darkness of my room and the dim, pearlescent light outside the window.

"Yes?"

"Father! Father Giovanni, it's Leon Poynsetter."

I forced my feet to the floor and sat up as straight as I could. "Leon, what's wrong? What is it?"

"It's Selene. Something's happened to her. Please, can you come, Father? Can you come right now?"

PART THREE

Hecate

Chapter Twenty-Six

armen was waiting for me at the obelisks. It was barely seven in the morning and a cold, misty dawn had risen over my shoulder as I sped away from Boston. The tall grasses that grew up around the obelisks were wet with dew and the air was clammy against my face when I got out of the car and opened my arms to her. She wrapped her arms around my waist and buried her face in my jacket, shivering a little in the chilly damp. After a moment, she pulled away and gave me a wan smile.

"Thank you for coming. Oh, thank you."

"Ah, *cara* . . . *cara*."

We got in the car and I drove the short distance down to Selene's house and turned into the driveway. Leon had evidently been watching from the parlor windows. The screen door slapped behind him as he hurried out to greet me, pumping my hand and thanking me all over again.

"Bet wanted me to call you last night as soon as we knew," he said, "but I figured you'd need most of a night's sleep."

"I know, Leon. I realized that."

"It's bad, Father," he said. "She's out like a light, but she keeps mumbling, talking, I don't even know in what language." He hunched his shoulders and led me up the wide steps to the door. "Bet says it's not Italian. She's with her now."

Bet Poynsetter was sitting by Selene's bed with her hands in her lap. I saw a rosary twisted through her fingers, but for some reason she slipped it into her pocket when she saw me in the doorway. She did not get up when I leaned down to kiss her forehead.

Selene was lying perfectly still under her white blanket; her arms were flat at her sides over the cover, her legs perfectly straight. She was so tall that her feet pressed slightly against the end of the bed frame. Her skin was the color of finest parchment and her silver hair, appearing to be recently brushed, was spread out over the pillow in a beautiful, gleaming wave. Her left hand was heavily bandaged. Except for the bandage and the loosened hair, she might have been a Pharaonic queen, prepared for burial.

I went to her and placed my hand lightly against her cheek. "Selene, *cara mia.* Selene. It's Vanni."

There was not so much as a twitch of an eyelid.

Without a word, the four of us left the room and went single file down to the kitchen. There was fresh coffee in Selene's old-fashioned percolator on the stove, and Carmen got cups while Bet went to the refrigerator for a carton of cream.

"Have you had a doctor for her?" I asked.

Leon nodded. "Came last night about eleven. Young kid in a sports car. Stayed twenty minutes and left."

"We thought we should have her in the hospital," Bet said, stirring sugar into her cup and sitting back in the wooden chair. "But he didn't seem to agree. Says her heart and everything is fine, pulse and so forth. Says she'll snap out of it."

"Something must have happened," I offered. "A shock. Some terrible thing. Why is her hand bandaged?"

Bet sighed and took a sip of her coffee. "She cut it, he said, the doctor. I didn't see. Dwight ... ohh ..."

I looked at Carmen. "Dwight's the one who found her." She gestured vaguely toward the refrigerator. "Right here in the kitchen, yesterday afternoon about four o'clock. He came and got Daddy and by the time we all ran over here—"

"Two minutes," Leon chimed in, "couldn't have been any more than two minutes."

"Yeah, she was on the floor, passed out. Dwight had bandaged her hand with some paper towels and duct tape and I thought it was better to leave it." Carmen never took her tired hazel eyes from mine as she said all that, leaning forward with her hands clasped around her cup.

"And where is Dwight?"

"Haven't seen him since," Leon said with a look at his pale wife. He stood up and leaned against the frame of the open back door.

None of us said anything for a moment and I found myself aware of the utter silence. Except for the clink of Bet's coffee spoon and Leon's breathing, there wasn't a sound. I went over to the screen door and looked out onto the tiles of the breezeway.

"Where are all the dogs?"

"Haven't seen them neither," said Leon. "Not since . . . Betty, when was that, honey?"

"Oh, I don't . . ." Bet was almost at the end of her tether, but she took a sip of her sweet coffee and tried to think.

"I guess I saw them Sunday? Yes, yesterday morning . . . or maybe it was night? Carmen dear, do you remember?"

"Want something to eat, Mommy?" Carmen said with an anxious look at me.

"No . . . no."

Carmen touched her mother's hair for a second and then busily got some food out of the refrigerator—butter and a jar of preserves, a bowl of enormous golden peaches. There was a package of rolls on the counter, and she arranged them on a plate, quickly setting the table with silver and Selene's white porcelain plates.

"Carmen, sweetie . . ."

"Mom, c'mon now, you should have a little something. Father? Please."

I sat at the table, actually glad of a bite of food. The post-Assumption buffet might have been weeks ago.

"Can't you tell me what happened?" I pleaded. "How any of this started? Did something happen at the farmers' market? When was that, Saturday?"

Leon kissed the top of Bet's head and stood with his hands on her shoulders. "You girls tell Father Giovanni here about the market and all and I'll stay upstairs with her."

And together, there in Selene's dim, quiet kitchen, mother and daughter told me what they knew. Bet, the coffee seeming to have partially restored her, took a deep breath and said that the Saturday of the market had dawned hot and bright, but with a fresh breeze from the northwest. "It was a beautiful day," she said in a dreamy, exhausted tone, "very warm, but with that tiny hint of fall that starts some years in the middle of August. I looked up into the sky that morning and I actually saw some of the maple leaves already starting to turn."

Bet said she'd been up and dressed before dawn. By eight she was loading frosted brownies and tall stalks of gladiolus into the back of the station wagon. Selene sauntered up the drive just in time to help her hoist two bushel baskets of tomatoes and zucchini onto the tailgate.

"Where's Carmen?" Selene said in a casual tone, climbing into the backseat to pull a basket from the other end.

"Oh, still asleep, poor darling; she and Victor got in from Boston so late last night, it must have been after eleven. Sissy, pile the tomatoes on top of the cukes, please ... She said not to wait. They'll come over later in the ... yes, good, just a little more ... Well! *That's* done!"

Bet slammed the tailgate and surveyed the filled station wagon with satisfaction, absentmindedly taking pink foam rollers out of her hair one by one, then putting them in the pockets of her skirt. As she did, she saw Selene looking up at the dormer window of Carmen's room. "Come on in and have some coffee while I comb out, dear," she said, heading up the steps. "Then we'll go."

By midmorning several hundred people were milling around the large grass field that had served for years as the venue for the market. They swarmed through the aisles of tables that sagged under the weight of all the fresh fruits and vegetables and flowers. Many people were selling prepared foods, jars of pickles and jellies and preserves and homemade candies. An immense display of pies, cakes, cookies, tarts, and pastries occupied almost the entire east end of the field.

The traditional flea market section had been set up in the swath of shade cast by the long side of an immense old rust-colored barn at the north end of the field. Bet and Selene wandered there for almost an hour, fascinated by the brave display of other people's sacrificed possessions. It was so sad, Bet thought, that they would let their things be seen this way, lined up in rows with small white stickers discreetly announcing the pathetic little price of each piece. Under most of the tables were large, dented cardboard cartons filled with additional items, those too large, too dirty, or too strange to claim a place on the table.

"Oh, aren't these *cute!*" Bet exclaimed. They were in front of a folding table covered with an assortment of crocheted toilet paper covers, all in shades of mauve or pink, as if the maker had gotten a bargain on the yarn.

"I got a green theme, too," the woman behind the table said to Bet, reaching under the overhang of her plastic lace tablecloth for an apple-green cover with magenta rosettes scattered across the top. "It's just a dollar, dear," the woman said, holding it up with her fingertips as if it were a tiny garment.

"Well," Bet said, looking at one that was done in shades of peach and cerise. "I don't know..."

"Two for a buck-fifty?"

"Oh... okay, sure. Here." Bet laughed and reached into her pocket for the money.

"Those things are garbage, Bet. Jesus," Selene hissed as they turned quickly away from the woman's thanks.

"Sissy, please," Bet said, stuffing the toilet paper cozies down into the bottom of her canvas shopping bag. "My goodness, you're in a stinky mood today," she whispered into Selene's ear. "You know these folks wouldn't sell stuff like this if they didn't need the money. It costs next to nothing."

A few minutes later, Bet went off to join her cronies in the baked goods section, but happened to glance back just in time to see Selene walk slowly around to the far side of the dilapidated barn. Over the wide doors, way up under the loft window, was a hand-painted sign:

J. C. ST. IVES ** BOOKSELLER

Bet told me the place had been there for more than sixty years. In the old days, on rainy afternoons when he was bored and out of sorts, Sterling would take Selene and they'd poke around for hours at a time. Old Mrs. St. Ives, widow of the original proprietor, still kept it open from April to October; at least two or three of her many grandkids were constantly prowling the aisles with big feather dusters, tidying up the thousands of moldy books under the old lady's eagle eye. She sat in an uncushioned rocking chair all season long, wrapped, even on the hottest days, in a fringed shawl. She knew the exact placement, provenance, and value of every book she had, and she presided over her offspring and her customers without moving a muscle.

Selene told Bet later that she'd stood just inside the door, waiting for her eyes to accommodate to the dimness. She drew the fetid air deeply into her nose—the ripe, slightly sweet scents of old hay and manure and of the ancient, rotted leather of bindings. The books were on waist-high trestle tables, each one rimmed with a lip that had been nailed on to keep the books from falling off. There were small signs on short stakes as in a garden, each one hand-lettered in faded copperplate script: LITERATURE, TRAVEL, HISTORY, WITCHCRAFT AND THE OCCULT, SCIENCE AND NATURE, ART.

Selene went slowly over to the travel table, well aware that Mrs. St. Ives was following her with her small, pale eyes, but damned if she would look in her direction. The books there were a neatly kept but shabby assortment of old Baedekers and Michelins, some decades out of date, though interesting for that alone. She picked them over at her own pace, opening several, looking at the photographs of travelers in business suits and pillbox hats, their own guidebooks in their hands, staring up at the Pyramids or the Statue of Liberty.

Selene tossed an old, cracked edition of *The Castles of Surrey* back into its bin, suddenly feeling very listless and all too aware of the unmoving gaze of the old woman in the rocking chair. Feeling slightly ill from the sickly smells, she turned to go, but just then, in the corner of another bin, under a little yellowed sign that said BOTANY in spidery letters, something caught her eye. The title was printed in faded gilt on the smooth brown cover of the book: *Fruit in Art.* She stood there for a moment, fanning the pages, inhaling the musty scent that rose from them, before she carried it to the door.

"How much?" Selene said, looking into the old woman's face, turning the book so she could see the title.

The woman said nothing.

"How much?" Selene asked again, holding out the book, waving it ever so slightly.

"You're Sterling Catcher's girl, aren't you?" Mrs. St. Ives said in a low, papery voice. "The elder one."

Selene didn't answer at first, feeling very annoyed but unsure whether to show her irritation. She just nodded.

The old woman made a gesture with her hand under the flowered shawl, a movement that Selene saw but did not care to interpret.

"I don't want your money," she said and turned her eyes away, focusing on the brilliant green patch of sunlit trees beyond the door. "Just take it if you want it."

Outside, Selene stood squinting into the brightness, gripping the book with both hands, filled with anger. A moment later, without realizing she had moved at all, she found herself around the corner of the book barn, facing the teeming market space. She shaded her eyes with her hand, looking for Bet, hoping she could convince her to go home.

The noon sun poured down on the vegetables and pies and antique kitchen tools and paperback romances and gimcrack mementos and pyramids of fruit arranged in brilliant rows that stretched all the way across the grass. Selene made her way through the crowd to the southwest corner, where most of the fruits and vegetables were being sold.

There were pears, peaches, nectarines, Bing cherries the size of Ping-Pong balls, bunches of carrots and onions, yellow and red and green bell peppers, beets and radishes, grocery bags overflowing with tomatoes and squash, and wicker baskets heaped with zucchini and cucumbers and peas in their pods.

Some of the fancier produce was wrapped in squares of green tissue paper or arranged in bright symmetry on beds of gold excelsior. On one table, enormous bouquets of broccoli and cauliflower were decorated with ribbons and bows, the entire design rimmed with cherry tomatoes. Under a yellow beach umbrella an old man sat drinking whiskey from a paper bag as he watched over his display of green apples and red potatoes. Across the narrow aisle from him a young boy was offering varieties of grapes from one of the small vineyards out toward the Vermont border; they were piled in Dionysian splendor on a long table covered with a "Merry Christmas" tablecloth.

And corn! Cartons and baskets and washtubs and plastic laundry carts overflowing with long thick ears, the brown and gold silk spilling out. Ten ears for half a dollar. One woman had painstakingly arranged about a hundred ears in an elaborate crisscross pattern that reminded Selene of the pioneer log-cabin building set Carmen had loved to play with years and years ago. The woman had shucked the top layers of the ears to show the rows of gleaming golden teeth.

And sunshine blasted down on everything, heightening the colors and the hot vegetable odors of the corn and artichokes and beets. The subtlest hint of rot, a sweet, ripe smell, hovered over everything in a thin, invisible cloud.

"And that's where I found her," Bet said, slowly eating pieces of a peach that Carmen sliced for her. "She'd been so tense and antsy all day, I was starting to worry about her, but when she told me about that bizarre incident in the bookstore, well, I knew it was time to start thinking about getting home."

Bet said she had been just a few yards away behind one of the large trestle tables, her purchases in plastic sacks and brown paper bags all around her, when she saw Selene looking with such an odd fascination at the displays of corn.

"Sissy! Oh, thank goodness! Look at this—isn't it simply gorgeous?" she cried, reaching into her big Jordan Marsh shopping bag for a large pear, already exquisitely ripened.

"Lovely. You about ready to go? It's too bloody hot out here, Bet. C'mon." Selene bent and grasped the handles of the nearest bag. "This stuff'll rot if you don't get it home. Oh, Christ, what's in here?" The heavy bag slumped to the ground and the twine handle pulled out of its fastening.

"Melons," Bet said, reaching for a huge, slick-skinned globe of honeydew. "And I have cantaloupe, too, and six . . . no, seven . . . muskmelons. Leon adores muskmelon, and look, Frieda Willis had strawberries, this late, imagine? I got some for Carmen. And plenty of corn . . . look!" Bet was on her knees opening each bag in turn, laughing up at Selene with delight.

"How are we going to get this stuff in the car?" Selene said, reaching for a bag full of corn, the tassels sagging over the rim.

"Bit by bit, I guess." As best she could, Bet straightened the sides of the Jordan Marsh bag, now filled with pears and peaches, and gave a dollar bill to a woman in a cobbler's apron. "Unless Victor and . . . oh, look! There they finally are! Carmen! Carmen dear! Over here, honey!"

Bet stood up, waving her sun visor toward the mountainous display of dahlias and chrysanthemums where Carmen was standing with Lido and Victor. Lido, wearing a wide raffia hat decorated with yellow flowers, put her arm around Carmen's shoulders, pointing to Bet and Selene.

Dwight stood just behind the other three, expressionless, his arms folded across his chest, eyes narrowed only slightly against the light.

"Carmen! Over here, sweetheart," Bet called again, finally getting Carmen's attention.

There was a flurry of greeting and exclaiming, Bet insisting that everyone admire all her vegetables and fruits. When they had done so to her satisfaction, she announced that she'd picked up more than enough for everyone, and she wouldn't hear one word about it. If the kids would just help her get it all into the station wagon, they could go off and enjoy themselves without having to worry about buying any more.

"How wonderful of you," Victor said, his hand gently touching Bet's shoulder. He and Carmen filled a borrowed wheelbarrow with all of Bet's purchases while Lido supervised, adding a large bag of grapes she had bought herself to the top of the pile. Carmen, hugging Bet's beautiful watermelon, which would not fit in the wheelbarrow, ran off toward the car, and Victor, laughing, grasped the handles and ran after her.

"Where was Selene?" I said, not sure why I asked.

Carmen shrugged. "Just watching, I guess. She and Dwight were standing off to the side and a few minutes later she and Mom went home, right, Mom?"

Bet nodded and took a deep, silent breath.

"Victor and Lido and I stuck around for an hour or so," Carmen said. "They had pizza and sausages and all that pastry, so we had ourselves a little picnic under the trees and then . . . I don't know, Father. I didn't see Selene again until, gee, I guess not until Dwight came over to get Daddy late yesterday afternoon."

"And Dwight didn't stay with you and Lido and Victor?" I asked, though I knew the answer.

Carmen made a face. "Are you kidding?"

Chapter Twenty-Seven

By midday, a steamy, unwilling sun had pressed through the clouds and flooded the air of the estate with a pale, shimmering light. It was sickly and indistinct, a washing-out rather than an illumination of the colors of the forest and the great field.

After Bet and Carmen went upstairs to sit with Selene, I went along the terra-cotta path to the *stùdiolo*. The heavy door was unlocked and I entered cautiously.

The large room was dim and humid and absolutely still. On the desk were piles of folders and loose manuscript pages, many yellow and ragged, and dozens of prints held down with rocks or half-full coffee mugs, some with actual paperweights, including one funny souvenir I knew Selene had gotten years ago in Florence. It was a snow dome of the Duomo, filled with water and fake snow—the kind you can buy in any one of the hundred tourist traps around the Piazza di San Giovanni. The Mantegna print underneath it was bent on one edge, all the corners curling in the damp air.

Papers and pictures also littered the sofa and chairs; several portfolios were in disarray under a broken chunk of terra-cotta tile on the low table by the sofa. On the east wall, books were tilted out of their places on the shelves; some had fallen (or been thrown) to the floor.

I stood in the middle of the dusty Persian carpet and swiveled slowly, taking it all in. The light seemed to ooze through the skylight, but it was an absence of darkness only, an excrescence of the brilliance that the sun could cast. The dreariness of it was depressing and sinister and had I not already been so occupied with my confused, unhappy thoughts, I'm sure I would have been horribly affected.

I went over to the tall, narrow south windows, which looked out to the side lawn and the edge of Sterling's forest. There, all along the floor, under the low window ledges, were arranged dozens of prints of contemporary portraits of the men who had once filled the streets and palazzos, the counting houses and brothels and piazzas of fifteenth-century Florence, Venice, and Rome.

They were aristocrats and artisans, princes and merchants, *condottieri*, divines and doges—and every sultry, hard-planed face looked, to my astonished eyes, almost exactly like Victor Bellacéra's.

Selene had obviously spent hours searching for his profile in Titians and Bronzinos, in Mantegnas and Parmigianinos, in frescoes, panels, and bronze medallions. She had seen his likeness in jaws and eyelids, in mouths and brows, hands, thighs, angle of neck and shoulder, and in the expressions—arrogant, thoughtful, alert, languid. It was almost as if the prediction of his coming was to be found in every one of those dark, canny faces of men dead five hundred years and more. But the horror of it was that I could see him, too.

The pictures had been carefully chosen; they were the most evocative, the most exact. Next to a stunning Andrea del Sarto portrait of a young aristocrat, Selene had placed the commissioned sketches for the monograph of Ludovico Sforza; these were the original renderings, all imaginary, of the great Sforza taking his ease in a Milanese garden. I stared into the black, charcoal eyes of my putative ancestor, knelt to trace the hard, vigorous hook of the nose with my finger, and knew that even in the moment she had placed the sketches on the floor, Selene had felt her own clawing, clutching fingers in that thick black hair.

In a line just in front of the Sforzas were several of the photographs she'd shown me some weeks before on the day I brought her the book of the Farnese collection. I remembered one of Piero seated on the stone edge of Carla's balcony in Florence, his eyes fixed on the haze of the landscape as if mystified to find it there.

There was another photo of Piero taken from the back, his solitary figure poised at the end of a long, dim *sottoportego* in Venice, the perspective created by the mouth of the passageway suggesting nothing so much as a tunnel, a look of finitude and enclosure. And even there, she had seen Victor Bellacéra.

One other picture was part of this fantastic collage. I didn't see it at first because it was propped up against the wall under the centermost window, as if presiding somehow over the Renaissance men spread out beneath. It was *The Death of Actaeon*: the Stag King and the Goddess he offended.

Slightly sick, nauseated with revulsion and distress over what I had surely never in a million years been meant to see, I wandered back to the desk and noticed something else. In the center of the mess, propped against the small brass easel that still held Carmen's beautifully reframed Fra Angelico, was a small volume covered in brown paper and neatly titled in gold letters on the front *Fruit in Art*. It was obviously the book Selene had gotten that day at the farmers' market, the one Bet had described to me.

It was the oddest collection. Many of the pictures were ordinary, rather poorly printed botanical illustrations labeled in Latin; others were second-rate reproductions of typical Dutch *nature mortes*, the sort with heavy, split melons and strangled game birds arranged next to tarnished urns and bunches of pale grapes. There were a number of contemporary (and very clumsy) photographic still lifes, and a few bold graphic sketches, brightly colored, of stylized apples, cucumbers, and squash.

I couldn't understand why a connoisseur like Selene would buy such an ugly book. The inescapable sense of it all was a kind of globular eroticism, a preoccupation with the roundness, the plumpness, the peculiar spacial quality of fruit. In every picture there was a full-to-bursting geometry that seemed to demand an analogy between the natural form of a pear or a melon and the shape of a breast or the swell of abdomen or buttock. This was a book compiled, I surmised, by someone teetering just on the edge of a fetish. I found it distasteful and embarrassing, even as I kept turning the pages.

Someone (Selene herself, of course) had cut pictures from other books and tucked them between the pages. Every single one was of a Renaissance Madonna surrounded by ripe globes of fruit; many were *Maestàs* or altarpieces, beautiful Crivelli, Bellini, and Mantegna renderings of the Virgin enthroned. I spread them side to side across the desk and backed slowly away to have a look.

One of the most beautiful was Bellini's exquisite *Madonna di Alzano*. The blue-robed Virgin was holding Her naked child on Her bent knee, gently, easily, with two hands. They were on a balcony with a still, blue-green Tuscan landscape behind Them. On the ledge of the balcony was a single pear, gold-green and perfect.

There were at least six Crivellis in the group, every one lush and Byzantine, from the opulent colors and rich patterns of the settings to the gleaming drapery of the Madonnas' robes and the ornate beaten gold of the halos.

Crivelli's fruit was most remarkable. His luminous, unblemished pears and peaches, gourds and melons were used as obvious symbols for the contemplative Lady and her pensive little Child. But in almost every one of his paintings the fruits were much larger than realistic size, suspended by vines above the heads of the figures.

My hand hovered over the pictures as if preparing to *pluck* the fruits from the pages. They were as beautiful as could be, but horrifying, somehow. The ripeness, the plenitude of the immense, heavy fruits seemed to represent something so earthy and, yes, unwholesome that I could not name it.

"But why pears?" Shocked, I knew I had whispered the words aloud. "There seem to be so many pears!"

The shape of a perfect pear, I thought. What is it like?

But then I noticed that in the center of my haphazard arrangement, without having particularly thought about it at the moment, I had placed Crivelli's wonderful *Madonna della Candeletta.* I picked it up with both hands and held it close to my eyes, drinking it in as if it were juice, some rich, pulpy distillation of the painting itself. The young Madonna, clothed in a dark blue and gold velvet robe, was gently touching the perfect golden pear that rested in the tiny palm of Her Son. The bower in which She was enthroned was decorated with huge pears and apples, cucumbers and figs. The Virgin's gown covered Her feet and was draped over the marble pedestal on which She sat, the lower step of which held a sumptuously decorated vase of roses and lilies. Beside that was one perfect, fallen rose and two cherries on a stem and, just below, the little burning candle from which the painting got its name.

Holding my breath, I touched the globes of hanging fruit with my fingertip and moved it slowly down the Virgin's rounded cheek and over Her little swelling breasts to the pear in the baby's hand. With a deep moan of feeling, shuddering at what I had done, I put the *Candeletta* back and picked up another Crivelli.

Here, the Child was standing on a red cloth spread across a ledge in front of the Virgin. She held His little bottom with one hand and the thin, elongated fingers of the other just touched His plump knee. Their halos were like heavy, metallic tiaras in which great pearls and cabochon sapphires had been embedded. The heads of both figures were centered between two enormous pears on one side and a firm, blushing peach on the other.

It was as if Their heads were fruits, too. The pears and the single peach were suspended, it seemed, into the frame from above the painting itself, forming a horizontal line with the Madonna's skull. The Child's face, with its rounded cheeks and narrow forehead, mimicked almost perfectly the heavy pears that hung above Him.

Starting to understand, I reached for the Tuscan Bellini I had laid on the desk a moment before.

In the Bellini there was only the one perfect pear resting on the edge of the balcony. It was so austere, so pious compared with the opulent Crivelli. The mood, the atmosphere was remarkably different in the two paintings and yet the symbol of the fruit was the obvious point of each picture, the powerful image to which my eyes were drawn.

What was happening? Whatever I was feeling, suspecting, had upset me terribly, but I couldn't understand why it would—why the Virgin, the Lady Madonna and Her Holy Child, surrounded by all this opulent fruit, would so affect me.

What is the pear *like*, I wondered, trying to look at all this more intellectually, thus to find distance and safety. With what could I compare it?

I thought the pear must symbolize something I couldn't quite remember. Purity? Or maybe it symbolizes the cross? I thought furiously, feeling tested, feeling confused, and angry at my confusion. And then, without in any way having planned to, I turned the Bellini upside down.

The pear on the balcony now looked like the nave and transept of a church, planned on the geometry of a cross, yes, but also . . . what? What did I see? I asked myself again. Trembling slightly, I held the upside-down Bellini at arm's length.

A pear is like *what*? The shape of a pear is like—ahh, God—like a uterus. It's like a womb.

I sank into the chair and let the Bellini flutter gently to the desk. And was this, then, the truest rendering of the Madonna, and therefore of the Great Goddess Herself? The womb? The bowl of life? Was a fifteenth-century Bellini painting only *technically* different from the bulbous sixth-millennium Goddess figurines at Tell Azmak?

I knew of course that the Madonna with fruit is everywhere in Renaissance painting. Selene had merely faced that knowledge, had brought together all those beautiful pictures of the Lady enthroned with Her Son-Consort and surrounded by symbols of ripe, powerful nature. Selene had searched for the essence, the idea of Her, and had had the courage to strip the details all away, to see that fruit—of the vine, of the tree, the bush, the womb—is the Goddess's symbol, as it is Mary's.

Selene knew that the womb is the core, the source of all birth and all rebirth—of renascence itself—and if you slice it open, you will find *seeds*.

This calling forth of the occult eroticism of the Goddess enthroned was Selene's doing. But *I* was the one who'd seen the image of a womb in Bellini's pear. *I* was the one who so readily found the metaphor in the lush shapes and tight, blushing skins of grapes and apples, figs and peaches and pomegranates. Selene's selection of the pictures had provoked me, of course, led me on, but *I* was the one who'd made the connection, and it was to *my* mind those images had come.

So this was the essence of her new book, her proof that the Goddess and Mary were one. She must have spent hours, probably on the night after the farmers' market—Diana's Day and the Feast of the Assumption of the Blessed Virgin—harvesting her books and portfolios of pictures of the Goddess with fruit. It must have been then that, finally, she'd understood the inspiration of the artists who had used the pear, the melon, the gourd to symbolize Her power. They knew that the idea of Her was best conveyed as a globe filled with seeds, densely packed.

I sensed that those beautiful pictures were the clues to whatever had happened to Selene, but it seemed impossible to piece them together, at least not until she herself returned from wherever she had gone.

Suddenly, I heard a slight movement only a few feet behind me and whirled in the chair, my heart pounding.

Dwight Desjardin stood on the other side of the desk. He had entered in his soundless, animal way through a door I had evidently left ajar. In his hand was one of Selene's makeshift paperweights—a large pink granite rock the size of a fist.

Chapter Twenty-Eight

gave her this rock," he said, turning it over and over in his powerful brown hands and looking at it as if he wasn't entirely sure what it was doing there.

"Dwight. My goodness. I didn't hear you come in."

I stood up, feeling irrationally but positively better on my feet, and looked carefully at him.

He was tanned and muscular, as hard as the rock he held; his blond hair had been bleached almost white from the sun and his pale gray eyes looked vaguely out upon the world, and me, from under smooth, winglike brows. A long scar just under his ear was white as inlaid ivory against the brown skin of his neck.

Ignoring me, perhaps not perfectly aware that I was there, he prowled the room with that surrealistic grace that I had observed before and to which others had so often alluded, remarking on the way Dwight had of slipping away into the forest, of vanishing somehow from a room or a conversation without being missed until much later.

I wondered aloud if he would tell me what happened to Selene.

"I didn't hurt her! I would never!"

"No, Dwight, I'm not saying you did. But can you tell me what happened Saturday at the market?"

I realized then that he was not unwilling to answer; it just seemed as if he didn't really know how to do it. But at length, in the abstract, hesitant way he had, speaking slowly in his deep, unused voice, he told me what he could and I filled in the rest.

He said he'd been unhappy at the farmers' market; it was not the sort of thing he ever did, but Victor insisted that he join them. The many smells, the crush of people, the burning sun, all confused and upset him. When Bet gave Carmen her fruits and vegetables and Victor took them in the wheelbarrow, Dwight stood to the side, not offering to help. He moved close to Selene, as close as he dared. She was watching Victor and Carmen with a strange expression on her face, and when Dwight came up beside her, blocking her view, she looked up at him with annoyance.

"Do you like my gifts?" he said, without preamble.

"Gifts?" Selene seemed to have no idea what he was talking about.

"The rock..." He cleared his throat and looked past her into the bright sky. "The pink rock, the one with all the lines... and the hawk feathers, and..."

"Ah." She closed her eyes and thought a minute. "Ah, the gifts. Yes, yes, the rock is beautiful," she said at last, turning to him and putting her hand on his arm below the elbow. With one finger she stroked the hair on his arm in the direction that it grew. He shivered.

"I keep it on my desk," she said, now stroking with three fingers, then resting her palm lightly on his arm. "It's very lovely. Didn't I thank you for it? No?"

Her hand moved again, a finger at a time, above his elbow. "It's beautiful."

"I didn't want to bother you," he said, his voice a low wind of sound, "but I wanted to tell you I took your storm windows out to the shed so I could—"

"Did you?" The cool fingers slid under the sleeve of his T-shirt.

"Isn't there anything else I can do for you?" he said. "Isn't there anything you want from me? I would do anything for you." He was afraid there was a rough, almost choking sound to his voice; he'd practiced the words many times but still failed to get them right.

"Would you?" Selene said. She moved past him toward Bet's car, her hand leaving his arm even as her shoulder grazed it.

"Yes," Dwight said. "Why wouldn't I?"

Selene turned back to him, smiling a little. "There could be something," she said, sliding her tongue across the edges of her top teeth. "Maybe there is something you could do for me. Come tonight."

"What did she mean, Dwight?" I asked, as softly as I could. He was obviously very distressed, either by his story or by having spoken at such length.

"I thought she might want the fruit, you know?" he said, looking up at me. As he'd told what happened at the market, he'd sunk to the floor and squatted like an Asian on the edge of the carpet. I remembered Carmen, or Bet, perhaps, once telling me that Dwight never sat in chairs if he could help it.

He said it was after midnight when he crept through the unlocked *stùdiolo* door and knelt beside Selene where she lay unmoving on the sofa, her eyes partly open but unseeing. The full Grain Moon threw angled beams through the skylight.

"I have your fruit," he whispered in his rough way. "You left your share at Bet's. I brought it for you. I'll cut it up, I'll feed you." He knelt over her, not daring to touch so much as a hair of her head.

She wet her lips and moved her head ever so slightly. "Go away," she whispered. "Go away."

"I brought you nine pears." He moved to lie on the floor beside the sofa, almost as close as he had been to her at the market. "Look."

She opened her eyes again, but she wouldn't look at him. "Leave me alone."

"I will do anything for you. Tell me what."

"Anything?"

"Yes . . . please."

"Then go." Her voice was soft, without strength. I imagined the one perfect Bosc pear Dwight must have had, pictured it held upside down in his strong, tanned fingers, a pear to match the one on the Virgin's balcony, less green than Bellini's, more truly golden in the moonlight. The slight blush through the skin was almost like circulating blood. A curled leaf still clung to the stem, which, vaginal and muscular, thrust up inside to the core of seeds. The rounded bottom was like the wet vault of the uterus, the transept of the cruciform church, the source of resurrection.

Dwight leaned toward her, his lips slightly parted as if begging for something, but Selene closed her eyes and turned her face away from him. Sighing, he placed the pear on her stomach, touched her outflung hair with the back of his hand, and left.

I had not fully understood that Selene's view of Dwight as a devoted, mindless slave was so completely in harmony with his need to be one. I'd been intrigued when she offhandedly mentioned all the strange tributes left by the *stùdiolo* door, but not until that moment did I realize that her opinion of him was as accurate as it was dispassionate.

I found such completely self-abnegating behavior very disturbing, but I knew that Selene reveled in Dwight's devotion, believing it no less than her due.

I remembered part of the conversation we'd had the afternoon we walked together in the woods. "I can't understand him," I'd said carefully, "not really. I've seen him at a distance so many times. Even today, he was across the river from where we were sitting."

"Oh, yes. He sleeps there most nights. Winter and summer."

A slow smile of amusement lit her eyes at my expression. "I suppose there are a lot of people who'd say Dwight needs 'structure,' needs to be given the direction he cannot give himself," she said. "That's all sanctimonious babble, of course, but to the extent that it might be true, he seems to find it serving me. He's always in the shadows or behind a tree wherever I go—always available, always there. I don't think there's a thing in the world he wouldn't do for me. He keeps bringing me little things from the forest, choice pine cones or a small jar of berries. That lovely pink rock you may have noticed on my desk is from last week. Naturally, those little gifts are trivial at best, but it's a start."

I had nothing to say to such a remark; it seemed to me she was spinning gold out of straw. But at the same time, and in her offhand, ironic way, she was telling me how badly she needed that utter devotion from a man. Victor Bellacéra was not about to give it. I certainly couldn't. Ludovico Sforza was five hundred years dead and Piero Corio (the last time Carla heard from him) was in Tibet.

What does that leave, I wondered, looking at Dwight. A schizophrenic boy? Surely not. Whether Dwight's devotion was as all-encompassing as Selene's queenly assertion suggested, I had no way of knowing, but the thought that it might be upset me terribly. But what in the world could she have wanted of him?

"Dwight, what did Selene mean when she said she had something she wanted you to do?" I thought I'd asked the question in a bland, even offhand way. But all at once he arched backward and stood up in a single, impossibly fluid movement.

"What else happened?" I pressed, reaching calmly to touch his arm.

"I don't know what."

"But when you ran to get Leon . . . when she cut her hand—"

"No. No! I wouldn't hurt her."

"Dwight, son, do you know what happened to the dogs?"

"I would never!" He choked as the words wrenched themselves from his throat. "I would never hurt her! Not *her!*"

And with that he flung out of the *studiolo* door and across the wide lawn and disappeared into the trees.

Chapter Twenty-Nine

n the middle of the afternoon I went up to Selene's bedroom to give Carmen a chance to go home and rest. When I looked in, Carmen was sitting in the plain wooden chair by the window, her elbows on her knees, chin propped on her folded hands, staring at her aunt's white face.

I gently touched her on the shoulder and, startled, she looked up and gave me a faint smile.

"Let me stay with her," I said. "You should rest, my dear."

"Okay. Yeah." She got up slowly and leaned over Selene for a moment, staring at the immobile features of her face before straightening up with a huge sigh.

"I've never seen her like this," Carmen said. "Never. I've seen her sleeping, of course, but never like this . . . gone."

When she left, I pulled the chair close to the bed and sat. The eerie, humid light that had oppressed the estate all day seemed to brighten, and then dimmed again. As I reached for Selene's right hand, all at once her lips began to move. I bent to listen, my ear inches from her mouth. And froze.

The words were, indeed, not Italian, as Bet had guessed. After a moment of careful attention, I realized they were the oath of the initiates to the Eleusinian Mysteries, the oath her father, as a young man, had taken at the Telesterion in Greece. The ancient words were low, almost inaudible, but seemed to be exactly what I had read in Sterling's manuscript of the cults of the Great Goddess. They were the vow of fidelity and silence.

"Selene," I whispered.

She remained quiet for a long time. Though she swallowed the small chip of ice I pushed between her lips, she never moved. I feared she'd had some cataleptic event, some stroke invisible but definite; I imagined a tiny blood vessel bursting deep inside that brain.

I have no idea how much time had passed, when slowly, so slowly, she began to move. I'd been at the window, looking out at the gloom, watching as the line of trees that defined the edge of the forest blurred into the misty vapor which swirled around their trunks, the leafy branches seeming to float into alien, disembodied forms.

When I turned back to the bed, Selene's eyes were open. She stared across the room and then at me. She reached for my hand and I let her take it, surprised at the strength in her grip.

"Shall I get your sister?"

"No. No, please."

Slowly but steadily, holding tight to my hand, she pulled herself into a sitting position on the edge of the bed and then got to her feet.

"Are you sure you're ready to get up, *cara*?"

"I'm sure. Yes. Wait downstairs. Please."

When, some time later, she came to me in the parlor, she was as she had always been—erect, regal, and absolutely alert. Her long, loose white linen dress flowed, unadorned, to her ankles. The silver hair was brushed back and held away from her neck with a silver barrette. Only the heavy bandage on her left hand revealed that anything had changed. She came to me, kissed both my cheeks, and stood back to look at me as if I were the one who'd been unconscious for more than a day.

"Where have you been, Selene?" I whispered.

"I'm not sure," she said in a calm voice, taking my question at face value. "I may have been in the Goddess's own world, Vanni. It was as if She threw a cloud over me and took me with Her. But the whole time I had the sense that there was some dark figure in the corner of the room, enchanting me. The Hecate in Her. Or in me." She smiled gently and touched my cheek with her fingertips. "I don't know."

I begged her to rest, to have some food, even a glass of brandy, but she would not. She took a thin white shawl from the back of a chair in the parlor and, at her insistence, we walked out past the obelisks and onto the county road. To the west, the early evening sky had lightened almost imperceptibly, a silvery glimmer seeming to emanate from the trees, the wisps of cloud, the road itself.

About three hundred yards to the east of the estate entrance was a narrow lane hidden by tree branches and a profusion of the wild red lilies, some still in bloom and more than five feet tall. There, invisible from the road, was an old-fashioned wooden bench covered with leaves and dust. Twining vines of dodder and honeysuckle had grown up around it. But the seat appeared sturdy enough and I brushed it off so we could sit.

With her right hand, Selene reached into her pocket for a cigarette. I lit it for her and she sat back, heedless of the creeping barberry that had wound itself over and through the rotted slats of the bench.

Showing no emotion to which I could give a name, motionless except for the hand that brought the cigarette to her mouth, she told me what had happened. She had deliberately set the stage for her story: the close atmosphere, the silent, cavelike enclosure of the trees and grasses. It was as if she was not entirely ready to emerge from the "cloud" she believed the Goddess had sent for her. Looking back now to that conversation, I think I see what set things off, what made her turn the corner, but still, even now, how can I be sure?

She told me that for days before the market she had thought of nothing but my invitation. "I spent hours, Vanni, with all my maps and books and old photographs of Florence, thinking what it would be like to walk those streets again."

The day of the market she'd been terribly distracted, finding herself riveted, at the oddest times, by visions of the color of the air in the Piazza della Signoria, of what Carlyle called "the deep indigo translucent skies of Italy." When I asked, she admitted she hadn't mentioned the invitation to Carmen, nor as yet made a decision for herself, but she thought of it constantly, she said, turning the question over and over in her mind as she wandered through the teeming market.

In only a few hours, she became bored and unnerved by the blinding heat and the oppressive, dizzying smells, the unpleasant experience in the book barn, and was eager to go home. But it had been just then that Carmen and the others had arrived.

As Carmen moved quickly through the crowd toward her and Bet, Selene watched the light grace with which she seemed to slide past the tables, the healthy look of her long, swinging hair, her laughing eyes. She moved backward and sideways, skipping, almost dancing, her sundress billowing around her tanned, bare legs. She had Victor by the wrist and he came willingly along behind her, smiling with an intensity of pleasure and compliance Selene could not remember ever seeing in a man's face. So obvious was his delight that Selene could not bear it that she had seen the moment at all, and quickly looked away.

For many years she had understood that Carmen was possessed of an absolutely pure, uncomplicated sensuality. From childhood, she had had the gift of taking immediate pleasure in her physical senses. Adulthood had unexpectedly intensified that, refining the tendency into a broader, more encompassing delight in the sensation of being simply alive. Carmen needed no perfume, no rich flavor, no sight or sound to call it forth. It was as if her enjoyment of each individual sense had been distilled into an appreciation of sensation itself that was almost primitive in its simplicity.

And now, her eyes narrowed against the merciless glare of the sun, Selene saw clearly how Victor Bellacéra's overwhelming and confident sexuality must have resonated with that—with Carmen's natural and earthy inner core.

Carmen's newly burgeoned womanliness was somehow enhanced by a childlike aspect she had never completely lost. As a consequence, she was able to reveal, if only by that uncalculating innocence, how a woman may best *be*, may most beautifully emerge from childhood into bloom, and wisdom. She was like a living incarnation of the changing phases of the Goddess.

"And then you and Bet came home," I said.

"I couldn't wait to get out of there."

If Selene guessed that I knew more than she told me of what had happened at the market, she gave no sign. She said only that she'd spent most of the late afternoon and evening looking through her beautiful art books, razoring out pictures of the Goddess with fruit, the great *Maestà* paintings that were, so many believed, the truest glory of the Renaissance. That the inspiration should have come from that shabby, vulgar book did not dismay her; she knew she must seize it when it came. Exhausted by her efforts, she had fallen onto the sofa, where Dwight, as he himself had told me, found her hours later.

When he was gone, she lay holding the pear he gave her, still thinking of Diana's Day and the Assumption of the Blessed Virgin, and of the paintings of the Goddess surrounded by Her court. She imagined the full

Grain Moon swelling in the western sky, the Goddess riding in Her course toward setting, while night Masses for the risen Madonna were sung and ended and all over the world the faithful blew out their smoking candles, one by one.

"I may have fallen asleep," she said simply, "because I think I had a dream. But I remember so much of it, Vanni, I believe I might not have been asleep at all."

Deep in the dream, she said, she had a sense of being touched, of her thighs and her breasts being stroked by an invisible hand. Soon the rhythm of the stroking turned into other rhythms, other cycles. She saw moon phases zoom by in accelerated motion; she recognized the flowering of trees, followed seconds later by autumn and silvery snow. She began to hear pounding and shouts and then the hooves of horses along a sea road, frightened into breaking the rhythm of their gallop by a monstrous form that rose from the moonlit sea, spitting foam.

Slowly, the foam congealed into a fruit, thickening with pulp and flesh and skin, and when it did the sense of rhythm came back into the dream. She became aware of the slicing of a knife biting through chaste fruit, deeper and deeper. At first, there was only a gentle sliding . . . and a stop. Then a less gentle sliding and a more sudden, more forceful stop. The knife was being pulled through by the contractions of the unresisting fruit itself, and a moment later she heard the sound of the knife's serrations scraping on the pit.

The fruit felt the sliding, the slicing, the splitting of its flesh; it flinched at the pressure when the pit, reached, was bruised and cut, yet willingly it enclosed the wet knife in its parted flesh, and the mouth of the wound filled with sea foam and milk and blood.

But just as the fruit capitulated, nearly in two now, split for sure, Selene sensed the aroma of forest in the air, the sweetness of baked pine needles and a stench, too, hotter and less sweet, as of heavy smoke, pungent with the odor of burning feathers. She almost woke at that, but the dream, like a feeding baby, sucked her down again.

Now that the pear, the nave, the womb was sliced and open, all the seeds slid wetly out, just as the knife had slid so wetly in. At first only tiny roots and yellow gouts of pulp came out, fibrous yet supple, but soon after them came flowers—red-blooming lilies, dahlias, and peonies— still clinging to the vines that anchored them. She felt a surge, a ripping away, and one enormous peony exploded into a thousand *Annunciations*, the doves and lilies, angels and Madonnas flying into every corner of the room. One tall Virgin crashed into the floor, and as Selene watched, amazed, Fra Angelico's Madonna, soaking wet, threw off Her long blue robe and revealed Herself, clad only in a short chiton, one breast exposed. Her quiver of arrows, embossed with silver, was hanging down Her back. She reached into the gaping fruit and, long bare legs braced for leverage, pulled with all Her strength and, gagging, grasped something in the dripping center of the fruit and yanked.

A host of giggling babies slid out, pulled by the ankles. Their wet wings, the feathers hot green and electric blue, fluttered in the cool moonlight, drying off, but again the Virgin tugged. The babies, still laughing, joined Her, and they pulled together, side by side, until out of the split fruit, only rind by now, he came at last: the Angel.

His powerful blue-black wings were drenched with foam. His gleaming teeth were square and ready. The Goddess, Her limbs trembling, leapt away and he reached into the pear's cavity alone, using his great strength to pull the last seed out of that wet pit: a Maiden, soaked with the juice from the rent fruit.

Exposed to air, the Maiden screamed and reached frantically toward the maw of the fruit that spawned her. Yet though it was empty and gaping, all pulp, all seeds expelled, just as her hand came close, the fruit clamped shut with the ringing sound of a portcullis gate slamming down on iron. *No!* the Maiden sobbed, pleading. *No!*

When they heard those sobs, all the doves came flying out from all the *Annunciation*s scattered everywhere, and with their gold beaks they split her skull. Arrows of light belched out in profusion, glowing and crackling, sizzling with sparks. The ruined Maiden lay there, paralyzed.

Then the Angel, his great black wings shining in the light from her split skull, came near. He plunged into her, his belly pressed to hers, the coiled muscles of his arms slick with her milk, lit by her sparks. With an immense, muscular tongue, he licked at the torn places where the doves had gashed her skull, and as he did he filled her with himself. As the Maiden awoke to his sucking kisses—Maiden no more—the beaming light flowed back into her head and she was born again. A woman now, a fruit, whole and sweet, she rose to meet him, filled with her own moist, willing *seeds*.

When she finished telling me about the dream of fruit and the black-winged Angel, Selene's breathing was ragged, her golden eyes, feverish since she began the story, hollow and dark. I had listened with sickened fascination. How could I not have known that this woman had whatever it took to dream a dream like that? All the affection, the love I felt for her, all the admiration, all the years of our friendship had not prepared me for such a dream. But it was the clearest signal yet that something had snapped in her, and what I had been watching for weeks was the elongated process of disintegration.

And though I felt responsible, I knew it was irrational to think there was a thing in the world I could have done, from the hour of my arrival in Boston months before to that very moment, to change a thing, to forestall or alter one instant of her vibrant, anguished life. But I knew I was more than a witness. I was somehow an accomplice, too. But to what? Had I missed some clues? Ignored them? Wasn't there anything at all I could have done for her? More to the point, was it too late?

I knew I'd been too smooth a vessel. All her stories had sluiced down my polished, willing gullet and, mesmerized, I'd offered no resistance; I hadn't uttered one distracting word. Yes, I had been fairly doubtful at times, been horrified, disbelieving, scandalized, moved to tears. But skepticism doesn't really count if you keep it to yourself.

A moment later Selene stood up from the bench and, reaching for my hand, led me back along the county road and through the obelisks.

The air had freshened and the waning full Grain Moon was rising in the southwestern sky. She appeared stark white that night, almost platinum. We passed the Poynsetter house, way off to the left, and I looked anxiously toward the front windows, hoping they would see us and come out, but they did not. When we got to the rock, I sat on one of the boulders at the base, but Selene stood on the path, looking across the darkening field.

Frowning at her own unspoken thoughts, she reached into her pocket for another cigarette, slowly rubbing it between her fingers before she put it in her mouth. She found a match and struck it on the edge of the rock, holding it straight up in the air, staring, fascinated, as the blue heart of the flame beat and shuddered in her hand. I watched her with held breath, but then, abruptly, she lit the cigarette and dropped the spent match on the road.

"I think it was the heat and color of the Renaissance that attracted me so much," she said quietly, reaching out to touch one of the long-stemmed red lilies still growing by the rock. "The hot, wet frescoes, the gilded angel wings, the Byzantine gold leaf of the Virgin's halo in the Martini *Annunciation*, the bright, sunny palazzos—the color of the fire in which Savonarola's bones were melted—all of it was hot and blinding, and I knew that it could sear me, polish me . . . and make me more powerful than my father."

She paused with her mouth slightly open and took a deep, shivering breath.

"And of course," she went on, "as you know, that all came true. There were years that I was more famous than my father had ever been. I was filled with the Renaissance the way the Angel filled Mary; I was pregnant with it, mad with it.

"I thought I had exceeded what he'd done, that because I'd kept myself celibate as he had not, and been so single-minded, that I was invulnerable to everything and the Goddess would deny me nothing. But what filled me up, of course, was pride. Nothing more."

She turned and looked carefully at me. "You, better than anyone," she said softly, "know how the ego *blooms* with chastity, because then you make love only to yourself, to your own mind. There is such a narcissism to it, Vanni, isn't there? You know the lure, the *temptation* of it, don't you?"

I couldn't say a word. I wanted to, thought I must, but nothing came out. Selene yanked a lily out by its roots and paced slowly back and forth in front of the rock.

"I have been pregnant with pride all my life. I thought that because I was chaste and cold, dominating everyone around me, beholden to no one, that I could do anything I wanted. But I've deceived myself."

She plucked a petal off the lily and looked up at the sky. "Vanni, listen to me. I have to get Carmen away from Victor; it's all gone on far too long. I am going to accept your lovely invitation, my dear, and in the morning I'm going to call Carla and tell her we'll be there next week."

"We?"

"Of course, yes. I'm bringing Carmen with me. I've already spent hours working out our itinerary. I'm going to write in the mornings and treat Carmen to a divine new restaurant for lunch and then to a different museum or gallery every afternoon. It will be *wonderful*."

At first, I was too shocked to speak. "But Carmen has her own life now, Selene," I said after a moment, as gently as I could. "She must make the decision for herself."

She turned and glared at me. "No, Vanni, she cannot stay here!"

I got up and took her shoulders in my hands. "We've been pretending, no? Something happened, something terrible. Selene, tell me what it was."

At that she put her head down, closed her eyes against whatever she remembered, and then looked up again, straight at me, her eyes blazing with amber light. "I watched that bastard ruin my girl."

Chapter Thirty

y God!" I said. "Selene, what are you talking about? What do you mean? Victor?"

"You think I don't know what he is?" she said angrily, waving the lily in vicious, sweeping arcs through the still air.

"Selene!"

"You don't understand. I saw ... I saw ..." She raised her arm as if to strike me, but lowered it almost at once.

"Selene," I said carefully, "what happened after Dwight brought you that fruit?"

"He told you that?" She growled the question into my face.

"Yes, he did. I was in the *studiolo* this morning and he came in. You must know I saw the pictures on the floor," I said, suddenly more sure of myself, "the Renaissance portraits and the old photos from Italy. *The Death of Actaeon.*"

She whirled on me, her eyes narrowed, blazing. "You didn't."

"Ah, Selene, you know I did."

When I said that, she took a deep, slow breath, looking at me with what may have been relief. "Yes, Dwight came ... very late that night. I don't know exactly when," she said more calmly. "I kicked him out."

"I know."

"I woke up about two in the morning," she said with a sigh. "I think it was at least that. I gathered some things from the desk and whistled to the dogs. The Grain Moon was almost full."

She said that when she reached Victor's house, she went round to the kitchen door, not really surprised to find it unlocked; when she went in she pulled it firmly shut behind her. The room was silent and hot, the humid moonlight slanting through the window. By the sink were the remains of a meal—soft cheese, a loaf of mill-ground bread, a jar of black olives, only four remaining, and fruit.

There were bowls and baskets filled with peaches and pears. They were the ones Bet bought that afternoon, but the day had been so hot that a few had ripened to the brink of rottenness. There was a pomegranate, partly peeled, on a white plate stained with its red juice and littered with the tiny seeds, to which small bits of the fruit's flesh still clung. On another white plate was half of a large Bosc pear, the twin of the one Dwight had given her. The dark skin was slightly roughened, the stem thick and straight. Resting on the edge of the plate was an old-fashioned fruit knife with a beautifully curved mother-of-pearl pistol handle. The pear half lay on its side, showing the knife's serrated pattern in its flesh, the exposed belly of seeds.

Selene took the knife and ran her tongue carefully along the edge, tasting both pear and pomegranate. Then she cut a slice from the pear half and speared it with the point of the knife, pulling the fruit away with her teeth. Only after she felt it in her mouth did her lips close over it. It was sweet as sugar, gritty with the hours that had passed since it first felt the knife. She picked up the open pomegranate and licked its inner cut surface, bursting one of the globules of the fruit with the force of her tongue.

She had with her a box in which she had saved the slashed and bloodied remains of her father's pictures of Aphrodite, those she had not destroyed in the fireplace. She opened it and stirred the fragments with the pistol-handled knife, seeing, even in the dim moonlight, a pink nipple, a trapezoid of pubic mound, a curve of lip, of thigh, of breast sliced, as it seemed, clean from the ribs. In her pocket, wrapped in a small white handkerchief, she had three strands of Victor's hair.

I realized she must have taken the hairs the same night she did... whatever she had done with the shirts in Victor's closet. The notion appalled me, but Selene ignored my expression and made no reference to whatever she may have guessed I knew.

"I placed the folded handkerchief in the box," she said in a precise, matter-of-fact tone. "Then I added the remains of the pomegranate and three of the black olives."

She then selected three overripened pears, the ones that gave between her fingers as she took them from their basket. A large peach nearly burst in her hand, the skin ruptured and dark, and she took that too, slowly licking the thick puree off her palm. Finally, she took the knife, running the tip of her tongue one last time along its length. Outside again, she called to Savo and moved silently away.

When they reached the oval in the forest clearing, the dogs lay down before every third stone, each knowing her accustomed place. The fuchsia rim of the sky showed clearly past the nave-like wall of trees that ringed the sacred space to the west. To the east, the moon sailed through the blackness of the night.

Selene took the half-eaten pomegranate and the shredded, bloodstained pieces of the Aphrodite paintings and arranged a small portion of each on a bed of dry, crumpled leaves on the nine stones the dogs were guarding, asking the Goddess, nine times, to find pleasure in the offering.

Then, with Victor's knife, she cut the olives, the rotten peach, and the pears into nine portions; she took the strands of Victor's hair, divided them equally, and imbedded the pieces, one at a time, into a slice of pear. Slowly, she went counterclockwise around the circle and placed each new offering in a nest of small twigs in the center of the stone just past the ones on which sacrifices were already arranged. The dogs lay silent as she passed; not even Tish whimpered in the darkness.

She went to the hollowed-out space in the center of the oval and dug deep until she found the shallow silver basin she kept there, hidden with clumps of moss and sodden leaves and decaying wood flowers. From the basin she took several loose matches kept in a small metal box and carefully went round the circle, clockwise this time, and set fire to each of the sacrifices.

When the purifying fires were all well lit and the eighteen sweet, smoky plumes began to rise into the moist air of the clearing, Selene took the knife again and with a firm stroke cut into the tips of the middle and ring fingers of her left hand, letting several drops of blood drip onto each of the nine remaining stones. Lastly, she took a small flask from her pocket and poured a few drops of oil on each of the eighteen slow-burning offerings. The nine stones she had sprinkled with drops of her own blood she left alone, knowing the Goddess demanded only that blood be spilled, not burned.

When she was done, she wiped her bloody fingers on the white hand-kerchief that had held Victor's hair, and placed the stained cloth on the stone before which Savo lay.

The moon, seeking to judge the beauty of these gifts, slid through the highest branches, passing quickly away from a small cloud to show the Goddess's approval. Selene, watching Her, lay down in the center of the oval, enclosed by the warm, fruity scent of the fires. She saw the smoky twirls of air cant slightly west with a new, stronger wind, and though she kept her gaze on the bright moon, her eyes, heavy with smoke and the rich odors that rose all around her, soon closed, perhaps in sleep, perhaps in some other abatement of consciousness for which there is no name.

With a wondering expression, as if she scarcely believed she was telling me all this, Selene lit a cigarette and inhaled it with a deep shudder before she continued. She said that although she was lying on the soft, giving earth of the sacred clearing, it seemed to her she lay on marble, on the floor of some great high-ceilinged chamber, a museum gallery, perhaps, or the salon of a grand old *palazzo*, rotting from the embrasures of the ceiling down, only the exquisite antique floors intact. Was this the Tribuna of the Uffizi, the air rosy with the shine off the marqueteried marble? Was it the inlaid loggia of the chapel of the Medici princes, the weathered tiles of the San Marco? Or might it be one of Ludovico Sforza's private apartments, the floors invisible under dense black pelts and thickly woven velvets, but marble all the same?

"Suddenly," she said in a low whisper, her eyes on the sky, "I saw great floating shapes of ancient trees: thin spires of cypress, oaks and banyans twisted like immense mandrakes—and poison yew, mysteriously carved to resemble lilies and phalluses—all growing from the marble. The shapes writhed and tangled themselves into swaying jungle trees looped with thick vines that seemed to lengthen right in front of me."

Soon the men came, queues of dark Renaissance men like the ones whose portraits she had spread out under the windows of the *stùdiolo*. They crashed through the forest of mutant trees in iron boots that struck sparks from the marble floor of the clearing. The men loomed above her, their naked arms heavy-muscled, wet with the trees' sap.

First came the zealot Savonarola with his hawk eyes and tiny penis. Then Galileo, his hair matted, his beard afire, pushed through the trees, followed by the first sons of the houses of Strozzi, de' Medici, and Gon-zaga. Piero Corio came, dressed in black silk, hooded and armed, holding a raised sword, its handle studded with sapphires and chunks of onyx ore.

The host of the Visconti and Rucellai heirs marched with him, their scarred, golden skin falling from their bones. And finally the Sforza lord himself, Il Moro, swathed in a sable cape, the expression in his eyes uncompromising, irresistible. At once, she rose to meet him, spread her legs wide apart and reached for him, roaring, even in her sleep.

At that, Selene turned her face away from the sky and faced me. To my everlasting horror, I knew she thought, just for a moment, that I might be Sforza himself. She took my chin in her hand, slowly running the nails along the curve of my jaw, and, letting go, looked away again.

"But he would not come to me. He moved away into the smoke from the stones. I saw the heavy fur of his robe swaying from his shoulders. And I screamed for him, again and again, pleading, demanding. '*Sforza!*' I screamed. '*Sforza!*'

"And only then, only when I shrieked his name the second time, did he turn back to me. He threw himself between my legs, his mouth sucked at my cut fingertips. '*Yes!*' I heard myself screaming it, Vanni. '*Now!*' I shouted.

"But just as I felt him, oh! ice cold inside me, he pulled away—and ran. He ran!"

In one leaping movement, wet and naked, her powerful arms stretched out to him, she rose from the floor, and the blood from her sliced fingertips sprayed over him like fountains as the antlers burst from his soaked forehead, branching, growing . . .

Now! she shouted to her dogs, hoarse as Hecate. *Now!* she roared in the voice of the Sorceress, as the Sforza, bloodied and terrified, raced away from her. The nine dogs, howling, tongues loose and dripping, closed upon him and tore him to pieces, limb from limb. They ripped his belly away from his pelvis, tore his thighs from their sockets and his heart from its red cavity, and his wounds gushed blood until his eyes, black as the cruel, educated eyes of all the Renaissance princes who were watching, closed in death.

I was completely thunderstruck. This vicious dream was more tortuous, more erotic than the one of the black-winged angel born from a rotting globe of fruit. I didn't understand how she could stay upright, telling me these things. But then I knew it was the telling that had rescued her. I could almost believe she had come back from her collapse just so she *could* tell me. This "confession" was a bizarre act of self-preservation, but in all my years as a priest I had never heard anything that could compare with it.

It occurred to me that the wind that brought the dream of marble floors and savage princes and blew out the sacrificial fires was like the wind the Goddess had caused to rise at Aulis, centuries ago in the year of the attack on Troy, the year King Agamemnon's daughter was to be sacrificed. To Selene's mind this new wind, like the old, must have been a sign of Artemis's pleasure at her offerings, for the Stag King's fruits and Aphrodite's images had turned to ashes, consumed in the fire, swept away on the Goddess's great breath.

And then I saw it, clear as could be. Selene's dream of Sforza was a *rival's* dream! A dream of contests, competition, possibly of conquest as well. And if it was a metaphor for leaving Victor, for dismantling his "seduction" of Carmen, she, Selene, would be the unflinching instrument the Great Goddess wanted her to be.

"It was less than an hour to dawn," she said, "when I started down from the clearing with the dogs. Only minutes later I was standing at the rim of trees at the western end of Victor's garden."

Looking far across to the salon windows, she was not surprised to see, even at such an hour, a small circle of dim lamplight somewhere in the room. She went to the ornamental iron fence at the edge of the forest— covered, even in the middle of August, with saucerlike, blood-red roses —and paused, breathing through her teeth, relishing that moment of wait- ing, oddly reluctant to let go of the surge of anticipation that had pro- pelled her down from the sacred oval.

She ran swiftly across the garden to the place where the first steel beam joined the estate house wall and stopped again, hearing, so faintly, chords of light, stringed music. She moved forward, inch by inch, until her face almost touched the tinted glass, and peered inside.

The light came from a cluster of small crystal hurricane lamps set in a circle on the map table, surrounded by vases of field flowers. Selene could not see their color, only the long stems that arched out of the vases, each bearing its burden of some kind of heavy, many-petaled bloom she could not identify. They appeared almost like fronds to her, primitive and unevolved, yet elegant and pliant as they sprayed from the mouths of the vases on the table.

"The music was clearer then," she said, her eyes fixed and staring, not on the sky as before, but on the trees on the far side of the road. "It was a strumming, plucking sound that seemed to fill the air of the room, sweeping up into the peak of the cathedral ceiling, then seeping out through invisible flaws in the glazing of the wall. Slowly—I don't know why it was so slow—I became aware that Victor was there in the center of the room. He was on his knees with his naked arms held out in front of him, and his attitude was just like Sforza's when he...when he... aaahhhhhh...Carmen!"

"Selene!" I cried, grasping her trembling hand. "What?"

"She was lying naked under Victor on the floor, on a soft, dark covering like the black furs from my dream. Her face was shining, glowing like the lamps, and she was laughing, Vanni! Laughing! I could hear her.

"Victor reached for her with his open hands, his back so straight, all his muscles tense and hard, and she came to him with such...such joy, such *readiness*. All their movements were so smooth, so natural. It was as if they were dancing."

As she lay down under him, Carmen's small breasts seemed to rise, as of their own accord, to meet Victor's hands, each one fitting to perfection in the hollow of his palm. He held them like small globes of fruit, rubbing his thumbs back and forth over their nipple stems until he let one go and slipped the hand behind her waist to hold her firm. His mouth came down instead to hold the round, freed breast upright, his tongue then gliding from her nipple to her stomach, his black hair silky on her thigh.

To Selene it was exactly as if the burned pictures of Aphrodite had grown whole again. Carmen welcomed her lover like a Botticelli Venus: her white arms moved to twine around his neck, her hands lay open and assured against the dark skin of his back as her smooth legs drew him toward her, circled him, gathered him, her calf and thigh muscles taut and strong around him.

Selene saw one bare leg slide slowly down the muscles of his hip, saw the slim feet lock languidly together, and then, her mouth wide with delight and expectation, Carmen arched her back and rose from the floor to pull the Stag King tighter into her.

Selene, her forehead pressed to the glass, was unable to absorb what she was seeing, or to tear her eyes away from it. She watched, repulsed but eager for more, her breath grainy and coarse in her throat, but Victor turned with Carmen in his arms and bore her slightly out of view...and Selene lurched, gagging, from the window.

By the time she finished her story, Selene was sobbing in my arms; my shirt was soaked with her tears.

"I couldn't believe it! I couldn't take it in. I have no idea if I cried out, or if I looked again, or heard the music, or if I ever saw the color of the flowers on the table. God! I *watched* while they did that! And then I ran, Vanni, I *ran!*"

Chapter Thirty-One

For one devastating moment, I was afraid she would relapse into the cataleptic state in which Leon and Bet had found her on the kitchen floor. But to my relief, in a matter of only a few minutes, she managed, by some incomprehensible act of will, to compose herself. She lit a fresh cigarette, inhaled deeply, and leaned her weight against the rock, staring straight ahead.

"Several hours after that," she said in a voice rigidly controlled, "I awoke on the sofa in the *stùdiolo* with a headache so terrible I almost didn't perceive it as pain. I have no memory of coming back to the house, none at all. But it was obvious from the slant of the sun through the south windows that many hours had passed since I'd seen . . . what I had."

Gradually, she said, she became aware of blanched, humid light and the sound of the dogs, whimpering and scratching at the locked door of the *stùdiolo*. She roused herself and went out, finding the dogs standing stiffly in a circle around the mutilated carcass of a small deer. Savo had blood on her mouth, and bits of wet fur and gristle stuck to Lorenza's bared teeth. Selene stared into Savo's eyes for a moment, then turned her back and went down to the kitchen, moving slowly, holding on to the side wall of the house.

When she went inside, the door banged shut behind her and all the dogs raced down the terra-cotta path, then put their paws up on the screen and barked hysterically.

But Selene never heard them. Fighting waves of nausea and the blinding pain in her eyes, she leaned into the sink and drank right from the faucet. The cold water sluiced over her face and neck, soaking her hair and shoulders, but she drank until she'd had her fill, turned the water off, and stood for a long time with a towel pressed to her eyes and mouth.

And then she saw the food. Someone had left a plate of fruit on the counter by the sink. It was almost exactly what she'd seen in Victor's kitchen—a white plate with several pears and two huge peaches, all over-ripe, and a knife. As if in a dream, she cut a piece from one of the pears: two quick strokes of the knife and the perfect crescent fell into her hand. She carefully licked the juice off the cut edge and all at once the taste evoked a perfect memory of what she'd seen—the silken legs, the strong, muscular arms, the lamplight on thighs and mouths. She bit her lips until blood came, but there was no forgetting, no way to drive out the sound of plucking music and the swaying shadows of the spears of flowers.

With a groan, Selene took the knife and cut without hesitation through her left hand diagonally across the palm, from the base of the index finger to the crease of skin at the wrist. In one motion. The knife never left her flesh. The palm of her left hand filled up with blood as quickly as if she'd dipped it in a well. The gash was deep and true and straight.

When they smelled the blood the dogs howled and threw themselves against the screen door. It was impossible that they didn't bring everybody running, but only Dwight came, a second later, racing across the lawn and through the kitchen door. The dogs streamed in behind him, all nine of them, filling the room with loud yelps of terror and confusion, crazy with the smell.

When he saw all the blood, Dwight stopped right in his tracks and made a keening, wailing sound, shrill and high in his throat. A sound a woman might make if she saw her child sliced open right before her eyes. He ran to Selene, grabbed her wrist, and held the ripped hand straight up as the blood pulsed down and flowed over the beautiful golden pears that his movement had knocked into the sink. He turned on the cold water and held her hand under it, but it just kept bleeding, bleeding, the dark blood running onto the white porcelain. The slick coating over the fruit turned pink for a moment, but became bright red again. And then, with a kind of roar, Dwight lifted the hand and covered the wound with his own mouth. He had his other arm around Selene; her face was in his bare shoulder and she could taste sweat and dirt and something bitter like grass.

Pinned to him, she couldn't move, couldn't turn her head, but she felt his mouth on her hand, licking, sucking the blood away. Then he thrust it under the running water again and pulled back to look down at her, his gray eyes wide and horrified. His mouth and chin were so smeared with her blood she thought for a minute someone had slashed off the bottom of his face. She tilted her head up and licked her own blood off his mouth.

She wiped her mouth and chin against the skin of his shoulder and looked up into his eyes.

"You said you would do anything for me."

When she said that, he shivered and inhaled with a soft, high sound and she licked him again and tasted her blood and his sweat; she could feel his teeth and lips with her tongue, the stubble on his chin and cheeks rough against her mouth.

"Yes," he said. "Yes."

I don't think I've ever been more horrified in all my life. Nothing that she'd told me, nothing she'd "confessed" before affected me like that did. Nothing. "God in heaven," I whispered under my breath. "Holy Mother of God."

Selene had been standing with her back flat against the sheer wall of the rock. All at once, she came forward and dropped to one knee in front of me. Then she held up her left hand, palm out in a gesture like the Virgin offering a blessing. And in a single motion, pulled off her bandage.

And the wound was there, red and swollen, almost like the stroke of a paintbrush, clear against the faint blush of her palm. Even in the dim evening light I could see that it ran in a perfectly straight line, ending at the wrist, just as she'd said. She'd deliberately mutilated herself and showed the gash if not with eagerness, certainly without apology, without restraint, perhaps with satisfaction.

I took a deep breath and gathered her into my arms, my heart pounding. Could I have lived through all the years of my life, all the way to that moment, and not have known such things go on? That people have such feelings, such passions and rages and compulsions? I was a priest who had taken holy vows, consciously made; I had heard confessions of foolish, inconsequential peccadillos and mortal sins alike; I treasured convictions fiercely kept for decades. What did my horror at her story say of *me?*

What she was telling me was worse than anything I had imagined. In my wildest, bitterest, most private speculations nothing so primitive, so unthinkable had ever crossed my mind.

When I let her go, Selene reached toward me, held my jaw in the fingers of her wounded hand, and looked hard into my eyes.

"And that," she said softly, "was when I knew that my sacrifice of hair and fruit, even my own blood, had not been enough for Her. She wanted more—a better gift, a more powerful offering. *My* blood was not enough because it was my own. You know, Vanni, years ago I used to wonder if the three of them—Selene, Artemis, Hecate—are really one and the same. But I don't wonder anymore. There is no difference. It is all hell and they are all Hecate."

"Oh, Selene. Oh, dear God in Heaven."

I wondered if she and Dwight had had sex, right there on the kitchen floor. I imagined the nine hysterical dogs throwing themselves against the walls while Dwight, powerful, sunburned, steaming, plowed into her. Dwight might not be as powerful as Sforza, not as dark, certainly not as vicious, not part of the original fantasy, but what would she demand of him? *You said you would do anything for me.* She might consider it indispensable in a lover for him to have spilled enough blood to make him worthy of being the next Stag King.

I cringed away from my own thought, filled with shame that the seeds of such ideas might be somewhere in my own mind, but filled with guilt as well to realize that I could think in such a hateful way about this woman for whom I had come to feel such devotion, such love.

But there was no forgetting Sterling's retelling of the legends of the King Stag, of the ceremonies that went back, or so he wrote, to neolithic times, with the ritual bridegroom brought forth to do the Goddess's pleasure for one year; then, each autumn, to be massacred, eaten and replaced, his successor doomed to the same. Was there, in any rational universe, a possibility that Selene had plans like that for Dwight?

I thought of the succession of lovers Selene had had in the years before she witnessed the Annunciation of the second coming of the Great Goddess in the fresco at San Marco. I thought, too, of my poor cousin Piero, not literally killed but dismissed, certainly, his days as "consort" ended, only to be replaced by fantasies of Sforza and the Archangel and all the cruel, dark men of the Renaissance—all of them safely dead and buried and historical, until Victor Bellacéra came to heat her up again.

I walked forward into the center of the path, inhaling the cool, darkening air, sick with the knowledge that I had absolutely no idea what to do; I had wits for nothing except to be terrified of what might happen if I didn't get her away from there.

A moment later, Selene got up and came slowly toward me, folding me in an embrace.

"Selene," I whispered into her hair, "Selene, let me take you to Italy now. Even tonight. Maybe Carmen can...join us later. We'll go to Carla's, to Florence."

She stood back and gently pushed my hair out of my face with her scarred hand. "Why would it matter, Vanni?" she said softly. "It is all hell and they are all Hecate."

Heartsick, I followed her along Sterling's road to the edge of her own driveway and watched as she climbed up the wide stairs to the porch. Standing there, wrapped in that beautiful white shawl, she looked, well, glorious. She gazed out over the great field exactly as if she were an empress about to enter a crowded ballroom, or perhaps a famous diva, *la prima donna*, accepting a wild curtain call, refusing to bow to the screaming mob who'd gone wild with her singing. There might have been an audience arrayed across that space, there might have been an army—or the thousand becalmed ships en route to Troy, lined up for her inspection.

Chapter Thirty-Two

e took a carafe of wine and some glasses from the kitchen and went back to the *stùdiolo*, surprised to find Carmen and Lido standing by the south windows, looking around in astonishment at the mess.

When we came in, Carmen gave a little cry and ran to Selene, throwing her arms around her. "Oh, Selene! I was so worried!"

"I'm fine, darling, perfectly well," she said in her Isabella voice. She kissed Carmen's face and gathered her into her arms as if it were Carmen, and not she, who had collapsed into unconsciousness after slicing her hand nearly in two.

"Vanni and I have just been walking in all that marvelous air," she said, "chatting, looking at the flowers." Selene might have been speaking of a garden party. How could such blithe conversation come from the mouth of the sobbing, anguished woman I'd held in my arms only minutes before?

"I'm so glad you're here, sweetheart," she said, "because I have something wonderful to tell you." She sat Carmen on the sofa, kissed her forehead, and then took the Fra Angelico from the easel on the desk and ceremoniously put it into Carmen's hands before snuggling down beside her.

"Do you remember when you told me we could use this for all family announcements?"

Carmen ran her fingers gently over the carving of the frame. "Of course," she said with a slow smile, "of course I do. It was the day of the vernal equinox, wasn't it?"

I was sitting in the flowered chair, facing them both. Selene looked up at me with a beatific smile and back to Carmen. Out of the corner of my eye I saw Lido in the shadows by the bookshelves, her arms folded across her chest. Behind her, the sun, more than an hour past setting, still flung pale streaks of lavender across the southwestern sky.

"So, what are you announcing, Selene?" Carmen said, suppressing a small frown of suspicion. "Tell me."

"Well, I have decided to spend the next several months in Florence."

"Oh? Well, that's great—"

"Perhaps longer. Carla Corio has invited me to use her house for as long as I like to work on my new book. I'll be leaving from Boston tomorrow night."

That was news to me, but I thought it best to keep my own counsel, at least for the moment.

"I'm happy for you."

"But that's not the best of it." Selene laughed and caressed Carmen's face again. She had left the bandage off and I could clearly see the dark red line of the wound as she touched Carmen. "My surprise for you, my darling, is that you're coming with me."

Suddenly, Carmen became absolutely quiet. At first, I guessed she was only tired from her long vigil, from the anxiety of worrying about Selene. And, naturally, stunned by Selene's announcement. But, all at once, she seemed terribly, terribly angry as well. She stood up and the Fra Angelico fell soundlessly to the carpet at her feet. Her face flushed into dark, frightening colors and her hazel eyes clouded with fury.

"It will be wonderful," Selene was saying, seeming to be oblivious to Carmen's reaction. "I've made such marvelous plans. As much fun as you had when we were there before, darling, you will love it even more this time."

Carmen seemed frozen to the spot. For a few seconds she stood perfectly still, then she backed away from the sofa into the middle of the room.

"You can't possibly have thought I would go with you," she said.

She shook her head as if Selene's assumption deserved no further response and started toward the door. But Selene, rising from the sofa, was more quick to anger than her niece.

"You *are* coming with me, Carmen! We're leaving tomorrow night. It's not up for discussion."

Carmen had backed up all the way to the doorsill. Selene came up to her and took both her wrists in a tight grip. The pain must have been terrible.

"You're just being silly, and you know it. After a few weeks in Florence, you'll forget all about that man. He's nothing, Carmen. You know he's nothing."

Carmen yanked her hands away and opened the door. "Selene, I'm not going to Italy and that's all there is to it. I can't believe you thought I would leave Victor."

Selene reached out with her wounded hand. It had started bleeding again and a smear of blood showed clearly on Carmen's blouse.

"You *are* coming!"

"Of course I'm not! Oh, God, don't do this to me, Selene! Don't!"

Lido had moved away from the bookshelves and stood very still behind Selene, only a tightness around her mouth betraying what she may have felt.

"Carmen," Selene said, "you know I've always known what's best for you."

"Stop it," Carmen said in a low, bitter voice. "Just stop it. This is crazy."

Though she was trying with all her might not to cry, the tears of anger and confusion spilled at last. It was all the provocation Lido needed.

"Leave her the hell *alone*," she hissed into Selene's face. "Leave her alone, damn you. Knock it off with all this manipulative bullshit! Once and for all."

An echolike silence followed Lido's words. Carmen's tearstained cheeks reddened again. Selene went absolutely rigid. She glared down at Lido and in her eyes was the tiny satisfaction of seeing Lido lean away, just a fraction.

"You little bitch."

"Sure," Lido said, "go to Italy, go right now. Just leave them alone so they can have a life together."

"Oh, Lido, please!" Carmen, sobbing now, opened the door and leaned, suddenly overcome, against the frame, her hands over her face.

"Look what you do to her! Look!" Lido screamed, but Selene merely turned away, her eyes filled with contempt. "You miserable slut," she said. "Get away from me."

"*Slut?* Hey, look who's talking! Holy Christ, you've been chasing after Victor since he got here. It's disgusting. We all knew she stole his fruit, by the way," she said, glancing at me for just a second. "Can you believe such shit? Followed him in the middle of the night, hung around the observatory in the dark like a crazy person. Went in his *house!* Everybody knew it. Victor's too decent to do anything about it, but everybody knew. Poor Bet begged us to tolerate you, humor you. 'Bear with her,' Bet would say, 'my Sissy's suffered so much.' Who's the slut, Selene?"

"Oh, God! Lido!" Carmen screamed and ran out onto the lawn, Lido mere steps behind her.

Selene's face was a mask of pain and disbelief. I went to her and reached for her bleeding hand, but she wrapped it in a fold of her white dress and shrank away from me.

"They love each other, *cara.* You refused to see it. You wouldn't let me tell you."

"He's ruined her."

"No, Selene, he adores her."

She shook her head, refusing to look at me, and for once I did not implore her. I ran out and reached the driveway just in time to see the two girls running down the road toward Victor's house, Lido clearly chasing Carmen. I followed them long enough to see Carmen stop, hunched over, and Lido embrace her from behind. They spoke for a minute or two, Carmen obviously crying bitterly, and then continued together down the road to the estate house. I did not go after them.

The sky had darkened to a somber, luminous purple. I stood in the center of the road watching as the color deepened and changed. Though the afternoon had been hot and still, there was a freshness in the small breeze that sprang up, pushing gently at the tall fronds of Queen Anne's lace that lined the road. I heard crickets, smelled something sweet floating on the air. The first stars winked on, high in the sky, and the moon, golden now, had risen high over the field, casting a spectral glow over the swaying grasses.

I was just starting back to the *stùdiolo* when, all at once, a black dog came through the grass, stopped in front of me, and growled. It was Lorenza. A moment later two more dogs joined her. Three more. Four more. Savo. They were all filthy, their usually sleek coats matted and rough. Selene had named her dogs for the greatest artists and geniuses of the Renaissance, but they were nothing but wild beasts, now starving. They looked almost gaunt, the bones of their rib cages actually visible under their dull, black fur. I knew from something Lido once said that everyone for miles around was scared to death of them. "Selene Catcher and all those dogs," people used to say. "Why does she keep those vicious, untrained dogs!"

Remembering the conversation with Carmen and Bet earlier in the day, I calculated that no one had fed them since perhaps the morning of the market; for almost three days, they'd had no food they hadn't killed themselves.

They moved closer to me, fanned out in a semicircle as they had that day at the worship circle in the forest. Carefully, I moved backward, keeping my face toward them, my hands rigidly at my sides. It cost every ounce of determination that I had to move slowly and keep my hands low. At some invisible signal from Savo, they turned and trotted away, but when, seconds later, I raced around the corner of the house to the *stùdiolo* door, they were waiting for me, tongues lolling, eyes glittering with attention. Fitzi blocked my way to the door. She put her muddy feet on my chest, pushing and baring her teeth. Only when Savo snapped at her shoulder, drawing blood, did she move away.

I snatched open the *stùdiolo* door and ran inside. Selene, standing motionless by the desk, looked up when I slammed the door.

"Selene," I gasped, "listen to me. Please, go to Carmen. She's down at Victor's house with Lido. Don't let things end like this."

She clenched her teeth and glanced away with a grunt of disgust.

"We can go to Italy, just you and I. Maybe as soon as tomorrow. But please don't leave it this way, Selene. I beg of you."

She turned angry, blazing eyes to me. "He's a pig. I don't know what she can be thinking. He ruined her. I *told* you what I saw."

"Selene, Selene," I pleaded, "he's everything to her, and she to him. You know it's true." I paused, considered my next words, and spoke them. "Your vow of chastity, Selene, is not compelling upon Carmen."

"How dare you," she hissed, backing away from my outstretched hand as if it were on fire, "you treacherous fucking *priest!*"

"You said you were like your father," I said, suddenly filled with a flood of anger so powerful, so ambiguous I did not recognize it as coming from myself. "You told me that a few weeks ago, but I didn't understand what you meant. Was it this, Selene? That you can't keep that vow any more than he could?"

All at once, she spun around to face me, her arms outstretched as on a rack, her hands like claws. Her scream raised the roots of my hair.

"*YESSSSSSS!* I wanted him! From the minute I saw him. I'd sworn I was through with it, that I belonged to the Goddess . . . that I wanted *that!* But that first night at Bet's he took my breath away!

"I couldn't get him out of my mind. I wondered what his skin would feel like, how it would be to touch him, to have him lying in my bed, looking at me the way he looked at Carmen. I could feel him in my hands, I could smell him, *taste* him. I was physically *hungry* for him, as if I could rip his flesh from his bones and swallow without chewing. And I was horrified at that, Vanni, terrified!"

Selene broke off with a high-pitched, croaking sound and raised her fists to the black skylight.

"Yes, I went to his house. I waited for him in the shadows by the observatory wall, sometimes for hours, and watched for him to come back from being with her. I knew he loved Carmen, *my* Carmen . . . that he wanted her, not me. I knew that with all I've had in my life, I never saw a man look at me the way Victor Bellacéra looked at Carmen. But I couldn't let her have him. No matter what I promised the Goddess, I couldn't let that happen."

From sheer exhaustion, she took a rasping breath and splashed some wine into a glass, gulping it all down as if it were water. She filled the glass again and sank into the chair behind the desk.

"The night of the Fourth of July, after everyone else had gone to the fireworks, I went in his kitchen door."

Sipping slowly at the wine, she told me she'd crept through the back hall and up to Victor's dark, cool bedroom. She looked carefully about and then went to the closet at the far end of the room. When she touched the louvered doors they slid soundlessly on their tracks. She stepped inside and saw his shirts, dim shadows in a neat row. She gathered half a dozen of them into her arms and pressed her nose and mouth against the cloth, inhaling his odor. Here had his arms been, here his chest, here his smooth, dark flank. She bent to inhale the nipples, the waist. She slipped one shirt off its hanger and draped the arms around her neck, rubbing her lips along the collar, biting the buttons, one by one, as she slowly pushed the fabric down over her breasts and stomach, grabbing the soft sleeve in her teeth as it slid off her shoulder. Slowly, she rubbed the shirt between her legs, back and forth, then faster and faster, pressing her legs together over the fine bunched fabric, her breath coming in gasps through her clenched teeth.

When at last she threw the damp shirt back in the closet, she went to the dresser on the other side of the room. On top there was a tray with some coins, the odd button, and a comb with just three coal-black hairs. She took them and left as silently as she had come.

"After that night," she said, "I almost never left the *studiolo*. Those weeks were agony for me. I'd sit here hour after hour, reading over the old notes I had from my monograph on Renaissance altarpieces, just trying to lose myself in the work, but it wasn't any good. I realized only later that there had been long stretches of lost time when I thought of nothing but him. I would come out of a waking dream of making love to him, and find a fresh cigarette burned out in the ashtray, and the damp marks of my fingers pressed into the Titian or Mantegna or Crivelli print I was holding."

Such interludes left her frightened by the audible beating of her heart, or the last scream of the fantasy, still in her throat. Alert again, filled with confusion and shame, she would force her attention back to the Goddess, seeking Her face in scores of pictures of the Madonna.

Selene put down the empty glass and hooked her hands through her long silver hair, freeing it from the barrette that had held it back. She sat like that for many minutes and at last looked up at me, her face wet with tears. "I saw him naked with these eyes," she said. "The man Carmen loves."

"When did you know?" I said.

"The first night. At Bet's dinner party," she said, getting slowly to her feet. "How could I not? But it doesn't seem to have mattered, does it?"

She came to me and stroked my face gently with her scarred, oozing hand. I shivered at her touch.

"I will not let Carmen leave me for him. Never. Yes, I wanted him, I followed him, I've thought about him day and night for months. But I don't love him. Understand that, Vanni: *I never loved him.* And now I despise him for what he did to us."

I did not know what to do for such despair. My years of scribbling out my meditations on confession, penance, and forgiveness were useless, all of it nothing but empty concepts that defied what I was seeing.

I went to the window beside the wall of *Annunciation*s and looked out into the darkness. All at once, I saw Victor striding across the wide lawn toward the *stùdiolo*. The white clothes he wore gleamed in the light of the fully risen moon. An instant later, Selene saw him, too.

She took her shawl from the back of the chair and gathered it imperially around her shoulders. Her face suddenly, magically became a mask of utter composure, unlined, as beautiful as it had been when I first saw her seventeen years before. I thought only later that Selene knew this was to be her last moment of clarity.

Chapter Thirty-Three

A second later, Victor was hammering on the *studiolo* door. When he came up on the tiles of the breezeway, we heard the dogs cluster around him, moving restlessly on the tips of their toes, but when Selene opened the door, they drew back, whimpering, as if they were afraid.

Victor walked past her into the dimly lit *studiolo* and was all the way into the center of the room before he so much as glanced her way. He nodded to me with no more than a muttered "Giovanni." No greeting, no smile of pleasure at finding me there. He crossed the carpet with his smooth, powerful gait and looked around at all the pictures, the furniture, the jumble of books on the shelves.

At some point, Selene had moved the print of *The Death of Actaeon* from the floor to the small brass easel on the desk. Victor stood looking at it from a slight distance, frowning with distaste. Then he picked it up and ran his finger down the Goddess's leg, down the curve of Her bow, and wordlessly replaced it, giving no sign that he knew the gruesome story.

Selene stood calmly behind the desk and watched as Victor continued to pace the large room, noting with interest those objects that seemed to catch his attention and those that didn't. It seemed to amuse her to watch what she may have taken for discomfiture.

I thought I knew better. Victor was so furious, so enveloped by anger he could barely speak. It seemed to me he was fighting that anger, waiting for it to recede before his better nature, so he could state his business and get out of there.

He leaned against the stone edge of the mantel and looked across the room to Selene, meeting her eyes; but he was clearly not as perfectly poised, as in control as she. Selene saw it and was delighted.

"Not ten minutes ago," Victor began with a sigh, "I found Carmen almost hysterical on the steps of my house, Selene. I was so afraid to leave her alone, I sent her home with Lido."

"I have no idea what you're talking about," Selene said with a small laugh, dismissing his remark.

Victor took a deep breath and pushed his hair out of his face. "She's not going to Italy with you, Selene. It's out of the question."

Selene got up and went toward him, but Victor moved away toward the west windows, always keeping several feet between them, until he stopped by the wall of *Annunciations*. Selene came so close to him that the fabric of her dress brushed against his sleeve. I could see her breath ruffle the clean black hair that had fallen over Victor's forehead. She looked straight at his profile, her face inches away from his, waiting with growing impatience for him to return her stare.

"Goddamn you. Look at me!"

Neither took a breath. They might have been underwater, or at an impossible altitude. I might have been invisible.

"I know why you came," she said. There was the thinnest glaze of seduction over the syllables. I couldn't believe it. Even now it seems impossible to me that she would approach him in that way.

"Oh, Selene," Victor said in a sad, clotted voice. "I came here to talk to you about Carmen, nothing else."

"Carmen?" she said, as if surprised. "Whatever for?"

"The sooner you go to Italy, the better for everyone, but Carmen isn't going and I want you to be damn sure of that right now."

"You don't know a thing about—"

"How could you have spoken to her the way you did?" The words burst from his lips. "You must know how she loves you, but now she's terrified of hurting your feelings, of being hurt!"

"I don't believe you for a second. How dare you speak about my girl that way!"

"Oh, Selene . . . Selene, she's not your 'girl'! Think about what you're doing to her. It didn't have to come to this." With that, he took a deep, shuddering breath, looked blindly up at the skylight for a moment, and walked back toward the fireplace, away from her.

"Damn you!" she shouted as the anger spurted up. "She is *mine*. I have loved her all her life! *I* was the one who cared for her, who taught her everything. You know nothing about our—"

"Taught her what?" Victor broke in, his voice suddenly rising with the anger he couldn't hide anymore. "About a bunch of sick aristocrats who steal from artists? About those bizarre articles you write? Christ's stomach muscles, for God's sake? Who wants to hear that? *Nobody cares!*"

Out on the tiles of the breezeway, the dogs began to whine and growl deep in their throats.

"Look, Selene, I know you think of yourself as some sort of queen, *la grande dame*, the *patronéssa*, whatever, but you don't seem to realize that nobody else sees you that way—"

"They certainly do!"

"They damn well don't. You flatter yourself and you have this way of demanding that everyone else flatter you, too. Oh, I know how you spent years dining out on being the brilliant daughter of the famous father, lionized for your books. I've heard all about it from Bet and Carmen, over and over. All that was finished years ago, but you've inflated it into one big insane *illusion*."

"You son of a bitch!" she screamed, hurling her glass toward him. It fell far short, shattering on the floor.

When Victor stood his ground, not even flinching as a shard of crystal hit him in the leg, Selene let out a terrible shriek.

"You fucking bastard!" she roared at him. "You stole her from me, you lied to her, seduced her . . ."

"Selene, none of that's true and you know it."

Suddenly, Victor seemed terribly tired. The resolve, the surging anger he must have felt when he came into the room vanished before his need to make her understand that he and Carmen loved each other, had from the moment they met, and would forever. Quietly, his voice filled with earnest pleading, he spoke his heart: "Selene, I love Carmen more than my own life, more than I ever loved anyone."

Selene ran to him and slapped him hard across the face. "*No!* You don't love her. You don't! You couldn't possibly want her!"

Victor made a sound, an expelling of his breath, as if it was only by a terrific force of will that he was able to restrain himself from crying out.

"For God's sake, Selene, you're making a fool of yourself."

She could not have failed to hear the regret, the utter honesty in his voice, but she was beyond reason, I think, even at that moment. His resistance was intolerable to her.

"You're the fool if you think that girl is what you need," she whispered, her voice dense with fury. "We've both known that from the start."

"You should be ashamed," Victor said in a low, wondering voice, seeming to choke for a moment on his own words. He passed his hand through his hair and then turned abruptly away from her.

"Where the hell do you get the nerve to speak to me about *shame!*" she screamed. She grabbed his sleeve and pulled with both hands, tearing the fabric.

He shook her off, but she dug her nails into his arm and I saw his face flush with the sudden pain.

"I didn't come here to fight with you," he said in a voice filled with sadness, "to have this scene, to be unkind. But you have some terrific problems, Selene, and I can't solve them for you. Your money can't. Your old reputation can't. Please. Just go to Italy and leave us alone."

Then, to my everlasting shame, he turned to me. "Ah, Giovanni, how could you let her get this far?"

Without another word, he started for the door and had almost reached it when Selene ran after him, seized his arm above the elbow, and yanked him toward her with a strength that surprised him so much he almost stumbled.

"You can't leave!" she shrieked. "I'm not finished with you!"

"Christ, Selene, get hold of yourself—stop it!" Victor grasped her hand and peeled the fingers away from his arm, one by one. He was breathing in a strange, uneven way, as if his momentary loss of balance had unnerved him, frightened him.

At that, without any warning, Selene burst into gulping, tearing sobs. She began to beat on him with closed fists, pummeling his chest, his shoulders, striking out at him with vicious, unaimed blows.

Victor kept reaching for her hands, trying to make her stop, but she fell to her knees and clawed his thighs, his hips with her nails until he finally grabbed her arms and managed to shove her into the chair behind the desk. The blood from her freshly bleeding hand was smeared all over the legs of his trousers.

I have never known how it feels to see the object of one's passion turn away. I have protected myself from such knowledge all my life. But somehow, even in my benighted, self-imposed, self-affirming excuse for chastity I knew that what I was watching was not jealousy; it was not that natural or simple. This was nearly a loss of self, an elevation and a plumbing of feeling that was a vivification of the Goddess and Her famous rages. This was an emergence of the Merciless Diana who lies dormant in all women, waiting to be brought to life by an emotion that can change the force of wind, that wrenches up the tidewaters of the world. Maybe Selene was right. Maybe it *is* all hell; maybe they *are* all Hecate.

Victor stood leaning over her, both of them out of breath, panting like racers. I tore myself out of my stupor and ran across the room to them, reaching for Selene, but Victor held me off with one strong hand against my chest, pushing me away.

"I won't let you do to Carmen what your father did to you," Victor said between gasps. "She isn't you, Selene. You know nothing about her at all because you judge her by yourself."

"You still don't understand, do you?" she said with a wide, bitter smile of false triumph. "Carmen can't have any plans, any ideas about what she wants, because she belongs to the Goddess!"

Repelled, Victor backed away from her, but Selene, springing to her feet, faced him squarely and came after him.

"She belongs to the Goddess and she always did! You tried to ruin Carmen and *the Goddess hates you for it!* You've offended Her and *She will make you pay!*"

Selene's voice suddenly became a hushed croak. "You made me forget what Carmen was to me. You made us both forget. The Goddess will not want her now."

"My God, you're completely crazy," he said with frank amazement. "I didn't actually believe it, but you . . . you really are out of your mind."

Victor, in his anguish, had seen right through her and she knew it. By some stroke of insight, he had seen every secret, every prideful assumption, every treasured illusion and had exposed them with the fewest of words.

Suddenly, Selene's golden eyes flickered from Victor's face to mine and back again. She stood still where she was, facing him and shivering, her body stuttering with small jerks. I thought she might be having some sort of seizure, her posture, her muscles were so tense, so contracted. Her hands, still in fists, were held stiffly in front of her. Victor looked down at her with an intense, bone-chilling disgust I hope I never see again. I think it may have been that repulsion that affected her, as his earlier, simpler anger had not. He found her disgusting, and she saw it.

"You're out of your mind," he said again. "I have nothing else to say to you."

At that Selene's mouth stretched into a grimace of unbearable pain. The sound that followed was unreproducible. It keened and flowed through the smoky air of the *studiolo* and bounced off the glass of the skylight, only to come back sounding like an animal dismembered.

When Victor went to the door, Selene dropped into the chair behind the desk, so overcome by what had happened she seemed, literally, unable to move. But then I saw her look up and her eyes fell on *The Death of Actaeon*, on the small easel, and on the carafe of wine beside it. She stood up and moved slowly toward the door.

Victor had gone outside. The dogs crouched back, forming a kind of gauntlet, but he wasn't frightened, not at all. He just walked through, clicking his teeth at them as he passed. By the time Selene got to the tile walk, he had already started across the grass. I don't remember her picking it up, but the carafe was in her hand.

"*Victor!*" she roared. "*Victor!*"

She moved across the lawn toward him, screaming his name. When he ignored her, Selene started to run. Just as she caught up with him, she dashed the wine from the carafe into his face. It splashed into his eyes and dripped onto his shirt. He stood there, blowing the droplets off his face, slapping at his shirt and his hair. He gave her one dismissive glance; his eyes filled with loathing. I was right behind her, but he didn't even look at me.

Chapter Thirty-Four

ictor had gone eighty, maybe a hundred yards into the field. He moved with such tense deliberation, I thought he might be trying to walk off his anger before going to Lido's house, where Carmen waited.

Selene would have followed him, but I held her back.

"Let him go," I begged. "Let him go!"

She was trembling, shaking inside her clothes. In spite of my grip on her arms, she kicked out at me, sobbing and moaning.

"No!" she screamed. "Vanni, damn you, *no!*"

Suddenly Dwight appeared around the side of the house. He passed me and Selene without a word or a glance, and moved like an animal through the high grasses after Victor, his legs moving in long, even strides.

When she saw Dwight, Selene twisted away and threw the empty wine carafe at me. It struck only a glancing blow to my cheek, but stunned, momentarily blinded, I instinctively covered my face with my hands, and in that instant she lurched away from me. Though I recovered myself almost at once, when I looked up she was already across the road and plunging wildly toward the middle of the field, crying out in high, hysterical wails.

Up ahead, Victor had cut straight across toward the rock. Hearing Selene's cries, he turned, saw Dwight close behind him, and began to run.

All of a sudden, I felt a sense of wind, like a wave of darkness flowing

past me. It was the dogs, running like the wolves I'd dreamed about...
gliding, streaming through the tall, swaying grasses, through the moonlight,
pack-silent, black as a single shadow. Frantic, terrified, I took a deep breath
and ran after them.

But I had gone only a few yards when I realized that two shadowy
figures were running toward me from the opposite direction. I flinched
and stopped, paralyzed with fear that it might be more of the dogs, but
a second later I heard my name, and in the pale illumination of the moon
and starlight, I could see that it was Carmen, with Lido close behind her,
calling out to me.

When Carmen reached me, she paused, panting, and fell into my arms.
Both girls were obviously frightened to death, glad to have found me
standing in the high grass of the field when they expected who knew what
horror.

"We were at Lido's house," Carmen said, pulling her long hair out of
her face, "waiting for Victor to come back, but then we heard those awful
screams."

"What's going on, Father? What's happened?" Lido said, almost out
of breath. "It's Selene, isn't it?" She went a few feet ahead of us and I
saw that she had one of her father's many shotguns gripped tightly in her
hands.

"For God's sake, Lido, give me the gun!" I cried, reaching for it. "Let
me take it. Please!"

To this day, I think she might have given it to me, but suddenly, from
the direction of the rock, not three hundred yards away, we heard another
scream—a man's voice—deep and filled with terror. It was Victor's voice.

All of us ran toward the sound, the girls quickly outdistancing me, and
Carmen, fastest of all, calling out Victor's name, over and over, as she
ran.

And then the night exploded into chaos.

The noise was horrific. The sleeping birds had been flushed out of the
grass and were wheeling and shrieking above us. The foxes and all the
animals in the field were wide awake and screaming, and the dogs, no
longer silent, were howling in high-pitched, primitive loops of sound,
roaring to wake the dead, and through it all...oh, God... *Victor's voice!*

"Victor! Victor!" It was Carmen. She'd reached the rock ahead of Lido,
just ahead of me. Lido rushed past, yelling to Carmen to stop. But it was
too late for that. When I ran around the field side of the rock, I knew
why she was screaming.

Victor was backed up flat against the granite face of the rock, his legs held stiffly, protectively together, his arms up in front of his face. He was absolutely terrified. Five of the dogs were spread out a few feet away from him, snapping and growling. Every time Victor tried to move, one of them would spring forward, bite his legs or his arms, and dart back, waiting for the next time.

When Carmen ran toward them, into the fury of thrashing bodies and swishing tails and all that clamor, one of the dogs lunged at her, knocking her to the ground.

I ventured closer, looking for a way through to where Victor cowered behind the wall of leaping black bodies.

And then I saw Dwight. He was outside the crescent of dogs, frantic, trying to get to Victor, but every time he moved, other dogs turned on him, biting his legs, throwing the weight of their bodies against him.

And all that time, Victor was screaming: "Selene! *Selene!* Call them off! Call them off!"

Selene stood only a few yards away, erect and absolutely motionless, directly in the path of the moon's light.

"Selene! For God's sake!" I ran to her, took her by both arms and shook her violently, but she didn't seem to know I was there, couldn't feel the pain of my fingers on her arms. She was transfixed by the sight, her eyes gleaming with excitement.

Shouting his name, I ran back toward Victor, but the dogs turned on me, too, and Fitzi, I'm sure it was, seeing her chance, leapt at me with all the force of her weight and power and sank her teeth into my leg. I had her by the throat even as her jaws snapped closer and closer to mine, ready to tear me apart. I don't know where I found the strength to hold her off, but all at once she seemed to lose interest in me and galloped back to the pack.

"Selene!" I yelled again. "Do something!"

Then, from my blind side, Lido, sobbing wildly, ran up with the shotgun in her hands and pointed it straight at Selene from only three feet away. "Make them stop!" she shrieked. "Selene! Damn you, make them stop!"

But in the split second that Lido hesitated, obviously afraid of hitting Victor or Dwight or me, Carmen saw what was happening.

"Lido! *No!* No!" She scrambled up from the grass, ran to Lido, violently slammed the gun out of her hands, and ran back toward Victor, who was still pinned against the rock.

This time she plunged straight through into the circle of dogs, fearlessly striking their faces, kicking at them, reaching out her arms to Victor. But no matter how she screamed, how hard her hysterical blows landed on their flanks, their bared teeth, the dogs did not attack her, only used the strength of their bodies to push her away from Victor.

At that moment their postures—Victor, in his terror drawn close into himself, his body curled over in futile self-protection, his hands crossed over his chest, and Carmen, her arms thrust urgently toward him, almost dipped to one knee in the grass—seemed a grotesque parody of the Fra Angelico.

And when Selene saw Carmen, reaching out so desperately, and Victor so paralyzed by his fear, both of them surrounded by the dogs, illuminated by the flood of moonlight, she flung out her arms and cried up into the sky:

"*Savo!*" she screamed. "*Savo!*" And Savo rushed out of the darkness from nowhere. She knocked Victor down at a dead run. And then they were all over him.

I crawled to my knees, weeping with terror and stabbing pain, wanting to cover my ears against the blood-chilling sounds Victor made while they tore his flesh off him. He was shrieking, sobbing at Selene—over and over and over—begging her to help him, and Carmen was right there in front of him, facing the dogs as if she could protect him with her own body. Savo butted her away, but Carmen came back, again and again, fighting to save Victor, reaching for his arms, his head, anything she could hold on to. His blood was all over her hair, her clothes; she was soaked with it.

"Oh, Mother of God," I groaned in a whisper, "Mother of God, let him die right now. Let him die . . . please let him die." As if it were not far too late for prayer or blessing.

Just then I heard shouts behind us, and from where I knelt on the ground I saw Leon and Bet come running with lanterns and flashlights, throwing the scene before me into sudden, hideous clarity—Victor's blood pouring onto the grass, Savo's gleaming teeth, and Carmen's blood-streaked face.

By the time Bet and Leon reached the rock, Victor had stopped screaming because he had no mouth, no throat to scream with. In less than a minute there seemed barely enough to bury, nothing left but blood and gristle. Carmen was covered with it. She was holding pieces of him and gasping out shrill, wordless torrents of agonized sound. Victor's face was gone, and his left arm was gone. His stomach muscles had been ripped away, his intestines snaking out onto the grass. Selene's dogs had torn him apart, exactly as Actaeon was savaged, exactly as the Goddess willed it.

Victor was probably already dead when Dwight finally, madly forced himself through the dogs. In spite of his own bleeding limbs, in spite of Tish, hanging by her teeth from his shoulder, somehow he grabbed Savo's head and started to drag her away, but she turned on him, slashing with her fangs against his leg, and just then I saw Lido running toward them with the shotgun in her hands.

"*Savo!*" she shouted. "*Savo!*" She was only a yard or two away and could have killed Savo with one shot, but all of a sudden Selene loomed up behind her, her wild, loose hair swirling about her face, knowing exactly what Lido was going to do. She grabbed Lido's neck, yanking her away. Lido shook her off, trying to take aim, but then Selene threw her whole body against Lido and the gun went off. I heard the concussion deep in my ears, felt the heat of the shot that grazed my own shoulder and slammed into Dwight's chest.

Spread-eagled, blood spurting out of his chest, he fell on top of Victor, and just as the dogs started in on him, too, Leon grabbed the shotgun away from Lido and pulled the trigger. The blast lifted Savo off her feet; the enormous black body spun around with the force of the shot before it fell at Carmen's feet.

"*No!*" Selene ran at Leon, reaching for the gun. He knocked her down with the barrel and she landed on her side in the bloody grass, gesturing violently toward the brilliant moon.

"Why? *Why!* I gave You what You wanted!"

And with that she fell, gagging on her screams, facedown into the grass.

Bet ran past her sister's crumpled body and through the ravening dogs to Carmen. She gathered her into her arms and away, and Leon, with a burst of booming, blazing gunfire, shot the rest of the dogs.

Selene was still lying in the grass. Bet guided Carmen into Lido's waiting arms before she went back to Selene and knelt beside her motionless body. She leaned toward her, her mouth inches from Selene's face.

"Can you hear me, Selene?"

Bet's voice was a whisper. She cradled her sister's head in her hands, almost with gentleness, moving it slightly as if expecting a response. None came. She touched her hair, her cheek, mumbling something I could not make out.

I crouched beside them, put my hands on Bet's trembling shoulders, and, as gently as I could, pulled her up and into my arms. I expected sobs, tears, even collapse, but no. When I looked down at her, Bet's face was like stone.

Epilogue

O n a clear, violet winter evening, five months later, I
drove through the obelisks and pulled up before Selene's dark, shuttered
house. There was only the sliver of the crescent moon, slender and white,
rising in the eastern sky to light my way, but I remembered the air's
strange, arctic glow as if the deep snow itself lit both the plowed road
and the laden trees that seemed to have grown in upon it in the months
I'd been away. Though the wind was still blowing from the northwest, it
had become an almost gentle breeze, just enough to stir the odd falling
flake into a lonely geometric spiral down the invisible currents of the air.

When I stepped out onto the fresh snow, it was pitch-black dark all
around me. It took me back, just a little, to see how dark it was, but I
resolutely took my small bag from the backseat, just as I had on my first
visit, exactly one year before. The keys Bet had mailed to Florence jingled
in my other hand.

They had arrived just a fortnight earlier, accompanied by a short letter:

Dear Father Giovanni,

*Selene has passed away in the hospital of the Convent House of St. Felice,
where our mother also died. As you know, it was Selene's last coherent wish that
she be allowed to do the same and, in spite of everything, I could not deny her.*

Leon, Carmen, and I will always be grateful to you for using your influence with the Church and handling those arrangements for us. The sisters tell me that from the time of her arrival in August, Selene spoke not one word to anyone. Toward the end, she neither ate, nor closed her eyes. Who knows where she might have gone during those last days before they found her dead?

Father, I ask you to try to find it in your heart to do one last thing for us: I am sending you the keys to the house and stùdiolo in the hope that you will dispose of Selene's papers and belongings as you see fit. Although the lawyers disagree with me, I place no restrictions at all on your manner of doing so. I cannot bear to do it myself. I told Selene I would never forgive her and, as I write this, that is still true.

If you cannot help me, I will understand. The estate property, with the exception of Lido's house and the few acres surrounding it, is to be sold in the spring. If you do feel you can help, I bless you for it.

Elisabetta Catcher Poynsetter

After a brief consultation with Carla, I agreed. Though it was wintertime, and severely so that year, I made the long journey from Italy to see what I could do—whether in this simple act of friendship I might, at long last, find a way to understand.

I settled in without delay. Bet had told me that the caretakers would prepare Selene's house for my arrival, and I found the warm kitchen well stocked with food and other necessities. Deciding to leave the *stùdiolo* for the morning, I made myself a bite of supper from the various covered dishes in the refrigerator. Though my appetite was not equal to the task of finishing my meal, I sat in the parlor with a glass of wine, watching the shadows, reluctant to face either thought or memory. In due course, I fell asleep and woke, still in the flowered chair in the parlor, to pale morning sunshine.

When I went out, I saw that the night's new fall of snow had drifted across the terra-cotta path to the *stùdiolo*. The air had begun to glow with the beginning of morning, a silvery pinkness just starting to define the dimensions of the white lawn and the shapes of the great trees at the edge of Sterling's forest. The light came without sunbeams, without direction; it seemed to grow from what it illuminated.

The *stùdiolo* faces west and south so it was fairly dim, but as I stood in the open doorway I could see that it had not been touched since the night Victor Bellacéra and Dwight Desjardin died. The bulb in the lamp on the desk had burned out months ago. The tray with one glass was as we'd left it on the desk. The wine had evaporated; a dusty maroon residue coated the bottom of the glass. *The Death of Actaeon* was still on the miniature easel. Pointlessly perhaps, but unable to resist the gesture, I replaced it with the lovely Fra Angelico *Annunciation* that still lay on the floor beside the sofa. Barely pausing to look at it, I put the Titian facedown on the papers that littered the top of the desk.

I spent most of that first day sorting through Selene's books and portfolios of art prints, scores of reprints and files, trying to bring some order to the incredible chaos, beginning the process of deciding what to save, what to discard, what to give away. Avery, who was still in Boston, though planning to depart for his little Tuscan villa as soon as it was warm enough, had told me he might be interested in some of it. There were private notebooks, too, at which I only glanced, but I saw enough to know why Bet had asked that I and I alone take care of this.

Late in the afternoon, weary and a bit disheartened by all the work still left to do, I bundled up against the growing chill and set off down the road toward Victor's house.

The whole place was deserted, cold and spectral in the pale light of the rising stars. I knew from Bet that the house had not been sold; I had no idea if anyone in Victor's family might have an interest in this splendid piece of real estate. But if he had left it to Carmen, as he may well have done, it would surely be sold along with the rest of Sterling Catcher's land.

I went along the snow-covered brick path beside the great veranda and down to the glass salon.

It astonished me that so fine and solid a structure could fall so rapidly into disrepair. It seemed to have been vacant for years, not just five months, though when I saw all the broken glass, it occurred to me that possibly some youngsters from the neighborhood may have had a hand in the amount of destruction that I saw.

I peered in through a section of the glass wall of which only shards remained. Aided by the last of the thin winter daylight, I took it all in in an instant. The louvered shades that had once covered the vast windows were mostly rotted through. Whole slats had fallen to the floor; in some places they had been down so long they were almost completely covered with dry leaves, branches and feathers, and small drifts of blown-in snow.

There was no furniture; someone, Bet and Carmen, perhaps, had taken care of that. And the telescope was gone as well. Scattered about, too, were large pieces of glass from gaping holes I could just barely see, high up toward the pitch of the ceiling. Entire panes were gone in some sections, the chunks of fallen glass covered with pine cones and brittle leaves, the tiny bones (did I imagine them?) of birds picked clean by other birds, and, in the far corner near the platform for the telescope, was the frozen carcass of a hawk, which had, in a moment of madness or inspiration, broken through. I couldn't bear to see any more and moved away into the garden.

Though the brick path was covered with drifted snow, I walked slowly down toward the old verdigris bench Eugenia Wallace had placed there long ago and which Victor had carefully restored. It reminded me of the desolate bench off the county road where, months before, Selene had offered me that anguished ghost of a confession.

I brushed away the snow and sat down, gazing with heavy-hearted fascination at the elegant proportions of the old garden and at the line of trees at the edge of the forest. In the late light, I imagined I could see tiny saplings, those that had taken root over the summer, creeping slowly toward the garden itself, coming to reclaim it.

I had the Fra Angelico with me, and after a few minutes I took it from inside my jacket. Five months before, in the instant before Victor Bellacéra's death, seeing him pressed in terror against the rock, and Carmen, in her own agony, reaching toward him, I had remembered the *Annunciation* and the posture of the figures—the Madonna, Her hands crossed over Her stomach, and the Archangel half-kneeling before Her.

But there in Victor's ruined garden, in the strange combination of reflected light from the snow and the rising crescent moon, in the waning daylight, the moment was so transcendent, so filled with sadness that I saw something I never had before:

In every *Annunciation* ever painted there is a *space* between the Angel and the Virgin. They are always separated by some painterly device—a pillar, a dove, a branch of silver lilies. The figures may be mere millimeters apart, but there is a space—and something in it.

What is in the space? I wondered, so fascinated by the question that I momentarily forgot the horrible scene that had brought it to mind. What is there, uncompleted, unexpressed?

Grace? Faith? Destiny? Is it God's love, flowing from the Angel to the waiting Lady? The promise of renascence, of the life to come? I let my mind sink into the question, into the wish that there truly was a promise, and that it would be kept.

After a time, becoming aware of the biting, windless cold, I knew that I'd been far away, lost in old, imperfect memories. I may have been thinking of the sunshine on the stones of my small, enclosed garden in Rome, perhaps of the candlelight on our family dinner table at the lakeside villa north of Milan the night I told my outraged, disbelieving father I would be a priest. Or I may have been swallowed by a memory of Selene's eyes, glowing in the rainy afternoon light of Berkeley Square, as she told me about chasing the Angel of the Annunciation across Europe.

When I looked up from my reverie, full darkness had come and with it the stars in their millions, just as I remembered them.

Years ago, when Carla and Piero and I were children, we used to go out on moonless winter nights to watch the stars: Callisto the Virgin, Orion and Betelgeuse (bright as could be), and Bellatrix and the brilliant Pleiades. At one time we knew all their names and their seasons and would find high, isolated places, far from the lights of the villa, where we could fill our eyes with them and nothing else. They are the one thing older than the Goddess and will outlast Her and us and all our dreams. And that night, in Victor Bellacéra's silent garden, I looked up at where they sparkled so wickedly in the clear, black sky, and oh! the comfort that I took in them, to have them up there to look at after what I saw down here.

I sat hunched over the Fra Angelico and rubbed the ornate frame mindlessly with my fingers while I thought about Carmen and Victor and that other starry night when Selene, in an act that destroyed so many lives, had found a way to propitiate the Great Goddess whom she had, with her passion for Victor and her betrayal of her precious Carmen, so grievously offended.

When she fell, screaming out at the Goddess, *"I gave You what You wanted!"* it was as if in the same breath she took full responsibility and none at all, as if it was the Goddess who had willed that horror, merely seizing Selene Catcher as Her instrument.

I'd been tormenting myself for months with that, with trying to define the act itself. Did Selene think she was killing the Angel of the Annunciation—the black-winged angel who came with an announcement meant for Carmen? Was she killing the Stag King, thus reviving the oldest ceremony of the cult of the Great Goddess? Or did she simply take a most human, primitive blood revenge on the man she could not have, and by consequence, by extension, on the rival they both loved?

Did the Goddess demand that of Selene? Did She require full blood sacrifice? Or did that pack of dogs tear Victor Bellacéra to pieces *because Selene Catcher told them to?*

There has been little comfort for me in the endless, coiling speculation with which I have tried, without success, to understand these things. Perhaps no one who has not thrived for forty years on a spiritual diet of submission and acceptance can understand the steadfastness with which I am accustomed to watching inevitabilities unfold before me. It's easy enough to say I had no idea, on that winter afternoon one year ago when I drove into this wilderness to see my old friend, that she was already well along toward the absolute madness in which her life would end.

Had I but known!

I've cried the words aloud a thousand times! *Had I but known!* But I did not. I have used up every act of contrition God gave me and yet I cannot name my sin.

What could I have done for her? For all of them? What did I miss? The depth of Selene's devotion to the Great Goddess, or the precise heat of her passion for Victor Bellacéra? I had lived my life believing there could be no Goddess but my own.

I have no experience with gods not bound by obligations of benevolence. The linchpin of Christianity is a belief in God's predisposition to forgive. But Selene Catcher lived as an acolyte of a pagan deity who demanded appeasement and sneered at love. And she died, an acolyte still, having paid with everything she had and everything she was, but at the end it was impossible to know if Artemis found pleasure in that offering. For when Selene fell into the grasses of the field that night, the Goddess, imperfectly convinced of her contrition, made her wait five long months to die. A suitable irony? Or justice?

Can we have it both ways: pagan power and Christian forgiveness? I believe that Selene's final torment came from her having somehow understood that what was in the space between the Archangel and the Virgin, between the announcement of life everlasting and the will to receive it, was a god's grace, the miracle of a love given without the precaution of blood sacrifice, without propitiation.

I wonder if the Goddess has a sense of humor, or a streak of cruelty more black, more ingrained, more sinister than any worshiper or scholar ever knew. When Ovid called Her "Merciless Diana," did he think it was a joke, or did he look over his shoulder, trembling, as he wrote the words? Or maybe Selene was right after all; maybe they are *all* Hecate. For in sending me to watch the unfolding of Selene's sin, the Goddess had devised the brilliant stroke by which She would teach us both a lesson: me, for my meagerness of passion, for my lifelong refusal to be brave enough for life, and Selene for her excesses, for what I saw as her relentless chewing down of life.

Contrition.
    Confession.
        Absolution.
            Forgiveness.
                Redemption.

I got up from the bench, tucked the beautiful *Annunciation* into my jacket, and set off toward the house. When I reached the rock, I paused to look up into the black, star-filled sky and saw the silver crescent of the virgin moon soaring past the trees, high above me. Was it the Renaissance Moon? I wondered. The one that may announce redemption for my friend, absolution of that sin for which confession never really came?

I don't know if rebirth is a natural consequence of all confession, or if we reap what we sow without exception, without forgiveness. The Goddess's justice may indeed be just that primitive. The skies and the wild places of the earth are filled with proof of Her vengeance, but She is also the first symbol of regeneration, of the seed, the pod, the tiny leaf, and then the fruit. The Renaissance that Selene Catcher chased all her life is to be found, after all, in that endless blooming, in those chains of harvest.